BANJO

BANJO

JACK CURTIS

THE MACMILLAN COMPANY
NEW YORK, NEW YORK

To Gi-Gi and Don,

for attics and high ceilings

"You can get in just as much trouble by being dumb and innocent as you can by breaking the law."

Billie Holiday, *Lady Sings the Blues*

BANJO

ONE

AUGUST, THE BOY, drawing up his new hand-me-down long pants, stepped out of the clean-swept and lime-dusted privy into the modest shelter of the latticework that screened the door. He was young, only seven, and his thoughts were wholly trapped by the holiday. From the barn, he could hear his father trying to gentle the hammerheads with sweet-talk nonsense, and from the kitchen the clang of iron on iron as his mother and sister, Kate, labored over the Thanksgiving dinner, and from the cowshed the ring of milk striking a tin bucket with its own particular music identified Jube playing the tits, and farther away, from the hired man's shack, past the granary, he could hear a brother twanging away on Jube's banjo.

It was like not quite awakening in the morning when the house was stirring and the sun coming up, and the comforters heavy and warm, and the curled-up bodies of his older brothers were without mischief or jealousy or anger.

Sometimes, after they'd said their prayers, they fought meanly, but the chill of night and the weight of the farm day were blessed peacemakers.

They made him sleep in the middle: Luther on the left, Martin on the right, and little August in no-man's-land.

The morning was crispy clear, and though the ice-gray cloud moving over the western horizon carried the first snow in it, Poppa was a thrifty farmer, and the fields were clean, corn was in the corncrib, hay was stacked, the wheat sold at a good price, and Jube had split a mountain of hardwood for the stoves. The coal-oil barrel was full and Momma had the root cellar racked with potatoes and cabbages in straw, and the storm-cellar shelves were heavy with canned green beans and kraut, and tomatoes. Wild plums were the only fruit because the little orchard was still too young for bearing, and the summers around Dodge City were too hot and searing for good growth.

"We will try, do or die," his father had said. It could be a motto for the Gilpin coat of arms. "We will try the apples, maybe they grow, maybe they don't." But inside that word "try" was the dull, endless cogwheel of drudgery.

Poppa had learned his farming in Iowa; Momma had come from Pennsylvania. Both were small towers of industry, dedicated to increase. Increase the yield per acre, increase the acreage per farm, increase the paper in the bank, increase the number of children, increase the cattle and pigs, and increase the devotion to the great creator, the God of Increase who gave his only begotten son too.

Their hired hand, Jube, had come drifting by in the spring when Poppa was breaking new ground for wheat.

"Are you a Christian?" Poppa asked him first off.

"Christian as I can be," Jube said.

"We're Lutheran," Poppa said.

"Yessir," Jube said. "I'm a good worker and I eat in the kitchen."

"You're not Catholic?" Poppa tried to lock eyes with the gaunt black man.

"I'm a Abyssinian Baptist," Jube said with his eyes down.

"Look here, Jube," Poppa said, you don't have to go around this farm with your eyes down. You're a free man. My father died fighting for your freedom."

"Yessir," Jube said, raising his shoebutton gaze to Poppa's knees. His smile was broad and set. "You don't mind if I play the banjo oncet in a while?"

"I don't see why not, if you have the time," Poppa said.

"Last place I worked, the man didn't like me playin' the banjo."

"I'm not a believer in all work and no play," Poppa had said, "any more than I'm a believer in all play and no work. You can start soon as you're ready."

Gus moved out of the latticework shelter toward the cowshed. In the yellow shadows Jube squatted on a milk stool, his ebony forehead fitted to the flank of the black and gold Guernsey, blending in such harmony of spirit and color and form, they were indivisible. Only his long spidery hands moved, ringing the milk out into the shiny tin bucket tucked between his knobby knees.

Gus made no sound as he watched the lean black man perform his shadowy ritual, fascinated by the rhythms, by the blackness, by the soft loamy sounds Jube hummed, until another bucket was brimming with foamy milk, and the wilted tits were stripped between those shiny banjo-picking fingers, and the tall man stood with his milk, stroking the cow's back with his left hand, murmuring, "So now, so now, Sheba, thanky for the cream," releasing the cow from her stanchion, ready to take the milk to the basement where mother or Katie would crank it through the separator.

"Jube," the boy said.

The tall man paused, turned, his eyes like polished walnut and white chinaware. "That you, Gus?"

"Yessir," the boy said. "I'm not spyin', I'm just watchin'."

"Sure, Gus," Jube said. "That's fine."

"I guess you really like to work—I mean it's fun for you."

Jube laughed. "It's life to me. Maybe I'd as soon be aplunkin' the old banjo, but life is work, or work is life, or somethin' the boss said like that."

Walking together toward the house, Gus asked, "Why don't you go to church with us, Jube?"

"Mainly because the nearest Pentecostal Abyssinian Washed in the Blood of the Lamb Church is somewhat south of K.C."

"K.C.?"

"Kansas City, Gus. A far piece."

As the tall man paused at the head of the steps, a bucket of golden milk in each hand, the boy impetuously touched Jube's wrist, unable to express his feeling any other way.

The tall man laughed again, displaying his white eyeteeth. "I like you, too, Gus, I like you better'n old Sheba in the mornin'."

"August," Momma called, "come get your coat on. August, we're going."

Katie had the light wagon partly filled with sacks stuffed with straw to cushion the jolts. Poppa sat on the seat reining in the restless team, while Momma assembled her brood and got them up over the tailgate and settled in the wagon box.

She was burned red as Indian corn by the summer's sun and constant wind, her hands were callused and tough as wheel spokes, but her manner was ever gentle, pushing all the time, but gently.

"All right, Poppa," she said, "hold 'em a minute?"

"I got 'em," Poppa said, watching the wild horses' ears as Momma climbed up beside him.

This was always a moment of expectation, the tick-tock bomb of disaster set to blast them all through the fence and over the moon.

"You'd think some day we could afford a honest team of mules," she said, as she had said a thousand times before.

"It's a good team," Poppa said, holding the reins wrapped around his big hands. "They'll learn."

"And then you'll sell 'em," Katie said.

"You just never mind," Momma said.

"Giddup," Poppa said, giving the mustangs a little slack, and off they paced down the road, swinging their hind ends sideways, throwing their heads about, and bowing their necks against the harness. But Poppa knew their tricks and played them like puppets on leather strings.

"They're a good team," he said. "Twice as fast as mules, and they'll bring an increase next spring."

As they rolled along the road, they exchanged comments about their neighbors' fields, of their value, of whether another quarter section could be absorbed this year, whether the bank would finance it.

Luther laughed and settled back lazily in his nest of straw pillows.

"Now what?" Marty demanded.

"Just thinking of how damned pretty it is right now before the snow, the dust all settled." Lu spoke in an undertone. "And the cottonwoods ruffled against the skyline."

"So?" Marty challenged.

"So why doesn't somebody see this country as a picture instead of another mortgage?"

"You one of them picture-paintin' fellers?" Marty asked, "bedding down with loose women and drinking wine?"

"I'd as lief that as try to eat all the dirt in Ford County the way we're-a-doin'." Lu closed his eyes and ended the discussion.

"When you goin' to fire the nigger?" Martin asked Poppa.

"What ever put that idea into your head? And don't say 'nigger,' say 'negra.'"

" 'Cause it's winter on us, and he won't be needed till spring," Martin said.

"I don't know," Poppa said mildly.

"He's a good hand," Momma said. "Might be he'd take less for the wintertime."

"You ain't said nothin' to him, have you, Martin?" Poppa asked.

"No, sir."

"You know you're goin' to do it anyways." Luther laughed to himself. "No work, no eat."

"It's no jest," Poppa said. "A farm don't prosper less'n it's thrifty. The land and animals, the buildings and the equipment and the hired hands—it all goes together."

"But I like him," Gus said.

"You like anything that gives you jawbreakers," Katie said. "He gives me the creeps."

"I haven't made up my mind," Poppa said. "Maybe because it's Thanksgiving, and even a negra ought to have a Thanksgiving after the harvest."

Lu laughed his crazy whinny that always seemed to say you're all crazy, and the world too.

"I tell you, Lu, you better stop that," Poppa said. "I'd hate to take a trace to you today."

"Yessir," Lu said solemnly. "I'd hate it too." And winked at Gus.

"Hush up back there," Poppa said.

The new church was taller than it was long. Its white spire could be seen for miles across the flat prairie. Its walls built of hand-split post rock, an ocher-colored limestone, rose to a steep shingled roof. To the left was a small graveyard fenced with wire running through chalk-rock posts. There were few graves in it. There wasn't time yet.

"Some day," Poppa said, "Dodge'll be out here. We should buy land."

But now there was nothing except unbroken, unswerving, unjagged prairie, golden yellow in the fall, stabbed by this yellow and white arrowhead of God.

The other farm families were arriving, and while they talked
and joshed and connived, the children tried to roughhouse silently,
invisibly, until the bell rang in the belfry, and the yard became
hushed as they moved inside the church and took their usual
places. In the high-ceilinged room lived a gaunt peace augmented
perhaps by the hymns they sang and abetted perhaps by the pastor's sermon on Thanksgiving. The pastor was not a hell's-molten-
cauldron type of preacher except once in a while in early summer, when the days were hot and humid and children were being
conceived.

His message was as soft as his habit, and pure as his color, and
reedy as his voice. He spoke of God, of Industry, of Increase, of
the evil of drink, and lastly of Thanksgiving for the harvest. It
was what the tough-grained, knobby-handed farmers needed to
complete their week's struggle.

Afterward, after praying and after shaking the pastor's hand,
they strolled easily into the yard as if they'd just had a good dinner. They gossiped some more, predicted weather, collected their
families, and went their separate ways again. Some in buggies,
but most of them in the familiar farm wagon.

Momma had to send Gus around to the bare double privy, with
its doors for men and women at opposite ends, to fetch the rest
of the children, who seemed to gravitate to that structure as dogs
to fireplugs.

Lu was inside, and Martin was with some other boys skylarking. Katie was with the girls, who seemed to be collectively admiring the back of the church, or the limestone marker for old
man Markle, the oldest occupant of the new graveyard, or anything at all except the yellow-painted privy where another girl
lodged for the moment of this ritual.

"Martin," Gus said, "Poppa said for us to go."

"Sure," Martin said, "there's work to do."

"Yes," Gus said.

"It'll wait," Martin said, watching the privy.

"You know how Poppa is," Gus said.

"I know, I know." Martin frowned.

Suddenly there was a dull thudding report from the privy and
a shriek of apparent fear as the left-hand door burst open and
Jeannette Koberman ran into the yard, clutching at her skirts. A

puff of gentle smoke followed her out of the door. The boys hee-hawed exaggerated laughter and slapped each other on the backs and spun around red-faced and wheezing. Gus was laughing as much as any.

The girls, trying to look stern and irate, sheltered Jeannette Koberman as she repaired her dress. And just as the laughter seemed to ebb, out came Lu from the other side, fixing his gaze on Jeannette Koberman, rolling his eyes, and very delicatedly holding his nose. The boys beat their sides with joy and the girls turned away like cats from cold water.

"Gosh, old Lu oughta be in vaudeville," Johnny Brewer gasped weakly. "The way he rolled his eyes at old Jeannette—wowee."

There were a few calls from the front of the church. "Come, kids, come along now. We've got to see to that old tom turkey."

Poppa had the team untied and ready. He didn't like to hold them in very long, especially when every neighbor in the county was hoping they'd wake skittish and kick at the harness, and hump and buck and bolt. He could buy a good wild horse out of Montana for thirty dollars and a year later sell him for a hundred. And that was Increase. And that's what he meant to show the neighbors. And if the blasted children would kindly quit frolicking around dumber'n these hammerheaded mustangs, and they would please the blazes get in and settled down whilst there was still a team and wagon more or less standing and waiting for their little highnesses . . .

"Dad blast it! Gus, I told you to fetch 'em, and where you all been?"

"It's O.K., Poppa," Momma said. "We're all in, say goodbye to the Watsons. Ya, ya, next week," she cried, waving her white handkerchief, which set the horses off at what would have been a breakaway gallop had not Poppa locked the reins doubled around his huge hands and humped his neck like a bull and braced his legs against the boxfront, and so it almost looked as if the team was prancing out of the churchyard if you hadn't seen the veins bulging out of Poppa's forehead, and the ridges of muscles jutting across his jaw.

"Momma," he said after a while, "don't never wave a hanky around these animals, they don't just yet understand everything."

"I'm sorry, Poppa," she said. "I forgot. You're such a wonder with horseflesh."

"All it takes is the right touch," Poppa said, letting off the chokehold. "You want to see them go?"

"No, Poppa, I already know they go good," she said, too late.

He didn't even need to say "giddup"; all they needed was a touch of slack, and away they went, towing the wagon like a kite. Poppa knew the road was straight for two miles and slightly up-hill. Wear them out, and they'd learn to behave. The children hung onto the sideboards as the wagon sailed over chuckholes and ruts, its wheels spinning swiftly.

"Lu threw a firecracker in the privy," Katie said.

"Couldn't hold it any longer, could you?" Lu said.

"Well, you did, and nearly scared Jeannette Koberman to death and burned her chemise."

"Bull," Lu said.

"Lu," Poppa said, "don't talk like that or I'll wash your mouth out with coal oil."

"Shush up, Katie," Momma said.

"Did you throw a firecracker in the privy, Lu?" Poppa asked carefully.

"Just a little dud left over from the Fourth."

"I think I told you about playin' the fool, didn't I?"

"Nobody was hurt. It was a joke. Everybody laughed."

"I don't imagine Jeannette laughed."

"Well, in a way she did."

"She was crying," Katie said.

"Shush, Katie."

"Well, she was."

"And tomorrow I got to borrow Gerald Koberman's feed mill. My saints in heaven, what are you thinking of when you do these tricks? You know how I hate to borrow, you know that."

"I forgot about the feed mill," Lu said, thinking of how to pay back Katie.

"Now all the neighbors are going around saying Mr. Gilpin has wild children," Poppa said. "Wild horses and wild children."

"Not me, Poppa," Martin said. "Don't mix me in on it."

"Lu, I mean to teach you a lesson. You will do without Thanksgiving dinner."

There was a moment of cold, feral silence. Momma felt like screaming. Katie felt a little sick at having pushed it all so far. Martin had no feelings, except a slight pleasure at the demonstration of who was top dog.

August said, "Oh, no, Poppa."

And Lu smiled and winked at Gus. "It's O.K. It's O.K., Gussie. I kind of felt like meditating on my sins and evil nature anyhow."

"Now look here," Poppa said, "you mind your tongue."

"He didn't mean to be bad," Katie said.

"Katie," Momma said.

"My mind's made up," Poppa said. "I'm sorry for it, but that's the way I am. A man has to stand to the job."

"Yessir," Lu said, winking again at Gus, whose terrified face was hidden in his hands.

The lathered team paced smartly through the neat farmyard to the stable and Poppa said, "Martin, you and Luther put the harness on the pegs and turn the horses into the corral. I don't want my suit dirtied."

Gus walked with Momma and Poppa along toward the house, a two-story chalk-rock practical dwelling that might have been beautiful if only the prairie would grow pine trees around it to soften its scoured square lines.

"Poppa," Momma said, "you know Lu, he's always full of mischief."

"He goes too far," Poppa said. "He's got to learn we're a solid family. If I'd a done such foolishness when I was a boy, my father would have sold me as chattel to a gypsy."

They met Jube coming out the back door.

He seemed to start guiltily, aware that he was in the wrong place at the wrong time.

"What is it, Jube?" Poppa asked.

"What is what, Mr. Gilpin?"

"What are you doin' in my house?"

"I knew I shouldn't have left that turkey in the oven," Momma said, giving him a way out even as she hustled past him into the kitchen.

"I think it's all right, Mrs. Gilpin," Jube said, stepping aside for her and moving easily down the steps to Poppa's level.

"Now what was it, Jube?" Poppa's voice was level, mild and inquisitive.

"You mean me bein' in the house, sir?"

"That's what I mean, Jubal. You know that's what I mean."

"Well, I don't know," Jubal said. "I don't want to start trouble."

"There's no trouble." Poppa's voice seemed to become more mild and Christian with each sentence. "But you can see I have to know. Someone has to keep track of everything on this farm in order that it produce and increase, and somehow I been elected to the job."

"That's right, Mr. Gilpin."

"So?"

"Well, long as you're keepin' track and I'm not stirrin' up any trouble, I'm missin' my banjo."

"And?"

"Well, I figured it might have wandered its way up here to the big house."

"But you didn't find it after searching high and low?"

"No, sir, I didn't search nothing. I just taken a look into the boys' bedroom. That banjo means quite a lot to me, especially on my day off."

"The instrument is definitely missing? I mean you didn't mislay it?"

"Everybody knows I hang the banjo on my wall and keep it nice and dry the same as you keep your crosscut saws sharp and in the right place."

"That's right. And you think my boys stole it."

"No, I just think it ain't on my wall and thinkin' how they like to tease, and thinkin' I'd surely like to pick out a tune, I figured it was fittin' I could look for it."

Somehow, Jube wasn't sweating the way he should have been. His tone had a little burry rasp to it. And Poppa's voice too picked up the edge, as if to say nobody has any more growl than me 'cause I'm top dog here.

Gus wanted to speak out and say he'd heard someone playin' it when Jube was milking, but he couldn't seem to get his words together at the right time. Poppa was in charge, and Poppa would fix it fairly and perpetually.

"Well, Jubal, you were mistaken," Poppa said. "You had no

right to enter their room, you should have waited until we got home."

"Yessir, I thought about that, but then I don't have too awful much free time and I do like to play that banjo."

"I hate a whiner," Poppa said. "Let's find the thing and settle it."

"Yessir," Jubal said, his eyes smoking up and murky.

Poppa led the way to the stable where Lu and Martin were finishing up with the mustangs. Neither one of them looked any guiltier than usual.

"Boys," Poppa said clearly, "seems Jubalee here has lost his banjo. You know anything about it?"

Lu had nothing to lose, having already been deleted from the feast, but he really didn't know.

They didn't answer.

"Yes or no," Poppa asked.

"No, sir," Lu said.

"No, sir," Martin said.

"Now wait, boys," Jube said, "I ain't spleeny or nothin', I am just lookin' for the old banjo. It's about the only thing I got for my own."

"We understand that," Poppa said. "Do you believe them?"

"I guess I better." Jube laughed. "Winter's comin'."

"What do you mean by that?" Poppa asked.

"Nothin', Mr. Gilpin." Jube smiled. "Don't worry about that old beat-up banjo, it'll turn up."

"No, it's not that way," Poppa said. "The way to run anything is to keep everything straight. That's why my saws are always sharp and hanging on the right nail."

"Yessir," Jube said agreeably.

"You're laughing a little, I think," Poppa said bleakly. "Let's look at your room."

He led on down past the barn to the old granary by the smokehouse where Jube slept.

He didn't wait for Jube; he just walked right in and looked around.

On the wall, on its accustomed nail, hung the banjo, a gash in its white skin, a broken string dangling from a bent post.

"Seems to me," Poppa said, "you're mistaken. Now tell the truth. Why was you in my house?"

Jube slipped by and took down the banjo wondrously.

"Sho' nuff," he said. "There she is. Busted. But there."

"I'd like an answer," Poppa said, "a truthful answer."

"I done told you the truth," Jube said without turning around. "It wasn't here an hour ago and now it is. Let's say it's a dee-vine miracle!"

Why he laughed then, just when Poppa might have let him off the hook, Gus never guessed until later.

"Let's have none of that." Poppa's voice was growly again.

"Lu," Jube said, "you or Marty done put it back, just now, didn't you?"

Neither answered.

"Well," Jube said, glancing from their frozen faces to Poppa's, "it don't make no nevermind just so it turns out all right."

"Jubalee, the boys said they didn't take it. You was coming out of my house and told me an outright lie. The evidence is right in your hand."

"Well," Jube said very slowly, "well, well."

"Is that all you can say?"

"I guess you're goin' to say it all soon enough, Mr. Gilpin," Jube said.

"What was you lookin' for to steal in the house?"

"Sure enough you meant to do it," Jube said. "I kind of had an idea that anybody keeps his saws sharp as a razor all the time and each one hanging on its own peg all the time would know how to do it, but then I kept tellin' myself to wait awhile, Jube, don't jump till your feet's burnin'."

"I mean to get the straight of this," Poppa said.

"Yessir, I know what you mean. You mean winter is comin', the harvest's in, the wood's chopped and snow's comin', why keep a banjo-pickin' Negro 'round."

"As near as I can tell you were inside my private house. And you give me no straight answer as to why."

"The truth is, Mr. Gilpin, my banjo wasn't on that wall when I came in here after turnin' the cows out. And the truth is I went lookin' for it and couldn't find it. And the truth of the matter is you're lookin' for an excuse to fire me and I'm tellin' you to give me my pay, I'm leavin', and the trouble is not about a busted banjo, it's about a black person workin' here."

"You lie in your teeth," Poppa said. "Get your gear together. I owe you thirty dollars."

"Indeed." Jubalee grinned.

Poppa counted out the bills from his purse and laid them on Jube's bed. "Don't ask me to recommend you anywhere in this county," he said.

"Yessir, Mr. Gilpin. God knows I ain't goin' to do that."

"It's only the charity of Christ that keeps me from turning you over to the sheriff. You might have been in my daughter's room."

"I can't hardly believe my ears," Jube said, already filling his bag with a couple of faded shirts and patched pants.

"I'm not lettin' you go because of the idle wintertime," Poppa said. "It's because you lied to me."

"Yessir, Mr. Gilpin. I ain't mad at you. You can't help it."

"I don't like your tone of voice." Poppa was getting stiff and cold as an anvil.

"I'm sorry. I'm just tryin' to be agreeable."

"You're smart-mouthin'. You want me to get my gun?"

"No, sir. I'm jus' old Jube, goin' down the road, singing a song, eatin' watermelon, apluckin' his old mangled banjo." Jube turned then and laughed wild as a hee-haw mule. Haw haw haw haw!

"You black devil," Poppa said, and knocked him across the room. Poppa had his feet set apart, his fists up, ready to charge like a wildcat when Gus howled.

Poppa gritted his teeth and clapped his hands together, holding down his violence. In a moment he said to Jube, "You git."

To the three boys he said, "You see how they are. Now come along."

TWO

GRIM AS A TOMMY GOING over the top, Gus leaped over a barbed-wire fence and ran for the McCoy farm. A mane of bright-yellow hair streamed from his head like a silken saffron flag. From the hedgerow he whistled Sally out from the washhouse the way they played Cowboys and Indians, only this time when she heard the bob-white whistle she knew it was for real.

He was waiting for her in the shade of the big cottonwood in the creek bottom.

The shadow of worry on her ruddy freckled face lifted away with a laugh as she saw him, standing with his back to a tree.

He was silent, already regretting his haste.

"Hurry up," she demanded. "Tell me. Quick, or I'll get a lickin'."

"I'm goin' to fight."

"Fight? Fight what? What're you talkin' about?"

"The Huns!"

"Oh gosh, Gussie," she said. "Why?"

"It's my duty. Lu's goin'."

"But you're only fourteen," she said, as though the number was the answer to the problem.

"I'm plenty big, and I can already shoot better'n most grown-ups."

"When're you leavin'?"

"Tomorrow morning."

"So soon?" Her thin face screwed up into an open mask of misery. "What'll I do?"

"You wait for me," he said. "You got to be true."

"I will, Gus, I promise. But suppose you're killed?"

"Would you give me a farewell kiss?" he asked bravely.

"I guess so," Sally answered, coming closer to him, looking at him carefully. "You're not just teasing, are you? Trying to get something for nothing?"

"It may be the last time I ever get to see you, Sally," he said, nearly broken with solemn nobility.

"I'll light a candle for you."

"I do want you to mention me in your prayers," he said. "And Lu too."

"I heard he got Maudie Koberman in trouble."

"Lu wouldn't do that."

"Everybody says it."

"Well, maybe he couldn't help himself as he was goin' off to war."

"Don't get any ideas, Gus," she said. "I'll kiss you goodbye, but that's all."

He leaned at her, missed her mouth, tried again and pressed his tight mouth against her thin dry lips. He clutched at her to keep his balance, felt her strong ribby cage, and pulled back. She was standing with her eyes closed, her red hair shaken out of its binding, her hands slowly pointing up together in an attitude of prayer.

"I'll be waiting for you, Gus," she whispered.

"Goodbye, little darling," he said, and turned away into the trees.

Strong and golden as Leif Ericson, he ran through the black forest of Prussia, all the way home.

After supper, Lu pushed his chair back, stood up tall as a tree, and said, "Time to tell you I'm joinin' up with the Canadian Army."

"When?" Poppa asked.

"In the morning," Lu said.

"Now see here, Luther—" Poppa tried to sound reasonable. "Is it not a fact that the Germans are on the offensive? They'll have the French broke gentle in a matter of weeks."

"That's all the more reason to go," Lu said, dark fawn eyes staring out the window at La Belle France prostrate before the German Beast.

"By the time you get there, it'll be all over."

"Maybe, maybe not. You always said not to shirk our duty."

"Your duty is right here, building up this farmstead. Hired help is scarce. I just can't pay DuPont factory wages."

"Quit buying up the land then." Lu laughed. "Be satisfied with your half of Ford County. It'll keep you out of trouble."

"I'm going too," Gus said.

"You shut up," Martin said. "You're only fourteen."

"Keep out of this," Poppa said.

"I'm taking the morning train east," Lu said, his jaw firm, his lips always smiling. "We will try, do or die."

Katie began to weep wetly, slobbering.

"You are not," Poppa said.

"Please—" Momma dabbed at her nose with her apron. "Please, Lu, don't."

"I can't stay here no more, Momma," Lu said, his voice very level, all the fun wrung out of it. "You got Poppa, he's got you, and you all got more ground than you can farm already. There just don't seem to be anybody laughing any more."

"Life is no joking matter," Poppa said. "And soldiers are a breed of common bums that always end up with nothing."

"Don't everybody?" Lu howled with his mocking laughter.

"I can see you've neglected your Bible training," Poppa said, his face reddening.

"Now, Poppa," Momma said, "maybe we better think some more about it."

"Sure," Lu said. "Think about it while I'm gettin' packed."

Katie was sniveling again.

"Can't I go, Lu?" Gus asked.

Lu smiled. "Sorry, Old Tagalong, not this time. I guess nobody around here can see it, but the whole times are changing. People don't want to plow the same furrow for fifty, sixty years and then be buried in it. I want to know something before I croak."

"You haven't even learned to work yet." Poppa glared at him.

"It wouldn't matter if I shoveled cow poop thirty-six hours a day for you, you'd still be singing that same old song."

"Lu!" Momma was shocked.

"Let him go," Martin said. "You never could talk sense to him."

Lu looked around the square wallpapered room in the lamplight, making himself look slowly and see every shadow and every line while he had the time. "Well, now, I don't expect to be no hero but I'd like to leave without everybody hatin' me for doin' what I think is best."

"I'm telling you no," Poppa said, trying to hang on and scowl down Lu's easy angel smile.

"You goin' to tie me up and choke me down like one of your hammerheads?" Lu laughed.

"Lu—" Momma said.

Lu pushed his hands together as if he were squeezing a loaf of bread.

"Got to look after the red sow," Poppa said, going to the door, but turning once more, he said directly to Lu, "You want to go off and fight somebody else's war, you'll have to walk from here to do it."

And when Poppa went out the door with the lantern, Lu went up the stairs two at a time.

Gus chased him up to the bedroom as Katie whimpered and Martin hissed at her to shut her damned trap, and Momma clucked her tongue.

Lu had already packed what little stuff he thought he might need. He would wear his one suit.

"Lu," Gus said, "I'm plenty big enough. I can pick off a jackrabbit on the run."

"Speakin' of jackrabbits," Lu said, teasing, "a stud fella like you has lots of fun comin' to him. You been lovin' up old Sally yet?"

"Now don't kid me," Gus said, feeling stung and cold and put off. "I want to go along."

"Nope. You ain't throwed the wagon tongue to little Sally yet, you can't go."

"You're never serious," Gus begged, "but I mean it."

"Heck, when I was your age," Lu continued, "I'd throwed it to every farmer's daughter for a distance as far as I could run in one night." He started laughing again.

"Is that why you're a-leavin?' 'Count of Maudie?"

"Say, now, you're smart for your age, ain't you?" Lu seesawed his heavy black eyebrows and shook his head.

"Well, is it?"

"I'm willing to say she's springing, and only God knows the sire, but if I stay here she'd sure try pinning it on to me, but if I leave, then she's sure goin' to pin it on one of the others."

"You mean a lot more besides you was with her?"

"Sure, Gus, you ought to give her a ride on the pitchfork whilst there's time. You be doin' her a favor, she likes it so much." And again Lu was darkly laughing.

"Can't you be serious?" Gus tried to break through the surf of cheer. "It's hard enough 'round here as it is."

"Seems like the more I feel good, the worse the old man feels. I can't seem to poke my head up for a look around without him pushin' for more increase."

"He's a-doin' it for us, he says."

"He's a-doin' it because he don't know any other way." Lu's smile faded away to a naked truth.

Gus had seen Poppa take a leather trace to Lu after a day's work of plowing with the wild team, take the leather trace to him for forgetting to water the team or keep their flynets straight or some such, but they'd always known it was an inborn hatred for the smile and white teeth and crinkled-up eyes of his son.

"Look here, punkin head, quit your worryin'." Lu laughed again, his dimples deep and his eyes clear. "I'm goin' off and have myself a wing dinger of a time."

"All the way to Winnipeg?"

"Maybe even to Montreal. French girls there."

Gus looked at his beloved brother, saw the tumbling black hair, dark, handsome, cheerful face, the straight back and squared-off shoulders and could have cried for the loss of his idol. Nobody but Lu could be so strong and yet so devil-may-care, so free and easy, so alive.

In the morning Lu was gone, as he had gone so many times before, no one knowing, simply drifting away through darkness, only his smile showing white and shining, and Martin complaining in the dawn at Gus that now he'd have to milk twice as many cows as before just because that worthless Lu had to go pull a stunt like that.

"I hope he gets shot right in the first battle," Martin snarled as he pulled on his boots. "And I hope then he realizes how he's made everybody so much trouble."

"You better shut up," Gus said. "He's coming back. He's coming back with the Kaiser's ear stuck on his bayonet and he'll be a hero and all you'll be is an old farmer eatin' dirt."

After the Armistice Lu didn't make it home as soon as the other boys did, so it wasn't much of a hero's welcome.

But Gus and Sally were there waiting at the depot, along with the rest of the family. And a few of the kids he'd run around with, only they weren't kids any more. As they shifted about uneasily, they kept saying things like "Remember how old Lu was always jokin'? Yessiree, he could get a laugh out of a baptized billy goat." They spoke nervously, hushed as an audience settling down for catharsis, aware that Lu, the repository of their revelry, just might not be what he'd been.

There was Benny Peacock, who'd married Maudie Koberman to keep out of the draft, and Donald Dodge, who'd taken over the pool hall, and one other friend, Grover Darby, who'd been appointed town marshal because he was big and slow-talking.

Katie's boy friend, Gerald Lundquist, had been delayed because his bull had rolled in the barbed wire.

Martin hadn't yet taken up with a girl. Some folks said he was too tight, but others said he was waiting for the best bargain. Martin said nothing at all; each year he became more and more reticent, honing a sharper nose and tightening the spring of his steel-trap mouth.

The yellow-painted depot stood at the edge of the old cow town, next to the tall cylindrical grain elevators, enduring monuments to memorialize the conquest of the plains.

The long, low wail of the whistle came from the east where the track was cut deep into soft sandstone, amplified and distorted, changing into a new music. Each engineer tried to play a different railroad song in the sandstone cut. This morning's song seemed to sing mournfully, "In the pines, in the pines, where the sun never shines . . ."

"I'll never forget," Benny said, "how old Lu stuffed the thunder mug . . ."

But Katie's elbow in his ribs stopped the tale there. He followed her stern gaze to the elder Gilpin, who appeared to be a monolith of post rock, standing rigidly on the platform.

"I'll never forget," Benny started again, "how old Lu and Gus used to go swimming down at the old hole. Boy howdy, he could dive like a kingfish and swim like a beaver."

No one listened to him.

"Gosh, what'll he look like?" Nervously Gus ran his big sun-burned hand through the unmanageable straw stack of loose yellow hair.

Sally had filled out into a tightly muscled, snub-nosed, red-cheeked maiden. "I don't know," she said. "I hardly remember him."

"I should have been on that train with him," Gus said.

"From the stories they tell, it's just as well you stayed to help your poppa," she said. "They say Charlie Brock had his head torn off by just one shell."

Gus stared blindly off down the track. He hadn't ever told how when he was sixteen he'd tried to lie his way into the Army and a big fat sergeant had turned him away. It was the first time he'd ever tried to lie, and he thought it ought to be the last if he couldn't do any better than that.

When the great black engine came clanking slowly by, the engineer smiling down at the crowd with his red neckerchief and striped bill cap, the way he looked at little crowds at every station, the hollow, fearful feeling grew into a near terror for Gus as he realized he didn't know what to expect.

And now home comes the rover, home from the far country, home from the war for democracy, home from Hun killing, home comes the boy who went off and faced them with cold steel.

The conductor set his little steel stool down by the steps and a traveling salesman carrying a heavy sample case stepped off in a hurry. Cory Hollingsworth stepped off and seemed surprised to see the Gilpins.

He smiled at Poppa. "Hello. I didn't expect a welcome-home party. I just went to Junction City yesterday."

"We're a-waitin' for Luther," Momma said. "Is he on this car?"

"No," Cory started to say and then remembered and shut off everything. "Well, now, maybe that was him down at the end, I just never really looked."

"I'll go get him," Gus said quickly to Sally and stepped to the conductor and said, "I'm goin' aboard to help my brother . . ."

The conductor started to object but he'd seen it all and knew it all, same as the engineer did, and nodded. "Far end of the car."

"Yessir," Gus said, and ran up the steps. Turning into the long car with the green velvet seats, he saw down at the end a soldier in a greenish uniform asleep.

Gus shook him, smelling whiskey. A silver-handled cane lay on the floor.

"C'mon," Gus said, "brother."

The soldier opened one eye and crooked a grin. "Say there, that you, Gus?"

"Lu, the folks are out there. Are you sober?"

"Maybe I better just set and ride on." Lu sighed and shut his eye.

Gus started, seeing the face then. The dished-out scar around the eye socket that was under the black patch, and the blue-green color of the man's face that almost matched his uniform, and the flabby skin around the neck, and the bony white hands.

"C'mon, let me help you," Gus said. "We got your room all ready so you can get some fresh air and rest out home."

"*Merci beaucoup*, young brother—I guess that's what I come for." That crooked grimace again as the muscles near the scar twisted the lip down. The eye opened again. "Where's my jaunty cane?"

Gus put the cane in Lu's right hand.

"Very valuable staff, my boy. Cost me three Iron Crosses and a silver-mounted Lüger." Lu transferred it grandly to his left.

"We got to hurry before the train pulls out," Gus said nervously.

"I just don't think they'd run off with a war-weary vet already, do you? I mean—never mind." Lu smiled again and slowly got to his feet, a faint ripple or muscle spasm flickering across his features.

"You got a bag?"

"A small oversight. It'll turn up somewhere," Lu replied with airy dignity.

The gray-green scarecrow wavered up the aisle, his cane thrusting forward, pegging down and poling the scant body along. The dark head, held high, lolling a moment, then picking up and mouthing a foreign word once in a while as some invisible agony hit him. "*Basta, basta, à bas . . .*"

The conductor faced him on the steps, ready to assist him to the platform where the family and friends watched in cowlike wonder, but Lu glowered and shrugged off his help, and carefully stepped his own measured pace down the treads.

Lu gazed out of his eye at them, made a mocking salute and announced, "Marshal Darby, we are here." His voice picked up a gasping wheeze which he tried to ignore, continuing from one to another. "There's old buddy Don Dodge, and Jerry Lundquist, glad to see you lookin' so well, and Benny . . ." His face lighted with sardonic joy. "Hi, there, Maudie. Somebody wrote you married Benny. How'd everything come out? All right?"

She nodded dumbly, her eyes wide as china saucers.

"And little Sal—I hope old Gus is takin' good care of you . . ."

And turning on one leg to Katie and Martin, he said, "Hi, Katie, you're looking well," and extending his chicken-bone hand to Martin, he said nothing, already turning to Momma, saying, "You're prettier'n any foreign beauty, Momma," and at last, turning to the monument of chalk rock, he extended the hand again and waited for the Word.

Poppa shook the hand as if it were a dead snake and said, "Well, I guess it wasn't all a picnic."

Lu twisted on the fractured half-teeth smile and started to wheeze, choking it out. "No, sir, I guess that's the simple truth. But if you all think I look bad, you oughta see the other guy!"

No one laughed.

"Let's get him to the wagon," Gus said before anyone could start a lot of questions. "He's been a long time on the road."

"I thought I'd stay in the hotel," Lu said.

"Now, now," Momma said, at last finding voice and contact with the living remains of her son, "we got everything all ready for you. You can come to town any time you feel like it."

"What do you think, Gus?" Lu asked.

"I think you better get home whilst you can."

Lu glanced at Poppa. "Well, it won't hurt to give it a try." Accompanying Gus and tagged along by the rest of them, Lu fixed a jaunty upcocked stance and gimped across the platform to the same old wagon hitched to a new team of mustangs.

"Thought you might have one of them autos by now," Lu said to Poppa.

"More increase in horses," Poppa replied.

"Yessir." Lu nodded. "Indeed."

Donald Dodge faded off to his pool room. Grover Darby trudged off to the jail, Benny and Maudie took off in their open new buggy with a two-year-old dark-haired boy, and the train sounded the lament for them all.

Lu lighted a cigarette and half closed his eyes, momentarily slipping under a slab of weariness. But Poppa kept him awake by pointing out the new farms he'd added to the home place.

"You been busy," Lu acknowledged.

Poppa's manner was not proud. "It don't take much special, a man just keeps movin' and nature increases."

"Who works the new ground?"

"We got a couple families of rednecks tryin' to make a start just now. They'll never last it out, but there'll always be another bunch wantin' to try."

"On shares?"

"That's right. Fifty-fifty. I provide the seed."

"Price of wheat's sky-high right now too."

"Bound to rise after a war. Foreigners are all burnt out and hungry. Only people got wheat is us."

"Then you're rich."

"Interest rates are mighty dear."

"Pay off the mortgages."

"Ain't got any money."

Hacking, wheezing more, Lu's unreconstructed mirth.

"Maybe if you didn't smoke them things you'd cure that cough."

"It's something else."

"Mmmm? I say what else?"

"Little touch of the phosgene."

"You shoulda worn a gas mask."

Wheezing, blue-faced, rolling eye, splinter grin, old Lu was drowning in his own joke. At last he whistled out a couple of words. "Too stuffy."

Poppa hated to be mocked, especially by laughter. He snapped at the team to cool off. The pair of spotted, shaggy-haired, Roman-nosed brutes tried a leap sideways but Poppa knew them and played them the way a man plays a fiddle for fun.

Momma decided to put Lu in the parlor on the ground floor so he wouldn't have to climb the stairs. She put china saucers on the piano and the mahogany floor stands so Lu wouldn't drop ashes on the rug.

She took the framed picture showing him tall and proud and smiling in his new uniform and put it in the bottom of a trunk.

Poppa and Martin and Gus still did their regular chores as they had done every day of their remembered lives. Milk the cows, slop the pigs, feed the horses, clean up after the animals, letting the women look after the chickens and the food and housekeeping.

It didn't seem as though Lu could do anything except sit in his room, or in the kitchen, or on the front porch.

A thick hedge of work and energy bloomed up between him and the others, no matter how they tried to make him feel welcome. They had nothing to talk about at mealtime except what the last job was and what the next one would be. And they couldn't ask him about his war experiences any more than he could tell them.

Poppa spent most of his day traveling from one farm to another, seeing that the land was worked the way he wanted it worked. Martin was in charge of the home ranch, and Gus was the jack of all trades, climbing windmills, putting in new gears, keeping up the mowers and wagons and cultivators and seeders.

Lu lasted about a day and a half in the rocking chair and poking around between the house and the chicken pen before he could get Gus alone.

"Gus," he said, "a small problem."

"Say the word, brother." Gus smiled. "What do you need?"

"A couple cartons of coffin nails, a couple bottles of rye whiskey, and one jolly piece of poontang."

Gus laughed.

"I'm serious."

"Gosh, Lu, you know what Poppa thinks about whiskey."

"I know what he thinks about cigarettes and nookie, too, but that's his razz-berries, not mine."

"Where'd I get whiskey anyways?"

"You go to the Long Branch Saloon. Ain't you ever been in a saloon?"

"Nope."

"How old are you?"

"Seventeen."

"Jesus H. Christ, when I was seventeen I'd drunk the barrel dry and tried every bed on Cherry Street."

"I ain't had time."

"What do you do besides work?"

"I hunt some."

"Well, it's something. I was afraid you was another Martin, only dumber."

"Where's Cherry Street?"

"K.C., but, Gus, that couldn't compare to Paree. Dear Lord, the cognac! And those French girls get a-hold of you, you been flipped and gripped and you come out o' there plumb pussy-whipped!"

"Did they charge?"

"'Course, if they needed the money, but mainly they just love to love. God, what a country! I'm going back as soon as I feel a little stronger."

"I know I'm dumber'n a drop calf, Lu, I can't help it."

"You got time, Gus." Lu smiled after getting his breath. "For me, nobody can help anything. Like Poppa said, I should have worn my gas mask."

"That wouldn't have helped your leg out much, though."

"There's worse hurts right here. Gus, these people around here are dead and don't even know it. They've got gut gangrene worse than any I ever saw, they got maggots swarming in their souls and think it's God scratching their ears."

Lu started coughing and wheezing again.

Gus was ready to cry. Ready to grab Lu in his arms and hug him to his chest and cry with him that something was wrong somewhere.

"Look, Gus, don't wait for life to come around the corner, don't wait for Poppa to give the command, goddamn it, grab it, every damned second of it, starting right now."

"I don't think I know how," Gus said.

"First thing is get on a horse and fetch me the whiskey."

"Now looky, Lu, I'll fetch the whiskey but I ain't goin' to drink it."

"Here's two dollars. Get me two quarts. I don't give a damn what you do," Lu said, suddenly worn out and gray-faced.

Gus took the money and rode his pony down the road between the stone fence posts whereon the meadowlark stood and sang and the wheat grew strong and green for miles to the Goshen hills.

It was an easy early-spring day, a lovely half hour's ride in golden sunshine. The prairie town was beginning to feel the spring. Merchants were sweeping sidewalks and washing windows.

Gus put the pony next to a couple of others at the hitch rail in front of the Long Branch Saloon. He knew everyone in town was watching him, but he reminded himself that what he did was none of their business. He carried his saddlebag over his arm into the dark unholy hall. He'd hardly dared peek through the doorway on summery Saturday nights, and he was on the alert for trouble.

But no one was there. He stopped inside the door, noted the old wooden bar, cuspidors, the mirror, and card and billiard tables with their overhead wires strung with counters.

The place smelled of stale beer and wintered-up men and old cigar smoke, and it felt smoothlike, like an old sheepskin jacket you get used to, worn in.

Behind the bar were bottles of whiskey. And beer barrels. Pictures of show girls in tights, and polished longhorns hung on the walls.

From behind a bead curtain in the back Gus heard boards creak, and in a moment, slipping through the screen, came Don Dodge, drying his hands on a towel. He looked an extra moment at Gus.

"Couldn't make it hisself?"

"I'd like two quarts of rye whiskey," Gus said.

Don went on behind the bar and reached up two brown bottles. "Two dollars. You shouldn't let him drink by hisself though."

"I ain't anything to say about it," Gus said, putting the money on the bar and slipping the bottles into the leather bag.

"You're big enough."

I'm in over my head, Gus thought. I just don't understand. I understand machinery, and guns, and dogs, and farm critters and dirt, but I don't know anything.

"I don't mean for you to drink it up with him," Don said. "I mean he ought to be in town."

"He ain't a drunkard," Gus said.

"That's right, son," Don said. "Remember that. But he's a human being and he always liked company, and he shore ain't got none out there."

"Yessir," Gus said, his face turning red.

"I guess he could stay at the Palace, they'd look after him all right. Get a yearly rate on a room."

"We'd like to build him up some, Mr. Dodge," Gus said.

"Lots of eggs and cream and fried steak? Well, chances are it won't kill him for a while, but you best bring him in when he starts losin' his appetite."

"Yessir," Gus said but didn't leave.

"You want a beer or some pretzels or something?"

"No, sir, I was just wonderin' where is everybody?"

"You mean the tinhorn gamblers and carousers and gunmen and fancy women?" Don Dodge glared at Gus. "Well, I could lie to you, Gus, but they just ain't nowhere in this town. At least before six o'clock in the evenin'."

Gus picked up the bag. "I see."

"You'll never learn anything if you stop up your ears like that, boy. Listen to me. There's some people have homes like yours and there's some didn't like 'em and left, and then some never had 'em and don't want 'em, so this is their home and family. It ain't much, maybe, but it's real."

"Yessir. Thank you, sir."

Gus left dumbly, stunned and horrified that men must call that echoing ancient hall home and family. He kept his eyes on the sidewalk and nearly knocked the barrel-chested Marshal down.

"Easy there, Gus," Grover said mildly.

"I'm sorry, I was thinkin' of something, Mr. Darby."

"Thinkin' about what, Gus?" The voice easy and gentle.

"Nothing, Marshal," Gus said and mounted his pony.

The high black autos bouncing over the rutted street bothered the pony, sending her off skittering sideways, her ears pointed and neck high.

"C'mon, Tops," Gus spoke, tightening his knees and forcing her on out of town, toward home. His mind was in a turmoil of wonder and guilt for his smug ignorance. For every time he'd mocked a drunkard, he felt a spur in his side, for every time he'd condemned card players and pool players as gamblers and riffraff, he felt the pain of a new awareness. Something was wrong. Why had he lived seventeen years in the same place and never learned anything except work, hunt, and church?

From this came the terrifying knowledge that he wasn't running his own life.

The freedom, the richness, the strength—what good were they if he went on through life as an ignorant hypocrite?

And the price for this painful knowledge was the maiming of his brother.

He hung the saddlebag in the stable, turned the pony out, and walked on across the yard to the porch where Lu sat rocking in the early sun.

He opened his eye a crack as Gus came up the steps.

"Have a good ride?"

"It's a nice day. I got the stuff."

"Well, fetch me a snort."

"Look, Lu, you know Poppa. Any drinking in the house he'd have a stroke. They're in my saddlebag."

"You'd think a man could have a drink of whiskey out in the open if he could pay for it," Lu said.

"Well, you can if you want, I'm just trying to think of Poppa and Momma."

"And Katie and Marty and Ford County and the Sunflower State of Kansas, locked in the middle of the red, white, and blue."

"Yes, I guess you'd think so," Gus said, feeling humbled and confused. "You do what you want, I got to get out there on that cultivator."

"Gus, you think I could go huntin' with you sometime? I ain't very fast but I can move."

"Sure, Lu," Gus said, "we'll go out to the hills Saturday in place of goin' to town."

He felt his spirits rise just from thinking of his wild domain. You never had problems in the Goshens except locating a rabbit track in the new grass or learning the song of the redwing blackbird.

Gus hurried to get his team onto the cultivator and started around their endless rows. He worked them hard, making up for lost time. The horses were still young and range-minded, still remembering Montana or Idaho, wherever they'd been captured and

abducted from their wild range, but they were learning, and Poppa
said hard work was good training.

At high noon, he unhitched them and walked them back to the
shade of the stable and went on into the house for midday dinner.

Martin met him halfway. A weird little smile worked over his
cramped mouth, and his eyes shone with some special delight. In
one glance, Gus read the whole story and was resigned to a punishment as certain as doom.

"You really did it, little brother," Martin said, his voice soft
and sandy. "This time you really . . ."

"Lu?" Gus interrupted.

"Let me finish."

"You ain't anything to say I don't already know." Gus pushed
on by.

"Wait," Martin said. "You go in there now Poppa'll take after
you with a singletree."

"What happened to Lu?"

"Bugs. Gone completely bugs. Singing songs, waving his cane,
offerin' everybody a drink of that rotgut you brung him."

"I was hopin' he'd nurse it along."

Gus hurried up the steps into the big kitchen, charging over the
top, against the machine guns and barbed wire and poison gas of
rigid minds.

Lu was nodding off in a kitchen chair. An empty bottle stood
on the checkered oil cloth. Poppa was at the sink pouring out the
second bottle, holding the brown bottle as if it were a nasty ser-
pent.

Hearing the door shut, Lu stirred, continuing his dreamy
thought, the words coming out in fluid buoyancy.

> "Mademoiselle from Armentières
> Went over the hill
> To kiss Kaiser Bill
> Down in the grass,
> She shoved a bayonet right up his . . ."

"Enough!" Poppa drowned out the word. "There's women in the
house."

> "Mademoiselle from Armentières
> O, mademoiselle from Armentières

> You might forget the gas and shell
> But you'll never forget that mademoiselle . . ."

Poppa glared at Gus. "This is your doing."

"Maybe, Poppa," Gus said.

"You can't blame it on to him. He couldn't even get outa the yard."

"I can blame the whole tribe," Gus said, keeping his eyes set on Poppa's.

"That'll be enough."

> "O, mademoiselle, mademoiselle . . ."

"If you don't ever listen you ain't ever goin' to understand."

"I ain't listening to a seventeen-year-old pup speak on the subject of a drunken, foul-mouthed . . . *cripple*—"

"Well, I guess I'll get back to the field, then."

"Gus, dimdam it, you stay here and you listen. From now on you don't do nothin' less'n I tell you to."

"Yessir, I ain't mad at you."

"I don't like your tone of voice."

"Poppa, I bet you don't remember our old hired hand, Jubal. Black Jube, the man with the banjo."

"I remember him for his uppity insolence."

> "The French they are a mucked-up race,
> Fight with their feet and save their face . . ."

"You fired him in the fall, remember?"

"He quit. He couldn't stick it out."

"No, I remember you was achin' to fire him, and you got after him on account of his banjo that Marty had busted, and you talked to him just like you're talkin' now."

Poppa seemed to rise up like a red-eyed wild horse. "That'll be enough! Carry this . . . this evil to his room and pray hard he sees the error of his ways."

"C'mon, Lu," the boy said, turning to the nodding, glassy-eyed man. "Beddy-bye."

Gus picked him up like an orphan lamb, shocked at how light a birdy the body was, all the more pitiful, remembering the powerful brown body swimming like a beaver across the river. A strong, heavy-shouldered plowboy carrying a fallen brother.

Laying him gently on the bed, Gus said, "I'm sorry, Lu, it ain't a-goin' to work."

But Lu was snoring and wheezing, dreaming of the lasses of La Belle France.

In the kitchen, Poppa and Katie and Martin were sitting down at the table while Momma put out platters of fried steak and potatoes and gravy.

"He's sleepin'," Gus said, taking his place.

"Dear God," Poppa said, shutting his eyes, "we pray for the redemption of Luther's soul, and thank thee for thy bounty."

They commenced eating, chewing, clattering silverware, slurping hot coffee. No one spoke. Gus looked around at them. He'd spent most of his life feeding generation on generation of animals, and these faces, Poppa's windburned hatchet, and the steely fox-face of Martin, and Katie's heavy cheeks, and Momma's thin hair and bright greedy eyes, seemed to be a composite of all those eating animals.

"I'll take him to town in the morning," Gus said loudly. "He's got his pension. He can spend it any way he wants."

"He stays here. He can still learn to live like a Christian."

"Poppa," Gus said, "maybe he's not a Christian. Maybe he's an old man."

"He ain't over twenty-two right now."

"And he weighs about ninety-eight pounds."

"Best you let me handle it."

"I'm tryin' to tell you he ain't a kid. He's been through so much more than you or me, we oughta call him granddad."

"Would you shut up!" Poppa mopped his mouth with his sleeve. "Just shut up and let me eat."

Gus started to get up, but Momma said, "Gus, better eat your dinner whilst it's hot."

"Yes'm," Gus said, sure that he was right, but overwhelmed by the forthright integrity and power of his father, by his father's endeavor and success and increase. How could a seventeen-year-old plowboy argue with that? If it only wasn't his brother, his idol, he'd have dropped it and admitted he was all wrong, but there was no hiding Lu: his scar, his eye socket, his ruined leg, his drowned lungs, the only thing left was his cheery spirit uncaged, and they were doing their damnedest to nail that to their cross of industry and increase.

"He ain't Jube, Poppa."

"You can leave the table," Poppa said without looking up.

Momma sighed. Martin smiled, and Katie scratched at a mole on her chin.

"Yessir," Gus said and went outside to the barn.

He sat a minute on a hay bale and tried to think on both sides of it. It'd been a hard day for him as well as the rest, harder perhaps because he was so far behind everyone else and he had so little confidence in his own judgment.

Still, he decided, chewing at a straw and spitting little pieces off into the still air, still, Lu was a man and oughta be treated like one and right was right.

He took the team out of their stalls and walked them back out into the field where the cultivator waited at the turn of the row, backed them into the traces, and gingerly hooked them up again, half expecting one or the other of them to kick his head off. A little rest and a bait of barley and they felt frisky and independent-minded.

Looping long reins around his neck, realizing too how he and the once wild horses were tied together, they commenced to route weeds out of the cornfield, around and around, through the spring swarmy day, and his thoughts were of Lu and of Sally and of Jubal with sweat on his round black face, stacking bundles of wheat for the thresher in August when the sun was blinding and the dust was strangling, and yet he had that wonderful, friendly grin for the little boy who napped and played by his big feet in their small shoes with the toes cut out and the slits in the side for the lump of little toe to feel free.

The wet heat seemed to rise out of the low ground and hang spermy and rich and aching to explode.

It started out like any other middle summer day, the chores, the breakfast, the hitching up of the new team, the flies biting, a heavy oppression in the air presaging a thunderstorm. Martin taking his team on to the north section, Gus taking his to the south.

Katie was helping Momma in the big garden, and the new hired hand was cultivating the west eighty.

Poppa was in town on some land business and Lu had all by himself managed earlier that spring to limp his way afoot down the road before anyone was even up, to settle in the Palace Hotel.

Lu was his own man, or half man. Whatever he was, he was himself. And except for Gus, he quietly despised his kin.

It was whispered that he consorted with Mrs. Larsen, who was a rather genteel, poverty-stricken widow with four children who had no hope except to lean upon the charity of the male community.

Even so, each day was a little quieter for Lu. It was harder to get up every morning and easier to go to bed after a couple of drinks down at the Long Branch. His cough was worse, his strength fading.

The heavy day went along steadily as the horses drew the four row cultivator. They resented the monotony and the sweat and the hard-biting flies. Gus kept a firm grip on them, outthinking them before they could ever get into mischief.

At noon as he'd done a thousand times before, he unhitched from the cultivator and walked the team back to the stable, fed and watered them. Washing his sweating, red-burned face under the pump, he heard Poppa ride into the yard and turn the horse into the corral. Gus could sense the storm in his father as he could sense the thunder coming across the prairie, but he said nothing.

When he said grace his voice was tight and strained. "Lord God, we thank thee for thy bounty and thy increase, and we pray for the redemption of the lost. We pray for the saving of the sinners."

Clue enough.

After he'd passed the mashed potatoes, Martin said, "You settle the Colorado land with the bank?"

"I did," Poppa said grimly. "At twelve percent interest."

"That's hard to make a profit on," Momma said. "Maybe we'd better set off awhile and swallow what we've already bit off."

"The land is going up, more people want it, and the price of wheat will keep right on a-goin'," Poppa declared.

There was nothing more said for a minute or two while they fed. After Poppa had pushed his bread-wiped plate away, he announced, "I better tell everybody plain out that I saw Lu in town this morning. He was stinking drunk in the morning if you can imagine such a thing. I saw him fall down and smack his head on the curb. Doc Winkleman hauled him off to the hotel. We're sunk in a total disgrace."

"Did he look hurt bad?" Momma asked.

"Just split his head a little. Don't worry, the Lord takes care of fools and drunks."

"I'll get the pie," Momma said, rising.

Gus looked around the table at the faces of his family and saw no pain, no worry, no nothing.

"No pie for me, Momma," he said. "I'm goin' in and see if Lu's all right."

"He'll disgrace us," Poppa said. "We're not going to have anything to do with him. I'm disownin' and disinheritin' him."

But Gus was already halfway across the room.

"Did you hear me?" Poppa said.

"I heard you, but you didn't hear me."

"I want that field cultivated before dark."

"Then you just better do it yourself," Gus said, afraid of his own voice. He'd never spoken so strongly before.

Poppa rose up, but the certain strength of young manhood was in Gus.

"Go on then!" Poppa yelled. "You worthless ingrate—and tell him to change his name and get out of the county before I take the whip to him and you too!"

The street was quiet. No convention of irate citizens met Gus in the square. Grover Darby sat in his heavy oaken chair in front of the jail, acting half asleep.

Lu's room was on the ground floor of the Palace, just off the lobby.

Dr. Winkleman opened the door at his tap. The room was so silent and the doctor's face so grave, Gus asked in a whisper, "Is he . . . ?"

"Take a look," the doctor said and turned to the bed.

Lu lay dazed, a thick gauze bandage around his forehead, his eye partly open.

"I've got him under," the doctor said. "Lacerated his scalp when he fell. Bled a lot, but he's done so much of that, a little more won't hurt him."

Gus looked at his brother with his own pain in his heart: the loss, the loss, knowing even as he felt this way, Lu might smile and ask, "Worryin' about the decrease?"

"He can't hear anything, Gus. I guess you're the one I have to talk to."

Gus turned, the fear in his chest deeper all the time.

"Lord knows your father ought to be here instead of you."

"He won't."

"I know he won't. How old are you, nineteen?"

"Eighteen, Doctor."

"Well, you can tell your dad that nobody'd ever got a look at Lu, excepting maybe Mrs. Larsen, until today when he was out."

"Yessir, he keeps sayin' he feels fine and gettin' better all the time."

"Well, the simple fact is that the Army doctors must've seen he was goin' to die on 'em, so they shipped him home. Save on paperwork. I never saw one mortal body that had so many mean things wrong with it. He fell this morning because his blood pressure is so low it's a wonder his toes and fingers aren't rotting off. Can't get any oxygen from the wet lungs. Only thing keepin' him alive at all is his youth. Youth hates to die no matter how much it hurts to stay alive."

"You mean it ain't the whiskey?"

"It ain't nothing to do with whiskey. Maybe whiskey is the only nourishment he can use. I'm sure he hadn't had a drink this morning. He fell because he didn't have the strength to stand up."

"What do we do?"

"You could order a wheelchair, but it'd be a waste of your father's hard-earned money. You just better get ready for a funeral."

"You've given up!" Gus was angry. "You're not tryin'."

"I'm telling you, son, he was a casualty when he left France. Youth, a sense of humor, and a little whiskey got him all the way to western Kansas, where I guess he wanted to come. I'm not giving up. I can give him pills, hop up his blood pressure, but there's no lung or kidney able to support it. Only reason I'm tellin' you this is because your father ought to know that his son may be dead in a week."

"I knew he was nothin' but skin and bone, but he kept smilin' and jokin' and talkin' about how he was a-proddin' all the girls in the county."

Even as Gus was turning away, he heard Martin yell from the street, "Doctor! Where's the doc?"

And somehow Gus knew right then in that moment what had happened, why it had happened, and who was guilty.

"That's Martin," Gus said. "C'mon, Doc, there's some bad trouble out at the farm."

The doctor had his bag in his hand and was halfway down the hall when Martin slammed through the door, his eyes wild and sharp.

He didn't waste any time or words. "It's Poppa, he's tangled up in the cultivator. Team broke and run on him." And turning to Gus, he spoke the simple indictment, "*Your* team."

"I'll take the Ford," the Doc said. "You boys better show me where to go."

The touring Model T was a little faster than a buggy and a lot noisier.

"The team?" Gus asked as they clattered highballing out of town, Grover Darby, Jake Zitzman, Don Dodge, Benny Peacock, Mr. Poffenberg and Joe Rosewurm, all out in the street watching them go, knowing already the emergency, the urgency.

"I cut 'em loose. They may be to hell and gone back to Montana by now."

"How'd he look?" the doctor asked, bending over the heavy wooden wheel and peering down the road, pulling down the gas and spark levers all the way.

"He was screamin'," Martin said, "just like a gutshot hog."

Down the rutted graveled road they raced, slewing around the squared-off corners, and gunning on to the east of town past the new Gilpin farms, past all the increase, past the home place.

The doctor found a fairly level spot and put the high-wheeled black machine into low gear and crossed the ditch into the field, let off the pedal, which sent it into high gear, and, seeing his target across the field by the walnut trees, charged across the new green corn, over the furrows and, yanking back the clutch lever, slammed his foot on the iron brake and leaped over the door to the wrecked cultivator and the man impaled on its steel teeth.

Poppa's eyes were grey green like a trapped animal's, his jaw set stubborn, refusing now to admit the steel in his bowel.

"Don't move, Mr. Gilpin," Doc said quietly, sighing, methodically bringing out a loaded hypodermic from the bag. And conversationally, he said to the boys, "Maybe you better ask his blessing while you can."

"Yessir," Gus said, and moved ahead of Martin with the queer urgency of the guilt driving him, bringing tears to his eyes. "Poppa, I'm sorry I took off like that, I'm sorry you're hurt."

And Martin added, "Poppa, what should I do now?"

"God, I ain't ready," Poppa said as the doctor eased the needle in and thumbed down the plunger.

"I guess nobody is," the doctor said gently. "You got any words for your boys?"

"Be good, boys, be a credit to me and Momma. Keep the name of Gilpin shining true." He started to ramble, great sobs breaking his voice. "You take care of the womenfolks and say your prayers, you work hard and watch the increase and . . ."

The opium finally melted his jaw and broke the ice in his eyes. His voice dwindled off like a gusty dust devil tailing across the prairie.

"Is he dead?" Martin asked.

Dr. Winkleman had his finger on the old man's inner wrist, and after a long minute turned and nodded.

"What was in that shot?" Martin's voice was cold and suspicious.

"Pain killer. I figured to save him all I could. I figured you'd want me to, but if you're worried about it, I won't charge you."

"Wait," Gus said, crying openly. "Don't be mad, Dr. Winkleman. What're we going to do now?"

"It ain't going to be pretty. Maybe you better have a drink of medicinal alcohol first." He took a brown bottle out of the black bag, took a drink, and handed it to Martin.

"I don't need it," Martin said. "I can stand up to it." And to Gus he said, "You don't need it neither."

"I need something or I'm goin' to fall down," Gus said weakly, going down on his knees. He took the bottle and drank the burning sweet brandy.

"That's enough," Martin said.

"I don't think there's much time," Doc said. "Folks'll be all around here, wantin' to help or wantin' to watch."

"Yessir," Gus said. "Poppa never liked folks pryin'."

"Heave up on that wheel then, boys, and turn this thing back up on an even keel. Then back it off the tree, and I'll try to unjam that damned shoe from his stomach."

The young men righted the rig and backed it away as the doctor wanted. Gus raised the cultivator shoes as high as the lever would go, while the doctor tried to ease the body free of the curved steel barb.

"Martin," the doctor said in a sweat, "lean down on the tongue so's to get him higher."

Martin put his weight on it and the doctor scrabbled on his knees, tugging this way and that, grunting to himself. "Must've been hooked." Putting his knee on the dead man's chest, he leaned his weight on the body until by brute strength the flanged shoe, shaped like a scooping arrowhead, ripped out and the body flopped flat to the ground. The doctor sighed.

"Hate bein' so rough, but he don't know it."

Gus was trying to hold down his stomach, trying to look off at the line of chalk-rock fence posts and the meadowlarks and the green plumes of corn sprouting up out of the freshly weeded earth.

Quickly the doctor had the body out in the open. He cleaned and composed the face and spread a blanket over it.

"I don't know what the hurry is," Martin said meanly.

"Right, Martin, yessir, you're right, only I know your Momma is goin' to be here in a minute and now she can look at a man instead of an ugly goddamned accident."

"It's O.K., Doctor," Gus said. "Here she comes."

Momma and Katie driving the grain wagon along with Mr. Westphal, the nearest neighbor to the west, pulled into the field. Mr. Westphal doffed his straw hat at the doc, and darted his quick brown eyes around, sizing up the still wet steel shoe and the blanketed form and nodding again to Doc.

Momma spoke to Martin. "How is he?"

"Dead, Momma. He died with a clear head and hardly any pain." Martin spoke the ancient formula, the first of a hundred false phrases that had to be said.

She knelt beside Poppa's body and pulled back the blanket from the face. Poppa's face seemed sublimely asleep. His hair was only a bit disheveled, his eyes were closed, a faint smile of glory on his clean lips. Momma touched the coarse white hair to straighten it, put the blanket back and got to her feet again, exposing her knobby, callused knees.

"I'm awfully sorry," the doctor said.

"I told him them horses'd kill him if he kept at it," Mr. Westphal started to say, but caught himself, realizing he was saying the right words but to the wrong people.

"Yes, ma'am," he said, "I always respected him for being a good Christian gentleman, and God knows he'll be missed."

She hardly heard him, but, turning to the boys again, she said, "Put him in the wagon, boys, and take him on in to Mr. Rosewurm. I expect Pastor Veitgengruber will make the arrangements. Me and Katie are going home."

"I'll be glad to take you, ma'am," the doctor said, "if you don't mind ridin' in my car."

"I think I'd rather walk, thanks," the hump-shouldered woman with the gray burning eyes said. "It's a nice little way. Come along, Katie."

Katie'd been dying for a ride, but she kept her eyes down and walked along about a half step behind Momma.

Mrs. Gilpin seemed to be inspecting the corn plants, estimating the probable harvest if the weather stayed anywhere decent and God didn't burn up the whole crop in July.

Gus kept thinking of his mother's stony red knees; he kept thinking of the bandaged one-eyed head of his beloved brother and the shiny iron barbed foot ripping through his father's stomach into his backbone, and the world and time seemed to be getting away from him, or, rather, inside him like a black furry bag growing and growing inside his ribs, crowding his heart and shortening his breath.

As the boys and Mr. Westphal drove slowly down the road in the wagon, Martin said, "Maybe you oughta drop off and tell the McCoys."

"Why them?"

" 'Cause they're next door, and they're Catholics. If you don't tell 'em they'll hold it against us."

Gus dropped over the side and walked into the driveway toward the farm yard, his mind turning over the elements of the day, trying to fit them into a true order, but the more he saw them, the more frustrated and confused he became, and there was just nothing for it when he saw Sally hanging up white sheets on the clothesline, reaching up high, a long, duck-billed clothespin between her lips, her back arched and her breasts high and the golden thighs bare through her gingham frock. No help. No direction. No nothing.

He simply went to her like a baffled bull who's been through the ring and still survives, groggy, bloody, but all bull. She turned on hearing his step and smiled lightly until she saw the blaze in his eyes and the firm set of his mouth.

"No, wait. Gus, wait a second," she said. "What's happened?"

And even as she spoke she was edging back into the washhouse where the boilers steamed and a great stack of sheets was piled on the floor.

"No. It's too late!" She wept tears of a curious remorse he hadn't time to question.

THREE

LU'S FRAIL PERSON never emerged from the shrouded depths, never spoke clearly, never knew of Poppa's death. He fell, he never got up again.

His death was sweet compared to Poppa's impaled pain. His loss was already wished for, accepted, and mourned, and he was buried next to his father in the plot next to St. Olaf's church.

But in the months that followed came the precarious summing up of what was and what was not, what was real estate and false estate, and how much trust it took to make a kite fly.

Gus couldn't have cared less that the Volstead Act prohibiting the sale of liquor in the United States was passed over the President's veto.

He was more concerned that Poppa had stretched his credit web as far as the banker, Mr. Hundertmarx, would let it spread, accepting the burden of an extra percent or two just to be first in farming the deep but untried Colorado land.

Martin tried bluffing, but he was still a novice and Mr. Hundertmarx was a professional.

"Consolidate," Mr. Hundertmarx advised through his neighborly jowels. "Best you all back up and take a breath. Your poppa was an expert in land development, but it took him years to gain the experience."

"Maybe so," Martin said. "I don't know where to turn. Momma's slowed down considerable, and the devil knows Gus ain't never been worth the powder to blow him to perdition."

"Better half a loaf than none." The banker smiled at Gus. "A man gets overextended and some little thing happens and next thing he's off workin' as hired help."

"I'm glad the home place is clear," Gus said.

"Not quite." Mr. Hundertmarx's face turned sad. "Your poppa was bound to get into the Western gamble." He picked up a paper and placed it under Gus's eyes. "Seven thousand dollars at twelve percent."

"When's it due?"

"Two years."

"What'll you settle for?" Martin asked sickly.

"Now, Martin, don't rush into anything," Mr. Hundertmarx said in his loafing dialect. "Your only problem is that you've been left long on debt and short on cash."

"I told him to sock it away, but he'd never listen," Martin sniped. "Now the price of wheat is dropping every day. And there ain't hardly time to harvest that Colorado crop either."

"You've got several farms in Ford County, boys, but unfortunately they're all mortgaged to the top." Mr. Hundertmarx was all worry and sorrow.

"What can we get for the Colorado section?" Martin asked bluntly. "It'll harvest fifteen thousand bushels of wheat sure."

"Nothing is all that sure, especially in dry-land farming, as you ought to know by now," Mr. Hundertmarx said.

"But say it brought in that big of a crop, say wheat is six bits a bushel, that runs about eleven thousand dollars."

"Say it hails, or rains, or the wind mats it down, what's it worth? Nothing, not to me, anyway."

"Half it," Martin said, not looking at Gus.

"Fifty-five hundred?"

"I want to get even, somehow."

"There's the Jorgenson farm," Mr. Hundertmarx said, digging out another stiff, crinkly paper. "It's worth, well, what's a tenant farm of a hundred and sixty acres worth?"

"Sixteen thousand," Martin said.

Mr. Hundertmarx chuckled. "I admire your courage, Martin, or your optimism, but you ought to know about tenant farms by now, and especially as wheat ain't two dollars any more. The Wall Street Jews are pushing it down more every day, and nobody knows where'll it stop."

"All right, what's your guess?" Martin asked sourly. "I mean what's your fair appraisal?"

"That's better," Mr. Hundertmarx said, and looked at the pressed-tin ceiling for a while. "Well, maybe it's not worth it and maybe the bank board will object, but just to be neighborly, and make sure you've got a fighting chance to get on, I believe I can say the Jorgenson farm is worth eight thousand. And the mortgage on it is six thousand, so you can cash these two papers in for a thousand dollars even."

"Watch him, Martin," Gus said. "He's offerin' a thousand dollars for two farms just before harvest."

"Shut up," Martin said. "Since when did you care anything about farmin'?"

"Just in reply," Mr. Hundertmarx said quietly, "if you can do better somewhere else, please go there. Your father was an honest, God-fearing man, and I trusted him much farther than most would."

"He made you rich," Gus said. "Him and the rest of us working for nothing."

"We'll take it," Martin said quickly.

"I don't want hard feelings or ill will." The banker toyed with his gold watch chain. "Money can't buy a good reputation and you'd better think again on it, because I wouldn't walk across this room to help someone that was going to bite my hand."

"I said we'd take it. I'll fetch Momma in this afternoon to sign it."

"Of course, you've got a plenty more paper here too, Martin," Mr. Hundertmarx said. "Sooner or later you'll have to do something about it. I'm always open, aboveboard, and foursquare. That's the way I live, and that's the way I do business."

"I'm sure beholden to you," Martin said, "but this is as big a bite as I can chaw today."

"Sure, Martin, you're young yet, and I'm just trying to teach you how your poppa did it. If he'd just lived another five years, he'd a had an empire. He'd a owned this bank and half the Western prairie, but of course he had to go out cultivating corn when he should have been elsewhere."

"Baloney!" Gus' voice came out in an unaccustomed gusty roar. "Even I can see everybody's working for you, and you're getting the gravy."

"You can leave right now," Mr. Hundertmarx said, nodding his head judiciously. "I'll have no such talk in this place of business. If you want to sweat, young man, I could sweat you. You have no idea of how I could sweat you. You could be arrested and put in a cell and starved and belittled until you rebelled, and then we could beat the pie-waddin' out of you and retry you for another charge and then send you to Leavenworth in chains for the rest of your life. Now I'm telling you, young man, for the sake of the memory of your father, I'll accept your apology."

At first Gus wasn't sure. But suddenly remembering Lu's free, merry face, Gus laughed at the fat, welted, red-faced, oily-talking bumptious crook and said, "I ought to sock you, Mr. Hundertmarx, you lying blood sucker, because this is America and you can't get away with it here. You just wish you could, that's all."

Martin had him by the arm, snarling, "You goddamn dumb kid, keep your trap shut and c'mon!"

And to the banker, Martin said, "You have to forgive him, Mr. Hundertmarx, he ain't been the same since we lost Poppa and Lu."

"You'd do well to send him off somewhere for his health. He sounds very much like an anarchist, like one of those I Won't Work people. Wants the world on a platter but won't turn a hand to get it."

"You've convinced yourself, so how could you be wrong?" Gus replied cheerfully and went with Martin.

On the street, Gus let his breath out in a long sigh. "I feel like I finally did something right."

"You damn fool, he was being decent because it'd have looked bad to take advantage, but now he's got us down."

"When are you goin' to start being some kind of a man instead of a tame mule owned by a bot-fly like him?" Gus asked, knowing there could be no answer.

"You're goin' to be spendin' time in the jailhouse," Martin said. "You just can't talk to respectable men like that."

"He just golloped up at least two years of our work in one gollop."

"That's his business. It's the system."

"It may be a system, but it sure ain't respectable."

They rode home in the wagon, neither speaking. Gus kept the team going steady, until Martin said, "I'm goin' to take that thousand dollars and buy a Ford, so's I can drive Momma to church."

"Fine with me." Gus felt tired. It was no good keeping the banker straight if Martin had no sense of himself. "While you're at it maybe you could trade a couple farms for a tractor."

"It ain't a bad idea," Martin agreed. "The country's going that way, everything modernizing."

Passing the McCoy turnoff and mailbox, Martin put a different edge to his voice. "Funny how them McCoys all pulled out right after Poppa's funeral, and nobody saw 'em go."

"Maybe to you a family going broke is funny," Gus said.

"You ain't sayin' much, I notice."

What is there to say? Gus thought. I loved her and I wronged her and they were gone before I could get clear of Poppa and Lu to make amends and ask her to be my wife. They left in the dead of night like chicken thieves.

After a while Gus said, "You know who owns that McCoy farm now?"

"Mr. Hundertmarx, I reckon."

"And that's why they left," Gus said. "Because he wasn't just satisfied to take half shares of all their labor. He wasn't just satisfied with that."

"You mean Fat Hundertmarx was a-cockwalkin' around your little Sally?" Martin crowed it out, a rising, strangling, cackling laugh.

"I told you so's you'd know who your friends are and who they ain't, and I hope you do more'n laugh when he starts cockwalkin' around Katie."

"He wouldn't dare," Martin said.

"I'd almost guess you'd trade her for an iron-wheeled Fordson tractor with five gallons of gas throwed in."

"You musta been pretty sweet on little Sally to get so all frothed up."

"I hate for the big hog to eat up the little folks, especially preachin' at 'em like it was his due, like it was owed him, like he was something God had picked out special. Well, I ain't never goin' to respect your eggsuckin' friend, and that's the end of it."

"You can think on it whilst you harrow the west quarter this afternoon," Martin said, thinking on it himself.

Katie had dinner ready for them, fried meat, potatoes and

gravy, biscuits, and plum jam. Her eyes were on the floor and she was silent in serving the two young men.

"Where's Momma?" Gus asked.

"She went over to the graveyard with some flowers."

"That why you been cryin', for grief?" Martin said.

"Maybe. Maybe it's none of your business," she said.

Gus noticed how heavy in the legs she was getting, a regular big-gutted farm woman. Her collie dog face was too much like Poppa's to win her any Gibson Girl awards.

"Maybe you oughta be gettin' married, Katie," Gus said, meaning well. "Get a husband and get your own place."

"What's the matter, you don't like my cookin'?" she retorted.

"No, I mean you got your own life to lead like everybody else. You ain't a slave to this farm or this family, either."

"I swear," Martin said, "you're just determined to rile up everybody today, ain't you?"

"I'm just tryin' to keep to the Golden Rule," Gus said. "I'm sorry if I hurt your feelings, Katie."

"Gus was tellin' me," Martin spoke slyly to her, "he was a-sayin' Mr. Hundertmarx might be a-sparkin' around here, checkin' the heifer."

The eight-day banjo clock ticked one, two, three, four, and the only other noise was an egg-free hen singing self-praise out in the yard.

"So?" Katie said at last, her face fixed solid as an iron frying pan.

"He ain't been yet, has he?" Martin's eyes were foxfire.

"Well, not out here least ways," Katie said quietly.

"What's this now?" Momma spoke from the doorway.

"We was just talkin' about the bank business," Martin said.

"Now, Martin," his mother said carefully, "please, I heard something different."

"Ask Katie," Martin said. "She knows. I don't."

Gus sat frozen. What he'd considered a remote possibility was unfolding to be an accomplished fact.

"Well, there's nothing to it," Katie sniffed. "I wouldn't have nothing to do with him. He's married and fat."

"But he's been sniffin' around down wind of you, ain't he?" Martin asked.

"Martin." Momma clucked her tongue.

"What else?" Gus asked, feeling sick, knowing it all, because he'd known Sally.

"What else, nothing, he seen me in town the other morning and said he was driving his new Buick down to Garden City and wouldn't I like to go for a drive, and I did."

Martin's face was beet red and his eyes were glinting like snow crystals. "What'd he do?"

"Nothing. I had a lot of fun in the machine."

"Now I know Mr. Hundertmarx is a charter member of our church and lodge, he was a good friend of your father's, and I wouldn't suspect him of one indecent thing toward our family," Momma said, watching Katie's face.

"That's right," Katie said in an unnatural voice with a wide crazy grin. "He's a fine gentleman with peculiar tastes in some ways, but at least he's alive!"

"What do you mean?" Momma asked.

"I mean I'm twenty-two years old and I just don't want to die an old maid."

"So he's had you already," Gus said quietly, rising from the table. "I guess I didn't quite get it all said this morning." And to Martin: "You comin'?"

"You set down a minute!" Martin yelled. "You're goin' to go off half cocked and throw us all into the poorhouse."

"Momma," Gus said, "I'm goin' in and beat him till he tells the whole town what a hog he is."

"What good'll that do our Katie?" Momma said, tears slowly leaking down her sun-barked face. "I don't know, I guess it's time for me to lay me down and die."

Martin leaped to his feet, yelling, "Now stop it! Momma, we don't never quit, and so he has been a-dickin' some around Katie, that don't hurt nothin', so long as nobody knows it!"

"I know it," Gus said and went out the door.

Martin caught him in the yard, saying breathlessly, "Don't do it, Gus, they'll throw you in jail and they'll throw away the key."

"He taken Sally, he taken Katie, he ain't takin' no more."

"Look, Gus, let's be reasonable. Maybe we can make a settlement, see, we'll get a lawyer. Get old Halmerschmidt, he'll work out a breach-of-promise case, and then we can settle."

"I said you'd sell her for a Fordson, but I didn't really think you would," Gus said, tossing the saddle onto his pony and reeving up the cinch hard.

"Oh, don't be so damned holy—look at what it got Lu."

"Lu? Holy?" Gus laughed.

"No, I mean goin' against the stream. You try to buck the bank, you're goin' to lose, boy, you're goin' to lose."

"O.K.," Gus said, "so I'm goin' to lose, but that hog ain't goin' to be buyin' up our womenfolk no more."

Gus coiled up a dusty braided horse whip and hung it over his saddle horn, bumped Martin aside as he mounted, and rode down the road toward town.

He had only one thing on his mind—to expose the animal. He meant simply to drag the banker out into the street and show him the animal whip and let the legend go from there.

Perhaps their next banker might be more interested in helping the community instead of eating it up.

But it never entered his mind that Martin would telephone Hundertmarx and spill the beans.

He rode into town the same as he'd hunt a deer up in the Goshen hills, coming in a way least expected. You never knew about winds or strange extra senses animals had. He came in from the east. Not hiding, or sloping through, just coming in at the springy trot his pony liked. He stopped at the hitchpost in front of the bank, where the bright black Buick sedan was parked with its Winged Victory statuette on its radiator. As he was dismounting, caught helplessly with one foot in the stirrup, one toe touching the ground, there was Grover Darby behind him saying, "Better come along with me, son."

So there was nothing for it but to walk along with the burly Marshal with his sleepy eyes and his big pistol in its holster.

"What is it, Marshal Darby?" Gus asked after a minute, still trying to figure how the spider webs were woven so fast, and noting the fat red face peeking out the dusty window of the bank, and the Marshal saying, "Heard you was on the prod."

"I'm just collectin' my own," Gus said slowly, still trying to think ahead.

"You can't win, Gus," the Marshal said placidly.

"I been livin' in this county eighteen years, Marshal Darby.

I ought to know something about it, especially what's right and wrong."

"You're young. Ain't broke to the harness yet. I'm tellin' you that it's a hard lesson to learn if you make it hard. Steel bars is a lots harder than a buggy whip."

"But what about a man bein' a man on his two hind legs? I mean, harness is for animals, ain't it?"

"Don't give me no sass, youngster, I'm goin' to show you the inside of a cell and let you make up your own mind."

"You just think so, Marshal," Gus said under his breath as he shifted his weight from the hip and brought his wheeling shoulder up with the ham fist springing out, crashing, stunning, dropping the lawman to the sidewalk like a pole-axed steer.

Gus didn't wait to see the damage. He turned running, grabbing the horse whip off his saddle and charging up the chalk-rock steps toward the double glass door, with its shades pulled down, busting right on through glass, doors, shades and all, leaping on over the counter into the office of the fat Mr. Hundertmarx with his red face and the little pistol in his hand firing and missing, firing and snagging a hunk of rib muscle, but by then Gus had him by the arm, twisting and snapping it, dragging him, the mottled sick green-faced hog, by the other arm out into the street where by then Benny Peacock, George Koberman, Donald Dodge, Gerald Lundquist, Mr. Poffenberg, Joe Rosewurm, Mrs. Larsen, Dr. Winkleman, Jake Zitzman, and Pastor Veitgengruber could see him whip the pig into the gutter dirt, once, twice, three times, and then to break the whip stock over his knee, walk to his pony and ride on out of town, dripping a slender trail of blood.

It wasn't so much Hundertmarx, but to knock down the Marshal was trouble, son. They'd hunt you down like a ratty coyote for that.

And as the road slowly corkscrewed before his eyes, the pain of the wound stabbing his side, and the dizziness making him clutch at leather, and knowing the cry already going, "Mad dog, mad dog!" and seeing the freight train loading wheat at the big elevators, he knew as well as he knew his own name that here was the way, the only way left, for him.

He slipped off the pony, slapped her hind end, and staggered across the gravel toward the rusty red boxcars.

Gus awakened in a transient terror. He wasn't sure where he was or where he'd been or where he was going, but no matter how he figured it, he'd done the only thing he could possibly do and still call himself a man named Gus Gilpin. It wasn't his fault that Grover Darby interfered. Still keeping his eyes closed, he said a little one-line prayer for the Marshal's health.

Then he opened his eyes to the splintery floor of the empty box-car rocking along steadily, clicking over every rail joint.

He was alone, going east.

The pain of the wound knifed into his side when he tried to get up. Somehow he'd blocked the shooting out of his memory, but it came back with a vengeance as he rolled up to his knees, a groan rasping through his teeth.

Dried blood caked his shirt. He reached inside the chambray and painfully separated it from the gouge across his ribs. The bullet had smacked against a middle rib and skimmed alongside it, tearing out a busy-bee furrow as it rammed on through.

It took him a half hour of painful patience to ease out of his jacket and shirt. He wanted to be clean.

But there was no water. The sky was dry and clear.

He tried kneading the dusty blood out of the cloth.

They passed through little lamplighted villages, but the train didn't stop.

Hunger made him weak. He'd always eaten regularly and heavily, burning up the fuel in the fields to bring in more food, always working for the extra increase. Now, supper was over and he'd missed it. Breakfast was coming and he was going to miss that too.

He dug in his pockets and found a couple of coins. He hadn't even brought his money. He laughed out loud, announcing to the east, "Here comes Gus Gilpin, folks, farmer boy on the road, forgot his purse and valise, wish him luck and treat him kindly!"

His laugh went out the open door and was crushed in the bleak rattle of iron wheels on iron rails.

Poor Momma, he thought. She'll feel all the more disgraced. Neighbors will be calling me a mad-dog outlaw. Shoot! Me, an outlaw!

He forced himself to think of something else. The pressure of rage and remorse threatened to split open his throbbing wound.

Dawn came on like a crystal of frost. Winter was around the corner. And hunger and a new world that'd never heard of Gus Gilpin or Ford County, Kansas.

He moved painfully to get the shirt back around his broad thews and tucked into his pants. The blue denim jacket went on over that. It was almost new and still dark blue. He could only hope it would hide most of the great stain on his side. He tried to comb his yellow hair back through his fingers and scrub his face with the flinty calluses of his hands.

The charnel stink of stockyards hit his nose before his eyes had gotten used to seeing the moldering brick tenements, soot-stained and inhuman, alongside the track, which became two tracks, then three, and then six. Boxcars rolled on either side, and remote-controlled switch points like destiny were shunting his car from here to there, left to right, and slowly slowing in a vast, noisy, hooting field of steel track and coal smoke and freight cars of every state in the nation.

He hadn't the vaguest idea of where to go, but knowing the hard sense of justice in western Kansas, he decided he'd best go along unknown and undercover for as long as he could.

The main thing was to move, move toward sanctuary somewhere, a job somewhere, a connection to this new world.

The freight slowed, the cinders were almost individually visible, and the smell of rotten blood and sledgehammered death of cattle and pigs was overpowering. He knelt in the open doorway of the car, trying to see some skyline, some point to aim for, but he could see only smoke-blackened, anonymous blocks, and at last despairing of anything but a life of roaming cinders and breathing the unholy stench, he edged to the door, favoring his wounded side, getting one leg over, grabbing a hold with his good right arm, and swinging off, running before his feet touched the cinders so as not to plow the road bed with his face.

His course took him diagonally toward a railroad work car where traveling section workers lived, an obsolete Pullman, gray-painted and dingy as the rest of the place. He leaned by its rusty stairway, taking in all the breath he could without getting sick. Looking back at the train he'd just left, he saw a squad of uniformed police move in on it, shouting at the engineer and brakemen, getting the wrong answers, looking under the cars at the

rods, and sending a couple of policemen topside to search while
the rest of them worked slowly through each boxcar, busy, hunting, a pack of dogs tracking a wounded animal.

Gus watched, unaware for a moment that the animal they
sought was himself.

The open doorway at the top of the stairway of the workers' car
beckoned like a sixth sense. In a flash he was backing up the stairs,
one at a time, facing the train yard.

"Hey there, you," a strong voice yelled.

He stopped moving and set himself to run.

"Hey there!" The voice belonged to a huge flat-nosed, red-
haired man in plain clothes coming around the end of the car.
Even a hayseed like Gus could see he was a man of officialdom
whether the state or the corporation paid his wage.

"Me?" Gus said.

"Yeah. You see anybody slip off that deadhead freight just come
in?"

"No. I just woke up," Gus said, realizing the redheaded officer
thought he lived in the workers' car.

"He shoulda been on that train." The beefy redhead glared.

Gus shrugged stupidly.

"Guess he coulda dropped off anywhere from here to Ford
County."

"Easy." Gus was feeling weaker every second, standing on the
run of the stairway, hung up like a Christmas goose.

The splay-nosed redhead looked at him a long moment. "Do I
know you?"

"I hope not." Gus smiled.

The cop cracked a small smile; he had still some sense of humor left. "Well, if you see a hard-case farmer sneaking out of
the yards give a whistle."

"What's he wanted for?" Gus asked.

"Bank robbery," the red-faced cop said, his eyes sharp and
bright, flicking glances into the dark holes of the jungle he lived
in.

"C'mon Whitey," another voice said behind him, "let's go."

The bull took them for a pair and turned away.

An older, craggy-faced, slope-shouldered man wearing clothes
almost identical to Gus's except for a billed blue cap came out
the doorway and down.

Gus moved ahead, wondering where the redheaded cop had gone.

"Mind if I walk with you?" Gus asked the older man.

"It's a free country," the old worker said defensively, and Gus walked along as if he knew where he was going and what he was going to do.

"Could you tell me the best way to get out of this train yard, mister?" Gus asked after a few steps.

"I'm goin' down to Third Street," the man said. "Where you from?"

"West," Gus said. "I'm lookin' for a job."

"What can you do?"

"Farm."

"Not in K.C., son. There ain't even a hunkie job open. There's hard times in K.C. I'm lucky to gandy-dance. Just don't get picked up for Vag. Never made any sense to me. Just big guys pushin' little guys around."

"That's why you didn't turn me in?" Gus asked.

"I'm a Wobbly. I wouldn't hand over any man to a bull. Come on, I'm after a drink."

"Don't you work today?" Gus wondered why the man was going off to drink.

"It's Sunday, boy," the worker said. "I gotta have a hair of that bulldog that bit me last night or die."

Gus hadn't the faintest idea of what he meant, but any way out of this hellhole was welcome.

They cut through lines of standing cars, through more tracks, past the machine shops and the great roundhouse, and finally to a street that had no steel tracks in it. The older man asked no questions, nor did Gus. He was learning the importance of a few words going a long way.

The first building was a tin-fronted shop with a blank painted door. It looked closed.

"Here's where I leave you, son," the old man said. "You go up Third Street about five miles, you'll be in the heart of Kansas City. But I tell you, if I was your age, I'd go right back the other way."

"Yessir," Gus said, thinking, Mister, I would if I could, but I can't.

He was thinking as he looked up the long sooted street that he'd best turn himself in and get it over with. The longer and the emptier the street looked, the emptier and longer and wasted was his future. He felt overcome by a massive sorrow that he'd left without the blessing of Momma.

This neighborhood of shanty tenements was the grimmest human habitation he'd ever seen. He tried to keep on the outside of the walk, sure that some maniac robber would leap out of a doorway with a gun or straight razor, killing first, looting later, and crying for more blood.

But no one was on the street or in the doorways. The whole city seemed to be asleep or empty. Cats and rats prowled through ash cans and garbage and broken brown bottles. And the stink of the foul slaughterhouses was an overpowering reek, signaling more than anything else that this city was the camp of death.

But where to go? The freight yards were blocked, the police were on the lookout. His legs were rubbery. His side ached, and he could only keep walking.

He had no friend here or destination, and if he could not hide or live unknown in this crowded shack town, where could he try?

Out of a dark narrow alley came not a robber or murderer but the same burly redheaded plainclothesman who'd directed the search in the freight yard.

"Been thinkin', big fella," the officer said. "What're you doing out in the streets this early of a Sunday morning?"

"Walking," Gus said, trying to hold down his fear.

"Funny," the officer said, "I thought you might be running."

"No, sir," Gus said.

"Where you from?"

"You mean my address?"

"I mean like are you from Ford County, Kansas?" The red-faced cop grinned with a sure instinct that he'd nailed his man. "And by God, if you deny it, I'll knock you down with a club. I wasn't fooled a bit, knew I'd got a bronco soon as I laid eyes on you."

As the officer ran his hands over Gus's flinching body, he said, "You're clean, except for the wound, and bringing you in will get me a raise. Lieutenant Moriarty—ah, now, don't that have a fine ring to it?"

Moriarty was jolly and proud as a cat after devouring a canary, prattling on about his future and his good work, and thank heaven he'd not stayed abed of a Sunday morning, for it was a well-known fact that the earliest bird caught the worm, which in this case was the Western desperado, Gus Gilpin.

"Stick your hands out, Gilpin, I'm putting the irons on you," Moriarty said. "I'm takin' no chances. I know how you country boys grow up big and wild as animals. I've seen 'em come through the yards many a time with their eyes rollin' white as a tiger in a cage, ready for any kind of strong arm stuff to stay free. Well, now . . ."

Gus was feeling exactly what the redheaded Moriarty was describing: a crazy anguish, a primal instinct driving him to batter and sledge through and over and gone.

"Please, sir," he said as calmly as he could, "first, I never robbed a bank, nor anything else, and I'm innocent. You've made a mistake."

"The judge'll decide that," Moriarty growled, as though he might be cheated of his prey. "You're guilty as sin or I never seen a crook, and, sonny boy, I seen a few, yes, a few. Now stick out your hands." Moriarty didn't like the look of the giant young man, the animal tenseness, a smell of panic, and drawing his police special, Moriarty leveled it at Gus's midriff and said steadily, "Once more, out with the hands or, by God, I'll blow a hole right through you."

"Well, I ain't ever begged anybody for anything yet." Gus's voice was soft, almost regretful. "And I guess I ain't goin' to start with you."

Gus extended his fists toward the redheaded officer. His huge callused hands looked like blocks of oak, the hands that could lift up the ponderous chalk-rock fence posts and set them upright into the ground, and in the same evening the same hands gently coax the milk from eleven cows without ever cramping or losing their fine touch.

With his left hand Moriarty pulled the handcuffs from his belt. He was dextrous enough and practiced enough, a veritable genius at coordinating the pistol and the handcuffs, but after snapping the first wrist into its manacle, he glanced into Gus's eyes.

Gus was staring at the once handsome face topped with red

curly hair, yellow buck teeth set in a humorless smile, fist-flattened nose.

"Golly, you look like Tom Mix," Gus said softly.

Moriarty beamed giddily and in that second Gus tagged him with a simple six-inch punch to the belly. The cop dropped, gagging.

Gus kicked the pistol as far as he could and ran. But Moriarty wouldn't chase anything for at least five minutes. He would only sit there propped up against the alley wall holding his belly and sucking wind. He would curse the big farm boy and would hunt and find his gun, but he'd not find the manacles fixed fast on Gus's left wrist. He'd think it over and decide it would look better for the report to say nothing just yet of the incident or the escaped fugitive. A sergeant never made lieutenant by losing his prisoner.

Ah, but there'd be a time. Sooner or later the big farmer would stick his head up and there would be Moriarty waiting to knock it off. No more kindness or charity of heart. Next time Gilpin would get everything he damned well deserved and a little extra.

Moriarty had a belly ache. He decided to go down to Cherry Avenue and roust out some whores.

FOUR

Gus ran as he'd run in the Goshen Hills, turning up trash-can alleys, down cross streets, over wooden fences and the barriers of slum debris. He charged past a boxy brick building with a cross mounted over the sidewalk. He ran back and tried the church door. A sign said "In Case of Emergency Call Police." The door was locked.

He ran with the manacle whipping his side until he was breathing too hard even to see where he was running. He staggered on into a red blur of fatigue, his legs sinking under him. He had no hope, no plan, only to go as far as he could.

A hardly noticeable stairwell dropped from the sidewalk to a basement den. Gus had no choice. The word was out. The dogs were loose. He had to hide. He had to rest. He had to find food. He had to get rid of the dreadful steel locked around his wrist. There was no friend, no haven, no man to see, no place left to go.

Incautiously he stumbled down the concrete stairway, which was amazingly clean compared to the street and walls and sky above him. As he descended, he tucked the flopping manacle inside his shirt sleeve.

A heavy oaken door, freshly polished and mounted on solid brass hinges, stopped him. A bell push was set alongside but there was no doorknob. Gus was at the end of his rope. He hadn't the courage to press the bell. He leaned against the wall and ran his fingers through his thick yellow hair.

How many times in the Goshen Hills had he tracked a rabbit to his hole and not wondered at the fear and pain of the little animal. But now he knew. He felt it in the very juices of his bones and the electric flashes in his nerves and in the implacable sense of doom in his spirit.

There was no point in weeping. A man was a man. He took his good with his bad. He did what he had to do and hoped for the best. What would Lu have done?

He only hoped that little poke with his fist hadn't injured Moriarty. He didn't want that on his conscience too. After all, the man was only doing his job.

Hunger gnawed at his vitals. His side was bleeding and throbbing, and the steel bracelet on his wrist seemed to mark him as a vicious animal. Once more he came to the basic point: There was no help. The only thing left was to turn himself in to the police and take whatever punishment they decided was right for him.

The thought of prison chilled him like a blue bruise all over his body.

O dear Lord, why hast thou forsaken me?

Better to kill yourself than put on the slimy gray prison uniform and peck out your life behind the granite of Leavenworth's walls.

He heard a faint scratch at the door and in his despair was ready to smash whoever would open that door. Whether it be an old lady or a child, a minister or a grizzly bear, he would knock it down and take over this cave and hide.

The door opened inward; Gus stood, waiting somehow for a sign. From the dark interior he heard the plinking of a banjo, and coming through the door itself was a small, skinny, shiny black man with a banjo strung around his neck and a push broom in his hand.

Gus couldn't hit him, not a blue-black, lantern-jawed man with a banjo and a broom who seemed to be almost expecting him.

"You too early, mister. We ain't open yet," the little black man said, his astonishing voice coming from deep caverns.

"Mister," Gus said, "I need help."

"Yessir." The black man smiled and scratched his close-cropped head. "Don't we all. But we don't open till noon."

"Open?" Gus asked, puzzled.

"What kind of help you need?" the black man asked, seeing

now that Gus wasn't just another thirsty customer. When Gus didn't answer, he added the guess, "You on the run?"

. Gus could only nod. How could he trust anyone, especially a black man in this hostile city in this evil neighborhood? He felt he was too lost ever to be saved. All he could do was go along with his destiny. In the end he had to trust someone.

"C'mon in, son. I ain't got much to offer but you're welcome to what there is." The shiny black man zinged a couple of notes off the banjo with his right hand.

Gus followed him into the dark room, which smelled of gin and stale cigar smoke and rancid perfumes.

When his eyes became accustomed to the darkness he saw the tables with chairs stacked on top, and the bar at the rear of the room, and the raised dance floor with chairs and music stands for a band, and a piano.

"My name is Jim. Jim Crispus."

"Gus. Gus Gilpin, Mr. Crispus. I don't know why you're doin' this, but . . ."

"Call me Jim. I ain't done nothing yet, less'n the cops was right on your tail."

"Well, I guess they're pretty close," Gus said wearily. "They think I robbed a bank out west, but I didn't."

"Come in on a freight?"

"From Ford County," Gus said, hanging on to the little bit of identity he still felt comfortable with.

Jim smiled. "You're lucky. I ain't never been outa K.C."

They went through a small kitchen and on into a little cubby-hole of a room lighted by an overhead bulb. Despite its smallness and absence of windows, it was clean and neat. Against one wall was an Army cot, against the other a chiffonier with a mirror.

"This is my room," Jim said. "Nobody bother you here."

"Look, mister," Gus said, "I haven't got any money. I mean I really didn't rob the bank."

"What did you do to get a bullet in your side for?" Jim asked, his round eyes blank.

Gus shook his head weakly in despair.

"I just horse-whipped the banker for fooling around with my sister. He had a gun."

"That's about the best thing you could have said, son." Jim

nodded his head. "Now set down. I ain't asked for no money yet. Get your shirt open. I seen a few bullet holes in folks before, maybe I better look at this one."

Gus had no course but to open his shirt, which in turn revealed the manacle hanging on his left wrist. Jim seemed hardly bothering to notice it.

"Say now, you didn't tell me you had that too." He looked at the wound carefully. "I'll get a saw and some iodine. You got to be careful. I seen a lot of big strong boys carried off by blood poisonin' from just such little scratches."

He left the room, while Gus slumped over weakly. His throat was dry, his stomach empty. His side was stiffening up and needling with pain. But still he wondered how the good Lord had managed to guide him to this savior and how he could ever repay the debt he was taking on.

Jim brought a pan of hot water and a clean cloth in one hand, a hacksaw in the other, a bottle of iodine in his pocket, and a swab in his teeth.

"Don't pass out on me just yet, Gus. Have to get that all cleaned out so's it heals right."

He washed the wound and the pain seemed to grow less.

"Now, then, Gus boy, this may smart some, but it's the best way." The deep voice was barely registering in Gus's ear.

"Go ahead," Gus murmured.

Jim dipped the swab into the bottle and gently flooded iodine over the wound. Gus sucked in his breath and clamped his jaw tight, until the worst of the bite was over.

"Best leave it unbandaged so long as you're just goin' to be restin' here. Heal faster. I got a spare shirt in the chest there that may be a little small for you, but it's clean."

"How am I ever going to pay you back, Jim?" Gus asked.

"Ain't nothin' to pay. We just play the game a card at a time and hope they all aces. I always figure it's better to bet on a man than against him. Now this swampin' job of mine ain't much, but it's the only job I can get, so I got to hustle. You can while away the time sawin' that bracelet off'n your arm." Jim picked up his broom and shut the door behind him.

Gus sawed at the case-hardened steel awkwardly. It was aggravating work but he had plenty of time. He'd notched halfway through it when the door opened and Jim came in carrying a tray loaded with sandwiches and a mug of hot coffee.

"These is leftovers from last night, Gus," Jim said, "but they're still good enough for po' folks."

"Gee whiz, Jim, I'm so hungry I could eat a raw cat." Gus grinned and folded one of the sandwiches into his mouth.

Jim laughed at the appetite of the big yellow-haired farm boy and commenced bending the sawed handcuff back and forth until the remaining steel crystallized and snapped.

"Hey, now, that's the kind of job I like," he said, laying the pieces in Gus's freed hand.

He went back to his janitoring. He sang a scatty little tune as he finished mopping and set the chairs down from the little round tables, covered them with fresh white cloths, and scrubbed off the bar top.

Gus felt unutterably weary. He was clean, fed, and free, but he felt the darkness of exhaustion closing around him. His head dropped, his eyes blurred, and he scarcely felt the rough Army blanket beneath his face.

When Jim returned and saw the young man slumped on the bed, he covered him with a quilt, shaking his head worriedly, wondering why, since he had so many other problems, should he add on another one. He didn't know the answer.

He picked up his old banjo, the only thing he owned beside his clothes, and strummed it softly.

What the heck was he goin' to tell the boss?

Gus was abruptly awakened by a blasting trumpet building in a screaming crescendo, backed up by a wailing saxophone, trombone, guitar, banjo, piano, and drums.

He'd never heard such a din except once when the Ringling Brothers came to Ford County. And even that music wasn't anything like this. It took him a minute to remember who he was and where he was. One thing he knew for sure, he was no longer a farmer.

The music was stomping fast and loud outside his door and he didn't dare open it, if only from fear of getting Jim into trouble. He snapped on the light and stood to look in the mirror. His big, sunburned face was creased with sleep lines. His yellow hair was wild as straw. He laughed sheepishly at his own image. Where could such a big horse go? What could he do?

He turned as the doorknob rattled. Jim scuttled in, locking the door behind him. Gus hardly recognized him in the peg-top pants and wildly striped jacket.

Jim started to ask him what he was staring at until he remembered Gus knew nothing of outside this little room.

"My band costume," Jim explained quickly. "I just wanted to see you was all right and tell you to lie low till I give you the high sign. We quit about four or five in the morning."

"Where am I?" Gus asked, puzzled.

"The Irish Rooster Club," Jim said. "You know, it's a blind tiger—a speakeasy. Look, it's a saloon that's illegal."

"Oh," Gus said, getting the idea. "Sorry I . . ."

"Don't be sorry too soon." Jim smiled at him. "I ain't told the boss you're here yet. Better you get your strength back before makin' any move just in case he says no, which he might. I'm just barely hangin' on here myself. If I didn't do the swampin' for nothin', he'd get along without any banjo player."

"Jim, don't take any chances for me," Gus said. "I can go it alone from now on, thanks to you."

The trumpet blew a note outside. Jim turned anxiously.

"That's my cue. Sleep awhile, get your side mended. I'll be back in the morning."

He disappeared again, a small dark saint in straw boater and broad striped blazer, peg-top pants and mustard-yellow shoes.

Gus lay down again on the cot and turned the light out and, despite the wild music and the occasional applause and squeals of women and hoarse hollering of men, he dreamed he was riding a freight train toward a long dark tunnel, and the song the engineer with his mournful whistle played was "St. James Infirmary."

"Yessir, Mr. Fitzgerald," Gus said, looking straight into the gun-metal-colored eyes of the white-haired man in the gray derby.

"You're untried." Mr. Fitzgerald toyed with a beaker of golden whiskey. "We don't know how you behave in the pinch. If you was raised in the street, we'd know and you'd know. But you was raised as a rube hayseed, so you don't know."

"I'm willing to learn," Gus said.

"You're askin' me to hide a fugitive."

Gus thought about it a moment. "I'm loyal."

"There are men who are loyal all the way to the electric chair, you know that?" the heavy-set Irishman asked. "I've known good men who were called beasts of the jungle, bloodthirsty cannibals and such by the newspapers, but they never peached on their friends. Every street kid knows that when he's born."

"So it's up to you," Gus replied. "All I can say is you can count on me."

Mr. Fitzgerald turned to Jim. "What do you think?"

"I ain't changed my mind," Jim said. "Sure, he's green, but he's level."

Mr. Fitzgerald put his opaque gray eyes again on Gus.

"We'll try it. You back up Jim at the door. Jim, keep your eyes open. Not so much for the cops, but Mickey Zirp's boys."

"Yessir," Gus said. "I'll do my best."

Fitzgerald looked at him across the white table cloth steadily. "You never know a man till you try him, but at least I'm pretty sure you ain't one of Mickey's rats." He let his face break into a chilly smile. "You can quit any time you like."

He dipped into his coat pocket and pulled out a hundred-dollar bill. "The money's for a new outfit." And, dipping into another pocket, he pulled out a solid, blunt Colt .45 and slid it after the bill. "You only shoot somebody trying to take over the club. That's all I ask. Jim, just to be sure, you tell him when to shoot."

"Yessir," Jim said.

Fitzgerald tossed off the shot of whiskey and rose quickly. "It's touch and go. If they'll stay on the other side of the river there won't be any bloodshed."

He picked up his briefcase and left without a goodbye.

Jim noticed the expensive material covering the sturdy shoulders of the older man and shook his head in despair.

"I'm lost," Gus groaned. "You got to teach me some things."

"Prohibition." Jim smiled. "It's an unnatural law put onto ordinary thirsty people. So it takes time to get the new rule figured out. I mean everybody's got to learn his place. Cop got to learn who he is, and how much money he needs to soothe his conscience, and real heavy guys like Mr. Fitzgerald and Mickey Zirp got to cut up the pie best way they can, and Mr. Pendergast, he got to line up all the government folks that can take a bribe, and so everything's shook loose for a while."

"I think I get it," Gus said. "This one law turned over the ant nest and the ants have to work out a new system to keep them going."

"You got it, antman." Jim laughed, relieved that Gus had passed Mr. Fitzgerald's approval. "C'mon, let's go spend that C note. I want a bodyguard that shows he's got some moxie!"

Gus stuck the big pistol into his waistband under his Levi jacket, feeling the twinges of scar tissue stretching in his side.

"You think it's safe for me out in the street?"

"You're working for Mr. Maurice Fitzgerald now," Jim said. "You're safe, 'cause he's working for you too. We all workin' together."

They stepped out into the bright sunshine.

"Wowee!" Gus blinked his eyes and smiled, feeling a great weight lifting off his spirit.

"Now what?" Jim asked.

"Jim, three days ago I was leaning against this door at the bitter end of my rope. Now, thanks to you, I've got a chance to do something."

"Forget it," Jim said.

On down the block they saw a sign, HABERDASHERY, and another new one painted on bunting, GOING OUT OF BUSINESS SALE.

"Maybe we can get a deal there," Jim said.

The store was long and narrow. On each side were glass showcases and in the rear were racks of suits. Near the door a small, sharp-nosed, ramrod-backed salesman waited, trying to get up a smile for the customers. He wore round spectacles that made him look like an owl.

"Howdy, boys." His voice carried over the typical Missouri twang. "What can I do for you?"

"Outfit the big man," Jim said.

"He's sure big enough, but I think we can do the job." The salesman wrung his hands together. "What are you? About a size forty-four?"

"I don't know," Gus said, "but I want somethin' that fits."

"Don't worry, we'll fit you. I'm not going out of business be-cause I don't fit people, it's just I got a better offer."

Gus was a size 46 long, and in a few minutes he was dressed in a chalk-striped blue suit with a clip-on bow tie, white and brown shoes and a lavender silk shirt. Through it all the salesman had skillfully managed not to see the big .45.

"Now a nice derby," the salesman said.

"I guess not."

"Ah, go on," Jim said, "you got money left."

"No, I'm a bare-headed country boy. I can't think right with an iron hat clamped down on my head. You get one for yourself."

Jim selected a pearl-gray derby with a silver bangle on its band and set it at a jaunty angle across his bare creased skull.

"Glom me!" Jim's deep voice boomed at the triple mirror. "Man, I feel refined. 'Minds me of my first banjo."

Gus laughed and paid the owl-faced salesman. "Where will you go from here?" he asked.

"Politics." The haberdasher smiled thinly, sharp eyes glittering through his glasses. "I've got friends."

"Good luck," Gus said, and followed Jim out into the street.

"We'd best be getting back." Gus was nervous as the mounting traffic of humans and animals and autos swirled and racketed by the open door.

"What's your hurry?" Jim asked. "I was thinking we could go visit my sis."

"Give me some time to get used to all this hustle bustle," Gus said. "I want to be in good shape for the job."

"Well," Jim said, understanding, "at least looky over yonder. That's the Muehlbach Hotel. Prettiest place in Kansas City. Oh, that's the cat's pajamas! Just the real rich folks can stay there."

The street traffic was overpowering. Gus's only previous vision of it had been on that quiet Sunday morning; now he was bumped and jostled by mobs of office workers, his ears were assaulted by the ringing of streetcar bells and the crashing sounds of steam engines and riveters banging together new high buildings. His nerves were set on edge for catastrophe.

They walked on back toward the club, which Gus by now called home and sanctuary.

"It's goin' to take me a while to get used to all this," he told Jim. "But I can do it."

The first night was easy enough. Gus acted as the unchainer and opener of the door, while Jim, relieved of his banjo, was at the peephole making sure who was right and who wasn't before giving Gus the high sign.

And though Gus seemed to be an extraneous flunky, his eyes were alert and memorizing every face, trying to connect each person to a job or a fact of some sort, an identification for the future. Toward the end of the night, Jim turned the door over to him while he joined the band, adding extra gusto and fun and clowning to the set.

Gus could see most of the whole room from his position in the hall. The dance floor was crowded. His eye nearly glided over a young, heavy-boned woman in a low-cut gown sitting at a table by herself, stirring her drink idly with her diamond-studded fingers.

Suddenly her eyes came up and locked to his. Her face was carefully made up but the predatory look of a hawk diving out of the sky could never be covered up by cosmetics.

He quickly forced his eyes to rove on, trying to keep his face fixed and unrevealing. He thought it worked, he thought he'd escaped. But when the night was over and she was leaving, she touched his broad shoulder, nodded, murmured, "For real," and moved on. It was only later the next day that he found the perfumed ten-dollar bill in his pocket and knew it came from her.

When he told Jim about it, his friend laughed and said, "Count your blessings. Suppose it was Mickey Zirp with a shotgun instead of a plain Jane with a barrel of money."

"But I don't like takin' money from women," Gus said.

"You didn't take it. Besides, if you don't somebody else will."

"That's O.K. with me," Gus said. "Just so I'm not somebody else."

The next night she came again.

Jim delightedly described her arrival from his peephole.

"Man, that's a Duesenberg if it's anything. I never seen such a big heap. And here she comes swinging a beaded purse full of ten-dollar billses. Lookin' for a big farm boy with a strong back and lots of noodles."

"Cut it out," Gus rumbled. "I don't want nothing like that."

"It ain't what you want, ain't I done taught you that?" Jim laughed. "It's what they let you get."

"There's better ways," Gus said. "I pick my own girl, I don't want nobody pickin' me."

"Open the door, Mr. High Wide and Handsome," Jim said, smiling, "and do your best."

Gus admitted her as politely as he had been taught. A slight bow, a firm resolve never to catch her eyes. But she stopped in the open doorway and laughed, sharp white teeth glittering between mauve-colored lips.

Gus felt trapped. He couldn't shut the door so long as she stood there neither in nor out.

"C'mon, big fella," she murmured, "look at me. I'm Rhonda Hellbaum."

Gus looked at her angrily, but tried to conceal his feelings the way Jim had told him, locking it all inside. She was what he regarded as a forward woman.

"Welcome to the Irish Rooster Club," Gus said as pleasantly formal as he could. "Please step inside."

He could feel Jim's eyes glow with approval and wonder at the manner, the firmness, courtesy, and cold purpose.

She obeyed. Her face lost its cheery contempt and became thoughtful, puzzled, curious.

"Say now, Champ," she said in her low voice, "you're a regular big tree, aren't you?"

"I'm just a hired hand, ma'am," Gus said.

"Live here?" she asked, and, not waiting for the answer, pushed on. "Where? In the back? Behind the kitchen, Jim's old room."

Gus nodded. "You seem to know the layout pretty well."

She laughed. "Layout. Yeah, that's a laugh. One of my ex-husbands used to own this blind pig when it was legit. Sure, I know it."

And with extra little switch of her ample rear end, she moved alone on into the main room, which was blue with smoke and loud voices and the tumbling riffs of Becket sax and Lewis clarinet and Keppard trumpet making Kansas City jazz.

"Hey there," Jim said, his tone saying all.

"Forget it," Gus said. "She's all yours."

"No, she don't play spade cards." Jim laughed. "But she's goin' to give you a free ride."

" 'Sposin' I don't take it?"

Jim never answered, as the buzzer at the door whirred quietly. He looked out and announced, "Mr. Cornelius Livermore, big in commodities."

Gus opened the door.

"By gosh, I don't know how you do it," Gus said after the corseted, florid-faced man passed by. "What do you know about the commodity market?"

"Nothin'. Only that's where the dough is. They say it moves fast in the pit."

"That's what's breakin' Ford County wheat," Gus said. "Can you imagine, some red-burnt farmer working like a draft horse sunup to sundown and working his wife and his little children like slave labor, and at the end of the year, his profit or his loss is decided by men like our Mr. Cornelius Livermore."

"Ain't that life." Jim smiled, trying to kid Gus out of his dark mood.

"Maybe it's life," Gus said, "but it ain't right."

"Gus," Jim said thoughtfully, "you're still a bald-faced boy. Do you know I got a kid sister hustles for money, and that's life and ain't right but it's the way it is."

"Couldn't you help her out?" Gus asked, startled.

"I couldn't when she really needed it. I didn't have a meal a day nor a bed to flop in. Now maybe I could keep her alive, but she don't want that kind of help any more."

"Gosh dang it," Gus groaned, "there's something real wrong somehow."

Jim grinned. "C'mon, now, Gussie, we ain't bein' paid for philosphizin', we're s'posed to be a-grinning like watermelon pickers. How's about fetchin' me a double shot of gin?"

"Sure," Gus said, glad to be able to move and knowing it was Jim's way of relieving the tension and the sordid sad mood that had crept up from the basement depths to strangle their happy spirits.

He'd forgotten Rhonda Hellbaum.

The bartender, a wizened-up little ex-jockey with a game leg, was busy on an order and Gus decided to go on back to his room for a fresh handkerchief. The kitchen people were busy making sandwiches and washing dishes. As he passed through, he noticed the old Negro cook, Johnny Washington, giving him an odd look, but he was too young, too inexperienced to respond. A street kid would have automatically loosened his elbows and gotten on his toes, but Gus pushed through the door to the hall and saw the light on in his room.

She was lying on his cot, smoking a cigarette in a long holder. A Tom Collins glass was empty on the floor. Smoke rolled up from her lips and obscured her eyes.

"High, wide and handsome," she said slowly and softly.

"Look, lady, I ain't tryin' to cut you down or nothin', but a man's room is his own."

"And his bed, dreamboat," she sighed and stirred, propping her chin on the back of her hand, gazing up at him. She patted the bed by her side.

"It ain't right," Gus said. "I mean you're you, and that's fine, and I'm me. And if I wanted a girl like you I'd first off send you a dozen roses."

"Lover man, I'm not waiting for roses." Her eyelashes hung long and low, her lower lip pushing up.

"I'm sorry, lady," Gus said, "but I do it my way."

"Come on in and shut the door behind you."

She rolled aside, her breasts pushing out of the low-cut feathery gown, and God knows Gus was tempted, but it went against the grain to be picked off like a banana from the bunch.

"No, ma'am."

"C'mon here before I yell rape," she said hoarsely.

He backed out the door and closed it just as the glass shattered where his head had been and an insult he'd never known a lady to say before came shrilling after him.

It was trouble. He knew it and he didn't know what to do about it, except to tell the truth.

He forgot about Jim's gin and searched the club room for Mr. Fitzgerald.

"Look upstairs," the bartender told him.

Gus went through a blank door, up a plain staircase and found himself in an ornately paneled office. Mr. Fitzgerald was at the desk, wearing glasses, going through a ledger.

"Sir," Gus said, "Mr. Fitzgerald."

The rosy-faced white-haired man looked up. "What's your trouble, Gus?"

"There's a woman in my room and she's threatening me with losin' my job and gosh knows what else if'n I don't settle her," Gus blurted out. "But I don't figure that's part of the job, or if it is, I want you to tell me."

Mr. Fitzgerald frowned, cut and lighted a big cigar, and cleared his throat. "Rhonda? Yes. Well, of course she's built like a brick privy and talks a hell of a line, but she's colder'n a dead Injun in an icehouse—but even at that, I figure a man that can't fornicate can't fight!"

"That ain't it, Mr. Fitzgerald, it's who's on top," Gus replied quietly.

"Well, you've sure made an enemy," the old man said. "But your job here is to do what I told you and I didn't tell you to be a whore."

"Yessir." Gus started to leave.

"Gus, I'll say this just one time." The old man's tone turned deadly. "In this town, you do or you don't, but you don't fool around halfway. In *anything*."

"What should I have done?" Gus asked, wholly bewildered.

"You should have laid her or beat the living crap out of her. Now get the hell out of here before I lose my patience."

Gus retreated in total confusion.

Trying to tell Jim about it later on, he was baffled by the turn of events. Here he'd been primed to defend his master and his business, but instead of something solid like a .45 automatic, he was in dutch over a sex-mad rich woman.

Jim listened through it all and shook his head.

"I don't know about you," Jim said at the end of the report. "I sent you for gin and you come back with dishwater."

"I hardly know her," Gus said.

"It's O.K., Gus." Jim shook his head in wonder. "Some are chasers and some are lovers, that's all there is to it. Whichever route you go you end up at the same river."

She was weaving unsteadily when she left early in the morning. Jim was playing banjo with the tired band and Gus was alone. She was accompanied by an off-duty bartender. Her mouth was twisted with lipstick and her dress was wrenched around, and her hair was too yellow for her skin. When they went out the door she glanced at Gus.

He tried at first to avoid that glance, but remembering what Mr. Fitzgerald had said, he turned to face her front on, his eyes flat to hers.

"By God, you've got eyes anyway," she said.

"I've got it all," Gus said, "and I put it where I want to when I want to."

"But you don't seem to know that four out of five have pyorrhea in Peoria," she giggled. He saw the tears in her eyes as she added, "Oh, you've got a lot to learn, dreamboat."

FIVE

●–•–•–•–•–•–•–•–•–•–•–•–•–••–•–•–•–•–•–•–•–•–•–•–•–•–•–•–•–•–●

MR. FITZGERALD GAVE Gus a raise after a month on the door and put him in charge of checking deliveries of liquor to the club, and, as expected, a substantial pilferage suddenly ceased.

"When the mice see a big cat like you watchin' the cheese, they'll move back downstairs," was the way Jim put it. "I'm glad to see you tie a can on the crummy thieves."

And it wasn't long before Mr. Fitzgerald decided Gus was old enough to learn the street payoff system.

"You'll go along with Jim to my other enterprises on Friday," the old man said. "You'll pick up a bag of money from each one, check the money and the slip, and initial a receipt, and somewhere along the route you'll meet up with Lieutenant Moriarty. You'll give him this envelope, which contains five hundred dollars."

"Just for one cop?" Gus asked, amazed.

"Oh, no, he passes most of it on up the line. Moriarty will help himself, maybe a hundred of it, if he's as greedy as I think he is."

"Supposin' he arrests me as a fugitive from Ford County?" Gus asked.

"Don't be foolish," Mr. Fitzgerald said bluntly. "Better remember you'll be carrying a large sum of money, and Mickey Zirp is never satisfied. There is a genuine risk."

"Yessir."

"Maybe you should have these." Mr. Fitzgerald reached into a cabinet behind his desk and lifted out a double harness of tooled leather. Each holster held a pearl-handled .45 automatic Colt. "Two is better than one, keeps the spine straight."

"Son of a gun!" Gus said, examining and hefting the silver-mounted and chased barrels. "Mr. Zirp better leave us alone."

He took the harness and guns to his room and adjusted the straps so that the weapons rode comfortably under each arm. With the two of them, they hardly showed more than muscle on his big frame. They were both loaded with full clips of soft-nosed bullets. There was no short-range weapon that could hit harder. Just tick a man on the finger with one of those heavy bullets and the shock would knock him down.

"Two-gun man!" Jim grinned, rubbing his long fingers over his creased scalp. "Say, now, I do feel safe."

"You don't carry any hardware?" Gus asked.

"Oh yeah, I carry my old razoo. That's my style," Jim said. "I can use it 'bout as good as you can rooty-toot-toot with them heaters."

"Hope we never have to use them," Gus said, slipping on his coat. "You got the money for Moriarty?"

"Right in the pocket," Jim said. "Let's go."

They walked easily and inconspicuously, the bulky-shouldered young man and his older black friend who moved like a greased ball bearing.

It was a hot Friday morning. The street hadn't cooled off and already the tar was bubbling in the pavement. The people on their way to work walked slowly and tried to keep to the shady side of the street. The voices of vendors and rag pickers seemed to be weaker, cracking out their cries for attention. Truckloads of ice were fanning out through the city. The windows of the tenements were open, but the air was too muggy to drift a curtain.

Their first stop was a bookie at a shoeshine stand.

" 'Lo, Jim," the bookie said. "Hot enough for you?" and handed over an envelope.

"Hot enough, Andy," Jim said. "Meet Gus. Gus may be makin' the route some day."

"You movin' up in the world?"

"All I ever want to do is plunk the old banjo," Jim said, grinning. "But I got to keep movin' on."

They stopped at a pool hall, a small beer joint, a candy store, a pawnshop, and a couple of small, malodorous hotels.

"God, I hate to take whore money," Jim said as they left the second shabby house. "Most of them girls are dumber'n cows, still some could make it out if they could save up a little nest egg, but the system keeps taking the money away as fast as they get it up."

"You said your sister hustled," Gus said.

"Yeah, but not in a crib," Jim said bitterly. "She got a telephone connection. It's just a matter of time, though. Damn it to hell." He swore with a depth of anger Gus had never realized existed.

"I'm sorry I mentioned it," Gus said. "Next time tell me to keep my trap shut, or belt me."

" 'Tain't your fault. 'Tain't no secret neither," Jim said. "And I ain't never been convinced a hustler is the worst broad in the world, either."

"Why can't people be what they want to be?" Gus said.

Jim laughed, his glistening humor and bounce coming back. "That's what I like to hear, boy."

"What?" Gus asked, puzzled.

"Hope for the human race," Jim said, handing over the satchel. "You carry the bag awhile. A big strong farm boy like you oughta be good for something."

"Sure," Gus said, reaching for the satchel, not seeing the big black Lincoln coming down the burning street behind them. But Jim's street sense was alert. He had time for a quick look over his shoulder, and, seeing the danger, lunged against Gus, knocking him to his knees as a blast of gunfire erupted from the big car.

"Come on, Gus," Jim yelled, rolling, scrabbling toward a doorway for cover.

It happened so fast Gus couldn't keep the little pictures straight. The bag lay in the open near the curb, where he'd never quite gotten hold of it. Off balance and angry, he stubbornly grabbed for it. Another volley of gunfire ricocheted off the sidewalk close beside him. Glancing back, Gus saw Jim coming out of the doorway toward him, hardly hearing him scream, "Let 'em have it, take cover, you dumb bunny!" because by then Gus had seen the black Lincoln sedan and the plug-ugly, ratty faces inside, their hand guns and sawed-off shotguns aimed at him, and he knew it was do or die. Cross-armed, he drew the .45s and faced the on-coming car on his knees.

The heavy kick of the automatics was reassuring in his big hands; each thud told him that his bullets were away and on target, one across the black car body, the next smashing through the windshield and the rest through the open side windows. He was outshooting four men, and he was hurting them. He saw a foxy little bug-eyed face disappear in a splurge of blood, and heard another voice yell, "Get the hell out." The driver, anticipating the order, had already jammed his foot on the gas, and the car thundered on down the street.

Gus held his fire. He was busy getting the satchel in his hand where it was supposed to be. How quick it all happened, he thought. He'd emptied both automatics. He'd run them off and saved the bag.

Jim was crumpled in the doorway; a straight-edge razor lay near his unmoving fingers. Gus ran to him, gently turned him over. There was street dirt on his glassy, obsidian forehead.

Jim opened his eyes, smiled tightly, and said, "Gus, you got some class."

"Where you hit?" Gus asked.

"Just a scratch. Try my sister's apartment," Jim said. "It's just around the corner."

Gus lifted the wounded man in his arms and, with the satchel in his left hand, carried his friend around the corner, where he found a stairway.

"That's it. Twenty-one," Jim said.

Going up the stairs swiftly, Gus said, "I'm going to call an ambulance."

"No, no, Gus, listen to me. Now you goin' to have to talk to law about this. Here's where you learn to save your breath and use your head."

"Don't worry about me," Gus said, coming to a varnished door embossed with the number 21, and, not bothering to knock, turned the knob and pushed on in.

For one instant he saw her stark naked in the light, coming from the shower, only a towel in her hand. A really tall woman, nearly as tall as he was, and yet all lovely curve and nipples, navel, and crowned crotch of glossy curls, and then she was gone, her long form disappearing soundlessly into a room so that in the state he was in, he wasn't sure he'd seen anything at all. He laid Jim on the couch and knelt beside him.

"Now, Jim," he said, "you're home. Let me call a doctor."

"Dr. Banjo." Jim smiled.

Gus stripped off the blood-soaked coat, shirt and undershirt, exposing the lean, bony torso which once had been a glowing pearl of black but which now was torn apart, splayed blood open, raw red and white flesh, the ugliest wound of all, twelve-bore double-ought buckshot.

"Say now, brother Jim," Gus said, "you taken on a little lead."

"It don't hurt," Jim said. "It's all numb down there."

"Jim," Gus said slowly, "I want to do something for you, but I just don't know what."

"Don't bother about me, mister farm boy," Jim said weakly, "but would you try to see after Bessie for me? I mean I let her down when she needed me."

"Hush now, Jim, I'll do my best. And that's a promise."

"Kind of dark in the back room, plowboy . . ." Jim breathed. "So long, old banjo."

"Jim," Gus said desperately, "hang on, hang on! Hang on."

Knowing there was nothing to hang onto except about a dozen slugs in his guts, and they were deaf, dumb, blind, cold and heavy.

There was a crashing against the door. The tall woman materialized, too late to open it.

Big, beefy, red-faced Moriarty, in a tight suit, a snub-nosed .38 in his hand, charged in to meet her.

"What the hell's goin' on, Bessie?" he asked, grabbing her hip with his free hand. "I followed a trail of blood to right here."

She didn't pull away.

Moriarty squeezed down, enjoying the pain he wrenched loose in her. "Speak up, bitch."

"Gimme a chance, honey," she said, coming closer to him, putting her body close to his. "My brother is hurt."

Moriarty moved away from her, his jaw down, his eyes drilling for truth and finding nothing.

"You're on that goddamned goofer dust again, ain't you? And I ain't had a cut from the man . . ."

"Over here, Moriarty," Gus said, rising from beside the divan. "I got your cut."

Moriarty raised his bulldog .38 and moved closer to Gus, peering in the dim light. "I think I know you, mister."

"Put away that peashooter before I stick it up your nose."

Moriarty leaned forward, puzzled, lowering the pistol.

"I'm takin' you in for murder," he said.

"Who'd I murder?" Gus asked.

"Tony Kerchansky is layin' down the block with his face blowed off."

"How about my friend Jim?" Gus asked.

Moriarty looked over the back of the couch and saw the body. "Bad business," he said.

"Good business for you," Gus said, reaching into Jim's coat, finding the blood-wet envelope and handing it over. "Here's yours. Here's what you live for and work for. Go buy yourself a testimonial dinner."

While Moriarty used the telephone, Gus turned to the woman in the shadows where she stood like a young majestic poplar. It was the darkness, the heavy deep velvet shadows she liked.

"Miss Crispus," Gus said, "Jim was my best friend."

She seemed to sway in the hot gloom, and with a curiously balanced and fluid movement she emerged into the dappled light and he could see her nut-brown features, the strong straight nose, lining up into dark sculptured brows.

Gus held his breath. Too much was happening too soon. She seemed to be someone he'd known forever, someone in a dream of long-lost Nubian beauty. She, Nefertiti of Imperial Egypt, and he, Hiram of Tyre, voyaging from Phoenicia, had lost his heart to her in Thebes, had suffered such a supreme ecstacy and anguish with her that their passion had overlapped time, that in this moment their time had come again, and the tragedy of their fiery love in those ancient days was upon them again, locking them into the rapture of instant knowing, instant response, instant and bronze-bound love.

"You're Gus," she said. He already knew how her voice would sound, low and singing. "I'm Bessie."

Her cavernous eyes were somehow false, the great pupils of darkness, the sleepy-time voice, and Moriarty's words of recognition all added up to cocaine. In his few months in K.C., Gus had learned the signs.

She read his mind. "Sure, Gus, I'm on a little white leaf. But it's all right. It's just there wasn't anything left for me to do, because you never came."

"O.K., Bessie," Gus said, "but now it's over. I'm here. I'm sorry it's this way, but it is, and we've got to go through with this and get it settled, right now."

"Sure, Mr. Beautiful," she said. "I know. I know."

Moriarty came back from the phone, his face sweating, his thick-folded eyes sharp, his .38 back in its holster. He started to grab Bessie's long haunch again, but she moved as gently as quicksilver and his beefy hand closed on nothing.

"Mister," Gus said, "from now on you don't touch her."

Moriarty snickered. "Give her a dollar bill and you can do more'n touch her. Look, hayseed, she's just a nigger hooker, forget her, we got to arrange these killings right. There's law in this town."

"Sure," Gus said. "All kinds of law."

"Never mind, just remember Tony Kerchansky tried to hold up Jim, and Jim shot it out with him, and both died. Cancelled out. Good riddance."

"Should have been more than this Tony," Gus said.

"They picked up a couple dead men in a big Lincoln down by the river."

"Who did they work for?"

"One guess."

"Mickey Zirp."

"You said it, I didn't. My job is to cancel this out and cut down on the paperwork."

"Then get out."

"Coroner'll be here to pick up the remains," Moriarty said going through a mental checklist. "I guess that's about it. You got the bag?"

"Darned right," Gus said. "And I'm keeping it."

"You keep proddin' me, you're goin' to have a headache," Moriarty said. "I'm just doing my job. Old Man Fitzgerald wanted to be sure where the bag was."

"I'll deliver it," Gus said.

"All right," Moriarty said, glancing at the tall girl contemptuously, "it's all settled. Take it from me, Gilpin, you better get the hell out of this town. You got a way of operatin' that don't go by the rules and somebody's goin' to put the bump on you. That somebody could be me."

"Go chase your tail," Gus said. "Go on, get to walkin', I'm sick of your dishwater."

"Well I never." Moriarty grinned from the door, his buck teeth yellow as an old mule's. "You thinkin' about playin' house with this coon whore, you're goin' to get what's comin' to you."

When the door closed, Gus turned to Bessie, who stood still and tall.

"Bessie," he said, "Jim told me he had a sister in trouble, but I didn't think she'd be like you."

"And he told me he had a friend in trouble," Bessie said, her voice husky soft. "He seemed to know we were like a hand and a glove, and he didn't know what to do about it."

"What's to do about it?" He felt a grim ache in his chest as he studied her tawny statuesque loveliness, the pale yellow robe accenting her hips and breasts, her long throat and sleepy face.

"Moriarty was right, you know. I'm a coon whore, you can buy me for a dollar."

"You're crazy," Gus yelled, a sudden rage burning up his spine. "You're beautiful, and you're done with the racket."

"They say once you sell it, it's sold," she said, smiling.

"They're wrong," Gus said, "and I'm goin' to prove it to you."

"I think you've got a conscience," she said gently. "Come on, Gus, you'd give a dollar for a good trick."

"You goddamned right," he said, the red rage flooding through his chest and drowning his mind. "If all it takes is a greenback dollar, I'll have some."

He jammed a bill into her hand and ripped apart the yellow gown, and O lordy, she was as lovely as Solomon's Shulamite.

"I'm black," she said, unmoving, her body glowing like old gold. "I am black but comely." Her high bossed breasts shining, her body swelling and diminishing as though shaped by the Master of all clay for His own Eye. The hip widening slightly, long and pliant, the soft black nest glowing over the mound of love, the long slim rhythmic legs, the glow of color burning out of her with life and love, the smell of lime and perfume of gardenias, her face still composed as a majestic woman, her arms slowly lifting to accept him, his burning fury, his insane rage at the fact of the dishonor of innocence, his only escape from it to implant himself, to drive his own wedge into the defiled innocence, to give himself, every breath and atom, every moment of his racial epoch from the time of Solomon and the Shulamite, and before, and from the future of the blood gene-germ, to give and force and insist and suck out every molecule of resource, every tabulation of blood, every barb of history and prehistory which had lodged in his cells for all life's long going, and all that he wanted to present to the beyond as his most precious and inalienable gift and obligation, and to make the moment as beautiful as God had made the body he thrust into, and his unconscious words as he surged against her seeking nesting were biblical, "O thou fairest of women . . . Behold thou art fair . . . thy two breasts are like two fawns that are twins of a roe . . . Thy lips are like a thread of scarlet . . .

"My beloved is white and ruddy . . . his head is the most fine gold . . .

"Thy belly is like a heap of wheat, set about with lilies . . .

"Thy left hand should be under my head and thy right hand should embrace me . . .

Perhaps neither of them knew they were murmuring the parts, perhaps neither knew they'd held themselves outside the stream since they were Solomon and the Shulamite. It didn't matter. They were as honey and pomegranate flower, they were like young deer upon green mountains. As the power joined with hers, his anger diminished and shifted to a sense of joy that time was no longer out of joint, a sense of promise of making things right for one and all, and a sense that his soul was so joined with hers, nothing could ever separate the twain again.

Fusion brought tears to his eyes, and his body moved in slow, long, deliberate arcs, seeding the great deep field with the gift, laying in each surge with animal grace and love, laying it in with the long arc, his body spending itself on the field, issuing the melt in the warm rippling stream.

When he was spent as a man who has given his mind to his body and finds it coming back in waves, the mind to say love, O why love, O why O why O love, O why should it be this way, and her misted nut-brown face so saturated with calm that a breath would make it ripple like a mill pond, and her eyes closed in complete satisfaction, her lips slightly open, her sex still taking each atom of him.

When at last he opened his eyes and smothered the sob in his breast, he knew he was a goner. His only hope for redemption was this lovely girl who had already bowed to the stormy winds of existence.

They were in her room. He couldn't remember the brutal rush that had brought them there.

She seemed asleep, the most beautifully sensual and delicate creature he'd ever seen.

He moved away from her and felt embarrassed, rose, and dressed. He reached for the greenback dollar clutched in her left hand.

But she held it tightly, opened her eyes and said, "No, no, Mr. Beautiful."

"Lady," he said, "I'm in love with you, I don't want you bought."

She smiled smoothly, her eyes warm as Egyptian spring. "But, Mr. Beautiful, you did, and that makes it all clear and all right, see?"

"No," he said stubbornly, "I don't buy."

"You're not listenin'." She smiled gently. "Once it's sold it's sold, like mammy and pappy on the block, and once it's bought it's bought, ain't that right?"

A knock on the door brought everything from outside inside. It meant business as usual. It meant the coroner, it meant Mr. Fitzgerald wanted the bag.

The thought of what he'd done while his friend lay dead in the next room appalled him. "I don't understand," Gus groaned. "I don't know what's happening to me."

The knock was repeated. Gus opened the door, afraid it might be one of Bessie's customers afraid of what he might do, but it was only two bored, faceless men in white smocks, carrying a stained stretcher.

"On the couch," he said.

They expertly rolled the stiffening body onto their stretcher, covered it with a sheet and breezed out with all the solemnity of cleaners hauling out a rug.

As he closed the door behind them, the telephone rang. He took the receiver from the wooden box on the wall. "Gus?" It was Mr. Fitzgerald's voice. "You all right?"

"Yessir," Gus said.

"I heard about Jim. And I promise you, he'll have a first-class send-off. Now you better bring the bag in."

Bessie was alongside him, nibbling on his ear.

"Yessir," Gus said. "Right away."

He put the receiver on the hook and turned to her. "Bessie, Jim's dead. How can you be so goofy?"

"I knew him like a brother," she said. "He's gone now, and the sooner we get used to it, the better."

"But can't you mourn? Can't you respect his memory for a few days?"

"Mr. Beautiful, you're crazy," she said. "I mourned him more the first second I seen him on your shoulder than you goin' to mourn him in a year. What are you? A big calendar? Your heart go tick tock, tick tock?"

He held her close. "It's like magic—more than love at first sight —it's more like the sun meeting the ground in the spring, and all of a sudden everything blooms."

"That's the way I feel too, Gus, but take my advice, love, go out that door and don't come back."

It was maddening. She never came back with the easy answer.

"You can quit the game. I make enough money for both of us."

"Maybe I spend a lot. Pretty clothes, diamonds, junk—"

"Bessie, you got to get yourself untangled and turned around."

"Supposin' it's too late?"

"It can't be. I'm trying to tell you, it's like I've known you a million years, not just this day, and in that million years I've loved you steady. Right from the first day of Eden, I guess."

"You'll kill me, that's what you'll do, Gus."

"I'm going to side you same as I would Jim only more. You're going to be all right."

"Yessir, Gus, you goin' to put me right in between the bulls and the guns."

"First thing you do is move out of here, change your phone number. No more of that call-girl stuff."

"I hear you," she said. "I may even try it."

He handed her three twenty-dollar bills. "When you're settled, call me at the club, and we can start fresh and clear."

"Yassah, mistah bawsman." Her lips were taunting and inviting, her eyes full of imps and devils.

He hugged her close again with a big laugh breaking out of his chest. She seemed light as a child, a feather, a woman, a beloved toy.

"Get on back to work, Gus," she said. "Make me some money."

"Call me."

"Sho' nuff." She gave him that extra-unbelievable grin again.

He kissed her and, taking the satchel, quickly got out the door and down the stairs before he could change his mind and stay with her.

On the street, he was alert for trouble. God, Lu was somewhere up in that smoky sky laughing at him, maybe him and Jim together now, busting their ribs at all his sweat and fear, and trying to get everything going on the right track.

"Go chase yourselves, you think you're so smart," he said to himself, thinking, God knows why she's black. It can't make any difference, she's mine. No matter what anyone thinks, we can be married.

Then he wondered what Poppa in heaven was thinking of him. "Poppa," he said, "I'm doing my best to live a Christian life and stay out of jail. Poppa," he added, "I wouldn't do it if I didn't think she was worth it." And he could almost hear the laughing jibes of Lu and Jim as he tried to square his conscience with a round fact.

"The heck with it," he muttered.

At the club he went directly upstairs to the main office. The bookeeper, a middle-aged, chubby-cheeked man, worked in a small anteroom, but hardly noticed Gus go by.

He knocked once and went on inside. Mr. Fitzgerald was speaking into the telephone. Gus set the bag on the desk. The white-haired man put the receiver into its cradle and, looking up at him gravely, said, "You did a good job, Gus. Maybe too good."

"No. I lost Jim," Gus said.

"Couldn't be helped, Gus. I told him to carry a rod, but he always laughed it off. The trouble is now you've killed three men today, and each one of those three has three friends, say, and what do you think they're planning for Gus Gilpin right now?"

"You got a spare box of shells, Mr. Fitzgerald?" Gus asked.

Mr. Fitzgerald brought a heavy paper box from a drawer and

spilled out a couple of dozen heavy-nosed, brass-bottomed shells. Gus loaded his spent clips from them methodically, trying to think of the best way out.

"I do whatever you say," he said. "You're the boss."

"Frankly, if I send you out on that street tomorrow, you wouldn't last a block. No profit to that, right?"

"No increase," Gus said.

"Ever been to Hot Springs?"

"No."

"In Arkansas. There's a very big man going to be there next week. And I'm supposed to send him a package."

"I can do it," Gus said, "only I'd like to take a friend along."

"What kind of a friend?"

"Jim's sister."

"Little Bessie? Gus, I don't want to butt into your business, but a doll like that can hurt a man, and she ain't exactly Swedish."

"I'm thinkin of marryin' her."

"Don't. She's a junkie," the burly Irishman said, his blue eyes as cold as a mountain stream. "You want to lay up with her, all right, but any more than that you're finished."

"With you?"

"Not just me, but K.C., the Middle West, the United States of America and all its possessions. I'm not kidding you. You saw what they did to Jack Johnson and he wasn't even a hophead."

"Nothing permanent's been decided yet, Mr. Fitzgerald," Gus said. "It isn't just that I owe Jim a promise. She's somehow, someway, a part of me."

"It's your business, Gus, but keep one of them forty-fives under your pillow, and sleep light."

"And Hot Springs?"

"You leave in the morning on the Sante Fe. Stay till the heat's off." Mr. Fitzgerald tossed a bundle of currency to him. "Spend this. Any time there's three less of the Zirp mob, the better I feel."

Later that afternoon when she called, he said, "Pack a bag, Bessie, we're goin' on a honeymoon."

"Mistah Gus," she answered, "you're outa your hayloft head."

"I know," he answered somberly, breaking the connection.

In his room, he tried to think it all through. He didn't really want to get mixed up in racketeering and he didn't want to shoot anybody, nor did he want to live with a woman without marrying her, but in this world you shot first and shot straight, or you weren't around any more.

That night, as floor manager of the club, he noticed a new undercurrent in the customers' mood. People were calling him Mister instead of Gus, and they were slanting looks at him out of the corners of their eyes.

Rhonda Hellbaum came in by herself and deliberately looked him up and down. "Dutch Gilpin, two-gun man," she said. "Farm boy makes good. You're famous."

"I don't know what you're talking about," Gus said quietly.

"Read this," she said, handing him the Kansas City *Star* folded to page two.

FOUR SLAIN IN SOUTHSIDE GANG WAR
Gunshots echoed through the Tenderloin this morning resulting in the deaths of four underworld hoodlums. Homicide Lieutenant Ronald Moriarty reported that Tony Kerchansky, Big Bill Buell, and Thomas (Tough Tom) Sinatra, members of the Mickey Zirp Syndicate, and James (Banjo) Crispus, bagman for a rival organization, were killed in a gangland battle on lower Eighth Avenue shortly before noon today.

A possible witness to the incident, identified as the notorious Gus (Dutch) Gilpin, is being sought for questioning. The investigation is continuing.

Bessie was ready and waiting. Her new apartment was little different from the other one, the exterior still a blackened, squat mass of bricks perforated by little windows.

Gus felt like leaping down the musty carpeted stairs with her under one arm, until he noticed the complete and unconscious fluid grace of her descending the stairs. Every jeweled joint of her structure moved in a contour of lightness. She might have been a soap bubble floating on air, she might have been a delighted child let loose in a meadow of blooming clover.

Mr. Fitzgerald's driver, Amos Lavender, a black man, said nothing as he opened the limousine for her. He was all right. His business was to drive dangerous people from one place to another and the only question he needed to ask was "Where to, please?"

"Union Station," Gus said.

It was a short drive and that early in the morning there was
only the traffic of produce trucks and milk wagons. Alert for ambush, Gus kept his eyes moving.

When they pulled up at the station, Lavender asked softly,
"Sir?"

"Yes," Gus answered, puzzled by the worried tone.

"Which entrance, sir?"

"The main one," Gus said.

"Let me off at the black," she said.

"Me too," Gus said, puzzled. "I'm with you."

"Your troubles are just starting, Mr. Beautiful," she said, her
voice turning husky and sad.

"Wrong," he said. "We're just beginning. And it's all goin'
to be springtime and flowers."

The driver carried their bags to the counter, accepted a tip from
Gus and was gone. The man behind the counter was a sallow-faced
Aryan with thick glasses.

"Two to Hot Springs, Arkansas."

"You and her? You go around the other side for your ticket."

"I'm with my niece from Alexandria. We always travel together," Gus said slowly, wanting to punch the bottle glasses off
the clerk's face.

"You'll have to set in the colored section."

"Why not?" Gus smiled.

"You ain't colored," the clerk said, but pinched his lips together when Gus laid a big ham fist on the marble counter under
his nose.

"Sir," Gus grated.

"Yes, sir," the clerk said faintly, taking the money and pounding out the tickets, and then spitting into the corner.

"Now look here," Gus said, barely able to contain his anger, "if
you're any kind of a man . . ."

"Come on, Mr. Beautiful," she said softly. "You ain't goin' to
be able to knock down every two-bit clerk for his two-cent lip and
still have time for me. Come on, you want it this way, you're goin'
to get it."

She picked up the tickets and guided him to the waiting train.
He was halfway across the enormous room before he cooled off
enough to talk.

"By criminy, that guy sure made me mad," he said.

"Simmer down, love, it's very good trainin' for you. We start playin' it rough like that, they say we goin' berserk, like apes, y'know, and any little old half-blind shrimp can pull out a pistol and cut you down and say, 'That nigger's goin' berserk!' They give him a medal."

"Forget it, Bessie, I'm sorry I lost my temper."

The conductor looked at him strangely, but was looking more at the fat-puppy prance of Bessie's breasts. He took a long time over her ticket, forcing her to lean toward him, studying the small print, bending this way and that, until Gus said, "You're goin' to get my fist instead of that tit in your mouth, mister."

The conductor froze a moment and said, "I guess you'll be all right. Just get off when they call out the station."

"Thanks a lot," Gus said.

"You better remember your manners," the conductor said thinly to him. "You ride back here, there's manners."

Again livid with sudden rage, Gus was ready to wring a scrawny neck when the warm, mocking voice came down the steps.

"Dutch, eh, two-gun Dutch—he's just an old goat. Come on, Mr. Beautiful, we got a ways to go." And she was giggling at him, at his bull elk hump-shouldered, bowed neck and blazing eyes.

He followed her into the car which bore a sign, simple and explicit: "COLORED." His yellow hair was beginning to stand on end like the mane of a Palomino stallion. She walked down the aisle all the way to the very back, past a grand assortment of dark-skinned people, some in business suits and two-tone shoes, some in overalls and cut-out brogans.

Gus tried to keep a set face, a pleasant but reserved countenance, but the numbers of the strange black mass were burying him with sharp obsidian stones.

The seat was worn threadbare; there were no white napkins on the greasy headrest.

"Gee whiz," Gus murmured, "why didn't I get us a private room?"

"You don't like my folk," she teased.

"No, it's just that soon as I start on my honeymoon, everybody's mad at me."

The train lurched, bumped, lurched again and was on its way, its wheels rattling over switchpoints. The stench of the slaughter-houses gradually lessened.

There were a few uneasy glances at Gus from the neighboring seats, but nothing was said. The old conductor came by and punched the tickets. A white butcher boy came by and Gus bought two apples at an exorbitant price, and from then on they were free to watch the scenery from the window.

The rising hills of Arkansas split up into the Ozarks. Oaks and lead mines and punched-up gray shacks on the edge of cleared meadowland moved by. Little things took their eyes and then were gone. A man skinning a pig which hung from an oak limb. A black boy on a mule waved a tattered hat wildly, and a white bull mounting a slim, poised Jersey heifer. They reminded Gus of home in Ford County.

He'd been cooped up in a walled hive for months, like a wild horse brought to the steeplechase for training. But he felt the pressure of angles and bricks and asphalt fading as the scene became more primitive and natural. The canyons they traversed became deeper and the country was as wild as it had ever been, undisturbed, except for the railroad itself winding up the green mountains, cresting and winding down a long, slow slope, until Gus heard the cry, "Hot Springs, Hot Springs," and awakened with his head on Bessie's silken shoulder.

Looking into her Egyptian eyes and her pleasant smile, he said, "That's for us."

Alighting from the train, they found themselves alone at the far end of the depot. Yonder a crowd of whites like maharajahs were being helped from the steps to the bricks and escorted on to their cars.

"Goddamn it," Gus said, "there ain't even a redcap down here."

Gus put his fingers in his mouth and whistled loudly. A confused gray-headed porter trotted down the line toward them, shaking his head at the daily mystery of what the white man was going to invent next.

Gus said, "Thank you," gave him the baggage checks and then said, "We'll be going to the hotel."

"*The* hotel?" the gray-haired porter asked fatalistically, rolling his eyes.

"Right," Gus said, and, taking Bessie's arm, he escorted her through the crowd of people clustered at the curb.

A cab pulled up and the old porter put the bags in the running-board section. Gus put a dollar in his hand.

"Where to?" the cabbie asked.

"*The* hotel," Gus said.

"I could take you to a place down the road, kind of a private place," the driver suggested.

"No, thanks," Gus said, "we'll try the hotel. I'm teaching my niece how to play golf."

"Well, she looks like she'd make a mighty fine hole in one," the driver said, cracking a slanting grin, until Gus laid a pearl-handled .45 behind his ear and said very quietly, "The lady will have an apology."

"Yessir, no harm intended," the driver wheezed. "My dumb ig-norant burrhead joking always gets me in trouble. No, sir, I wasn't thinkin' of anything wrong, no, sir, that's a wonderful-looking niece you got and I swear to that. Yes, sir. I'm sorry, madam."

The hotel was a grand white-painted, turreted building of many wings and no logical plan. The desk clerk was a bald, short dum-pling ever wary and impeccably bland. When he saw Bessie com-ing along with Gus, his blandness turned to cold beeswax.

"Mr. Gilpin," he said, turning over the reservation card, "we have no notice of another—"

"My secretary," Gus said. "Takes care of my money and cleans my guns after I get 'em dirty."

"I'm sorry we didn't expect . . ." Beeswax to granite.

Gus fluttered a bill near the elbow of the small mound of re-spectability in the biggest gangster resort in the country.

"I bet I know what you're thinking," Gus said, now sure of him-self. "It's very embarrassing to her when it happens, which isn't too often, but it happens she's a daughter of King Farouk of Egypt, and she expects to be treated as a princess."

The bill had disappeared; a faint smile thawed the stone back into wax. "Indeed, Princess, we're delighted to have you stay with us. We have some lovely cottages next to the golf course, perhaps you'd rather have that sort of privacy."

"Exactly," Gus said.

The clerk banged the bell and yelled, "Front!" The ultimate seal of approval.

Bessie's face altered and came through from the somber, impenetrable racial wall to a glowing, childishly pleased gamin's expression. Her shoulders inched back a fraction, her head a shade higher, and she was as tall as Pharaoh's daughter or any pure Watusi maiden.

The clerk had been wise, and Gus promised himself to remember him, because the cottage was large and clean and comfortable.

To one side was a white-tiled pool of constantly flowing warm mineral water; to the left was the fairway of the eighteenth hole. Big pecan trees shaded the cottage and provided the dignity nature makes with time.

Gus tipped the bellboys at the door, and, as they left, he turned to Bessie, took her in his arms, and her happy kiss was sweet as a springtime morning. He lifted her high and carried her into the cottage.

On through the sitting room, he carried her into the large airy bedroom and to the great canopied edifice piled high with feather-beds.

She was biting his ear and crying, quick little sobs, then giggling low and husky, and kneading his shoulders with her golden fingers.

All day it was a springtime idyll, all that wonderful day. They splashed and laved naked in their pool, his eyes ever studying the loveliness of her body, the way an artist studies the perfect composition. There was never an end to the flowing, unexpectedly perfect lines and forms.

And she was singing, letting go with a blue velvet voice, songs he didn't know but, whatever the lyrics, she was singing of the joy that can come only after courage defeats despair.

"I love my man, 'cause he's all mine . . .

"I love Mr. Beautiful, 'cause he treats me fine . . ."

When she sang, her smile was all the more open and sweet and especially real. Nobody, he thought, can smile any more except her. Most people smile like dogs wanting a handout, but she smiles because she's happy.

She was just enough overweight, he decided, to make her the most beautiful woman in the world. She was just enough of a leopard to make her a member of the big world.

They made love in the warm water like laughing swamp creatures, and later, lying on a blanket in the grass, peeking through the shrubbery, they watched the golfers in knickers and caps, battling their way through the day's heat toward the final green. His milk-white skin was turning red, but her golden-brown body seemed to burn a welcome to the sun. A bellhop brought cold champagne and a dish of cold chicken and summer sausages and poppyseed rolls.

When the sun settled red and rank on the western ridge, she was giggling and sobbing again, murmuring little disjointed phrases, "I can't take it . . . I gave up once . . . Why dream on . . . I'm goin' to wake up in a minute . . . There'll be a big-bellied old freak chewin' . . . but oh, it's such a sweet dream . . . sweet as Coke . . . O sweet . . . O Gus, don't wake me up . . ."

He lay with his head between her strong pointed breasts, his arm lying loose between her long soft legs, listening and not listening, surfeit, half asleep, all the cares of the world outside somewhere in a different world where he himself was a complete stranger.

"Soo now," he whispered, "soo now, soo now, girl."

"How come you picked me? You? How come?"

"I didn't. It happened."

"How long you goin' to tell me that?"

" 'Nother thousand more years," Gus said.

"I can't get over it . . . I don't deserve . . ." and she was singing again, "My blues tonight are apple pie, 'cause me and my Gus are high as the sky . . ."

"You've got the creepiest, sweetest voice I ever heard. When I hear it I remember nightbirds singing, and corn a-growin', I could listen all night. You oughta be on a stage."

"Most managers want a cut of flesh, too, and that kills the song."

"No more. Nobody even thinks about a cut of my girl. You want to sing on stage, it's O.K."

"I don't know . . . Why me? Oh, Gus, I love you too much . . . Don't you know how much hurt there is everywhere, oh everywhere I went they hurt, and I was young and kind of lovely . . ."

"You're just starting," Gus said. "Young and kind of lovely, Princess Cleopatra."

Happy, happy, happy, and singing again,

Cherries, cherries, red berries, berries sweet,

O heav-en wel-come me . . .

He called for a dinner of everything he could think of. Oysters, duck, and Smithfield ham. Strawberries, cherries, and baked Alaska.

It was served on the screened porch, in the deepening night now lustered by a rising harvest moon. Old liveried flat-footed waiters moved from the great silver-covered dishes on mahogany carts and returned with the next course. One silver-haired old retainer wearing a red coat stood nearby silently supervising, deigning only to pour the correct wines at the correct moment.

Hand in hand in the moonlight they strolled down the clipped grass turf of the fairways, and sometimes she would break away and whirl like a seraph, her arms heavenward, her pleated silk skirt whirling out. And she would suddenly be close, turning into his arms, a gentle loving kiss, and on to stroll again. He'd say, "Sing some more," and she'd let it all out of her heart like the gold from the lonely moon.

> "Oh, it's been a while since I seen a smile,
> But now my heart knows happiness . . ."

They were half asleep by the time they returned to the cottage, and joined together, the long lovely honey, and the heavy-boned milk white, in the incredibly light and yielding featherbeds. It was a night God gives seldom, and they both savored it, treasured the black velvet tone, the sorcery of bliss, the sea surge and tidal moontime.

After coffee in the late morning, both suffused and basking on a high plateau, Gus heard the phone ring faintly through his bliss.

"Gus Gilpin?"

"Me," Gus murmured.

"Sounds like that dinge hooker broke your back."

"Who the hell is this?" Gus said, waking up.

"A.C. Goetz," the voice replied with amusement. "What's the matter, you don't like a spade called a spade? You prefer dark meat, O.K., but it's still dark meat. Black ass is black ass, ain't it?"

"Get off it," Gus said.

"Jigaboo is still all darkie. No matter. Point is the meet."

"Right." Gus could barely speak through his rising anger to the man he'd been sent to serve.

"Meet you in the bar about noon, bring that shine nauch along with you."

"Noon," Gus said and hung up.

"A.C. Goetz," he tried to explain to Bessie, "is the syndicate man, top dog of St. Louis and St. Joe. Mr. Fitzgerald pays him and works for his job, Goetz pays Mr. Pendergast and works for his job."

"And what about Gus Gilpin?"

"I don't pay anybody, I just work to be Mr. Gilpin," he said.

"How long can you?" she asked.

"Long as it takes."

"I don't know, Gus," she said. "I been down awhile, I'm not used to bein' up."

"Princess Cleo, we're going to the lounge and meet Mr. Goetz and pass him over his tax, and pay our humble respects to the Lord of St. Loo and then run like the dickens back here."

She smiled, because he'd conquered his unexplained anger and didn't need it explained.

But he paid special attention to the Colts. Jacked in a shell, jacked it out, and replaced it in the clip, making sure the pieces were perfect and the ammunition clean. Lastly he jacked a fresh bullet into each breech, leaving the guns cocked and ready to fire.

"You take it easy," he said directly to her. "Just pretend you're my wife, or my hunk of fat beef or my foot stool, or whatever, just so you recall you're mine and naturally I'm goin' to take care of you."

"Gus," she said softly, "I can stay here. I'm not pushin'."

"Come 'long, princess," he said, "I want to show you off."

He was determined to keep his mouth shut and his hands ready for action. By the time they strolled on the path toward the grand white-towered building his face was as solid and mean-eyed as a grizzly bear with a belly ache

His hands were slightly fisted, huge mauls, unconsciously ready to ball and smash.

Inside, a small group of men waited for seats, or doubled up at the crowded bar.

The room's noise, the garrulous din of men's joshing, seemed to diminish to a steady swarming buzz as Gus escorted Bessie to a booth. Waiters and the maître d' seemed to have conveniently disappeared.

It was a big booth, adequate for eight people. Gus let her slide in ahead of him.

"My man," she said gently, "Ain't no need to prove it any more. I'm a one hundred percent believer."

He ignored her and the cut was enough to remind her she was a woman, his woman, and her place was beside him, and her sound was to be silence.

No waiter arrived, but a tall, sandy-haired, mustachioed man turned from the bar, surveyed them for an instant, and stepped easily through the tables to the booth. There was an air of disdain in his loose-jointed nonchalance.

"This table is reserved for Mr. Goetz."

"Where is he?" Gus asked.

"I'm he," the tall man said, his lips not smiling, his lips quite thin and pale.

Gus rose. "Gilpin," he said, not extending his hand. "My companion, Princess Cleo."

Goetz bowed suavely to her, but his eyes were flicking off each nub of nipple, each crease of crotch, measuring, pressuring, buying, selling.

"May I sit down?" he said to her. "Princess?"

"Please do," she answered.

"How are things in K.C.?" Goetz turned to Gus.

"Warm," Gus said. "Mr. Fitzgerald asked me to bring you this." Gus took a fat envelope out of his side pocket and slid it over to the tall fox-faced gentleman in fine clothes.

"I heard you're an excellent messenger."

Gus didn't answer, but kept his eyes tight and fixed on the thin and dangerous man. A.C. Goetz didn't get to be bigger than Mr. Fitzgerald by simply being suave.

"Reliable. Brave. And a rare marksman. Are you ambitious?"

"Sure," Gus said. "Up to a point."

"And the point?"

"I don't sell people."

"I don't get you."

"I don't sell out my boss, or my girl. I don't kill anybody unless he tries to take something from us we don't want to give."

"Funny, I was thinking you'd want the princess to be some sort of entertainer. I bet she can sing like a canary. I own an interest in some clubs in St. Louis, could carry her awhile till she got a good start."

"There's clubs in K.C.," Gus said.

"I've an opening for a middleman too, a fixer. Pays double what you're getting from Honeyfitz. You could stay with her while she was singing."

"No," Gus said, a strange emotion boiling in his chest, a sixth sense saying he was being laughed at, toyed with, that this lean, immaculate gentleman had only to touch his pencil mustache with his little finger and Gus would be knocking at the pearly gates.

"We'll be going," Gus said carefully.

"No hurry," Goetz protested mildly. "The princess hasn't had time to get acquainted yet."

"I'm acquainted," she said. "One whoremaster looks like any other."

"Oh—" The fox face twitched. "Then you already know."

"We don't play," Gus said.

"Gilpin, I'm not asking any favors from a hayseed punk. I'm going to make a proposition and you'd better take it while you can."

Gus silently studied the rapacious countenance, knowing it was touch and go from here on out.

"That's better. Now the princess and I will take a little stroll upstairs and you'll both have a nice fat bundle out of it."

"You're crazy," Gus said.

"She'll make more off me than she ever made on Cherry Street in a week."

"Why pick her? Because she's mine?"

"Because she's got class. And that's worth the price."

"Better learn to live without it," Gus said. "The answer is no."

"You know I run all this. You know the bartender and waiters and lugs are all mine. I blink an eye and you're dead, and after I finish with her, she's got no home to go to. No big strong protector. She just hustles her butt to niggers."

Gus slowly lifted his big damask napkin to his lips and when he settled it down to his lap, his right hand stayed with it.

"Mr. Goetz, that's the end of face-up. I don't like your dirty mouth, especially in front of my lady."

"Oh, aren't you a brave bucko." Goetz grinned.

"I get braver when I got a big solid piece of cocked Colt in my hand," Gus said. "Especially when it's under the table aimed right about at your puckered-up belly button."

"You're bluffing," Goetz said, unafraid.

"Now pick up the envelope and stick it in your pocket. No signals, no nothing. It's a lot easier and safer for me to bump you right here. Just blink that eye and I'll blow you clear over the bar."

"You're digging your own grave," Goetz said.

"Gus," she said, "he's right."

"One step at a time," Gus said. "Maybe he's right, but I'm betting he's sensible."

"Think about it. You're trading your life for a black pig. I only want her tonight. You make yourself a grand, and take up where you left off."

"Stand up nice and easy," Gus said, his tone a conversational command. "We'll be walkin' out of the garden door and down the path to our cottage. We're goin' down there and study out this generous proposition where we don't have any audience."

"Kid, you're goin' to regret this," Goetz snarled, his aplomb fading as he suddenly realized Gus was solid, that Gus didn't give a damn whether he lived or died, just so he did what he thought he should do.

"I just hope a bug don't get in your eye," Gus murmured, " 'cause if you blink, I'm droppin' the hammer."

"You'll never make it."

"I'll carry your jacket, Bessie," Gus said, taking the jacket and laying it over the gun in his lap, putting the napkin on the table. "Bessie, stay on my left. Mr. Goetz will be on my right, smiling like he knew he had a long life ahead of him."

Goetz looked around the room carefully, spotting his people, weighing the odds, and knowing all along in the marrow of his bones that Gus was going to do exactly what he said he was going to do, no matter if A.C. Goetz was the head man of a tri-state organization, no matter, if it were a golden afternoon in a fancy dining room, no matter, he had no way out, none at all, nothing mattered except the guts of the man with the gun.

Goetz glanced at Gus and nodded. "All right, let's go, maybe I can talk some sense into you on the way. I don't really want the coon bitch any more. She's a loser."

"Move," Gus said, starting to rise, Bessie's jacket loose over his wrist and hand.

The tall man unfolded his legs like a crane and stepped forward. Bessie followed Gus, who moved with uncanny swiftness and grace, invisibly, quickly, so that he seemed to be politely steering the left elbow of Goetz as they walked slowly out of the room toward the side garden door.

A heavy beer barrel of a man rose from a table to greet Goetz.

"Ace! Haven't seen you in a coon's age."

"Hello, Manny," Goetz said easily. "This is Mr. Gilpin and his friend, the Princess of Fatima."

Gus nodded. The fat man froze awkwardly, knowing danger was there but not how or why.

"I'll talk to you later," the fat man said.

"Fine," Goetz said. "Nice seeing you, Manny."

Gus gave an imperceptible iron nudge to the elbow and Goetz continued across the room. At the door Goetz said, "You're damned near a dead man already. Gilpin, give it up now while you can."

"Mr. Goetz, I'm goin' to pray for your soul."

Goetz paled slightly under the intensity of Gus's eyes and moved through the door.

"I didn't know this was going to happen, Bessie," Gus said, "or I'd never let you in for it."

"I could as well have turned the trick," she said.

"You couldn't and lived and you know it," Gus said. "The skin of this snake has got a poison in it."

"Mister," Goetz said, "I own six two-story whorehouses down by the docks. There's probably a hundred twenty of the toughest old humpers in the country down there, worn out old nauch that'd do anything, anything at all, for half a dollar. We get a strange type of clientele down there. When this is over you know what I'm going to do with this smoke bitch?"

"I don't know why you want to die," Gus said. "I'm a peaceable person. I ain't kill crazy or I'd already punched out your backbone, but you seem determined you're a big he-dog who can lift his leg on anybody."

"Everyone in that room knows there was something wrong," Goetz said. "In a minute they'll figure it out and you won't ever leave. There's people stayin' in this hotel shoot people for nothing, they get a big jolly off it."

"Inside," Gus said, opening the door.

"Gus," she said.

"Bessie, I'm sorry, but we got to hoe the row, whatever it is. Time's past when we let this breed of skunk pee on us. Right?"

"Right."

"It's better to kill him and face the music, ain't it?"

"Better?" she said.

"I mean I'd as soon be dead as peed on by anybody."

"That's because you never hustled." She smiled. "You just don't know."

"You never had a chance to learn different till now."

The phone was already ringing. Bessie answered it.

She listened and spoke to Gus. "Somebody wants to talk to Mr. Goetz."

Goetz grinned.

"I'll take it," Gus said, flipping Bessie's jacket off the silver-mounted Colt. "Yes, no, he's got a case of trench mouth," Gus said. "Call back. Operator, I want long distance. Mr. Maurice Fitzgerald, in Kansas City."

Gus gave the number and waited through the various operators lining up the wires. He hoped Mr. Fitzgerald was at the office. "Be too bad," he mused aloud, "if Mr. Fitzgerald went to the ball game today."

It took a few minutes. Goetz sat down and stared at the wall. Bessie offered him a drink, which he refused.

Mr. Fitzgerald sounded like a voice from the cellar but Gus breathed a small sigh of relief.

"Got a problem," he explained. "Mr. Goetz wanted more than the payoff. He wanted my girl, too, but I couldn't swaller it, so I got him here settin' in my room, waitin' for me to make a wrong move."

There was a long silence, broken at last by the old man's sigh. "Jesus Christ, Gus. It's my fault. I forgot Goetz has this adultery-freak thing. He's got to top every dame he sees with a man like you. It's his way of lettin' you live in his world."

"Well now, Mr. Fitzgerald, I'm not certain how long he's goin' to continue in any world." Gus laughed. "His people got us sort of penned in here. Most likely they all got their ears in the switch-board. I just want to know shall I kill him now or later."

"No, don't kill him yet, just set there with him." Mr. Fitzgerald's voice seemed urgently concerned. "I'll have to make a couple phone calls. Are you all right?"

"Fine as new twine," Gus said. "Only I don't know what the sharpies are fixin' up, so if you don't call back in half an hour, I'll punch his ticket and then we'll make our move."

Gus broke the connection, leaned back on the sofa, and glared at Goetz. "Kinda makes me grouchy," he said, "the way you're clutterin' up my honeymoon."

Goetz kept his mouth shut.

Gus had a beer as the phone sat silent. He watched the clock tick off the minutes.

Goetz glanced at the clock, shifted his feet and looked at the floor, and said, "O.K., I'm sorry. I admit I was wrong."

"That's big of you," Gus said. "Any other last words?"

"You bastard," Goetz said, "you dirty nigger-lovin' bastard."

"Twenty-nine minutes," Gus said, lifting the pistol, sighting across the notch to the blade to the pale damp forehead. Butt safety off, thumb safety off.

"Wait a second," Goetz said. "I'll cut you in on my operation. You can stash the dinge off somewhere. I don't want nothing to do with her."

"Goodbye, Goetz," Gus said a moment before a knock on the door broke the spell.

"Who is it?" Bessie asked.

"George Morton Pendergast," the man at the door replied.

"Let him in," Gus said, "but stay on the other side of the room."

A portly man with red-veined cheeks and a big walrus mustache entered alone. He was dressed richly and was short of breath from moving unnaturally fast. He went to the center of the room, eyed Gus, the .45, Bessie, and at last the object of his wrath, Goetz.

"I warned you," he said. "I told you and I told you. Leave other guys' dolls alone. I give you fifty pretty virgins, but no, you got to pick on this Negress and get yourself twixt a rock and a hard place, and I guess that's all I got to say to you. You don't learn."

Turning to Gus, he said, "I had a call from your boss, and I'm his boss, and this one's boss too. Understand?"

"Yessir," Gus said, "I understand."

"Well, onliest thing you can do is to walk him down the road. There's a truck there. You shoot him or you don't. If you don't, you lose. But it's up to you. If he didn't have this cravin' for other men's pokin'-poozle he'd be a first-rate man."

"George," Goetz said, "you're joking me."

"I never joke about business," the portly gentleman said, and added to Gus, "There'll be no reprisals or anything, no matter what. This is a clean resort and I run a clean business over six states."

"Yessir," Gus said. "I counted on it."

George Morton Pendergast turned at that, caught by the simplicity of the truth. "You're a sharp youngster. Honeyfitz told me, but I didn't really believe him. Yes, I see now. You got a woman problem, otherwise you'd do well."

"I don't have that big a problem. We ain't tryin' to prove anything except that a man can love a woman and she can love him back. Happens all the time."

"Certainly," Mr. Pendergast said. "Every man has a woman problem. Only some got it worse. Maybe I'll see you later."

"You're bluffing," Goetz said to the already closed door.

"Come on," Gus said. "You're going down to the end of the road with me."

"You don't really think he means it, do you?" the skull-faced man asked. "He's just puttin' you to the test. Makin' sure you got the moxie."

Gus shrugged. "Let's go."

"Sure," Goetz said, his tone capitulating, comfortable.

"You try something fancy, it'll be your last mistake," Gus said. "I hope it is a test. Cold killin' goes against my grain."

Goetz at the door turned to Bessie. "You look like a hophead to me, a dime-a-dozen snowbird. You ain't goin' to live long enough to be a fat nigger mammy."

"Move." Gus jammed the iron into Goetz's side. "If someone knocks you off real soon you can blame your rotten mouth for it."

Outside Gus indicated the path. "Just walk."

"Sure thing, farmer." Goetz smiled.

Gus was thinking it was too easy. Goetz had never gotten to the top of his mountain without foul blows and backshooting. And Gus knew in his own heart that he could never simply execute this man, no matter how evil or dangerous he seemed. He'd always had trouble executing a chicken for Momma's Sunday dinner.

The evening was balmy and the fragrance of petunias and nicotiana saturated the air. The old pecans stood tall and immense, like guards over the grounds.

"Nice night," Gus said.

"Depends," Goetz said. "You don't really think the boss would put me down and put you up, do you?"

"I believe that's what he said," Gus said. "It's all right with me if he changes his mind."

Walking down the leafy sweet evening, Gus tried to keep close to Goetz. He knew a man backed into a corner will fight like a bagful of bobcats. But as they passed through deeper shadows, Goetz seemed to stumble and in catching himself had to move awkwardly. For a split second as he whirled aside the moonlight showed a tiny derringer in his right hand.

"You're the one taking the truck!" Goetz's voice came fast and tight as he squeezed the stubby little trigger.

The force of the high-velocity slug spun Gus half around, and he knew his shot had to be good or it would be his last. The heavy .45 thumped hard in the heel of his hand as he squeezed, the lead was low, going toward the rising moon, but Goetz's throat was in the way and the top of his head sprayed off like catsup pounded from a bottle.

Gus knelt on one knee for an instant, queasy from the horror and the violence and the angry burning in his shoulder.

He shook his head like a prize fighter after a knockdown. At last the spiral let him off and the big pecans stood up the way they should and the moon was surely firm in its place.

He found the little derringer near Goetz's twitching hand. A two-shot beauty, a regular miniature bulldog. Jamming the .45 in his belt, he found the envelope in Goetz's breast pocket and put it in his own pocket, then awkwardly with his right hand dragged the lean corpse on down the path, hoping it wasn't too far to the truck. The blood welling down from his shoulder was going to ruin his brand-new forty-dollar suit.

Two men waited by a smelly Diamond T truck. They didn't step forward to help. Gus let the body drop in front of them. He couldn't see their faces. They were simply muscle men willing to do a disposal job.

"He's yours," Gus said, his hand resting on the .45 in his belt, not sure, not trusting anything or anyone in this lovely moonlight.

"Easy, boss," one of them said. "We just the movers. It don't make no never mind one way or the other, just so's I ain't late to the crap game."

"That's all there is to it?" Gus asked, hanging on, even as the men took arms and legs, tossed the late Mr. A.C. Goetz into the back of the garbage truck.

"Yessir," the talker said, "that's all. No fuss, no muss, call us."

Gus turned away. It was over and he couldn't believe it. Too much was turning over and over. The field was too big and the plow too small and the horses too wild.

He staggered weakly, trying to keep his eyes on the light of the path which would lead him back to the arms of Bessie. But it was hard going. His legs didn't want to mind. They wanted to let go, to veer and yaw, but he set his jaw until the sweat poured, and said to his heavy muscles and bones and guts, "You go. You will go. You will."

Crazy-legged, he made it back to the cottage and through the door, already looking for a place to fall. He'd made no noise coming in and as he staggered toward the bedroom he saw Bessie in the bathroom, a paper of snowy powder in her right hand.

He was already losing consciousness; all he could think of was dropping flat on that bed and letting the sleep drown him. He wanted to cry out, Don't, Bessie, don't do it. But he was already disappearing into his own pain.

SIX

WHEN THE DOCTOR had gone, Gus looked up directly into Bessie's sultry eyes and said, "I want you to marry me."

She smiled. "Mr. Beautiful, you aren't even healed up yet."

"It's not right," he insisted. "It makes you less than you really are. You know what I mean."

"Sure, like any ofay dude can have a colored mistress, but nobody ever marries one."

"Bess, I'm saying I love you and that just means man and wife to me."

She kissed him gently as a cherry blossom touching his lips.

"Takes two to say yes, Gus, and I say no. Because you got something else on your lily-white mind."

"O.K. I remember seeing the coke."

"So I take a little leaf," she said.

"You don't need to, but you don't believe it. If we were married, then you'd be sure."

"Sure you wouldn't stray off as soon as the kick's gone? Sure that a man ain't a rabbit?"

"Yes. That's what I'm saying. Marriage is sacred to me. I'd never betray it."

"I ain't a hard user," she said. "Really. You use the stuff 'cause there ain't anything else and because there's plenty of lice in the world pure delighted to take a bite out of you and pay it back with snow."

"Call up a preacher."

"No, Gus. Never, never. I'll quit the coke, but I'm not marryin'. Besides, I think it's illegal in Arkansas."

"Marriage?" Gus asked.

"Miscegenation." She smiled.

Gus tried to reach for her, but she eluded him, her face absolutely set in a determination as fine and concrete as his own.

"All right," he said after a tall still moment. "All right. Main thing is for you to have your own free soul."

"Now, now," she said, coming close, settling her silken cheek on his and kissing his throat and ear. "Now, now, I love you, Gus, I love you. O Lordy, how I love you great big beautiful puddinhead." And the song started there, rising up from her sweet murmurings. "Oh, Mr. Happiness, listen to this beat of mine, O hear the blues I sing for this goldie man so fine . . ."

His shoulder was taped, and his arm was laced to his chest with a swaddling of bandages, but he still had his good right arm. She bore down on him, her great brown breasts floating across his face, her long limber legs twining around his own, the little catchy, throaty laugh coming off her lips, and for a moment they held each other like that, clinched solidly, the stresses blending between their bodies, balancing, rising, opening, going along on that rise until her face was damp, and she was biting his lip while he was blanking out into another time.

Next morning, Gus was pacing on the patio, letting the sun draw the wound in his shoulder, when a missile from nowhere drove directly at his head. He instantly dived to the turf as he felt the breath of it going by his ear.

In a moment he searched on hands and knees through the grass and found the white golf ball.

"Guess I'm gettin' buck fever," Gus said to Bessie when she came. "Thought somebody was after my neck. Damned golfers."

"Hello," a voice called. "Anyone there?"

"You darned right," Gus yelled. "Beat it."

"Now looky here, mister, I lost my ball." The voice was cut strictly to pure Brooklyn twang.

"You gonna lose more than that," Gus answered the man coming into the patio, followed by a trotting, shrunken ex-jockey of a caddy carrying a huge bag of golf clubs.

"Jeez, mister, don't be so touchy," the cheery stranger said. "I'm just pipin' this new game."

Coming closer, he saw the bandage and Gus's arm in a sling. "No wonder you're such a spud." He grinned sympathetically. "I had one of them once and I growled for a week."

As the other three men of the foursome drifted in, Gus began to wonder. He'd left his .45. He glanced at Bessie.

"Now, now, we don't mean you no harm, Dutch," the cheerful, pock-marked Brooklynite said. "If I was aimin' to put you in a wooden kimono, I wouldn't be shootin' golf balls."

"You know me?" Gus was more and more puzzled.

"Heard about you, Dutch. My name is Johnny. This here is Al, and there's Doc, and that baby-faced boy over there in the check-ered knee britches is name of Floyd."

The men nodded with quiet respect.

They were a stolid solid group, not hurrying, not skylarking, al-most like heavy herd bulls sleepy-eyed, powerful.

"We're all on vacation," Al said. "Just takin' the waters, right, friends?"

The three nodded agreeably, and their caddies nodded behind them.

Gus put the ball in Johnny's hand. "Sorry I acted like a stump-tailed bull in fly time," he said. "Care for a beer or champagne or something?"

"Brothers?" Johnny put the question to his friends.

"Why not?" Al answered for them.

Bessie went into the cottage for the refreshments.

Al reached deep inside the leather golf bag and extracted a strange weapon. "You own one of these, Dutch?"

"I never even saw one before," Gus said.

"Thompson submachine gun," Al explained. "Call 'em Tommys or Banjos for short."

Gus took the piece, hefted it by its forestock grip, and tried to sight it like a rifle.

The caddies retreated to the other side of the hedge.

"No, you don't need to sight it," Al said. "You just aim old Banjo and cut her loose."

"You all carry them?" Gus asked carefully.

"Oh, sure. 'Course, we all favor some small hand gun too, for

old time's sake, but, son, the feds carry 'em, and we all got to keep
up with the neighbors."

Bessie returned with a tray carrying an iced bottle of Mumms
and five hollow-stemmed glasses. She let Floyd work the cork.

"Where could I get one?" Gus asked.

"I've got a couple extra I borrowed out of the Jacksonville
Armory." Doc spoke for the first time.

"How much?"

"The Banjo and a thousand rounds of ammo you already won."

"I'm willing," Gus said, "but how'd I win the prize?"

"There was a fella named Goetz used to be bothersome . . ."
Doc said, his long sorrowful face settling into a seamy grimace.

The cork popped. In one split instant the four men instinctively drew their pistols and were blazing away at the soaring
target, shredding it into cork confetti.

Gus looked at bug-eyed Bessie and burst out into a huge Kansas guffaw. "By golly," he said, "you boys really take the cake!"

Bessie handed the crystal glasses full of bubbling champagne
around to the gunmen.

"Long as it was your golf ball," Gus said, "you get to make
the toast."

Johnny, his deep-socketed eyes glowing, lifted his glass and
said through his chipped teeth, "Here's to peace and freedom."

They clinked their glasses together, drank deeply, shook hands
and politely took their leave from Bessie.

In a moment, Gus heard Johnny holler from the fairway, "Fore!"

Bessie shivered. "Times like that sends me onto the candy."

"They're in a line of business that's unpopular just now," Gus
said, "but so am I. We can't help that."

"I guess you're learnin' something," she said, "but don't forget
there's cannibals all over. Like the late Mr. Goetz and the men
who killed Jim."

"Don't worry about the past," Gus said. "I'm just sorry we have
to leave in the morning."

"We broke?" she asked.

"No, there's aplenty money. I think it was meant for us."

He gave her the envelope from Goetz's pocket.

She flipped through hundred-dollar bills.

"Jackpot!" She laughed with excitement. "Baby beautiful, you pulled down the right number. My, ain't all them little goose eggs pretty!"

"Let's buy a car and drive back." He smiled.

"Know how to drive?"

"Sure," Gus said. "I rode a Montana bronco, I guess I can top one of them newfangled machines."

The man from the agency brought out a Stutz Bearcat and took them for a drive, explaining the shift and clutch and its other virtues. He claimed it would go eighty miles an hour, although the roads were made for a maximum of ten for a racing horse and buggy; still, times were changing and the roads would some day catch up with the cars.

The roadster was a pretty lemon yellow with a black canvas top that could be folded up or down, saving the passengers the need for dusters.

Gus discarded the arm sling, but the shoulder was still stiff, and angry twinges of pain reminded him to treat it gently.

But it was fun spinning around the gravel roads, feeling the wind blowing their hair, opening the cutout, scaring roadside chickens and zooming by farmers in mule-drawn wagons.

Gus was loose and easy behind the wheel; speed was a release to him, he realized, perhaps something like a snort of coke would be for Bessie.

"It's the coming thing," he said. "If we had any sense at all we'd buy into a car factory and retire."

"Then do it."

He laughed. "You sound like a high financier."

"There's two ways I know to makin' money, legal and illegal."

That afternoon, Gus called a stockbroker and bought five hundred shares of a wildcat stock called General Motors.

"It's money down the drain," the broker told him. "If it were me, I'd buy into the streetcar lines. They're a seasoned investment."

Gus turned from the telephone and laughed. "You rather have streetcars?"

"I want auto cars," she said, making a blackface. "We want the biggest, best and mostest legal money-maker out."

"Five hundred General Motors," the broker grumbled. "And good luck."

"Thanks," Gus said. "While you're about it, get me a hundred shares of that new telephone company."

"Yessir," the broker said with complete exasperation, his contempt for the amateur coming clear across the magnetic wire. "If you'll forgive me, there's a company called Western Union, deals in messages by wire. It's paid dividends ever since 1868. AT and T is still in a dream world."

"Never argue with an expert," Gus said and laughed. "My lady says we like telephones."

"Yes, sir. Why does she like telephones?"

"Why?" Gus asked her.

" 'Cause they're black." She giggled.

" 'Cause they're black," Gus repeated.

"Very good, sir," the broker said. "Thank you for your business," and hung up his telephone rather snappily.

When they checked out of the hotel, Gus let Bessie take the wheel. She drove the way she walked, loose and easy, without effort. "Lady Oldfield" Gus called her as she tooled around a section corner, easing by a wagonload of hay, scooting up another rise and down the open road.

Coming through beautiful hill country, Bessie drove slowly down a winding valley of fertile soil wooded with chestnuts and oaks, hickory and maple, walnut and cherry, all fevered with the first colors of autumn.

"I never had it so good," Gus said. "The only thing I could wish it was spring instead of fall, and I could love you all the summer long."

"You plan on hibernatin' through the winter, beautiful Mr. Bear?" Bessie asked.

He lay his head on her shoulder. "Lady, I'm gonna love you through the snow and hail and ice, I'm gonna work you down to a flake of gold."

"Baby!" She smiled.

She slowed, going by a small apple orchard where a family of youngsters were filling baskets with bright-red apples. When Gus said, "Let's buy an apple," Bessie braked the roadster to a stop and shifted into reverse.

"You get the best ideas for a blue-eyed American boy," she said agreeably, backing into the driveway where an ancient log cabin still served as a home for the family. The yard was bare dirt, but it was neatly swept. A few roses bloomed by the doorway. The air was rich with the spicy perfume of ripe Spys and McIntoshes and Spitzenbergs.

The harvest had stopped when the car stopped. Gus saw the family standing stiff and afraid. There seemed to be about eight dark-haired children and one worn middle-aged woman. She had her apron full of fruit.

"Hello," Gus called.

"Maybe it's me," Bessie said.

"No, no, it's just we're strangers."

The children were copper-skinned, straight-haired and lean as pilgrims.

"Hello," Gus said again, walking into the orchard toward the mother. "We only want to buy a couple apples."

The mother seemed to consider this, cocking an eye at the new yellow car, the tall cattail Bessie following, and back on to Gus's broad sunburned, guileless face. "Please," she said, "you folks just help yourselves. We have plenty."

"That's the best part," Gus said, "being able to pick one right off the branch." He searched through the leaves carefully, picking out just exactly the reddest and roundest he could find. Bessie had chosen a crimson-splotched McIntosh. Gus took a bite of his Winesap, and the juice spurted as his teeth crunched into the fragrant white flesh.

"Dear heaven." He sighed. "That is the cat's meow!"

The woman was smiling and the children were grouping up close to her and smiling too. Gus indicated the car. "You want to look?"

They didn't bother to say yes or no, but were scampering on their way like a flock of squirrels.

"Looks like you'll make a good crop," Gus observed.

"Yes," she said, "it's been a good year for fruit."

"Maybe too good," Gus guessed. "The price down?"

The mother nodded. "Hardly pays to pick, but I can't stand seeing them go to waste."

"How come you was so scared when we drove in?" Bessie asked quietly.

"Figured you for somebody else. There's a man coming, and

the sheriff. I pray every night he will not come, but I know he will. You see, when my husband died, the funeral expenses were higher than we expected, and I put my cross on paper. At the time I just wanted my husband laid to rest in a decent way. I'd have marked anything."

"A mortgage?"

"I guess it said if I didn't pay the bill right off they could take what they wanted to make it good, and I reckon that's the way it should be. Right is right."

"Sure," Gus said. "But what about people are people?"

Even as they spoke a long black Hupmobile drove into the yard.

A fat slug of a man got out of the driver's side, while a lanky coyote-faced lawman stepped out of the other.

"That's them," she whispered, her face pale.

"Afternoon, Ada," the fat man said unctuously and nodded perfunctorily at Gus and Bessie.

"You must be the local undertaker," Gus said.

"That is my profession."

"And you're his hired gun." Gus spoke to the man with the star.

"Don't reckon it makes any difference to you." The lawman's voice was flat and indifferent. "But I'm the sheriff, and I'd as liefer throw you and your blacktail mammy in jail as not."

"Easy there, highpockets." Gus smiled. "Guess I'd be kinda touchy too if I had to do your work."

"Well, Ada, we didn't come to gossip with outsiders," the mortician said smoothly. "Have you got the money?"

"I'm doin' my best," she quavered.

"I surely hate to do this, but the law is the law, and right is right."

"Mister, happens I owe this lady a considerable debt. I figure she wants me to see the papers before her family goes walkin' down the road."

"It's none of your business," the sheriff said.

"Well now, Sheriff, I guess I'm goin' to see those papers."

"Show him the papers, Fred," the mortician said. "Let's get it over with."

The sheriff handed a sheaf of documents over to Gus and bit off a chew of tobacco.

It took only a minute to see that the mother had signed a chattel

note and that the sum of seven hundred dollars was due for em-
balming, plot, and "services."

"Seems a little high for a country planting," Gus murmured.

"She had free choice," the mortician said. "She took the best
casket I had. And the best always costs more. I'm sorrier than anybody about this, but I've got to make a living too."

"I guess you're eating all right from the looks of you," Gus
said easily. "Now it looks to me like if you cut this bill down to a
fair number, say two hundred, what I owe this lady would about
cover it."

"Two hundred!" the fat mortician gasped. "Get on with it, Fred,
serve the damned paper."

Fred had a pistol in his hand, a long-barreled single-action
Colt. "I'll serve it, Mr. Fircken, soon as I tame down this darkie-
lovin' city boy."

"Honey," Gus said over the sheriff's shoulder, "you know I
don't like you to play with my Banjo gun. You never know when
it'll go off."

The fat man looked at Gus in disbelief and turned slowly, like
a mechanical toy, terror holding him rigid. He saw exactly what
Gus saw: Bessie aiming the Tommy gun over the high fender of
the Stutz.

She had a big wild grin on her face and Gus wasn't exactly sure
whether she'd reached a limit of patience at being called dog.

"Put an apple on top of that pea-brained sheriff, honey," she
drawled. "I wanta see if I can knock it off."

"She means it, Fred," the undertaker whispered.

Fred's shoulders hunched. His face twitched. His hand trembled
as he settled the old Colt into its holster and turned too, to half
face the black princess.

"I apologize," the sheriff said. "I do. I mean I really do. I
mean it."

"And I guess you can settle that debt for two hundred cash,"
Gus said.

"Yessir," the undertaker agreed.

"Heck, I was hopin' you'd argue and then I could ask you what
price casket you wanted so I wouldn't have to bedevil your be-
reaved widow."

"Two hundred, sir. That'll be just right."

"You're not being pressured, are you? I mean, it's out of the goodness of your heart you're doin' this. Like people are people, blacks, whites, Indians, rich, and poor."

"Yessir. I always admired old Charley Breedlove. That's why we sent him off in style."

"Just write all that down on the paper," Gus said, taking a pair of hundred-dollar bills from the envelope.

The undertaker quickly complied and gave Gus the receipted bill, as well as the attachment writ. Gus handed the money over.

"Right's right," Gus said. "People are people."

"Yessir. Ready, Fred?"

"No," Gus said, "Fred isn't ready just yet. He's too busy thinking out how he's going to dry-gulch us when we leave here and claim we was running off or some real smart trick."

"No sir," Fred said, "I'm done with you."

"Fred, believe me, there's other people like me, good friends of mine, and if something happened to me, they'd come a thousand miles just for the pure pleasure of stopping your clock. You understand that? I mean they got guns."

"I don't like it, maybe, but you got the high cards."

Gus looked around at the mother, who was clutching at her children clustered around her. "All right, get going, and don't be botherin' this lady no more or I'll hear about it."

"Yessir. Goodbye, sir," the mortician said, scuttling off toward his big car like a fat hog on ice.

The sheriff tried to amble slowly, making a show of belated courage, but Gus didn't bother to watch.

He gave Mrs. Breedlove the papers. "You keep these," he said. "They prove you're in the clear. And after this don't sign anything until one of your children reads it to you."

"I can't send them to school much," she said. "We have a hard time because we don't know things like that. We can grow apples, but we need learnin' to keep up."

Gus took ten bills from the envelope and stuffed them into her tough, knotted hand. "Now, Mother," he said, "that's to go for education. Not a car, not a new sofa, just education."

"Oh, mister, oh, mister," the woman cried, "what's your name?"

"Gus Gilpin, and this is my lady, Bessie."

"You are the truest people I ever knowed," the mother said. "How can I ever pay you back?"

"Ma'am, you offered a stranger an apple, that's all the pay I could ever want."

Gus went over to the car, where Bessie was gently revving the engine. "And you see those kids get to school," Gus added, " 'cause I may be back and want another apple some day."

He stepped into the car as the mother bit her lips to keep from crying, her hands full of the documents and the green bills.

"I can't believe it," she said. "I prayed and angels came!"

"Goodbye, Mother," Gus said.

"Goodbye, Mother," Bessie said gently. "Goodbye, you beautiful kids," and she drove out onto the road, the Tommy gun across her lap.

Gus was smiling. "I wish you could have seen that bald knobber's face."

"Amazing," she said, "how a little black girl like me just plunkin' with a little old secondhand banjo can make a growed-up sheriff shake."

"Bessie, no matter what happens, you remember we were riding through a little valley on a windy road and the trees were all red and purple and yellow, and I said, 'Bessie, I love you so much there's never been a word made up that could come close to saying it.' "

"Listen to that big beautiful Scandihoovian yatter on," Bessie murmured.

SEVEN

•─•

DURING THE GRAY WINTER, Gus managed the Irish Rooster Club, collected and delivered the bag money for Mr. Fitzgerald, and was rewarded with another raise and a bonus. He was known as a quiet and dependable organization man.

Over Mr. Fitzgerald's doubts, he put Bessie on as a singer in front of a small combo. And he persuaded Fats King, the five-by-five piano player, to work with her. Fats, who was also a classical organist, knew Kansas City jazz like he knew apple pie, and played it for sheer joy. He was an energetic exemplar, and, hearing Bessie's natural tone, helped her line out a pleasant original style from which she could develop any way she chose. She could handle the intricate rhythms with no trouble, and learned to phrase a certain melancholy into any song, even in the joyful, bouncy tunes like "Ain't Misbehavin" or "Riffin' the Scotch," because she not only had it, she was willing to share it.

Gus put her on with no fanfare or grand debut, because of the club's clandestine reputation, but he passed the word around that a singer worth listening to was opening at his place, and in a matter of weeks it was Standing Room Only when Bessie was on.

By spring she was well launched and solidly experienced. As young as she was, she could sing as a pro anywhere. Fronting Fats's group, she cut a couple of records for Mellyfone, but the company was too obscure to reach a wide audience, and the public hadn't really heard the Kansas City jazz-blues yet.

She was excited by the work, weak and shaky by night's end, and she sometimes trembled in her sleep and clung close to Gus as if she were afraid of being torn away from him by the invisible demons of fated lovers.

Best of all, for Gus, was the knowing she'd kicked the dope. Once she felt truly loved by a real man, she could lean on him whenever the devils of the past rose up, and she could borrow on his strength to turn away the buzzard-eyed pushers and hop-jockeys.

The snow melted black and sooty into the gutters; the poor came out of their brick boxes to greet spring. It was a lovely green spring day, even in the smoky brick battlements of Kansas City, when Mr. Fitzgerald called Gus into his office. He was pacing the room when Gus entered.

Gus tried to settle the old man down. "O.K., Mr. Fixit is here. Take it easy."

"Ah yes, good, Gus. I'm going to ask you to do a rough job." Mr. Fitzgerald's tone was more than worried. "You can turn me down and I won't hold it against you."

"You already know how I feel about rubouts," Gus said.

"I know. I can pick up a contract jayhawker anytime for a due bill, but this operation is going to take more brains than guns and a lot of luck too."

"Name it," Gus said.

"We're opening up west Kansas. It's not the richest territory in the country, but I got word that Mickey Zirp's Cicerinos are moving against us from Denver."

"What about the local back-seat bootleggers?"

"They would rather join up with us."

"I'm elected because I come from out that way?"

"Yes, Gus, that's part of it. And maybe you don't want to go back. I have to know."

"I guess I can go back, but I don't want to stay," Gus said.

"This is a one-time deal. A regular convoy. Six big trucks, loaded with alky. A shotgun guard on with each driver. A smaller truck with gas and oil, spare parts and supplies. All you have to do is get it to the icehouse in Dodge City. Once there, I've arranged for the rest of the campaign."

"Lots of heat along the way besides Zirp's boys?"

"Bulls. You'll have plenty of fix money, but you'll have to be tough with it or they'll graft you to death before you make Wichita. You only pay one at a time, and only once."

"And if they come back for more?"

"I'll have a due-bill jayhawker on call."

"And the T men?"

"Outsmart 'em."

"I see what you mean about it's not being just a little run across the river and back." Gus smiled. "A hundred-thousand-dollar cargo of booze to haul clear across the state. And we fight Mickey Zirp's hoods every foot of the way, besides the state cops, every local constable, and the Treasury boys too."

"There's ten thousand dollars for you as a bonus."

"That's the profit."

"It's cheap if we can put a breathing space between us and Zirp, otherwise there's going to be all-out war right in the middle of Kansas.

"One thing more," Mr. Fitzgerald said. "You best not take Bessie. You'll have enough to do."

"I wouldn't want her around if we start burning powder anyway," Gus said. "But you'll look after her till I get back, right? I won't have anybody pushing on her."

"Just as you say."

"When do we go?"

"Sooner the better. I've got six brand-new Mack trucks loaded in the warehouse. Drivers and extras will be with their trucks. We've tried to keep all this quiet but chances are there's a birdie in the organization somewhere."

"I pick my own route and lead them with the Stutz," Gus said. "I ought to have someone to carry messages."

"Salty Saltz is the best."

"Why not? He's pretty old, but game as they come."

Mr. Fitzgerald opened his wall safe and took out a bundle of greenbacks. "It's in small numbers," he said and smiled. "You can't hardly ask a shade-tree constable for change."

"Yessir," Gus said, jamming the bundle into his pocket, going to the door. "And you'll look after Bessie?"

"I will, Gus. That don't mean any woman is going to do what I say, but I give you my word I'll do my best."

"That's all I need. I'll be back in less than two weeks."

"I hope."

Gus broke the news to Bessie as easily as he could, and he put the best face on it. They could buy a house of their own with the bonus, and he'd certainly get a raise and a step up in the organization.

"I guess it's time to find out if I can stand up by myself or not," she said slowly, worried. "I can do two weeks, I guess I can do anything, but please, Gus, don't make it much longer than that. I get to fretting about you."

"I'm goin' right into my home country. I'm safer there than walkin' across Cherry Street right now," Gus said. "And maybe I can buy us a real record company, or take you right into New York City and show 'em how my K.C. thrush sings."

He kissed her lightly, hardly goodbye.

In the huge liquor warehouse by the river, Gus checked the trucks carefully. Each was stowed with wooden cases of gin, bourbon, and Scotch, which had been barged upriver from New Orleans. He ordered each load covered with double tarps and he checked the rigging to make sure nothing slipped or shifted loose. He knew how the six big square black trucks would appear to the people along the highway.

There was bound to be a few heroes out there with nothing better to do than try to rustle a chunk of the herd.

He already knew most of the drivers, tough, greasy men who liked machines better than women. They were men who could drive day and night over the potholed prairie roads, pounding on and on. They were the offspring of the Texas drovers, the toughest men in the world, and the least complaining.

The six guards were a different breed. They came from the crowded streets, and their crimes were street crimes: murder, robbery, rape. Each lived by the street code every minute of his chancey life. Gus knew four of them personally, knew their wives or girl friends, their kids or their parents, knew they actually did lead a personal worrisome life underneath the dirty, jumbled bricks of the street. The other two were from the same neighborhood but had just been sprung from Leavenworth and needed a stake to make up for lost time. It was a motley group in too tight, too dark, too cheap suits, in shiny black shoes with rubber heels, and creased gray Fedoras, with the snap brim warped down over their constantly shifting eyes.

"Everybody knows where we're goin' and why?" Gus asked.

They nodded.

"Let me check the guns then."

Each man carried a pocket gun, and each truck held an automatic sawed-off shotgun. Satisfied with the arms, but knowing he had to beat Mickey Zirp to the punch, he went to the phone and called Mr. Fitzgerald.

"We're leaving," Gus said.

"When?" Mr. Fitzgerald asked.

"Right now. They'll never expect it. No one's been out."

There was a long pause as Mr. Fitzgerald considered the sudden move. "It's your show, Gus," he said at last.

"Tell Bessie it had to be this way. Early bird stays alive."

"Good luck."

"Yessir," Gus said and hung up.

He walked back to the group of men lounging around the great blocky machines. "Twenty bucks to the best shot. One at a time. Let's see you put out the light."

At the far end of the warehouse a small forty-watt bulb glowed dimly. Behind it was a brick wall. The men didn't wait for a second invitation.

"Start with Salty and deal to the right," Gus said.

Old Salty laid his bulldog .38 over a shiny serge forearm and shakily snapped off six echoing shots which smacked against the brick wall.

"Get him some cheaters, boss!" someone yelled.

The men laughed and the next man, Lefty Streeter, cut loose with an automatic and with the same results.

Catfish Murdoch, a long-armed beer barrel, steadily pumped slugs out of a Lüger. Next was Tiny Feldkamp, a huge hairy bear of a man, whose bullets flew steadily and close, but the target seemed impossibly small for these guns.

"Lemme show you boys." Fid Muhlhausen's prison-pale face appeared anxious and determined. "I ain't had much practice, but I'm lucky." He cut loose with a brand-new Police Special and had no luck.

The next, Snake Miller, a taciturn and despondent creature of the same pearly pallor, shrugged, took his turn with the same results, though he made the bulb sway with the close shave of the flying lead.

Cracker Zack, pinched cheeks, his eyes always hidden behind dark glasses, used a short-barreled .44 with no better success.

The huge room was blue with gunsmoke and smelled sharply of burned powder.

"Hell, Gus, your money's safe." Catfish laughed. "Ain't nobody can hit that puny little light."

Gus reached inside the Stutz for the banjo in its hideaway behind the seat. These men made their living with guns and staked their lives on them. They were necessarily avid devotees of weapons, and the chopper was the most advanced tool of their trade.

Gus checked the magazine, clicked off the safety, jacked a shell into the chamber, and without pausing fired from the hip, hosing the blue gloom with chattering lead. In an instant the light and socket and cord were splattered into sparking, smoking junk.

Gus said nothing. He snapped on the safety and let the gunners examine the banjo.

"Grace God," Lefty said, "that baby can talk, walk, and waltz!"

Gus spoke a terse command. "Time to roll. Right now."

"Now?" Catfish asked.

"Right now."

"Jeez, I thought it would be tomorrow morning," Big Tiny said in his high little voice.

"I ain't said goodbye to my new girl," Snake protested.

"Better we say nothing to nobody. You can make a phone call tonight from someplace along the line. The less chance they get to shoot at us, the bigger chance we have of gettin' there in one piece."

"I'm for that," Cracker Zack said. "I ain't got anybody to say goodbye to but myself anyways."

"Where at we goin'?" Lefty asked.

"West," Gus said. "Six trucks and the candy wagon go out of here in line. Take the regular road to Olathe. I'll be bringin' up the rear for a while, just in case Zirp has a tail outside."

"I'm ready," Lafe, the lead driver, said, and, climbing up into the high cab, he started his engine.

The whole warehouse vibrated with the roar of heavy cast-iron motors.

Gus and Salty opened the huge doors and checked out each truck

and the tail-end candy-wagon supply truck. Gus, eying the opposite buildings for a suspicious sign, drew a blank.

"I can't believe Zirp's all that dumb," he said to Salty as the
caravan thundered slowly down the street. "Let 'em get a good
start."

Gus took his time reloading the Tommy gun. He glanced at his
watch, saw that Salty was ready, climbed behind the wheel, and
gunned the Stutz out into the street, quickly turning right on the
trail of his convoy.

They passed through the littered, brick-lined streets, over the
bridge and through some modest residential districts, always bearing south and west until the townhouses became scattered, became
farmhouses and barns, became open countryside.

Once in the open, Gus stepped on the gas. He was already worried that he'd given them too much head start.

"That Lafe surely knows the road to Olathe," he muttered.

"We'll catch him soon enough," Salty said, aware of the tension
in Gus's voice.

On a far rise, Gus saw a giant, square-topped truck cross and
disappear on beyond.

He smiled with relief until he saw the big blue Lincoln cruising
along behind the candy wagon.

"There's the Zirp watchdog."

He reduced his speed and tried to look like an ordinary driver
on an ordinary day.

"Open the windshield, Salty," Gus said, slowly gaining on the
blue Lincoln dogging the long convoy.

Salty loosened the butterfly nuts on the windshield's hinges and
locked it open. Steering with his left hand, Gus lifted the banjo
and rested it on the dashboard, its barrel barely visible over the
hood.

"What you want me to do, Gus?" Salty rasped.

"No point in killing."

"You won't get a better chance," Salty advised.

They crested a steep hill and started down. Without warning
Gus hit the gas and gunned the Stutz up close behind the big
sedan, the banjo bucked in his big right hand, the bullets ripped
into the sedan's rear tires.

There were pale Italian faces turning, staring out the back

window, but the heavy car was already slewing down the graveled roadbed as the driver fought to keep control. In the loose gravel on the steep downhill grade, it was impossible. The rear end skidded sidewise, hung on the edge of the ditch, where weight and momentum took it rolling on over.

Gus didn't pause to watch. He was already whipping the Stutz forward at full throttle to catch the candy wagon, moving at a steady thirty miles an hour toward Olathe.

"Poor Mr. Zirp done lost his watchdogs." Salty smiled.

"Too bad." Gus clucked his tongue.

They reached the little country town of Olathe in another half hour, and as the lead truck started to pull over to the side, Gus drove by the convoy.

"Tell 'em to keep coming," Gus said to Salty.

As they cruised by the lead truck, Salty passed the word to Lafe, "Follow us!"

Lafe nodded agreeably and shifted the stiff gears.

Gus held the speed down as they went through the unpaved main street of the old town, but as they left he picked it up to thirty again.

"Check me, Salty, I want to take a turn west to Baldwin City. Won't be much of a road."

"I know it blindfolded. I hauled a lots of alky out this way. Be about three miles on."

Salty's memory was dead right. The narrow dirt road bore sharply to the right. It looked more like a driveway than a thoroughfare, but Gus relied on Salty's knowledge. The lumbering trucks made the sharp right with difficulty, shifted down, revved their thunderous engines. Gus had to cut the speed to a top of twenty.

"How much of this?" Gus asked as they passed a lonely little farm set in the midst of a huge high field of rank corn.

"Eleven more miles, then smoothes out, straight as an arrow," Salty said. "Straight west. Ain't no towns, though."

"Fine," Gus said. "I want as far away from K.C. as we can get without anybody noticing us."

The fields were in beautiful condition, the rich bottom land flooding the area with stiff, stalky green corn. The farmers and their wives and children were all out in their fields cultivating.

Gus remembered the endless hours of being tied to the hind end of a horse, working back and forth through the hot muggy days for the increase, and that cultivator Poppa had fallen under. Forget it, he told himself, put it under a chalk-rock fence post.

As the road straightened and the surface improved, Gus added a few more miles per hour. The sun was a yellow fire in the west, blinding the drivers, but they pressed on, sometimes scaring little flocks of scratching chickens out of the way, and sometimes turning to miss the great black snakes looping slow as ropes across the narrow back road.

At a junction, Gus pulled off to one side. The trucks followed his example, lining up like boxcars behind the perky little Stutz.

"Take a break. Stretch your legs," Gus called. "Lefty, take the lookout."

The drivers and guards wearily creaked out of their places and moved to the ditch sides, where they stretched their arms and stamped their legs.

As they moved around, kicking the tires, lighting up their pipes and cigarettes, Gus kept a sharp eye out on the road behind.

"You ain't expectin' no more from Mickey's bunch, are you? I seen the way you put 'em over the side," Tiny said. "They'll be a week gettin' started again."

"You never know," Gus said. "I don't take anyone for granted. I'd surely like Mr. Mickey Zirp himself to show up, though. I could settle the territory's boundaries with him right soon."

"Ever seen him?" Salty asked.

"No," Gus said. "You?"

"Once," Salty said. "Still gives me the creeps. Save the worst of the Irish and the worst of the dago-Jew, put 'em together and that's him. He's got a nose like a buzzard and red, frizzly hair. Eyes like a lizard. He's taller than Tiny, and he's got a twist back. He's an expert with a shiv and a fast gun. He's always thinkin', too, all the time plottin' up some dirty work."

"I heard he was a cutter," Lefty said. "Gets a big jag offa cuttin' a man. Strikes low. I heard you never want to let him get within six feet of you, 'cause he moves so fast with the steel. I heard he's made a many a man a gelding just for his own spite."

"Spite?"

Lefty nodded. "They say that he's like a stud horse that's been cut proud. Took a slug through his stones, so's he's more rogue than most men. Only thing he cares about is the bastard son he sired while he could."

"How come someone ain't just shot him twixt the eyes?" Catfish asked.

"He's taken plenty lead, but seems he's lucky with his life. Some say you need a silver bullet to take him out."

"I put a load of double-ought buck into him, he won't care whether it's money, marbles, or chalk," Cracker Zack said.

"We'll eat at the next stop," Gus said. "Let's roll 'em."

He was thinking of the red frizzle-haired, buzzard-beaked, proud-cut enemy scheming out there somewhere in the beyond, perhaps even around the next corner. Never let him get within six feet of you, because he can strike his full length before you even know it, and he strikes low with his curved knife.

He was thinking it was bound to come, sooner or later. Man to man. Because Mickey Zirp owed him Jim's life.

Stepping over the door into the seat, he waved them on.

The huge trucks, like blocky insects riddling the stillness of the fields with the racket of their engines, followed along single file into the oncoming darkness.

Gus hated the darkness. You could only see lights; you couldn't tell if a man with a gun or a box of hand grenades was riding behind those lights.

One or two cars came from the west, and Gus had the banjo ready for each of them until he could identify them as farmers going home in their Model T's.

In an hour they reached a small hamlet. Gus saw no billboard of welcome, but Salty said the place was called Overbrook.

A lunch counter had a sign out with a light bulb burning over it. The street itself was empty of cars or wagons.

"Looks O.K.," Gus said. "We got to eat somewhere."

He drove to the curb, parking parallel in case of need for a fast start, though the rule was still the old hitch-rail policy: aim your transport at the curb and tie it up.

"Go ahead," Gus told Salty, "bring me out a sandwich or something, and make sure the men get plenty of everything except beer."

"You goin' to stand guard all by yourself?"

"Me and banjo," Gus said.

Salty smiled raggedly and led the drivers and guards like an alien horde into the sleepy, empty restaurant.

Two yellow street lights defined the graveled main street at each end. Gus walked down the sidewalk toward the rear of the caravan, checking to see that tarps were tied down and nothing was out of place. The last thing he wanted was to draw attention to the truck fleet, though the very bulk of it was enough to cause a scandal. It was like trying to hide an elephant, he decided. You just had to act as though it was business as usual.

He thought a moment of the darkness of Kansas City and Bessie dressing for her evening's work at the club. A terrible pang of remorse and loneliness crossed his mind, but he forced his thoughts to move on to the future, each crossroad, each bridge ideal for ambush. He dared not think of anything else.

As he reached the tarped-over candy wagon, a figure emerged from a doorway down the street. An old bone-handled Colt hung at his hip, and Gus could make out the stooped, thin shoulders and grizzled mustache of the village constable.

Gus waited for the first move.

"Just passin' through?" the old man asked, thumbing his ancient vest pockets.

"Like to stay," Gus said, "it looks like a nice town. But we'll just feed and move on."

"Well, you're making Red Wolford happy. He ain't sold so many dinners since he opened seventeen years ago."

"They'll leave a good tip for him too," Gus said.

"Funny you parked this way 'stead of the other way."

"Funny?" Gus asked.

"See, you're breakin' the law. We park on the angle in Overbrook, like everybody else. What're you carrying in them big trucks?"

"Special kind of seed grain. We're goin' west with it and start a new crop."

"Real good for drouthy folks, I suppose." The old marshal smiled faintly. "Maybe I ought to take a look at it."

"Too much trouble unstrappin' all those tarps," Gus said.

"You ain't parked legal," the marshal said. "Likely I got to give you all a ticket."

"Six vans, a pickup and a car. How much?"

"Two dollars apiece," the old man said. "That's for parking wrong."

"That's pretty steep, especially we ain't bothering anybody, and making Red Wolford rich to boot."

"Red Wolford don't need money, 'cause he don't spend it," the grizzled old man said. "I was a cowboy on the trail from Texas to Abilene, and I always spent my pay like it was goin' out of style. I figure money goes dead and stinks if it sets in a man's pocket."

Gus smiled and palmed a hundred-dollar bill. "That's exactly my feelin', too, Marshal, and I bet this town could use a contribution from an outsider just passing peaceably through."

"Likely," the marshal said as Gus passed the bill. "That's a mighty nice contribution. Now maybe I ought to ask if you was connected to a big Pierce Arrow sedan painted dark blue. Had five men in it. One of them was a frizzly sorrel with a Roman nose. They was two other big cars with 'em, and they wasn't so contributin' as you."

"I've heard of someone like that," Gus said, "and I surely thank you for letting me know they're hereabouts."

"Point is, I don't want nothin' untoward happenin' here on my bed ground. You rannies want to frolic, you frolic yonder outa my jurisdiction."

"Yessir," Gus said, "I'll do my best. I'd as liefer not have a ruckus a-tall."

"Wish't I could." The old handlebars quivered, the rheumy eyes looked backward fifty years. "Oh, I wish't I could!"

Gus smiled. "I'd surely like you on my side of the barn was there something untoward to happen."

His men were straggling out of the restaurant now, full of food and coffee, contented and ready for another hour or two of the hard night driving.

"I wonder," the marshal said faintly, wishfully, "I wonder if . . . No, I got to stay. I don't know why I got to stay, but once an old stump jumper goes out to pasture, he's got to abide it."

"Well, you got a job to do here," Gus said gently, "and you want to do it right. You'll get the smell of gunsmoke again one day."

"Naw, these farm clodhoppers are still bufflered by the buckaroo. They just dumb as sheep and some less interestin'."

Gus walked along with the marshal to the Stutz, where Salty had a paper bag waiting for him.

The marshal said, "Reckon I'll have a sup of coffee and cow juice soon as you leave, mister."

"Thanks again," Gus said.

He took the paper sack from old Salty and spoke in a quiet tone. "Pass the word that Mickey Zirp is ahead of us."

Salty's contented face registered a sudden spasm of fear but quickly sealed the break. "Yessir," he said, and strolled back to the knot of men chewing on toothpicks and poking cigarettes into the corners of their mouths.

Gus could think of no sure defense for the caravan on the move at night. The big trucks were simply too slow for a fast-mounted hit-and-run attack.

He bit into a succulent roast-beef sandwich and walked over to the lighted doorway of the restaurant, where the tall old cowboy with his drooping, grizzled mustache watched and waited.

"Where does the circus camp when it comes to town?" Gus asked.

"They generally take that level field out west by the cemetery," the marshal said gravely.

"Reckon you could show me where? I'd kind of like to rent it for the night."

"You don't need no guide. And it's county land. Just go straight out a mile even. You'll see a boot hill on the left and the circus field is on the right. Just high prairie, never broke. No fence nor ditch. Just go on in and set up."

Gus passed another bill into the old arthritic hand, its dally finger amputated long ago.

"You drive," Gus said to Salty. "I'm going to want a look-around."

"The boys is set," Salty said, getting behind the wheel.

The street reverberated with the mighty engines, and, like a slow freight train, the convoy moved out.

Gus gave the old marshal a salute as they left, and the old prairie-burned face under the battered Stetson lighted for an instant as though the moment was to come again when six-guns would leap from their holsters and men would die in the dusty streets. And then it faded as the twinges scraped through his bony

hinges, and he had it twice hammered home that he was nothing
more than a beached relic of another time and place and energy
and ambition, when men were absolutely men, and a Texas drover
in liquor could yell, "Half-horse, half-alligator! Raised in a cane-
brake, fed in a hog trough, suckled by a she-bear, the click of a
six-shooter is music to my ear! I'm the purple blossom of Gingham
mountain, and where is the son of thunder to rap his antlers to my
yell?"

Gus held the chopper in both hands, and as Salty drove slowly
out of town, Gus climbed out on the running board, free to fight.

The hair on the back of his neck was crawling, and his eyes
seemed to see threatening bulks and shapes that were only shadows
of trees and barns. Far up the road, coming over a rise, he saw
the yellow glow of headlights. Was it a farmer homeward bound,
or was it the humpbacked cutter?

A little coupe rattled by, its driver never knowing how close he
was to death that night.

Dogs barked. Owls hooted. The corn crackled like a million
clocks ticking as it grew in the warm humid night.

Gus saw the iron fence and arched gateway first, the sign peeling and leaning. "Mount of Olives."

"Turn right first chance," Gus yelled in to Salty.

The tracks were hardly visible in the faint light, but other trucks
had once crossed the buffalo grass, and Salty followed them into
a level field where there were no dwellings or buildings. As the
marshal had said, it was high ground.

"Make a circle," Gus said. "We'll camp here."

Salty drove around to the tail of the candy wagon, while Gus
hopped off the running board and spoke to each driver, urging
him to close up the gaps, closing the trucks in a circle, bumper to
bumper. Once they had the idea, he gave the signal for Salty to
stop. The vans locked into a tight ring.

"Sleep with your guns," Gus called out. "Catfish, you and
Tiny take the first watch."

The men knew Gus well enough to be sure he wasn't being so
careful just for the sake of discipline.

They laid out blankets and tried to sleep in the unfamiliar fresh
air and bright stars lighting up the enormous marquee of heaven.
Cicadas sang, owls hooted, and the city-bred men grumbled at the

hard ground. Several of them preferred to sleep in the cramped cabs because of a primordial fear of snakes.

Gus walked the circle outside the trucks, checking the terrain for anything unusual, but, except for a jumbled pile of never used chalk-rock posts, it was simply flat unbroken prairie, littered some with the debris of other campers, shimmering under the banks of stars.

At midnight Gus aroused Lefty and Fid to relieve the guard. But instead of letting Catfish and Tiny retire inside the circle, he sent them off outside, to the pile of post-rock fence posts.

Gus was almost certain that Mickey Zirp would force a show-down before dawn. Zirp would think he had the element of surprise on his side. And he would hit with everything he had. No one had ever said a word about Mickey Zirp having a streak of kindness or mercy.

At four he awakened Cracker Zack and Snake, but he didn't retire Lefty and Fid. "Keep your eyes on that graveyard across the road," he warned. "If they come from anywhere, they'll try it from there."

"How many you suppose he has?" Fid whispered.

"Marshal said there were three limousines. That would mean at least fifteen, maybe twenty guns."

"How do you suppose he tailed us?" Salty asked.

"I'd like to know that myself," Gus said grimly.

"They're going to a lot of trouble just to hijack some booze," Salty said.

"They may like to get the cargo, but that ain't what they want most," Gus explained. "Mainly they want to stop us. Stop those trucks from getting through. If they get a couple thousand cases of whiskey out of it, all the better, but it's the territory they really want—"

The rattle of a tin can interrupted him, followed by a faint curse in the darkness. They barely had time to dive into positions before a barrage of gunfire roared out of the darkness and the starlit night was afire with muzzle blasts.

Gus picked out their sites and tried to guess the numbers of the attackers. Over a dozen at least. He was outnumbered but he held the ring and they'd need all the guns they could get to take it. Once he had their positions in his mind, he moved his men to better defensive spots. They lay behind heavy wheels or crouched behind the iron engines and kept up a counterfire designed to stop any concerted rush. According to orders, Tiny and Lefty had not fired yet from their outside, ace-in-the-hole position. Gus tried to imagine where Zirp would be stationed. He'd be behind one of the armored limousines, probably near the center of his line in order to keep track of the battle.

Gus waited until he saw several flashes of an automatic bloom from that area. Leaning over the Mack engine, he stitched the night with the banjo. Red fiery tracers arced through the darkness. The effect was devastating as he hosed out the stream of hot lead. A scream rose over the stuttering battlefield, and Gus dropped, even as a new barrage smashed at his position.

"You got one of 'em!" Fid yelled.

"But it wasn't Zirp," Gus growled disgustedly, knowing the battle would end if he could finish off their leader.

He crawled to another spot, lying flat on the ground this time, and lined up the chopper on another steady-firing night hawk.

He wondered if it might be a decoy, just the muzzle of a pistol exposed while gunners on either side waited for him to open up on it. That would be Zirp's style, he decided, and, aiming well off to the left, he raked a steady stream of bullets in an arc and quickly rolled behind a wheel. The tire exploded from the counterfire, but it stopped the bullets.

"Give it up, Gilpin," a voice yelled from the perimeter. "Give it up and we'll let you loose."

Gus was already running to another area, checking to see that his men were still firing, were unhurt and in protected positions. Even the drivers had borrowed spare guns and were pumping lead out into the night.

"Soooo, pigs," Gus hooted in a traditional hog call that reached every ear. "Soooeee, come git it, Zirp!"

His men laughed, but there was an increased blast of shotguns, rifles and hand guns. Bullets had splintered into the trucks and the night reeked of raw whiskey and burned powder fumes.

A lurid burning limned the distant darkness and suddenly a new roar filled the night as an armor-plated Pierce-Arrow limousine charged against their line.

"Hit it, everybody!" Gus yelled, standing and pounding the machine with the banjo.

Suddenly the limousine's protected door opened and an arm threw a burning torch arching onto a van.

The limousine slewed around a tight circle, gunning back toward its own line with its engine howling. Gus held his tracers onto it, ignoring the torch, ignoring the bullets whistling by him. That car was vulnerable. It had to be. He drove another magazine of hard-nose slugs into it, and every fifth one was incendiary, showing him he was on target.

Salty was already leaping up to put out the fire; wounded, he fell back only to be replaced by Lafe.

Even as Gus despaired of penetrating any part of the car, an explosion rocked the field and burning gasoline sprayed high, igniting the crippled car and its screaming occupants. Another explosion lifted it into the air and in a moment the entire machine was a fiery white tomb.

No one escaped. And, as Gus with his Tommy gun empty watched transfixed, a bullet whizzed in so close to his ear it drew blood, but the bullet smacked the side of the truck in front of him. Gus dived, drew a .45, rolled, and fired.

A figure moaned, rose up to its knees convulsively, and pitched forward. Gus moved quickly to the man and rolled him over. Snake Miller had sold out and was now paid out.

Gus wasted little time in sympathy. Zirp would have to make one more play. And he'd have to make it before dawn and before his men felt the deep soul sock of seeing their comrades burn.

They came in a rush at the weak side, Salty and Snake's station, a dozen running, hard-shouldered killers firing and charging. By God, Gus thought as he fired, that Zirp must pay well.

They were nearly into the perimeter as a second attack came in from the other side, and Gus, with both .45s blazing, yelled out into the night, "Tiny!"

Tiny and Catfish did exactly what they'd been impatiently waiting to do. They smashed their own hail of lead into the flank of the attackers, confusing and turning them in the darkness, forcing them to fire even at each other in the howling, screaming, cursing melee.

Gus, seeing the smaller rush turn and retreat, turned his guns against the others who were trying their best to get untangled and back to safety. Few of them made it. Gus and his men had held the line.

The gray dawn was split once more by the howl of the straight-eights as the two remaining armor-plated limousines churned out of the field and raced west.

Gus looked at Salty's shoulder wound and saw that Zack had made a neat bandage for it.

"Don't worry," Salty said, "just help me out there. I want to see how much we hurt 'em."

Gus glanced at the body of a man named Snake and said, "He was one of them, a backshooter. He'll have a roll of bills on him. You're welcome to it."

In the still glowing, smoldering car were tiny piles of ashes of a different color than the rest. You could put all of them in a paper bag like flapjack flour.

"That's four," Gus said, and, circling over to the left where the main charge had failed, they found Tiny and Catfish looking over the scattered bodies of four more blood-sullied, gray-suited gunsels. In life they'd been terrors of men, in death they were pathetic, dirty-smudged mannequins, all awry on the green curls of buffalo grass.

They scouted on and found two more bodies on the far perimeter. One of them had been shot to ribbons.

"That banjo sure tears the meat," Salty grinned.

But Gus felt sick. "Get some shovels. We got to bury 'em before any visitors turn up."

The men fell to the work in the cool dawn, wanting more than anything to get the sight of twisted death underground.

"Lafe," Gus said, "take one of the big trucks and bull that hunk of iron off into that far ravine. Somebody'll find it, but they'll never be able to connect it up with anything. Maybe some day little kids will play in it."

Lafe took the least damaged of the trucks and put the front bumper against the still hot steel shell and pushed it far off into a little gully clogged with chokecherry bushes. Only the scar across the earth remained to tell that tale.

Seven bodies were buried near the pile of stone posts, and when they were covered and the ground leveled off, the men dragged seven of the posts over the grave, setting them side by side, like ancient druid markers.

In time the field would be called haunted. It would be named Seven-eleven Hill, and the yarns would grow bigger and wider until at last some day dreamers would dig for treasure and find belt buckles and raging teeth.

Gus was only concerned to get the caravan moving west. While the graves were being dug, the drivers were repairing tires and camouflaging bullet holes.

At last the engines ran, the radiators were patched, the tires fixed, and every machine was ready to move.

"All set," Lafe reported.

"I want to say a little prayer for these boys," Gus said, "then we'll drive on out."

The drivers parked their trucks over the burned scar and left the engines idling, returning to Gus standing by the seven stone posts.

Gus nodded as the boys removed their pearly snap-brimmed fedoras.

"Lord God, You're for everybody, I always heard, even the wrong ones, and for that we thank Thee and ask Thy mercy upon the souls of these dead men here and those in the Pierce Arrow. They were brave enough, and loyal enough, and if they worked for the wrong outfit, they probably didn't have much choice. So, Lord, if You've got a special barrelhouse for torpedoes up there, we pray You'll open up the pearly gates to these fighting hoods who just ran out of luck. Amen."

As Gus raised his head, he saw the lean, bowed-over marshal walking an old gray cow pony across the field toward them.

"Morning," he said to Gus, letting his gaze wander slowly over the scene, "did I hear you say 'amen'?"

"Yessir," Gus said. "We always have a prayer before we start out in the morning."

"Probably don't hurt none." The Marshal nodded. "Sleep well last night?"

"Like an honest man," Gus said, "tired from a hard day's work."

"Thought I heard a little racket out this way."

"These boys *do* snore!" Gus smiled.

The marshal's leathery face split, his old blue eyes twinkling. "Yessir, yessir, they shore do. Why, they snore just like those Earps snored down at the O.K. Corral some time past."

"Well, sir, we'll be goin' on west. My name is Gus Gilpin. Anytime you need some help, just ask for me in Kansas City, and I'll remember."

"Yessir, Mr. Gilpin." The marshal wasn't listening, he was still laughing. "Yessir, they *do* snore! Just like old Johnny Hardin snored in Abilene!"

"So long, Marshal," Gus said. "We got some miles to make today."

"Maybe you better touch a little iodine on that earmark," the marshal said vacantly, touching his big Stetson and managing to get the old steel-dust pony into a stately if racking trot, going off the buffalo grass to the dirt road and turning as a lonely and nearly obsolete person, back down the road to his quiet little town.

Gus wondered what all those blue eyes had seen in the past seventy years. Imagine!

"All right, here comes ol' Hannah," Gus yelled into the warm morning. "Head 'em up and move 'em out!"

He got behind the wheel of the Stutz, letting Salty ride shotgun again, and led them out of the pasture onto the road, turned west into the tracks Mickey Zirp made in his screaming retreat.

"Think he'll be back?" Salty asked.

"Take a while. He'll have to send clear back to Cicero for more troops. But he's a long ways from being done. Likely he'll try to get somebody else to do his dirty work for him."

"Like what?" Salty asked, puzzled.

"Like local bulls," Gus said, guessing already how it might go.

They drove westerly at a steady twenty-five miles an hour. Gus was beginning to feel the letdown. It had been a long night.

"You want me to drive awhile?" Salty asked. "You could get a little shut-eye."

"Tonight I'll sleep," Gus said.

"We goin' through Wichita?"

"No," Gus said. "I know it's shorter, but we'll go by Great Bend, cross the river there."

"Ain't much at Great Bend."

"That's the idea. Wichita has too many Zirp connections."

They stopped at a farmer's house to gas up the trucks from the candy wagon and to drink a pot of coffee provided by a farmer's wife. They were just outside the little crossroads town of McPherson where great wooden derricks were rising in the long wheat fields.

"You goin' to get rich on oil?" Gus asked the woman.

"Not us," she said tiredly. "We sold out our oil rights to Rockefeller before we ever knew there was any value to it."

"I'm sorry," Gus said.

"I guess it'll take a lot of oil to run these machines we're building," Lafe said. "Don't seem to be any end of it. Tractors and trucks and they're making the harvesters to run on gas too. Fella'd be smart to buy leases if he just knew where the oil was."

"That's a dirty business," Gus said. "John D. Rockefeller, going to be king of the U.S. with a golden crown, but the little farm folk suffer for the greed of the big ones."

"But old John D. is sure making a pile," Salty said.

"You know how much he's going to leave when he dies?" Gus asked.

"No," Salty replied. "How much?"

"All of it," Gus said.

The caravan moved on steadily. It was an efficient organization now. The candy wagon's mechanics were quick to replace flat tires and always managed to keep the crew in food and coffee, rolling on through the long hot day.

"Those boys on the candy wagon goin' to earn themselves a bonus," Gus said. "We're a half day ahead of schedule already."

"That's good, ain't it?" Salty asked, wondering why Gus should be worrying.

"It's sort of like walking a high wire over the Niagara Falls. You go too slow, you're liable to lose your balance; you go too fast, you're goin' to meet the wrong guy at the end. But it's all right. I had a notion when we started we might need a spot for a layover and happens I know one."

Gus tried to avoid the larger towns, and when there was no other way, he led the convoy through slowly, without stopping. He could already visualize the word being passed on ahead of the alien cargo slogging heavily westward. There could be plenty of Zirp-inspired small-town cops waiting to nab them for any small infraction.

Coming into Larned, the county seat, he noticed the barren side-walk under the tin awnings, empty except for one small vagrant child, whose mother burst out of a millinery store in daredevil defiance to grab up her babe before the demons devoured it.

"This looks like it," Gus said softly to Salty. "These here country boys want a little lick of the gravy ladle. Now, if I get pulled over, you know what to do."

"Yessir," Salty said. "I lead 'em out real slow, and if you ain't on the candy wagon, we come back fast with guns blazin', chasin' the bulls."

"Right, but be sure you don't hurt anybody except bulls."

In the middle of the main intersection stood a ruddy-joweled modern police chief in a tight blue uniform and black billed cap. Another villager in the antiquated uniform of an Army captain stood at the ready on his left, and on his right the local post of the American Legion was assembled at parade rest on the cross street. They all wore blue overseas caps embroidered with gold, decorated with medals. The rest of the attire was democratic American, from the optometrist's suit to the butcher's apron. Their fowling pieces and varmint rifles were grounded.

As Gus observed their soft, pale, alcoholic faces, he believed that even they knew how foolish they looked.

"Whatever," Gus said, "don't stop. It's too hard to get started."

He slowed the Stutz, but never let it come to a complete stop. Salty pressed close to him, sliding in his place as Gus jumped to the pavement.

Gus was moving swiftly ahead of the Stutz, a big smile on his face, which the chief realized could mean the big blonde man enjoyed a battering brawl, or it could mean he had a message of glad tidings to deliver. The chief was already awed by the size of the convoy. Everything about it was big. He was beginning to regret taking Mr. Zirp's fifty dollars to stop the liquor traffic.

He moved slightly aside to accommodate Gus and get clear of the oncoming Stutz, and then he had to take another side step to avoid the noise and listen to what Gus was saying, before he could even start to say, "Halt in the name of the law."

Because Gus was simply bursting over with beneficence, playing his own part in a heavier game than Larned's chief of police or the post captain and his Legionnaires with their goose guns imagined. He was declaring to the bespectacled captain and the red-nosed chief, "Hello, hello! I knew we could count on you and the great city of Larned to greet our seed train going west."

In order to demonstrate his appreciation, Gus dug carefully into his coat pocket and extracted ten hundreds and counted them one at a time into the pudgy, boozy hand of the chief where all could see, and looked him square in the eyes, softly saying, "I'd rather choke a cat with cream than lead any day."

And the chief was cursing himself for putting it all out in public, which meant he'd have to split with the rest now that they'd seen it, even as each huge truck slowly lumbered by in low gear, the drivers looking straight ahead, the shotguns looking the crowd over as if hoping for a little country mischief, and the truth of it finally socked home to the chief.

This was really a *big* deal, and they meant *business*, and a man could get his little self killed dead just looking cross-eyed around here, and he began to shake before Gus's steely eyes. His jowels quivered out of control. He lost one of the bills, which floated back and forth in the thunderous air, evading his frantic grasp until he had to snatch it out of the dirt, and Gus still stood balanced like one of his trucks, enormous, powerful, lethal, his two heavy pistol butts exposed, ready to go, the great broad country smile still on his face.

"Yessir, yessir," the chief said. "Yessir, glad to have you visit the town. Come anytime. We'll accommodate you. Yessir, yessir."

"I'm going to see that a case of refreshment is sent to these patriotic Legionnaires who are always in the forefront—of law and order," Gus said.

The fifth truck was passing right then, the driver chewing his tobacco cud, ignoring the world except for the road ahead. Cracker Zack looked bored and detached, thinking he'd like a vacation or a horse race or something to break the monotony.

"Yessir." The chief's voice was cracking to stuttering pieces. "You go right ahead."

"Thanks, Chief. Give my regards to the rest of the loyal citizens and Mr. Zirp."

"Who? Who? Who? Who?"

"Me? I'm Gus Gilpin. Used to live on a farm west of here."

"Gilpin. Sure, I know the Gilpins. Mighty fine people."

The sixth truck was by and the candy wagon stacked with tires and barrels came along like a caboose behind the great black train.

Gus reached out and caught a windshield stanchion, letting his weight carry him up on to the running board, and, turning to the troops of the ranked Legionnaires, he gave them a level look of inspection and lifted his hand to his forehead in a fine salute, his jaw big and firm, his attitude so military they were caught in its magic, and their captain, with his Sam Browne belt and holstered pistol, arched his back, clicked his heels, and bellowed, "Present arms!" The troops snapped to as he raised his hand to return the salute with equal military ferocity.

Gus eyed the troops and the captain sternly, and at last snapped his hand down simultaneously with the captain's. The inspection was over and the troops dismissed.

Gus grinned at Porky, the candy-wagon driver. "Cut on around fast now and get me back to the Bearcat."

"We may slow down some, General, but we never stop." Salty laughed as he relinquished the driver's seat to Gus.

"We have to stop somewhere. In two hours we'll be moving into Dodge and that's the wrong way to do it," Gus said.

He thought about the problem for which he had the easy solution if he wanted to push his luck a little. He turned it over in his mind.

"My folks had a farm about two miles off the highway," Gus said thoughtfully. "My brother runs it, I guess, now. It'd sure hold this convoy for over night with nobody any the wiser."

"You get along with your brother?"

"It's been quite a while and lots of water over the dam since I left," Gus said. "He likes money better'n his kinfolk, but I don't mind putting a few bills into his tomato can."

"Dodge is the problem," Salty said. "Zirp could already be there selling and buying people."

"My people?" Gus asked, already knowing it could be true.

"You know it," the seamy-faced man said. "And your head is on the block."

"I can't deliver so late in the day and I don't trust the darkness."

"It's your deal, Gus," Salty said, glad it wasn't his decision to make.

"It's a terrible thing to say, but I can't gamble that much on my brother," Gus said. "We'll make camp in the Goshen Hills."

He led them off the highway to the uninhabited north where he'd hunted jackrabbits long ago. A little box canyon with a windmill and stock tank seemed to be an ideal hideout.

"Park 'em facing out," Gus said. "Just in case we need to move in a hurry."

When the trucks were positioned as he wanted, he told the tired crew he intended to check the layout and also bring back chow for the night. He set Lefty and Murdock as lookouts. Taking Salty in the Stutz and followed by the candy wagon, he drove back down the tracks to an unmarked crossroads and turned right.

"My brother will be glad to sell us supplies," Gus said.

At the next familiar intersection of country roads he turned right and drove up the same dirt road he'd once ridden his pony over, and made the wagon trip into town with Poppa and Momma, and there on the little rise was the soft yellow ascending shaft of St. Olaf's, its steeple sticking heaven and the far, far horizon of yellow wheat.

The little graveyard inside the chalk-rock fence beside the church was becoming crowded.

They drove up the road past the weed-grown McCoy property, past the tenant farms of the bank, owned at least on paper by Poppa for his increase, and Gus felt the terrible pang of homecoming, the helpless anguish that no matter how a man returns, he feels the racking of its riddle of past and present and future, naming off those great, magnificent, explosive years when all was sensual and nothing made any sense.

They drove on over the rise and turned into the driveway of the original Gilpin homestead, the real land of the pioneer family who were contested by cattle barons who were contested by Indians, who were contested by bison. Now who will contest it? John D. Rockefeller, Mr. Pendergast, or General Pershing? Who will take it away from the last man who won it?

A red iron-wheeled tractor stood in front of the stable. The house needed paint. There were weeds where Momma would never have allowed them, and a stooped man in overalls and straw hat was turning from the tractor, his slitted eyes angry and calculating.

The eyes snapped and locked up the Stutz and candy wagon like a lizard's tongue grabs bugs.

Gus was shocked at how Martin had aged in such a few short

years. Had he not strengthened and refined those rabbit eyes into the glowing savagery of a lynx, he'd have looked exactly like ten thousand other worked-thin wheat farmers on the great prairies. But those young phosphor eyes set him apart. Gus had learned about the eyes of his fellow men, how they could lie to you and cheat and kill you, or they could tell you the simple affirmative truth of respect and honor, but he could not penetrate the outer greenish glow that filmed the truth in Martin's mind.

"Hello, Marty." Gus climbed out of the Stutz and said, "It's me, Gus."

"I knew you, Gus," Martin said. "Looks like you been makin' a good increase." The voice was dry as a corncob; the hand felt rusty and small.

"How is everybody?" Gus asked.

"So-so. Momma went loony, had to send her out to the county farm. Katie's turned into a brood sow, litterin' the country with bastards. I'm hitched to Lily Veitgengruber. That's about it."

"Things don't seem to have improved much since I left," Gus said, feeling the dusty gloom of Martin's mood stifling him.

"It ain't so bad," Martin said. "I managed to hang onto a couple of the farms, and wheat's up again. They's talk of making me a board member of the bank."

"What about Hundertmarx? He claimed I robbed his bank."

"There was a rumor going around that there was a shortage, 'count of he was playing the commodity exchange, and maybe he was trying to lay it off on anybody he could. Anyways, the auditors never found anything wrong. He's a mighty powerful man around these parts. Highly respected and all."

"Don't worry," Gus said, "I don't hold grudges."

"What business brought you here?" Martin was adding up Salty and the candy wagon.

"We need grub for about fifteen hungry men. Some good thick steaks, spuds, and coffee. We'll be going into town at daybreak."

"Lucky I butchered last week, but I don't know as I care to sell to such-like." Martin was canny. "Trouble breeds trouble."

"They're my such-like. And they don't like trouble any more than anybody else."

Gus saw the faint sneer twisting on the weathered, crafty face, and realized he was talking to a man about a whole world he could never understand.

"You know Momma deeded everything to me. This is all my ground."

"I wouldn't insult you by offerin' bribe money," Gus said, "but I can throw a twenty in the pot to buy Lily a washin' machine or somethin'."

"Fifteen men. Regular army." Martin seemed to be studying his scarred-toed brogans, splashed with cow manure.

"Make it twenty-five," Gus said. "And count your blessings."

"Just the one time?"

The tension broke in Gus's heart and his laughter rolled out through the yard. It was such a relief to know he'd escaped this dry-leaf, thin-souled existence, to know that no name would ever strike any fear in his heart, neither Mickey Zirp or a marshal named Grover Darby. He knew he'd crossed a bridge and thrown fear and despair behind; he could begin to live like a mindful human being.

The more Gus laughed, the more sour Martin's face looked.

"Here's a C note," Gus said, peeling a bill off the roll. "You know what happens to squealers in our business?"

"Never heard."

"They go for a ride. And they don't come back."

"Lily will be down with the victuals directly," Martin said, turning on his heel and going up the steps of the back porch.

Gus realized he'd purposely not been asked inside.

Turning from the door, Martin said through the still gloom, "I figured you'd ask about that McCoy woman you got in trouble."

"Tell me."

"She's the town whore. Lays out above Chester's Place, four bits a crack. Takes on greasers and niggers."

Gus turned away, not in fear nor despair, but in wonder that his brother could be so outrageously vile.

Little freckled-faced Sally, her ragged cotton dresses and her tomboy laugh and joy. And, oh, it wasn't Gus had gotten her in the trouble, it was that rotten banker.

Gus walked back through the barnyard to where Salty waited.

"What's the matter, boss?" Salty asked. "You sick?"

"I got to get into town," he said quietly. "You know Dodge?"

"Some," Salty said, his grizzled face showing his worry that a new problem had come on the wind.

"There's an icehouse back of Front Street. Big place."

"I know it."

"All you need to do is drive those trucks into the warehouse at daybreak and unload 'em. The man that runs the icehouse is named Hess. He's our man."

"How about the law?"

"Marshal Grover Darby. He's supposed to be bought, but Mr. Fitzgerald wasn't too sure of him. Wanted to wait and see before putting too much weight on him."

"I get it," Salty said.

Gus divided the bankroll with Salty. "Just in case I don't make it back, you know what to do."

"Maybe you oughtn't go alone, boss." Salty's voice betrayed his anxiety. "Porky can haul back the chow."

"This is something I have to do by myself. Thanks," Gus said, moving to the Stutz. "I should be back at camp in a couple of hours."

Gus drove out past the old house and turned toward town. He was worn thin from the hard trip, but he didn't see how he could avoid moving immediately.

He knew well enough where Chester's Place was. It had been a decayed foul dive on the wrong side of the tracks even before he'd left town.

He parked at the curb littered with rusty cans and broken glass and slowly surveyed the place for a possible ambush. If there was something wrong the old panhandlers hanging around the door didn't know about it. He gave away all his pocket change and went into the old barrelhouse that had started as a home away from home for lonely, bone-weary cowboys but now was the last stop for the meachy, penny-pinching grifters of the wheat town. The place stank of an unclean bathroom and chronically spilled green beer, and a foul aroma he associated with overage goats.

Behind the bar was a little gnome of a man with eyeglasses shaded by a green celluloid visor. Gus tried to place him, but he could not. He tried to think of him as a Fitzgerald, or a Zirp, and he came out Zirp.

"Somethin'?"

"Girl upstairs?"

"A couple. Take your choice. Four bits. Pay here."

"I . . ." Gus was going to explain but decided to save his breath. He tossed over a dollar bill and said, "Buy the house a drink with the change," and went up the stairway to the second floor. The gnome of a man put the dollar in his pocket and pushed a concealed button.

In a little alcove were seated two women, one a fat, gross Mexican. The other was thin, with nervous lines in her tight freckled cheeks, her loud hennaed hair looped around in spit curls on her forehead.

Gus spoke quickly, before he could change his mind. "Come on, Sal."

"Hey!" she shrieked, "you're lucky, you're gettin' a eight-hour virgin. How come you know my real name?" she added, leading him into a narrow cubicle hardly large enough to hold the bed. The room smelled like salted cod.

She came close to him, putting an arm around his waist, rubbing a bony hand up his leg.

He looked at her vacant eyes. No help. Whatever she had to say was blanked off. She wasn't on heroin anyway, maybe a pill or a tonic of some kind.

"Sal," he said, "it's me. Gus. Gus Gilpin. Get your things together. I want you out of here."

"Gus!" Her voice was a shrill, jangling howl. "Good old Gus! My little baby-faced sweetie! By God, Gus, I can't hardly believe it!"

"Sal, I haven't got much time but I want to see you get a decent break."

"Yeah," she sneered, "I heard all about that kind of help, like when the price of wheat dropped and the banker come by for his interest." Her voice rose again to a high shriek, nearly hysterical with an unspeakable joke.

Gus was stunned. There was nothing he could say.

"Look, honey," she said, "you wasn't the one. You understand. Hundertmarx was collecting. I thought it would help out the family. And that's the way the world goes around," she howled, laughing a scream of pure madness.

"Sally, I didn't even know," he said. "You folks just took off like the field had opened and swallowed you down. I taken the whip to Hundertmarx for you and for my own sister. That's all I could do."

"Quitcha worryin', big boy." She laughed. "It's all over, and I'm doin' fine. Me'n my boy friend is goin' to buy us a little hotel some day, soon as we get enough saved up."

"Sal, I'm not payin' off any pimp, but I'll give you a thousand dollars right now if you'll let me take you to K.C. and send you to business college."

"You ain't plannin' on throwin' a marriage certificate in the bargain." She giggled again. "I just don't put out for nothin'."

"You wouldn't live with me," Gus said, "or nothin' like that."

"You mean you already got a sweetie, eh, Gus?" She grinned, the face a horror of lipstick and rouge and dripping mascara. Why'n't you just give me the grand, I'll throw you in the cooshayvoo. O.K., sweetie?"

"No, thanks, it's too late, I guess. I mean it's too late for me to make sense with you."

"Aw, you just wanted to remember a little frisky sorrel filly instead of a bought and sold hunk of horseflesh. Hell with it, honey."

"Dear Sally," he said humbly, "I'm sorry. I'm truly sorry."

It reached her. The murk in those blue eyes unclouded, and she came to earth.

"Gus," she said softly, "most everything I said was right, but one thing I didn't say. There's some kind of a setup for you. They figured you'd come."

"Who?" he asked.

"All kinds of bulls, state, fed, even your friend and mine, Grover Darby, and even someone else a lot saltier than them. It stinks. It stinks to me." Her voice started to rise again into that shrill laugh. "But then, we all pull a boner and for some it's sooner than later, right, honey?"

"Any other way out of here, Sal?" he asked.

But she was giggling hysterically again, rubbing her cold hand up his leg.

He slapped her hard. She seemed to freeze. "Any other way out, Sal?" he asked.

"Naw," she said. "They're too cheap to put in a fire escape."

He went to the window overlooking a dark alley. It was a long drop. Too long.

He heard the heavy boots of state troopers clumping up the stairs. He had no choice.

"Thanks, Sal, thanks."

He lifted the grimy window and crawled outside, digging his toes into the ancient red bricks, and hoped there was some sort of shed to break his fall.

He heard the official knock on Sal's door and let go.

The next to last thing he remembered was a splintering pain in his left leg as he hit a trash barrel and solid concrete.

Lastly, he had that one vision to go out on: the dark, oily beak, the vulture eyes, and the scarred mouth of Mickey Zirp. He tried to dive at the hunchbacked buzzard, tried to defend himself, but a club sapped him behind the ear and caved in his mind.

"All right," Grover Darby said, "don't kill him here."

The hunchbacked killer clubbed at the yellow head one more time to prove he could do it.

"I got him," Zirp yelled over Sally's screaming from the up- stairs window. "Shut the dame up," he ordered, and in a moment Sally's scream ended abruptly in a bubbling gasping fight for air as a pair of hairy-backed hands locked on her throat.

Gus was dimly aware of pain and of a gathering knot of men.

"Wake up," the stony voice said, and he felt a hard-pointed toe of shoe rip into his ribs. "Wake up. Wake up. Wake up."

Gus knew that his .45s had been lifted and his left leg was too numb to carry his weight.

The pointed shoe dug into his stomach. "Wake up. Wake up."

"O.K. What do you want?" Gus opened his eyes and got a good look at his tormentor. It was enough to last him a lifetime. The obscene beak, the slaty, reptilian eyes, the twisted crocodile lips, the fetid odor coming off him like grave damp.

Gus let his gaze drift off easily to the others ringing him. Three hoods backing up Zirp, and Grover Darby chewing laconically on a toothpick, his brass star tarnished and drooping. There were two state troopers in puttees and Boy Scout hats, and four more cops in gray suits. These were uglier, heavier jawed, more sullen in spirit than the hoods.

His eyes made the circle, the completed circle of Mafia, local cops, state cops, T men and G men, all united in a single enterprise.

"Where's the trucks?" Zirp demanded.

"Strange bed pardners," Gus said, studying the group, "but you all have the same stink."

Zirp hit him across the face with a Lüger, knocking his head back against the bricks, and Gus fell forward unconscious.

He came to behind bars. Old Doc Winkleman was packing his bag, and Gus felt the splints firmly gripping his aching leg.

"Thanks, Doc," Gus said.

"Don't thank me. I took an oath. I'd do it for a dog."

"I ain't a dog, Doc."

"Maybe not, but you been running with a bad pack." The old country doctor shook his head, his little boozy eyes diddling, and Gus knew right then what card he had to play.

"Doc, I have to get a message out. It won't make any trouble, but it's worth five thousand dollars to you."

"Probably get myself killed," Doc said, his eyes watering and his mouth deprecating.

"Doc, I have a man and some trucks parked out south of town at a little place we used to call Buffalo Hump. You know it?"

"Sure. I delivered a pair of twins out there one winter when the snow was so deep my mare could hardly pull the buggy."

"You get out there and tell my man to skedaddle. That's all you need to tell him. Tell him I'm in the jailhouse, and he's to light a shuck back east."

"I guess I can remember that," the doc said, "but who pays me?"

Gus put his hand into his now empty pocket. "My man will pay you. His name is Saltz. Tell him I said to."

"All right, Gus, I'll do my best."

The benign-looking medico, bowed down by the weight of ten thousand mistakes in his venerable career, moved carefully out the door, where Grover Darby appeared with his key ring.

Gus had to stare at the floor to avoid seeing the big wink Doc gave Darby as the door closed and the lock turned.

Gus felt he could breathe easier now. Mickey Zirp and the bulls would be decoyed to Buffalo Hump, while Salty would come in at dawn from the north, and once the stuff was there, it'd take a civil war and presidential action to get it out except through the Fitzgerald organization.

All he had to do was stick it out. Just stick it out till dawn.

He didn't realize the full extent of what that meant.

Zirp came in as he was checking the splints and wrappings on his lower leg. He didn't bother to look up.

Darby opened the door for the hunchbacked gangster and his behemoth bodyguard, who smelled of garlic and olive oil the same as Zirp smelled of decaying flesh.

Behind him, he could make out the shadowy form of a fat man dressed expensively with an elk tooth dangling from a gold chain across his paunch. Hundertmarx.

"All right, Gilpin, they're out checkin', but I don't believe a word of it."

Gus looked at the big old Regulator clock ticking on the far wall. Only eleven o'clock. Dawn would be about five. Six hours to stick it out.

"You listening," Zirp asked, "or you want me to clean your ears out with a Lüger?"

"I'm listening," Gus said. "I'm wondering how you get to be so buddy-buddy with the bulls."

"Simple. Al and the Attorney General made a deal. It goes all the way to Sicily. You can't win."

"You got the Army, Navy, and Marines too?"

Zirp snickered. "It's so perfect you wouldn't believe it. We need the National Guard, we got 'em. Big Al has the whole country in his pocket."

"Who has Big Al in his pocket?"

"One guess."

"John D."

"Fitzgerald and Pendergast are going to be ground down to goofer dust, boy," Zirp said, "but you're first. Now where's the stuff?"

"Gone east."

"Liar. Shake him up a little, Bonzo."

Bonzo swung low with a quick hook. Gus felt a bomb explode in his midriff. He barely made it to the slop pail to retch.

"See how it is?" Zirp asked. "Bonzo gets a lift out of breakin' up guys, especially big pretty blonds."

"No," Gus said simply.

"It ain't like bein' a stoolie," Zirp said. "You ain't blowin' any whistle on anybody. Just the trucks. The men go free."

"No," Gus said. "You know I can't sell out the job."

"I think we got enough time." Zirp grinned with his thin white lips. "I'm goin' to poke that red-haired hooker seven ways from Sunday while you think about it."

Another curtain of doom fell over Gus's heart as he realized the fetid hunchback meant to have his fun with Sally, while Bonzo had his own weird play with Gus.

"Funny," Bonzo said, "funny how it goes. Old Mickey, he's got the syph. Gets a kick outa passin' it on. Me, I like it this way."

Gus tried to block the blow, but even his own mighty forearm was small protection against the giant fist that crashed to his cheekbone. Gus swung his own right and connected to the jaw, but only hurt his hand. He tried it again, and still the giant Bonzo only smiled, extending his jaw for another. Gus hit him with everything he had. Bonzo nodded absently like a winetaster and murmured, "Mighty fine, mighty fine," and abruptly uncorked a full-powered uppercut.

Blood dripped down Gus's chin, and he spat a tooth on the floor. He tried to stand up, tried at least to make it some kind of a fight, but his splintered leg wouldn't hold him and he fell into the bars. A rocketing left cross snapped his head the other way, nearly tearing his eyeball out. He was pinned against the bars by the force of the rapid blows. Gus futiley hit the giant two times in the belly.

Bonzo's eyes were bright, the creamy froth on his mouth sucked in and out, his hands alternating, smashing crashing blows to Gus's face. Each time the foam sucked out Bonzo sighed, and it continued until Gus slipped and slanted like a wounded bird, side-slipping and flopping to the concrete floor.

A sloshing bucket of water brought him back. He tasted the blood and vomit in his mouth and tried to think. Stick it out. Stick it out, Gus, till five o'clock.

Through a purple pinwheel haze he saw the hands of the clock pass midnight. Only an hour gone, and oh, Lord, he hurt. His leg was screaming, his face was no longer recognizable.

"Easy now, kid," a kindly voice said, "you're going to be all right."

He opened his one good eye again and saw Grover Darby sponging at his face.

"My leg," Gus said.

"Yeah, I know, them boys is pretty rough," Grover said. "I pulled that big stud off you. Told him I wouldn't stand for such a thing in Ford County."

"Thanks, Grover," Gus said. "I knew you wouldn't sell out."

"It ain't easy hewin' to the middle of the road," Grover said, "but I do my best. And I'll do my best to keep them broncos off'n you, if you'll just level with me."

"Level?"

"Well, I'm in the dark. I don't know what's goin' on .They make a lot of rough charges against you, and I want to stand up for you, but I don't know your side of it." Grover's voice was frontier-style hospitality, fried steak and gravy. Good old Uncle Grover.

"Gosh, if I told you, they'd try to beat it out of you."

"Don't tell 'em I know."

"No. Be safer if you didn't. Maybe they've already gone," Gus said thoughtfully.

"Gone where?"

"If I ain't back by midnight they're supposed to drive west on the river road to Norton, then hightail it east for Lincoln Center."

"You sure worked yourself into a quicksand, didn't you, Gus?" Grover said sadly. "I told Lu a long time ago I was afraid you'd get on the wrong trail."

"Grover, get me outa here. I haven't done a thing, or even been charged with anything."

"Wish I could."

"It's the law, Grover. You stand up for the law, don't you?"

" 'Course I do. Simple law and order. Don't be spoutin' off like a legal eagle at me. I know my duty and I do it."

He went out, locking the door after him.

Maybe his ruse would hold them through the night. Darby had played his part well enough for a country boy.

He tried to rest, knowing he was powerless to break out of the cell in his weakened condition.

It was just one o'clock when Marshal Darby opened the cell

door again and said mournfully, "Well, son, I guess you've picked up the bad habit of lying to police officers."

"Not much choice, Marshal," Gus said.

"Come along. The feds claim they can break a man in record time."

"It's a waste of time, Marshal," Gus said. "They want me to squeal on my men and my boss and I ain't goin' to do it."

"Maybe so, I get paid either way, but I'm plumb curious in these new scientific law-and-order methods they're workin' out."

Gus had to hop on one leg down the corridor to the office where three of the blue-jawed, liver-eyed federal bulls waited. They sat him down in a straight-back chair. They looked so much alike that Gus couldn't keep them apart. He tried to remember that once even they had been human and that if they could ever see themselves as trained police dogs, each one with pointed ears and liver eyes and blood in his nostrils, they could come back into humanity and be saved.

"Cigarette?"

"No, thanks," Gus said, "never use them."

"That's good," the federal bull said, grinding the lighted cigarette into Gus's hand.

A rage rose up in Gus's heart that these animals who were supposed to be paragons of virtue, animals made fat with taxpayer money, should so abuse his American person.

The hot blinding light snapped on. His one eye blinked shut.

Someone slapped him. "Open eyes."

The black eye wouldn't open. Another cigarette burned into his hand.

"Where is it?" they asked. "Where is it? Where is it?" they asked in rotation, bored, meaning absolutely to have their way because the federal agent was taught that he should have his way and however he got it was right.

Rage sustained Gus. It was like strong drink and rich broth to him, and he had enough to keep him silent and alive! His raw flesh smoldered, his eye was blind, his brain ached from the Oriental torture, but he had more than enough of the honest native-son rage to keep him going against all their third degree.

After a couple hours of it, he was strong and they were tired.

They yawned, loosened their neckties, they scratched their ribs, they hardly spoke the words any more: Where is it?

Zirp came in and quickly understood how it was going. Enraged, he leaped at Gus and hit him in the face with the Lüger.

When Gus awakened again, he was in the basement. He couldn't keep track any more. The last thing he remembered was someone saying it was past three. Maybe it was past four now. An hour to go.

He tried to keep his eyes closed and his breathing hoarse, but they'd quit waiting. He saw the leather puttees and knew the state troopers were ready for him.

"Play baseball?" a voice said.

"I like the Yanks. I like the way young Ruth swats the ball."

"We could play ball with this dumb krauthead," another said.

"I want to pay him off a couple licks for keepin' me up all night, but you ain't goin' to get beans out of him."

"I stick my night stick up his hind end, you never know," another said.

"Oh, hell," another said, "it's late and we'll just get our uniforms dirty."

Somebody's boot kicked Gus in the back. Another threw a chair that splintered against his macerated face.

"See," one said, "I know these dumbos, I know 'em. The more you beat on 'em the dumber they get."

"We could give him a double dose of salts, that might clean him out."

"You're always wantin' to work him out through the hind end, Griesiedick, I don't know about you."

"I'm just tryin' to do my job," Griesiedick said.

"All I can think of is throw him out in the yard and shoot him for tryin' to escape."

"What time you got?" Gus asked.

"Quarter past six," Ronnie's craggy, faggy voice answered before anyone thought how to cheat.

"Then it's all over," Gus said. "We win."

"You win!" a voice guffawed.

"You goin' to wake up in the pen, mister, and you ain't winnin' nothin'."

Gus tried to place that voice. Was it a trooper, or Darby, or was it a fed doberman, or was it the fetid Zirp saying, "We're keeping you on ice. On ice right where we can get you when we want you. You are going back to Leavenworth for life, Mr. Charles G. Belinski."

"Belinski," Gus murmured. "He's a . . . He killed them little girls . . ."

"You're Belinski from now on."

Gus was fading out. The relief of doing the job against all ob-stacles and pain and disillusionment was flooding over him like a warm sweet river.

"I'm not Belinski. My name is Gus Gilpin," he whispered.

"No longer," the voice of stench reeked out, "no more, baby raper, Charles G. Belinski, number 907862. That's you. For life."

EIGHT

DARKNESS. Thick soft lightless darkness.

He touched the wall in front of him, rough, wet stone and ancient mortar.

He listened, but there was no sound, not a breath nor mouse scamper nor drip of moisture. Nothing. A full-grown man reborn blind and deaf.

There was a slop can in one corner of the pit and his fingers told him there was a hatch in one wall so small a man would have to crawl through it or be dragged through it to enter. That was his universe. Still, he knew if he were alive and in this ghostly tomb, someone had put him here, and someone might think he should be fed.

Suddenly a noise slammed into his aching brain like rolling thunder. Distant footfalls amplified to reverberating kettle drums. He listened as the steps came closer to his hatchway.

They came near, two men with rubber heels and leather soles. They stopped in front of his cell. A dry crackery voice yelled, "Belinski."

The man without a memory wasn't so sure then. Maybe he was Belinski. He took a deep breath and tried to think it out again.

But the voice was impatient. "Belinski, you in there? Belinski, you dead?"

"That's not my name!" he howled back.

The voice said, "Slop him, Coalie. Today he's no-name, tomorrow he's Calvin Coolidge."

"Yessir," Coalie replied.

The hatch opened and a tin bowl of stew with some bread on top of it was thrust into the cell. The hatch closed, the footsteps continued on.

At least he was sure he wasn't dead. This would be too strange a holding corral for heaven's waiting list, even allowing for the whims of the Creator.

He ate the bread and stew hungrily, though its flavor was foul. He hadn't realized how starved he was. What would the next serving bring?"

It turned out, as he fitted into the routine, that once a day he was given a bowl of oatmeal and once a day he was given a bowl of stew or beans. And that was that.

The same voices served him each meal, and they always called him Charles G. Belinski, no matter how he tried to convince them otherwise. They ignored his arguments, treating him like a lunatic.

But time became a fact, measured twice a day by oatmeal and stew.

"Charles G. Belinski!"

I'm somebody else. They've crossed up the system and put me in here. Listen to me. I'm somebody else.

"Slop Belinski anyway. Tomorrow he'll be callin' hisself the Prince of Wales."

Day by day, hair and beard grew longer, his wounds healed, and his leg carried his weight. A greasy clamminess seemed to encase him, and his mind began to chatter as if cold. He shivered uncontrolled as he tried to exercise, tried to keep some tone, but in time his whole existence became dreadful, a vicious, foul, unspeakable sin against the spirit of a man, and his mind had little to sustain it except the belief that man was essentially a good creature, made to bring harmony and peace and freedom to the world.

In such a prurient environment, it became harder and harder to hang on to the conviction that sooner or later a man was a man, capable of building instead of destroying, capable of creating a beautiful world for himself if he used the courage and good sense God gave him to begin with.

Under this still vacuum, this lonely isolation, his carefree attitude changed. He was forced to use his mind to review what little he knew, and seek for answers, but each time he attacked the problem, it became all the more evident that he hadn't enough education to arrive at a solid logic of what man was.

He longed for a banjo to play and sing to, but there was none, and though sometimes the new harmonies grew grandly in his mind, other times he found there was no tune, no nothing, as if all the strings were slack and silent.

"Belinski! Charles G. Belinski!"

"No."

"Slop him anyway. Tomorrow he'll claim he's the Czar of Russia."

In time he began to see that he must change. That he must know more, feel more, think more clearly without the bias and prejudices planted by the generations before him. He must become a full and complete human being.

Revelation.

Unimportant what his name was. He became an identity in the name of mankind, convinced that there was no individual anywhere, only a massive global gene reproduction and spirit building river from which no one escaped with a name.

What difference then so long as the floating consciousness knew the answer, so long as the disorderly mind discovered there was no riddle, discovered there was no rule, no law, no government, only the renewing mass of mankind blessed with the divine intent to achieve human harmony. And that was heaven, and the pursuit of power over others was hell.

"Belinski!"

"Here, sir."

"Charles G. Belinski?"

"Yessir."

"Slop him, Coalie, and remember to tell the warden."

Stew and bread was handed through the hatch.

Through the long night with the constant darkness, he waited.

He counted the buttons on his shirt and divided the number by the buttons on his pants. He did his calisthenics until sweat dripped off his beard. He tried to sleep without dreams, but always the mysterious Bessie waited there, not to torment him but to remind him of perished days and nights.

"Belinski!"

"Here, sir."

"Charles G. Belinski?"

"Yessir."

"Warden wants to see you. Come on."

All it took was a name. The Czar of Russia, the Prince of Wales, the Red Baron, or Charles G. Belinski.

What difference in Leavenworth prison, where your name was a number anyway?

Dressed in a new gray uniform, the guard led him down a long corridor and up a flight of stairs.

In a bare, gray-walled room, he was instructed to sit on a wooden bench. He sat, ignoring the various doors and peekholes. Obviously he was being observed, but he found nothing to wonder about that.

In his heightened sensitivity, he could feel the eyes looking at the back of his head, and in a moment through another little peekhole the eyes stared at his profile, and at last the eyes moved to the little glass plate in front of him, looking him full in the face. They were red-veined and opaque with dishonesty, ferretlike with fear and blind with righteousness.

As he was led out he asked the fat guard, "Who was that, sir?"

"Assistant Warden Ronald Griesiedick. Know him?"

"Looks like a bad actor," he said, shaking his head.

"You're smarter'n you look," the guard said, "but you still got to work."

"I want to help all I can," Belinski said.

"Fellas comin' out of the hole usually feel that way." The guard smiled. "You did three weeks longer than anybody I ever heard of. You must not have any feelings at all."

"It helps," Belinski said.

"I dunno where to put you. You sound like the library type, if we had a library."

"Put me at the bottom, so I can work up."

"Time you started learnin' about bein' smart-mouth, Belinski. I got some respect, a man who can kill five little girls like they was mice in a shoebox, and still do seven months in the hole, I got some respect, but, mister, here you don't smart-mouth. You just hope to hell you get to live through each day."

"Yessir," Belinski said.

"You start in the laundry with the rest of the incorrigibles."

"Yessir."

Waiting in the laundry room was the fox-jawed, bland-eyed official named Ronald Griesiedick, who seemed to have a special interest in Belinski.

"No talking, just work." Griesiedick's voice was familiar. "I heard of you, and I'll be watchin' too. Got it?"

"Yessir," Belinski said.

"How's your sex?" Griesiedick asked, trying to hold his eyes hard and failing as they bleared off.

"Normal," Belinski said.

"After what you did with a knife to them girls' privates?"

"That's long gone," Belinski said carefully, thinking to himself that guilt was guilt the same as life was life, and the innocent could bear it better than the guilty.

"I mean what do you like?"

"My woman is outside," Belinski said, "that's it."

"Yeah," Griesiedick muttered. "You ever know anyone name of Zirp?"

"No."

"Gilpin?"

"No. Doesn't ring any bell."

Ronnie Griesiedick grinned and directed Belinski to a huge steaming vat full of greasy water and gray blankets.

"You win the crap-dip machine," Griesiedick said. "You dip out them blankets when they're washed, wrench the water out of 'em, and hang 'em up."

"Yessir," Belinski said, taking a long bleached paddle and stirring the vat.

He could feel the others of the laundry crew sizing him up, but he felt a terrible weariness. A sense of complete exhaustion eroded his consciousness, though his hands continued to move the paddle and the work continued.

A scarfaced black man, bare to the waist, heavily muscled and glistening like an ebony sculpture, came alongside and spoke in the Leavenworth *sotto voce*. "They's clean enough, you got to wrench 'em out."

Belinski was ready to drop. Seven months in the hole had destroyed him as a man.

"I'm going to fall down in a minute," he said tiredly to a void.

"You fall down, somebody goin' to kick your butt up again."

Belinski leaned against the paddle trying to find a bit of energy tucked somewhere away before he should fall and be kicked.

A bell rang.

"Chow time," the black man said, rolling his eyes at Belinski's pale greenish face.

"Manna from heaven." Belinski smiled, closing his eyes for a moment in silent prayer of gratitude.

He followed the half-bare man to an enormous mess hall where thousands of men carrying tinware went past the lines of cursing belly-robbers. The laundry crew sat in their own corner in numerical order with the screw standing by. They ate the stew and the bread. Someone down the table—Belinski never knew and in a way was glad he never knew—threw him a piece of extra bread. He devoured it like a wolf eats a rabbit.

There were a few murmurs of compassion around the table.

"By Joe, the ofay is sho nuff beat."

"Kep' him seven months in the box."

" 'Tain't possible."

"They did. Coalie tol' me."

"Bet you a bag of smoking he ain't goin' to last."

"That's no bet, he goin' to take a long bath right soon."

His eyes were beginning to see again after the nourishment. Fifty men sat at the long table. He was the color of catfish belly, but they were black, brown, yellow, and red. And they were united in their color. Only he and the screw were white.

It was a day of watching and waiting. The men who worked in the flooded, steaming room had every reason to resent him as a nickel-dropping informer planted by the warden. Maybe bought his way out of the hole with a fink chit.

And as Belinski felt these undercurrents of mistrust, his next thought was what did they wish to protect? A small backroom crap game? A little larceny? Illicit movement? No. There was something else, a powerful motion, a deep movement swelling up, and he was placed right in the middle of it.

They whispered rapid fire Afro-Spanish argot and never moved their lips. He could feel their dark eyes peeling the skin off his back.

When the bell rang, they had beans and bread. The bread was

moldy, but Belinski ate it. There was the angry silence as the prisoners glared at their tin plates, the bitter shuffling of feet, the banjo twang of a spoon striking the plate in hateful derision.

As they were marched out the door toward their cell block, Griesiedick held Belinski back to the end of the line, and as the men turned into their cells, he could see the tiers and tiers of barred-in black and browns and yellows and red. It was like a nation, like an army of murderous galley slaves.

Belinski was taken across the small hall to a different cell block, a segregated area of tiers and tiers of whites.

He wondered about that. Why they would segregate him to one side all day and segregate him on the other at night. It was a good way to get killed, he realized.

The tiers of white faces stared out through their bars at the pallid scarecrow being brought across the hall, across the color line to the first open door.

"In here," Griesiedick said, holding the door of the cage wide.

Belinski turned in like a docile eunuch, even then thinking with perception that, yes, he was that already. A steer, a stag, a cut barrow, a sexless subhuman. Yet, he cautioned himself, no matter what, you're still human!

The door slammed with the inhuman discordancy of iron on iron, and his world became a concrete compartment. Two bunks. Gray blankets. Slop pail. Iron on iron. Concrete painted gray, frosted with salts of dampness. The fetid smell, ever pervasive, vapored the tiers on tiers and blocks on blocks and cells on cells, and the incense of moldering men.

Belinski nodded to the man stretched out on the bottom bunk.

"Fresh fish," the man grunted, staring at the bunk above. "I get all the luck, a change-over nigger for a china."

The man was handsome enough to have been Rudolph Valentino, but the expression of his mouth showed such contempt for life that his dark face was twisted from its natural poetic quality into the mask of a killer.

"They call me Charles G. Belinski," Belinski said.

"I'm Rocky Luciano."

"Chicago?"

"Detroit. Purple Mob. Doin' five to twenty for a snatch."

"Ninety-nine years for nothing."

"I peg you now," Rocky said. "You're that freak. Cut girls.

Yeah. Lemme tell you, pal, one of them girls was Italian. And you're liable to wake up dead first time you look cross-eyed at me."

"Learned my lesson," Belinski said, his voice gentle and sincere.

"How'd you get in the hole?" Rocky sneered. "Pinch a screw?"

"Dunno," Belinski said. "Can't remember. Woke up in the darkness. Had a lump on my head, some aches and pains. Tried to figure it out and I finally decided it didn't make any difference what they called me."

"Aw, shut up, punk," Rocky said.

"Dunno why," Belinski said, "but they're settin' me up for a pigeon. Maybe they give me to the blacks, then use it as an excuse to fry them."

"T'hell with them spades."

Belinski crawled into the top bunk, he too staring at the nothingness above him.

"I guess we could be pals," Rocky muttered, his voice carrying a yearning.

Belinski heard the monotonous rustle of the thousands of eunuchs in their cells settling down for the night. There were a few loud yells, a few curses, a few swishy giggles.

"A man's got to do something," Rocky said softly, "it ain't healthy livin' like this."

"The only way out," Belinski said carefully, "is to think. You play the muscle game, they've got you. They can't make you think what you don't want to. And they can't stop you either."

"A zip slug between the eyes," Rocky said, his voice hoarse, "a shovel splitting your spine, a truck running over you accidental like. They'll stop you thinkin' anytime they want."

"But then you're free of it," Belinski said. "They can't stop you at all from then on."

"I don't give a damn," Rocky said. "You're my cellmate, and you're goin' to be my chicken."

"No," Belinski said. "It's like trying to breed a rooster to a horse. It can't be done. What can be done is for all of us to start thinking how to make this place into our own. Make it livable for us."

"They'll loan you a million volts for agitatin' like that."

"Not talkin' about wrecking the place, talkin' about asking for better food, volunteering our people to help cook it, or grow more of it."

"Shut up, you Bolshevik. How'd you like a shiv 'tween your ribs tonight?"

"Fine." Belinski chuckled. "Turn me loose."

The bell rang. The lights dimmed and Rocky slept with nightmares. Groaning, grinding his teeth, he thrashed hotly under his blanket, and the air was wet with the breath of thousands of men.

Belinski slept like a rock in the middle of the earth. When the bell rang in the morning he awakened refreshed. His back felt stronger, his chin was lifting. There was a peculiar joy of renewal bubbling in his blood.

Sure, the odds against him were enormous and a superhuman labor awaited him, but at the moment of awakening he believed he could do it.

Rocky wouldn't look at him. His pock-marked face was fixed in a perpetual snarl.

Ronnie Griesiedick personally sent Belinski like a white crow off with the blacks. Belinski knew what the black crows did to the albinos.

But by then it made no difference. They were going to have to listen to him before they killed him. And if they listened they might learn, and if they learned, something might be saved.

The boilers were hot, and the walls were wet with condensation. The laundry gang worked through the jets of steam and dragged the wet clothing and blankets from one vat to another. Belinski was given the paddle to punch the boiling mass down, and today he felt the strength run through his arms as it had not for months. Each minute gave him more confidence.

The giant Negro jostled him, nearly spilling him into the boiling vat, but Belinski caught himself and twisted free, staring in wonder at the big black man.

"Why?" he asked.

"You're a cool one." The big man laughed. "Maybe we don't need no finks in here."

"You're wrong. Best friend I ever had was black."

"He have a name?"

It was torture to bring it out. Sweat beaded Belinski's brow.

"I didn't think so," the huge man said, and, speaking to a tall, wiry Mexican, he said, "Come on, Jesus, they throw us a fish, we throw him in the soup."

Jesus said, "Hokay, Pearly."

"Wait," Belinski said. "You know K.C.?"

"Born next to the stockyards," Pearly said.

"My old man was a U.P. section hand," Jesus said.

"My friend was Jim . . . Jim Crispus."

"He play in a band?" Pearly asked incredulously.

"Can't remember."

"Any family?" Jesus asked.

"Can't remember at all."

"How come I never heard of you?"

"Maybe because I'm not sure who I am," Belinski said. "Got a knock on the head and then I'm a name. And what's a name? Might as well call me Charlie Chaplin or Sun Yat-sen. I'm Joe No-name."

"Why'd they send you down here?"

"Maybe they don't think I'm any use saving."

"A double setup," Jesus whispered, his flat-planed face alert. "We bump him for them, and they use the job to wipe us out."

"Don't tell me any secrets," Belinski said. "I can already feel the whole place is ready to blow."

Before Jesus or Pearly could answer, Griesiedick suddenly appeared. His face was eager and expectant, but seeing the three of them together shook his confidence, and his eyes wavered to left and right. "All right, you men," he yelled, "break it up and get this slush moving."

Pearly gave a sharp glance at Jesus; the meaning was clear. Griesiedick's setup was tried all right, but it didn't work.

The rest of the working day Belinski felt the hostility of his co-workers diminish as the word spread. He knew Jim Crispus. Maybe he ain't Belinski. Maybe it's just another setup and knockdown.

That night, high, low, far and wide, stacked like greasy spoons, were men oozing and stinking their virility into the concrete and fetid air, and there was not a woman, not one single God-blessed woman in the whole reeking joint.

Rocky looked Belinski up and down and sneered, "You lived through it. You must be either dumb or lucky."

"Dumb."

"Give me a little bit and I'll smarten you up," Rocky suggested, keeping his tone light and persuasive.

"Top pansy's just as fruity as the bottom one," Belinski said. "My way is with a woman."

"Show me where she is." Rocky laughed scornfully. "Show me where anything real is."

"She's not here and she's not coming."

"You don't know, baby, till you've tried it."

"I've seen the faces of those who tried it and didn't like it."

"I'm goin' to kill you, baby." Rocky smiled. "I had a good offer today."

"Rocky, you've got to get muscle out of your system. There's times a man must kill to stay alive, but you're playin' their game to kill for simple favors."

"So? What do you mean to me? Nothing. You got a better offer? Nope, you got words comin' out like wind outa the west."

"Who's payin' you?"

"The top brass. They decided you wasn't worth the ice to keep you fresh."

"How you ever going to amount to anything?" Belinski admonished the handsome Italian, "if you don't learn anything besides the knife? You live by the sword, you die by the sword, everybody knows that."

Rocky's face changed slightly as he looked into the sincere, unafraid countenance of his cellmate. "What's the matter with you? You some kind of a religious bug or somethin'?"

"Rocky, I don't know how many months in that hole it took to figure what was good about the good people and what was bad about the bad people."

"Sure, and then you got the perfect answer, right?"

"No. But if I can show you where hired killing is just a way of killing yourself, I've done something."

"Saved your neck, you mean."

"No. First of all, just first of all—" Belinski spoke with absolute sincerety—"no threat or anything, but you try me and you'll be deader'n the iron in that door."

Rocky's face shifted again. "You're pickin' up moxie mighty fast."

"Peace," Belinski said.

"What can I do?" Rocky complained. "Somebody's fingered, I rub him out. Everybody knows that. I mean that's me."

"You can change your own course. You really can."

"And so what? Sell Bibles?"

"Get a job washing dishes and go to school."

"Me? School!" Rocky whistled, but he was charmed with the notion.

"Think about it," Belinski said, closing his eyes and joining into the mass dream of the muttering, murky, funky men.

Each morning afterward, Pearly would smile his big shoe-peg grin and say, "Well, I do declare, there's Mr. Belinski still alive and walkin'."

And Jesus would flick his obsidian arrowhead eyes and murmur, "Tonight they will kill him."

And Pearly would guffaw and slap his great thigh, while Jesus would only slit his eyes all the more and arch his back with a proud upthrust toreador stance.

Yet each day the muscles revived in his great shoulders and legs. The time when any bully could have killed him with a tap on the chin was long gone, though he could never survive a fight with Pearly, who was so quick and so huge, or Jesus, who had the Yaqui ferocity of a rattlesnake bred into him.

Each day Rocky grew more bemused with the idea of learning. By now, he was borrowing the few books in the prison, finding new wonders and arguing directly with the books. "Now, watch it, buddy, you tryin' to tell me there's stars outside *our* stars? You mean it's all there somewhere but we don't know it? Well, how the hell do you get to be such a smart pants?"

Belinski encouraged him to read on and explore not only the infinite solar system but poetry too, and Rocky took "The Ballad of Reading Gaol" to heart so much he would burst out reciting it at the drop of a club. It became a game among his friends to see how long they could evade the recitation by keeping the subject of conversation away from poetry, jails, England, Oscar Wilde, homosexuals, crime and punishment, but sooner or later in their hourly yard time, Rocky would sneak the subject around to where suddenly he could throw out his chest, cast down his dark-lashed eyes, and declaim:

> "And all the woe that moved him so
>   That he gave that bitter cry,
> And the wild regrets and the bloody sweats,
>   None knew so well as I.
> For he who lives more lives than one
>   More deaths than one must die."

Belinski himself worked to learn Spanish and Indian phrases and the fantastically complicated Sufi fables of the blacks. And once they saw him having his own stupendous struggle because his brain like theirs wasn't trained to learn abstractly, some were willing to follow his example.

He tried to stay out of the conspiracy and revolt so close to boiling over. He couldn't blame them, of course. The food wasn't fit for hogs and there was not a baseball, not a marble, not a woodshop or craft center. For recreation they were given only the bare dirt of the yard to walk, cursing, cursing.

Over a hundred black men lay as permanent cripples in the infirmary because they'd cut their Achilles tendons in protest.

The phony library was an afterthought of a warden who'd inherited some moldy books from a presumptuous uncle, and having no place to store them for himself, he had dumped them in a barracks abandoned because of an epidemic of smallpox. Over the years, to present a picture of enlightened penal system to visiting Congressmen, one or another custodian had dressed it up with various signs: LIBRARY. HOURS 2 TO 4. TAKE GOOD CARE OF THE BOOKS AND THEY WILL TAKE CARE OF YOU.

Hoping to prevent the incipient bloodbath Ronald Griesiedick was provoking, Belinski worked hard among the blacks and browns and reds, hammering the message: Each one teach one.

When Belinski discovered a green-covered magazine called *The American Mercury*, he read it with wonder. Its editorial views seemed to be lifted right out of his mind. So impressed was he with the editor's acid humor that he wrote a simple letter to Mr. Mencken telling of his appreciation and asking for a grant of books of any kind to the Leavenworth library.

The letter was printed without comment in the next issue of the *Mercury*, and, wonder of wonders, books from all over the world began to arrive in the mail sacks!

There was nothing for Warden Spritz or Griesiedick to do except to put Belinski in full-time charge of the growing library and study room.

The first thing Belinski did was replace the dusty, phony signs and put up his own sign: ANYBODY CAN LEARN SOMETHING ELSE, IF HE'S GOT THE TIME.

The seething of the inmates gradually simmered down, until Pearly was learning to read the Constitution and the Declaration of Independence, Jesus the history of the Catholic Church, and Charley Foxwalk was reading about land grants and Indian treaties.

Oddly, Warden Spritz was more nervous now than when the insurrection was ready to explode in his face. The dullest flat-eyed field laborers were learning to read and write, and their huge hands seemed to take more pleasure writing a word than in rolling a Duke's Mixture cigarette.

Griesiedick spent a lot of time inspecting the books, but Belinski managed to keep anything incendiary out of his sight. It became a nerve-wracking cat-and-mouse game. Once, when Griesiedick was reaching for a volume of Prudhon's *Revolution in the Nineteenth Century*, Belinski was able to stop him only by upsetting the entire bookcase and, in the confusion, jamming the quiet little book under his blouse.

Belinski tried to be persuasive. "They're just books, Mr. Griesiedick. Some day the guys will get outside and they'll have some idea of what can be done besides committing crimes."

"Save your breath, scum."

"You're welcome to read any of this stuff," Belinski persisted. "I mean, it's all knowledge and it's good for you."

"You callin' me a moron or something?" Ronnie Griesiedick puffed up like a toad crossed on a gunslinger. "You think I don't know what's goin' on, think I don't know? Well, mister, you want a bloodbath, let's get it started right now."

Some of the cons were willing to kill Ronald Griesiedick, but Belinski persuaded them there would only be another sick spoil-brain coming along right behind him.

All Belinski could do was work all the harder. He wrote to Mencken asking him to commend the warden for his farsighted approach to penology. The wise editor understood.

Through Mencken's planted articles, Warden Spritz was enjoying a national reputation as an enlightened penologist, a man more interested in rehabilitation and education than punishment and repression. With Spritz's blessing the library had a breather and Belinski hustled all the harder for more books and more recruits.

But the evening that Warden Spritz was addressing the Brothers of the Moose in Omaha, almost at the same time he was declaring that boot-strap self-help was the way to solve the taxpayers' problems as well as to keep the prisons free of riot and rebellion, his second in command, Ronald Griesiedick, was in his office examining a new box of books.

The collection of Oriental religious books were for the most part dull fare, until after tossing aside the Vedantas and the Liu Tsao and the Tale of Genji, he turned up an illustrated Kama Sutra. One glance and he knew he held the bomb that would blow up the whole rotten system.

"Coalie," he ordered, "bring Belinski in here right away."

"Yessir." Coalie hurried off.

Griesiedick wondered how much he could even trust Coalie. He'd been infected almost as badly as the rest.

Belinski came into the office warily. He too had learned from the library. He had just read *Les Miserables*, and he had read the mind of Ronald Griesiedick well.

"Yessir."

"Got a box of books for you." Griesiedick smiled engagingly.

"Yessir." Belinski wanted no quarrel over something he didn't have in the first place.

"You want to know what they are?"

"No, sir."

"Just guess."

"*Police Gazettes?*"

"Oh, no, a lot more interesting than that."

"Maybe you should take it up with Warden Spritz instead of me."

"This stuff is obscene. Griesiedick held out the book opened to the thirty-seventh position.

"I'm running a library. The people make up their own minds.

"Filth, that's what you're peddling. Damned dirty filth!"

"That material is three thousand years old and I'm not peddling it. It's common knowledge like the Bible, the history of the United States, Shakespeare, *Moby Dick*, Robin Hood, *The Call of the Wild*. As far as I'm concerned it's a free choice."

"No more." Griesiedick started ripping the pages from the book. "Coalie, return this bastard to his cell."

"Yessir."

Belinski tried not to show his worry. As far as he was concerned the library was vital, and he was willing to be punished to preserve it. He could have destroyed Ronald Griesiedick in laughter because the red-lipped catamite was nothing more than a vaudeville clown, but they all needed the books.

"Wait just a second, Coalie," Griesiedick said. "First we shut down that hotbed of anarchy and filth."

Too late Belinski saw that the officer meant it, that his neurosis was like a long-term cancerous growth rooted in Griesiedick's mind, forcing a confrontation which he could justify any number of ways later on.

"Mr. Griesiedick," Belinski said, "I don't want to tell you your business, but it's not fair to punish the library for anything I might have done."

In the Moose Hall in Omaha, Warden Spritz was explaining that in spite of additional overcrowding of prisoners and consequently a lower quality of food for the ration, there were fewer cases of insanity, fewer suicides, fewer self-mutilations, and fewer murders than before, primarily because the men had something interesting to do.

"It's settled," Griesiedick said, picking up a telephone and ordering a contingent of guards to meet him in the hall.

"I'm not saying what the consequences will be," Belinski said, shocked that a madman should be placed in charge of six thousand human beings.

"Consequences?" Griesiedick smiled like a thin-lipped cat with feathers in its teeth. "look, baby, you don't threaten old Ron Griesiedick. You threaten Ron Griesiedick, you're goin' back in the hole!"

"They're books!"

"Handcuffs on him, Coalie."

Coalie stared at Griesiedick.

"Handcuffs!"

"Yessir," Coalie said, fitting the manacles around Belinski's wrists, but making sure they were loose enough to slip his hands free if there were a need.

"Mr. Griesiedick, you try to shut down that library for no reason at all, you're goin' to have a yard full of dead men in the morning."

"If they want a bloodbath, then let's get at it." Ronnie Griesiedick cocked his fox jaw proudly.

And in Omaha, the warden was declaring that all it took to make a model prison was a minimum of hard, iron-fisted discipline and a maximum of freedom to learn a new way of life. He was forecasting some great scholars and scientists might graduate from Leavenworth some day.

In the hallway were six professional guards, career men.

"Come along," Griesiedick said. "Keep an eye out. Grab off anybody even smiling."

Griesiedick marched out of the administration building, across the long, bare yard to the old barracks where the library was located and men in their one free hour of the day were congregated, silently reading.

Sitting on the floors or on boxes, off in corners, poring over the tattered tomes of charity, many were quietly teaching other individuals to learn the shape of the letter and the word and the linkage that held the world and time together.

"Everybody out!" Griesiedick yelled into the quiet room. "Back out in the yard. And leave the damned books here. We're shutting it down."

The men looked about, hardly comprehending, but seeing Belinski in manacles sent the message faster than anything the Sub-warden had said.

The moment was like a burning fuse racing into a bomb.

"Move!" Griesiedick yelled.

Jesus lobbed a dictionary, Pearly and Charley Foxwalk threw chairs at Griesiedick, the others threw anything at hand at the guards.

"Sound the alarm!" Griesiedick yelled, and jerked his pistol, meaning to gun down Belinski first.

But Belinski was already loose and diving aside.

The shot missed and struck a small Negro named Little Jim. The bullet cut Jimmy across the eyes and his blind terror produced an incredible scream of pain and panic. It seemed never to stop, the scream rising and falling from an ancient common outrage and binding them all into the river of justice for the sake of justice. Even the great siren atop the jute factory couldn't drown out Little Jim's call.

The men in their steel-barred tiers heard it and began a stamping chant, and their guards came running to beat at them through the bars. Fires were started, keys were taken, the great yard became a swarm of angry men absolutely determined to declare themselves men.

At first the battle surged back and forth, hit and miss, but Griesiedick, separated from the other guards, was being crowded to the wall. He was firing and killing, but there were too many human bodies for his bullets. In terror he fired his last smashing shot into great Pearly's chest, but Pearly kept coming with strength enough to seize the red-lipped sodomite and slowly wring his neck bones even as the blood gushed from Pearly's mouth and his eyes glazed off into sightless unlearned clay.

Belinski yelled one last recognizable word at Jesus. "The gates!"

Jesus saw the need. His mind worked like cactus and lightning though the battle still swirled around him within the walls.

Rocky saw four guards clubbing Belinski.

Rocky had a gun and, firing as he ran, killed two of the guards. The others ran for the walls. Coming to his side, Rocky caught Belinski's dead weight up on his shoulder and tried for the gates. A shotgun blast took him in the back. Three slow, heavy, unbelieving strides carried him nearly to freedom, and then he fell. The helpless Belinski slipped gently from his arms as he whispered his own epitaph into the howling, smoking sky. "For he who lives more lives than one, more deaths than one shall die . . ."

Coalie took Belinski from the dying man and dragged him into the cover of the wall as machine guns opened up from the towers.

Men died and died hard then. The machine guns swept the yard without minds or eyes, simply sweeping the living into the deathbin for happening to be where they were at the moment.

But there were corners and coverts where the fifty-caliber brooms couldn't reach. Springfield rifles looted from the armory were firing back and the men who murdered with the broom were being picked off by the big black hands of squirrel hunters and pitching in sorry rags off their perches.

The old buildings were burning. The factories, the cell blocks were ablaze. The smoke of burning jute blew on the west wind.

Jesus was asking each guard, "Will you open the gate for us?"

And each guard said the universal criminal word. "No."

Jesus methodically cut the throats of four guards, one at a time. They died in disbelieving terror that any one man could kill so methodically to gain such a simple thing as freedom.

The fifth one saw the light. His word was "Yes." Gladly, thankfully, joyously, he gave over the key, and the huge gates were opened.

Men by the hundreds, bringing their wounded, still had to fight every foot of the way.

They carried their wounded friends on their backs. No man was abandoned, no man was left behind unless he asked to be left. Little Jim, still screaming the awful battle cry, was led by Charlie Foxwalk. Jesus carried the unconscious Belinski, steadily forging their way down a lovely boulevard they'd polished with their sweat and good behavior. The siren still bayed and howled, but the yard was empty of life. Thousands of dead men in gray and blue uniforms lay together. The fires burned luridly within the falling stone casements, and the stench of the gutted prison was carried clear to Kansas City.

Gus stirred and heard the Mexican ask, "You O.K., Ski?"

"I'm O.K.," Gus said, wondering what was happening. The headache was squeezing his body into a pure pearl of pain. "What's going on?"

"We bust out. We head for the goddamn border."

"My God," Gus said, "I'm mixed up. I don't know!" He was suddenly afraid. His life seemed to have stopped somewhere and started somewhere else. He was afraid of the crevasse in the midst of his existence. "How far?"

"A thousand miles. We'll make it," Jesus said. "We'll steal cars, we'll fight our way. And we'll all meet in Sonora and start over in the mountains. We can make our own goddamn country and nobody tell us we can't read books."

"Books?" Gus asked.

"Man, you took a knock on the head. But you're alive. That's the main thing."

"How much time have we got?" Gus asked.

"Don't worry," Charlie Foxwalk said, "time don't mean anything to us."

But the National Guardsmen, the misfits and draft dodgers in uniform were already groping their way toward the battle scene. They brought not only Browning machine guns but cannon as well.

It became a futile, stupid massacre. There were at the most, in the one group still trying to stay together, marching down the road, a thousand men. In an hour they'd been shot down to three hundred, and in another hour there were only a hundred and they were running in stolen cars and trucks, going as far away from Leavenworth as they could, no matter in which direction, so long as it was away, away, away.

Jesus was driving a new Essex at full throttle. There were fourteen brave men in it, on it, hanging to it by their fingertips, and Jesus had not learned anything about driving in the library.

He was driving eighty miles an hour when he hit the bridge abutment, and he never knew what killed him.

NINE

•··•

"YOUR NAME? Who are you? We need your identity, please."

"Identity?"

Gus smelled sweet ether and carbolic acid. Only one hand was free. It touched his face: a mummy-wrapped pad of gauze, only a little hole to breathe and drink through.

"Your name? We'd like to notify your friends or relatives. Your identity?"

The voice was soft and girlish, a strangely lovely sound.

"August. August Gilpin," Gus croaked.

"There seems to be some confusion, sir. You aren't Charles G. Belinski?"

"No," Gus' voice funneled out of the bandages. "Who's he?"

"A revolutionary agitator at the prison. They burned it down last week. But some escaped," the girl's voice rippled, replying.

"What prison?" Gus was confused. His head hurt inside and outside.

"Leavenworth. But don't worry about it, Mr. Gilpin. Better get some sleep now. We don't want to overdo it, do we?"

"Could you call Mr. Maurice Fitzgerald in K.C.?"

"Very well, I'll try. Now you get some rest."

The advice was unnecessary. Gus was already back into a limbo where the pain was only heavy numbness.

But when he heard the firm modulation of the Irishman, humoring the nurse, he knew he was home.

"Mr. Fitzgerald," Gus said, feeling tears well from eyes that could not weep.

"There he comes. Excuse me, lassie, we've a few things to discuss."

"Mr. Fitzgerald, it's Gus."

"Yes, Gus. I know. Welcome back to the land of the living. Where've you been?"

"I don't know," Gus said, his head beginning to ache. "Zirp was clubbing my head. I remember that. Then I think he said I was Charles G. Belinski. I can't seem to remember—"

"Don't worry about it, Gus—we were afraid you'd gone for a one-way ride after you beat Zirp out of Dodge City. We owe you a lot, Gus."

"Bessie?" Gus asked, wondering in fear why Mr. Fitzgerald hadn't mentioned her name.

"Bessie has had a little problem, Gus, but now that you're back, maybe we can get her straightened out." The voice was gruff and compassionate. "Just take it easy and get yourself knitted together again. Won't be long we'll be rolling in high gear again. Nurse!"

Gus heard rubber-soled footsteps and the strong Irishman speak to the nurse.

"This gentleman is Mr. Gus Gilpin of my organization. He's to have the best of everything and the cost is not to be considered. I'll send over my own doctor."

"Bessie, Bessie, Bessie!" Gus despaired over the smoothness with which Mr. Fitzgerald had passed her by.

And the books. The thousands of books! He suddenly remembered the old barracks burning red and black. The books he'd worked to bring to the losers were now nothing but ashes. What had Mencken said when he had heard the news?

Gus was burning with the memory of those last minutes with his comrades. He could have wept, remembering the enormous kegheaded Pearly, trying and succeeding in translating an inked page into a thoughtful statement of life. Remembering Rocky, who'd shaken loose from the gutter to take a book of poems gently in his hands, and remembering the tall Jesus, who had joined his Yaqui flint-edge heritage with the rest in the education movement for peace and freedom, and Charley Foxwalk, even farther from the inked page than Jesus, but still stolidly learning and, like the others, teaching too.

All were dead. And of all the books Gus had read, none could answer his cry for justice, his appeal for mercy, his demand for fair play.

His room was crowded in the morning with vases of roses and sprays of gladioli and potted chrysanthemums. He could smell them, but his eyes were bandaged closed.

"Please share them out," Gus told the nurse. "I don't need them."

"Yes, sir."

"How long before I can leave?" Gus asked the doctor.

"Hard to say. The burns are healing well, and your skull fracture is coming along without complication. You're a quick healer."

"My eyes?" Gus growled at the evasive medico.

"We'll take the bandages off tomorrow and see the extent of the damage."

"You mean I might not see?"

"We don't know, and we aren't taking any chances. There was some trauma when you were thrown out of the wreck."

"You're good at saying nothing, Doc," Gus said.

How much of life had he lost waiting for a wound to heal or a prison to burn? And was he to be blinded now? Was he to be a scruffy old man tapping a white cane down some eternally dark avenue?

He went to sleep in a mist of roses.

And awakened to the smell of carbolic hands spreading a cooling unguent over his blistered chest. There were people in the room.

"We'll start cutting the bandages, Mr. Gilpin," the doctor said.

Gus felt the scissors snipping the gauze mask from around his face.

"Wish me luck," he said.

"Luck," Mr. Fitzgerald said.

Dear Father in Heaven, I can give you everything but my eyes. If you must have them, then take the rest of me too.

"Steady now." The doctor's voice sounded like strong lye soap. "I'm going slow, easier on you that way."

"Was my face burned?"

"Not by the gasoline. No, it was from plowing the roadbed with your face. I took about a pound of gravel out of your forehead. Your eyes . . . We couldn't tell, especially with the skull fracture taking priority. I can see the time coming when the medical profession will have a branch devoted strictly to automobile accidents. Doctors have their offices at the worst highway intersections. Get richer. Any pain?"

"No, sir." Gus was settled in his mind now. Perhaps he could live without sight, perhaps not. If he could not, he had the means to end it.

Pearly and Coalie, both gone. And Little Jim, and Rocky, Jesus and Charley, all gone. All gone.

And where, oh where, was Bessie?

"Nurse," the surgeon's voice cut through, "lower the shades. I want a minimum of light."

Gus heard the rustle of heavy curtains.

"Now then, Mr. Gilpin, we'll remove the bandages. Try to be calm, and keep your eyes closed for a few moments."

"I'll try," Gus said as the doctor lifted the thick bandages from his face.

Gus kept his eyelids shut. He felt the doctor's cool fingers testing the flesh of his forehead and nose.

"You've healed like a doctor's testimonial," the surgeon said. "There's some involvement of your eyelids. Open your eyes now, please."

Gus forced his mind to stand fast and willed his eyes to open.

A faint light filtered in, but whatever he was looking at was too blurred to recognize.

"Anything?" the doctor asked.

"Not much," Gus said.

"But something? Yes?"

"Yes," Gus said.

"Splendid," the doctor said. "It will take a few minutes. After all, it's been eight days."

"I see something white."

"That's me," the doctor said. "Take it easy. I find no scar tissue on the cornea. The blood serum has drained out of the retina, and there appears to be no detachment."

The doctor was leaning over him, sighting into his eyes. He could see the face emerging from the mists, an old man with a white mustache, protruding eyeballs, studying his own eyes.

The scene was rushing on him now, the view bigger and clearer.

Behind the doctor was a young nurse with horn-rimmed glasses, and to one side stood Mr. Fitzgerald, older, yes, but still in ruddy good health, his back straight, his head high, his hands holding a black homburg hat. His eyes were on Gus, compassion and hope on his face.

"Mr. Fitzgerald, I'm sure glad to see you again." Gus smiled.

"Oh, my boy!" Mr. Fitzgerald's voice cracked. "You don't know how pleased I am to know you can."

Mr. Fitzgerald tried to hold his smile, but the shadow of worry was apparent.

"Easy now," the doctor said, "not too much right off. It takes time and patience."

"Fine with me, Doctor," Gus said. "I was some worried."

"Most people are," the doctor said, "even when they go through life never seeing anything." The doctor turned to Mr. Fitzgerald. "You can have him in four or five days, practically good as new."

The doctor and nurse withdrew, leaving Gus alone with Mr. Fitzgerald.

"I'll need a set of forty-fives and a banjo," Gus said.

"I managed to retrieve yours, figuring all along you'd turn up again."

"Lazarus."

"The Count of Monte Cristo." Mr. Fitzgerald smiled. "I'll rent an apartment for you and we'll get the tailor in and a barber, and you'll be top chop."

"What's the business problem?" Gus asked.

"Too much to tell right now."

"Something close by?"

"Right in our town. Mickey and his friends from Cicero think we don't shear the poor people close enough. Well, you know how it goes. I'm not all that greedy. I just want everybody to share in the business that wants to."

"I want to," Gus said.

"You're first."

"Can Bessie visit me here?" Gus asked.

Mr. Fitzgerald sighed. "Gus," she doesn't know you're here. Nobody does. You're too vulnerable. If Zirp knew you were here, flat on your back, he'd have already sent a rod man."

"Where is she?"

"She's singing in a club in Chicago. Supposed to be doing real well. I've sent a messenger. He'll bring her back on the first train. By Monday you'll be in your own place and able to hold your own, and she'll be with you."

"Then what's the problem?"

"She's a junkie." Mr. Fitzgerald said it carefully, resentfully, as if it were a curse he'd rather forget.

"Bad?" Gus asked.

"Yes. I promised to look after her, and believe me, Gus, I did my level best, but I finally had to face it: a junkie is a junkie. Like a horse player is crazy and incurable, so is that lovely lady."

"She'll straighten out," Gus said confidently. "What's it like out in the world?"

"The stock market's still falling off, money's scarcer, hard to say where we're going right now. Hoover claims there's no problem, but an old duck my age can see something's gone wrong."

"And our business?"

"Better than ever in fact. But somehow those Easterners don't understand ethics, only the fast buck. Make it on girls, booze, strong arm, dope, sell their own mother, nothing seems to bother 'em. And Scarface Capone has gotten to be nearly as big as old John D."

The nurse entered, glancing at Mr. Fitzgerald, who'd not noticed Gus slowly going to sleep, unthinking and uncaring that the year was 1931, and his world had changed since 1928 for the worse.

True to his word, Mr. Fitzgerald moved Gus into a large, beautifully furnished penthouse overlooking the park. The latest electrical gadgets were installed, including a new Philco heterodyne radio and a Westinghouse electric clock that never needed winding.

The tailor took his measurements and made clothes for the pale-faced patient who still limped slightly on the game leg and whose eyes held a pain and sorrow of soul this Polish Jew understood very well.

Peg-bottom pants, tight double-breasted coat, white silk shirts with close collar points, yellow shoes, ebony cane with ivory handle.

Once dressed, Gus took to walking in the park, trying to build up his legs again, trying to train his eyes to seeing green things again, alert to quick movements and widest possible peripheral vision, training to stay alive.

He was anxious about Bessie, who was due to arrive on Saturday.

"It's covered," Mr. Fitzgerald said. "You'll be as safe as anywhere. But they'll know the tiger's loose and if Zirp is as smart as I think he is, he'll try to buy you first. You're worth a lot of money to anyone."

"If they want me," Gus said, "they'll have to kill me."

"The time may come, Gus, when it's kill or be killed."

"I don't like killing," Gus said. "But I don't like dying for nothing either."

"One more thing. You know the hard cocaine users generally keep somebody around to make sure there's a supply. It's the system."

"You mean Bessie is liable to have an escort?"

"A couple punk creeps. Means nothing except they keep her fixed on the junk. She makes a lot of money. But they get it."

"I understand."

"Maybe you don't. I mean I went through this already, Gus. They'll stick like fleas. You belt 'em and she'll throw a hizzy. It isn't that she likes them. It's the dope. She has to have it, and only the creeps bring it."

"Can you get me about a pound of the white stuff?" Gus asked.

"I'll send it over this afternoon. And, Gus, as soon as you feel up to it, you're promoted to top assistant."

"Monday," Gus said, "and thanks."

"Nine o'clock. We have a suite of new offices in the Union Bank Building."

"Suite?"

"A pool and a solarium, too, so you can keep in shape. We're trying to run our business like a corporation. Keep the executives happy."

Trying to catch up, he studied the Kansas City *Star* and the *Journal Post*. The *Star* was conservative and stately. The *Post* was more liberal but with overtones of cheap corruption. Which to believe? Neither. He read the words and tried to guess at the facts. Yes, there were ten million men unemployed. Both papers tried so hard to hide that simple statistic that it shone out like a block headline. The price of wheat was down to thirty-five cents a bushel. Good God, wheat would be cheaper than coal. Japan wanted a bigger navy and was probably already building it. Capone was happy. Hoover was somber. Jimmy Walker of New York was in Miami with his latest mistress. Jack Dempsey was strong. Gene Tunney was cerebral. Sacco and Vanzetti were reborn. e.e. cummings wrote a poem: a politician is an arse upon which everyone has sat except a man.

Johnny Dillinger was in the papers too. And Alvin Karpis and Pretty Boy Floyd, Baby Face Nelson, Doc Barker, and Dutch Shultz. All doing their best. Still golfing occasionally.

New bloods elbowed up. You could catch their names in the blurred type and the grainy pictures. Legs Diamond, Big Joe Wintergreen, Dino Luchesi, Fat Gutt. Hired guns. Assembly-line enforcers.

Melvin Purvis appeared as the Knight of the Federal Bureau, his thin steady smile and cool gray eyes denoting instant justice to wrongdoers.

All over the country millions of gray men in patched gray clothes were aimlessly patrolling the gray streets of the brick cities like prisoners in Leavenworth, and Gus kept wondering, Why don't they burn it all down? Light a match and announce you want a job. Announce, by God, you want a vote. You want a piece of the country. Come on, John D., fork over or watch the barbecue!

But they didn't, or hadn't yet, and Gus kept wondering why all the way to Saturday afternoon.

He had practiced hours with the .45s. He could flash them out of their spring-loaded holsters in an instant and keep those heavy barrels steady for at least the first two shots, and though he hadn't a chance to try out the chopper in the special banjo case, he knew the old familiar feel of it.

The great smoky Union Station was crowded with the gray people going nowhere because it was a shelter from the cold and the wilderness outside. Railroad bulls kept the people moving, never allowing them to sleep, but unable to keep them outside.

Gus gave a dollar to every panhandler sloping up on stooped shoulder and inclined eye to make the little murmuring pitch: Say, buddy, I'm a vet, can you spare a dime?

It hurt Gus. For every dime they begged, they paid over a dollar's worth of self-respect.

The smoky gloom of the great station, an edifice of the Union Pacific and the Santa Fe, was numbing. The moving horde of lonely paupers wending through the huge columned shed was a ghastly outrageous vision of the underbelly of America.

They had believed they were building a bigger and better country. They had believed the cops were there to protect them. They had believed their church was built to help them live Christian lives. They had believed their politicians would be their faithful stewards. They had believed any man could get a job if he really tried, and they had discovered the horrible, insidious truth that no matter how good a man was, he could not get a job. The speechifiers could talk your arms off about rugged individualism, but good strong men were not able to bring home bread for their children. Good strong men were being crushed into spit and mud by this split between beautiful ideal and hideous fact.

Across the great smoky room Gus could hear a band tootling, a bass drum booming, a chorus of lassies singing, "Onward, Christian Soldiers." He made a mental note to pass that way as soon as he had collected Bessie.

The Chicago Streak was already pulling in with great swaths of steam and the stench of acrid coal smoke.

Gus felt a sense of fear and joy, not knowing what she might look like now, nor even knowing whether she'd recognize him. His face was healed, but it held scars no surgeon could hide, and Gus had cared nothing about them until just now. O Lord, he said to himself, if I could just go back three years, wipe them out, those years, try a different way. But he knew as well as anyone could know that he'd never had a choice once he'd decided what was really right and really wrong.

As always the cars were segregated, black and white, and he knew which way to go. The old silver-haired porter at the step was black. His eyes were golden, his manner that of the imperative slave. He helped no old ladies down the step. He guarded.

"Gus, you're getting all bogged down in nothing," Gus warned himself. "He's a man, he's worthy."

She appeared like an angel, the little smile on her noble features, not a line of care, not a blemish of age. If anything, she

looked younger, more the new bride of Solomon, more the innocent fey child of Nubia, more the leopard passion of Sheba.

A white silk dress concealed her incredibly long and lovely legs
and contained the fullness of her bosom. Two strands of coral
beads dangled to her waist, and her hat was wide as a floppy
umbrella.

Gus's heart leaped at the sheer beauty of her.

He waited, hoping, praying that she would recognize him.

He felt none of the fears that the worry of Mr. Fitzgerald had
wished on him. Whatever stuff she was on hadn't hurt her.

"Gus!" she cried, her great Egyptian eyes ablaze.

And she was in his arms like a vivid, rippling-muscled cat. Her
mouth bursting on his, her arms crushing his back. She smelled
of white gardenias.

Gus nearly fainted under the storm of joy, the release of ten-
sions of years which had been slowly webbing his soul into another
corner away from hers. But they knew each other in the infinite
instant, the way all lovers know each other, unquestioning, and
positive.

It was the longest and the shortest kiss in history. They wanted
it to last forever but the world wouldn't wait. Jostling people
and envious bystanders, they couldn't wait.

"Gosh, honey," Gus said, letting her go, "are we goin' to have
a lifetime!"

Her eyes were big, the pupils dilated.

"There you go, Mr. Beautiful," she said, "talking instead of
doing."

Gus noticed a couple of small black men dressed in wild check-
ered suits of the most radical cut, big watch chains draped out
of the vest pockets. Their eyes were moving, their pupils wide.

"These guys do some work for me. This one is Cal, he's my arranger." She laughed. "And this one is Reagan, he's my arranger's
arranger."

"Hello," Gus said, testing their small limp hands. "You can
put Bessie's bags in the green Duesenberg."

They looked questioningly at her like twin fawns.

"Get rid of 'em, Bessie, I got a ton of coke. You don't need
arrangers any more."

"O.K., Beautiful," she said, and spoke to Reagan. "Find a room somewhere, and stay loose. If you find a better deal, go for it."

"You owe me a C note," Cal said.

Gus put a hundred-dollar bill in Cal's breast pocket and looked at the imitation face of Reagan. He didn't like it. This little hophead would destroy anything to make his own little world seem shinier.

"Don't try selling us out." Gus set his big hand on Reagan's padded shoulder.

"Come on, love," Bessie said, "Reagan ain't any good but he knows which side of the plate the beans is."

Gus cooled off, turned and took her arm. "Let's go. A million years with you wouldn't be enough for me."

They were crossing through the slow-moving, gray, sleepless parade, and Bessie slowed a second, stared at the faceless, anonymous, moving mass of human beings, gripping his arm.

"We have too much," she said, and yonder, far across the way, she heard the Salvation Army band, the big bass drum and castanets and cornet tootling away.

"Come on, Beautiful," she said, "we can share a little."

She didn't wait to be asked, any more than the Salvation Army ever held back when help was needed. She strode magnificently across to the hard-working brass band and, with a single gesture of her arm, she created a grand stage out of the grimy concrete.

" 'Battle Hymn of the Republic,' " she said to the puff-cheeked cornet player blasting out a favorite tune.

His cornet nodded and the drum beat picked up as "Throw Out the Lifeline" merged into the stately majestic beat of the universal hymn.

> Mine eyes have seen the glory
>   of the coming of the Lord,
> He is stamping out the vintage
>   where the grapes of wrath are stored,
> He will make men holy,
>   He will make men free . . .

Never before, perhaps never again was the determinedly impersonal antihuman warehouse of the smoky railroad temple absolutely still and silent, except for the power and pathos of her voice ringing through the rafters and around the huge gray columns.

When the hymn ended, the silence was too much. A man groaned. A woman sobbed.

"Now then, one for Bessie!" she cried. " 'Pack Up Your Troubles'!"

The band picked it up, while the entire gray wave of humanity in the temple abandoned despair to sing the rollicky ballad together.

" 'Pack up your troubles in your old kit bag, and smile, smile, smile . . .'!"

Thousands of miserable, beaten creatures stood with their chests out and their heads up, the men taking off their greasy, floppy fedoras and holding them over their hearts, no doubt that, by God, they were decent human beings, giving each to each as only a man can when there is a need, each singing the rousing song.

". . . and smile, smile, smile'!"

Tears in their eyes, embittered men and women on tiptoe tried to see Bessie and thank her with their thoughts.

She felt like crying herself, but she cupped her hands and shouted to the rapt, still audience, "Hurray for you!"

And then Gus had her moving out to the street.

The great gray room broke down again into the sickening sound of shoe slipping, shuffling slowly over the grimy concrete and the voices saying, "Move on, you can't sleep here. Mister, please, I hate to ask, but could you spare a vet a dime? I'm sorry, but I'm hungry."

The bags were in the trunk and Gus spoke to Mr. Fitzgerald's driver, "Home, James."

"What's our driver's real name?" she teased.

"Lavender." Gus smiled. "And don't get any wrong ideas. He's taken more top guns for a ride than you can count. He's also an expert with nitroglycerine and oxyacetylene."

"Oh, doll, doll, my big old white and yellow-haired speckled rooster doll." She smiled, kissing his ear and closing her drowsy eyes.

The driver, who wore dark glasses and a golfing cap, smiled, steering through traffic, thinking. This dame was ostrich-feather woman. Big whoosh of a woman. Basketfull of brown eggs woman.

Black sapphire leopard woman. And O she smell of white gardenias.

The driver could love a woman without trying to own her or pirate her from another man. God knows if she were free, he'd have stolen the Duesenberg for her, but she was not. She belonged to Gus, and that was fine. Gus was a good man, he ought to have her. Lavender was a good man, and if the luck was right he'd find a beautiful full-out woman too. It took nerve to pick black, but if you had it, you won the best prize of all.

"Will you be needin' me any more this evenin', Mr. Gilpin?" Lavender asked.

"No, I guess not," Gus replied, stepping out and helping Bessie to the street.

"Mr. Fitzgerald suggested I take him to a dinner party on the hill."

"Of course," Gus agreed. "If I need a car I can drive the La-Salle."

Gus escorted Bessie past the liveried doorman, who welcomed them warmly into the marble lobby to the elevator.

"Say now, Mr. Beautiful, you have come up in the world!" Bessie smiled at the pomp and posh.

"Yeah, and all it took was three years under another name," Gus said as the middle-aged, baldheaded elevator boy punched the button and let the machinery take over. "I'm learning the top office now. Getting acquainted with the bookkeepers, outer managers, and so on."

"Sort of like vice-president of the corporation."

"That's right. You'd be surprised how big this operation is."

Gus was watching the elevator boy's ears. They seemed to redden as he faced away from them.

"The first thing I learned was that finks and squealers, no matter how high or low, were bumped without delay." Gus set a .45 against the bald head. "Who are you and why?"

"Me, sir?" The elevator boy's voice quavered.

"You listen well, do you talk too?"

"No, sir. Not me."

"I never saw you before. Where's the regular man?"

"He's my brother-in-law. And he's sick. He didn't want to take a chance on losin' this good job, so he begged me to take over for him. He's married to my sister and got four kids. You don't know how hard jobs is to get, sir."

Gus had the Colt back in its holster, sorry that he had reacted so quickly. Somehow he sensed trouble, but he couldn't put his finger on it. He put a bill in the man's trembly fingers.

"I don't want anybody to know anything about me. Got it?"

"Absolutely, positively, yes, sir," the man quavered.

Gus disliked it. The performance was bad, his instinct smelled deceit, but there wasn't anything he could do about it. Bessie was already frightened and nervous.

Gus fixed the red-veined eyes for a moment. "Believe me, give it up while you're ahead. That's more warning than most get."

There was an acid hatred in those eyes that weren't going to give up anything.

The elevator doors shut behind them and Gus led Bessie down the short carpeted hall to the carved walnut door.

"How come you giggin' that elevator hop?" she asked, entering the big living room.

"Something's rumbling like thunder," Gus said, taking her hat. "I feel it. On the farm, if I felt this way I'd head for the barn because for sure there'd be a heck of a storm comin' in from the west. Spooky kinda feelin', but that old boy is in on it. He knows it and so do I."

"Darlin', I love you," Bessie said, her voice husky and sweet, kissing him long and deep.

She clung to him a moment, all rich and svelte and animal.

"You want a drink, a shot of coke, whatever?" Gus asked.

"Nothing now," she said, going out on the roof garden through the glass doors.

The phone rang. It was Mr. Fitzgerald. The feeling of disaster was too much to ignore.

"Yes," the voice of his old friend agreed, "I feel it too. We can go hunting now or wait to hit back."

"But do you know what to hit?"

"I got word a few minutes ago. Mickey Zirp, Big Joe Wintergreen, Marty Lansky, Frankie Madigan, Fat Gutt, Legs Genovese and an ape named Bonzo came in from Chicago this morning."

"Where are they?" Gus asked, his stomach tight.

"I rather wish I knew. Had the best tails on them, but they've dropped out of sight. Gus—" the tone of the voice changed—"be careful."

"I think they're after you," Gus said. "I'm too green. Let me go along with you for a while as a little extra protection."

"Gus—" Mr. Fitzgerald's voice was firm and unafraid—"if they take me out, you move into my chair. Don't waste a minute. If I can learn where they are I'll call you and the rest of our people. Otherwise play out each day like it was a sure winning hand."

"Yessir." Gus admired the cool courage of the man who had been living under the threat of murder for years and had never faltered. "Goodbye, sir."

As the gray day silvered and dwindled toward a chilly darkness, his heart rose with a light joy when he saw Bessie on the terrace.

Across the way was the Muelbach Hotel. Far downwind were the stockyards, and in the distance were the enormous grain elevators overflowing with cheap wheat. From north to south the wide old Missouri snaked through the city and pushed on toward the mighty Mississippi.

The fading February day was too ineffably crisp and beautiful. The smell of fresh snow and smoke and the certain sense prevailed of spring winding up, ready to drive out before you could even know it.

"Fine," she said at last. "Gus, it's fine as wine."

"We don't own anything," Gus said, "just what we see this minute."

"Sure, Mr. Beautiful," she said, "that's life. Come on inside. I'm not one for looking at sunsets."

He made a drink for them as she poked through the rich suite muttering little cries of amazement over the appointments.

"Lordy, gold faucets! Oh my, looky—that great big bed! Gussie, love, come looky this here giant bed!"

Gus laughed and joined her in the bedroom.

"You ain't goin' to believe it, but you're the last man I've known, and, baby, that's a long time."

"Me too," Gus said, "and I believe you because I love you like the other half of me."

They lay on the silk sheets of the huge oval bed. Her ebony limbs long and relaxed, her full thighs and round abdomen and tall taut breasts dark as ancient bronze on the white silk. And his own heavy-shouldered bulk, red and white and gold beside the dusky form of fire. She was counting the stitches on his body, murmuring with sorrow and making mock fun.

"Mr. Beautiful, that's thirty-seven just to your elbow."

"You going to give me any points for unremoved lead?" Gus smiled.

"Ten points apiece," she said.

"Add a thirty-point bonus then."

"Ever think of bulletproofing your vest?" she asked, snuggling up to him, fevering his skin with the heat of her body.

She was counting again, a teasing kitten, girlish, counting each surgeon's scar with the tip of her tongue, trembling hot wet tongue, counting the welted scars across his yellow-haired chest and slabbed abdomen.

"That's sixty-nine already." She paused, not changing her position, grinning like a goofy elf, sighting up his abdomen through the cleft of his chest to his eyes.

"Bessie, Bessie, Bessie," Gus sighed.

Later, long later, he broke the deep peace.

"Bessie, marry me."

"No, Mr. Beautiful, no, sir. We're O.K. now, I'm not goin' to let you ruin it with a preacher."

"I can't protect you enough," Gus said, "and I want to."

"We're past protection," she replied.

She leaned off the bed and turned on the Philco heterodyne. A late-evening program of jazz. Paul Whiteman, King Oliver, Alvino Rey.

"You know," she said into the darkness, "I'm kind of taken with the leaf."

"I heard," he said.

"Don't it bother you?" she asked.

"You're the most beautiful woman in the world."

"It costs some too," she said.

"I can get it for you wholesale." He smiled.

"Gus, you're unbelievable. Why aren't you a dingdamned do-gooder trying to make me unhappy?"

"Lady, oh Lady, if I could tell you of Pearly and Coalie, and Charley and Jesus, and Willie and Rocky—well, we're just luckier than anybody because we have each other."

The radio was playing a set of jazz blues.

"Listen," she said.

"Now what?" he asked drowsily.

"This is for you," she said.

He heard her voice coming over the radio backed by a full orchestra: "O my man I love him so, he'll never know . . ."

"That's you?" he asked. "Really you?"

"That's me, singing to you, Mr. Beautiful," she said. "Just listenin', I could cry."

"I didn't know you'd made records."

"Oh sure, lots. I'm pretty good. You're about the only one in the country that doesn't know it."

"Hush, let me listen. I haven't heard you sing blues for years."

Her voice had all the power of a Cadillac V-12, but she used it only for establishing the dimensions, working more at smoothing out and simplifying the song line into its blood beat.

When the song ended, the announcer said, "That was Bessie Crispus, our own Kansas City thrush, strictly velvet and white gardenias, and in case you missed the news, she's been signed to sing the first live jazz concert in Carnegie Hall, and, ladies and gentlemen, that's in New York City."

Gus stared at her. "Bess, I'm the one guy in the world who isn't surprised. I always knew you were the tops."

She smiled.

"But Carnegie Hall? That's Walter Damrosch and the long-haired Philharmonic country."

"No more," she said. "Not after I move in. Me and Benny and the Count and Jack Teagarden and Bix and Artie and Teddy Wilson and Pres—we're goin' to blow 'em down. Just blow 'em down."

"I believe it," Gus said. "It must have been a battle."

"Gussie, there's no prison any lonelier than backstage in a back street speakeasy. You can kind of see the world from the wrong end of the spyglass," she said, trying to explain something. "Seedy, sordid, and the smell of old, old make-up in old, old powder rooms would gag a skunk, especially when you think of those youngsters who've gone through the mill ahead of you, leaving only their smell behind. And your man ain't there when every club manager thinks he has flesh rights. Always a battle. No wonder we go on the dreamy stuff and no wonder some of it gets into the song."

"Marry me," Gus said.

"Not a chance. You're too good a man. I don't want no permit to make love to you. Man gives a permit figures he can take it away, too."

"I love you, Bess, I love you, love you."

"All we need. Like always, you and me. We goin' to beat the times. We really are." And she began to sing softly.

> "A rock, a wind, a stream a-grieving,
> A willow weaving in the evening,
> A woman walking all the way
> Just to see the light of day . . . "

The tune was hauntingly poignant and simple. She sang herself into the lyrics.

"Make a nice song, wouldn't it?" she asked.

"It's the sweetest, saddest song I ever heard," Gus said.

The hours passed by, each one making up a year of lost time, each one more beautiful, more tender, more pure and essential, more of a swing into the darkness outside time and place, peeling off each time another layer of ancient cosmetic, swinging closer and closer to the instant when in the beginning of heaven and earth they were the one perfect creation, each swing closing the distance, healing that terrible wound that had split them apart, each swing making it back over that ripping pain, that awful loss, that divided soul and body, closing the gap, closing it all back, healing the wound, and bringing themselves to the moment of one perfect person.

The telephone rang its insistent ding until Gus stumbled out of that ancient sleep to the other room and answered it.

"Yes," he said, "hello."

"Gilpin," Zirp's voice whispered from a larynx crushed by a bullet and scarred beyond repair, "Gilpin, I got a valentine for you. Better get downstairs right away."

The receiver clicked and Gus was wide awake. Quickly he slipped into his clothes and, making sure his Colts were loaded, hurried to the elevator.

The same old baldy with the yellow eyes waited at the door.

Gus didn't know what was going on but it was no time to talk. His first thoughts had been of fear for Bessie, but it had taken only a second to see her safely sleeping like a dark angel, her breasts high, the long curve of her hip like a hill in spring.

Zirp wouldn't bother him about old Salty or any of the working regulars, so it had to be Mr. Fitzgerald.

The elevator cables purred as Gus wished he'd killed Zirp when he had the chance, knowing all the time he could never kill anyone helplessly beneath his guns. But if only Zirp had taken a slug in the head that night of the Cemetery Ridge fight. A big if.

The elevator doors opened and Gus hurried through the lobby to the front doors. The doorman was long gone. People were supposed to be asleep at this hour. Strange that the elevator operator stayed on duty.

He looked back. The elevator was closed, the indicator moving to the basement. Gus kept to the side, hunching a bit, peering into the street, waiting for the worst. Surely they hadn't called him down here for popgun fun. No. Their humor was more like concrete and steel bars than telephone tricks.

From a distance he heard the rising scream of a high-powered engine racing down empty Linwood Boulevard. Like a rocket streaking through the sky on the Fourth of July, it was power, machined iron power tearing loose, aiming straight at him.

His feet wanted to run, but his mind refused. He held a heavy Colt in either hand and waited for them to do their damnedest.

A monstrous black limousine with gunports in its armored sides loomed into view over the far rise of the deserted street and charged on at seventy miles an hour.

He let them take the first shot and, crouched like a wolf at bay, he hammered at the car with his .45 slugs.

A Tommy gun traced a staccato ribbon toward him and he dived behind a concrete urn as the bullets cracked stone splinters into his face.

The black sedan slowed a moment, the rear doors opened and discharged cargo, and the engine howled again like a maniac's glee, like a shrike high on fresh blood, like a jackal giddy with murder.

Gus ran to the first form spraddled without dignity in the gutter. Mr. Fitzgerald. A single hole bored between his vacant eyes told the story instantly. He ran on to the crumpled figure of Lavender. They had put their bullets in his chest. He lived.

But he lasted only to say, "Mr. Gus, get your banjo . . ."

His eyes never opened. He knew he'd done his best, knew he'd met the master of death and accepted it once he'd said what he wanted to say.

Gus carried him to the sidewalk beside Mr. Fitzgerald.

He could hear sirens. Bulls. Ambulances. Let them come for two good men deader than coffin nails.

Mr. Fitzgerald, the only man he could come to for help in any trouble and be sure of getting it. Gus felt a strangling remorse that he'd not really known the older man better. There'd always been a wall of age and experience and practical business between them. Never had they touched. Never had they spoken of family, of church, of trees or immortality. Always it had been day-to-day affairs, from the first time he'd taken Gus as a farm kid off the street to the last time he'd called bequeathing his work to his heir. Always thinking ahead, always thinking of someone else and keeping the organization moving.

Gus touched the silvered, disheveled hair, brushing it back into place. "It's all right, Mr. Fitzgerald, it's all right. I'll take care of it."

A sporty little cop sedan was coming down the rise. Gus eased on inside the lobby. The elevator was waiting, but the operator was gone.

Instantly, exultantly, Gus knew where to begin.

He ran down the corridor and saw a red uniform sprinting around the corner beyond. Ignoring his weak leg, Gus ran at full speed, giving it all.

The corridor led to a locked door. Gus ducked to the floor even as a small gun roared in his ear. The baldheaded operator never got a second shot because Gus had him locked in his big hands, sorting him out, bone by bone. The baldheaded man tried to bite him and took an elbow across his false teeth for his trouble. He quit.

"Upstairs," Gus said. "We use the freight elevator."

The big lift rose slowly with a whirring of machinery. Gus let it go all the way to the roof without speaking. He didn't intend to say much. They'd brought the death game on, he hadn't.

They were on a landing behind the penthouse. Tarred roof, pigeon droppings and gray dawn coming over the stockyards.

"Your move," Gus said. "Tell all of it."

"You scared me." The man tried a con, an unconvincing con; he knew it wasn't going to work, but still, like the set lines of tragedy, he had to go through them until Gus smashed him on the cheekbone, sending him back against the low wall that held him from falling into the alley eight stories below.

"O.K., O.K. I'm done," the baldheaded man said quickly. "What do you want?"

"All of it."

"I'm just a tail. I'm supposed to let Mickey know all your moves. That's all."

"Not quite," Gus said. "Give me the number you call and how you name yourself."

"Poplar 4711," the man said. "Charley's my name."

"You're going over the side."

"Poplar 3711," the man said. "My name is Sherman. That's all, honest to Pete, that's all."

"Who was in that car? And where are they now?"

"I dunno nothin' about that."

Gus, in a blue rage, seized Sherman by the waist and lifted him high.

"Wait!" the man sputtered, turning his head to see the long drop. "They's all out of Chi. Six of 'em. Big Joe, Lansky, Frankie, Dino Luchesi, Fat Gutt, and Bonzo."

"And where do I find 'em?"

"Too late. They're goin' to stash the big car in the City Garage and hop a rattler back to Chi. That's what I heard."

"Thanks," Gus said, starting to let the tall man down.

Trying to use the unguarded moment, Sherman kicked out with the sharp toe of his shoe, catching Gus in the Adam's apple. For an instant Gus was paralyzed; his hands froze open and the force of the kick sent Sherman across the low wall.

He screamed and grabbed at the wall. One hand clutched at the bricks. Gus tried to reach him but his nerves were paralyzed and his legs wouldn't move. He saw the fingers claw the brick; he saw the brick shift, heard the scream, saw the long, nicotine-stained fingers squeeze blood out of the brick, but the brick's mortar was thin and old, the brick went with the hand, the hand went with the body, the body went with the towering scream.

Enough, Gus thought, enough of blood and terror. He leaned weakly against a chimney, gulping in air through his quivering throat. But he knew there wasn't enough. Not yet.

He moved across the roof, climbed over a brick wall into his own roof garden, and slipped quietly through the door.

Bessie hadn't awakened; she was still in a dream of velvet and white gardenias.

He reloaded his .45s, watched his steady hands, went to the phone, and dialed Poplar 3711.

A man's voice answered. "Kansas City Hair Tonic."

"Sherman," Gus said. "Gilpin's running. It's all ours."

"Good deal, Sherm," the voice said. "You come in now. We'll open a bottle at the garage."

"I'll be there." Gus hung up and called another number.

"Pendergast Transportation Company," the voice said.

"The Boss," Gus said.

"In Florida. Anyone else?"

"Anyone else is me." Gus closed the connection and called once more.

"Salty? Gus. Can you drive a big one?"

"Name it," Salty's voice rasped back.

"Now. You and me, the fastest thing on wheels. I'll be at the front door of the office."

Gus went to the closet, loaded the big pockets of his tan trench coat with submachine gun clips, picked up his banjo case and went back across the roof to the freight elevator.

He rode it to the basement, took the steps to the side entrance by the coal chute and came out far enough down the alley that the harness bulls standing around Sherman's flattened remains, blowing on their cold hands and jigging around, didn't notice his broad back going on around the corner.

Once on the street, Gus stayed close to the store fronts, a .45 ready in his concealed right hand, the banjo case in the other. A musician going home after a long hard night at the dance.

It was only a block to the Union Bank Building, where the home offices, the center of a vast distribution network spreading into Missouri, Oklahoma, Nebraska, Kansas, Texas, and Arkansas, were located. Gus knew how big it was. Knew it was the prize Zirp wanted.

He waited only a few seconds in the doorway before a low, long open car pulled up. The two-seater looked like a green whip snake. Gus had never seen anything like it. But Salty was at the wheel and that's all he needed.

He hopped over the door into the leather seat and spoke quietly. "They knocked off Mr. Fitzgerald and Lavender about ten minutes ago. I'm in charge. You want in or out?"

"In, Gus, you know that."

"I'm going to make a fast bump," Gus said, "so fast they won't expect us. The City Garage. Roll it."

Gus was already opening the banjo case and removing the chopper. He jammed a full magazine onto the breech and jacked in a shell. Now it was alive and deadly as a thousand outraged rattlesnakes.

"I'm sorry about our people," Salty rasped, deftly shifting and turning the sleek foreign car across town.

"It's the business," Gus said, "but it don't have to be that way. I just hope to God that Zirp is there in the celebration. This heap reliable?"

"The best. A Bugatti. Belonged to a Sicilian who brought it in loaded with Horse."

"The Sicilian?"

"Too much Horse. Checked out with an overdose."

Growling like an angry wolf, the long green roadster whipped over the early-morning streets, dodging milk wagons and green-grocers, aiming toward the west side of the city, which until today had been accepted as no man's land.

The sun hadn't come up yet. The blue morning dawn was enough to see by.

"Front door?" Salty asked, a block from the garage.

"Right," Gus said. "Meet me in the back. I'm going right straight through."

"You be there," Salty said, letting the throttle off so that the Bugatti cruised silently to the front of the big building like a canoe coming into a reed-covered bank.

Gus hefted the banjo under his right arm, his pistols snug in the deep trench-coat pockets.

The big old brick building was a dingy blue-red in the cold morning. The main car doors were closed, but a small door cut into the big one had a shiny brass knob. Gus tried it and the door opened. He stopped a moment to smell the trouble.

They should have had a guard at the door. But they expected good old Sherm to come along for a few free drinks.

Small explosions to the rear of the building stopped him for a moment, but when he heard the guffaws, he realized they were popping champagne bottles, passing them around, toasting the glorious future. Ah yes, ah yes, the future.

Banjo at the ready, Gus moved silently through the shadows toward the lighted area in the back. Among several cars parked inside was a big black armored Packard. Metal smelled hot.

Gus went slow and easy. He was in. They couldn't leave. He didn't care how many there were, he only cared that Zirp should be among them.

But in the darkness, his shoe brushed a loose wrench. It rang on the brick floor like a doorbell.

The laughter chopped off. A voice yelled, "That you, Sherm?"

Gus had to go all the way now. If Zirp was there, wonderful; if he wasn't there was no help for it.

"Howdy," he said, coming through a double line of cars. Six of them, standing around a broken case of champagne. Each one had a fat green bottle of bubbly in his hand. He had seen them all at one time or another. Big Joe Wintergreen looking like a cave man in a sport suit; Marty Lansky, a jockey knifeman; Frankie Madigan, an ex-bull turned killer; Dino Luchesi with jowls as blue as lead; Fat Gutt with his famous yellow walrus mustache; and faithful, stupid Bonzo, the monstrously big freak from southern Italy —the same who had cold-cocked him in Dodge City.

When they saw his face they froze in incredulous cold fear. They were of the breed of men who knew death constantly but never expected to see it in the face of one man.

"Gus," Lansky said, "give us a chance."

"Same chance you gave Mr. Fitzgerald." Gus turned toward Lansky.

Dino whirled away, snapping out a flat automatic, and the others were fast and firing wildly, but Gus stood solid and touched the trigger of the jolting submachine gun and sprayed the room from left to right, right to left. Bottles smashed. Men cried out and sobbed in pain and death. Slugs whined bloodily off the white-washed wall behind them.

In twenty seconds six corpses lay sprawled like driftwood on the floor, huddled against the white and bloody wall.

Gus hunched by them, uncaring, still hoping to find his mortal enemy. He hardly felt the wound in his side, so charged up was his spirit, like a bulldog in a pit. His nostrils were flared and strained, and his eyes blazed over the area, hunting for more of the same.

A single shot came from the darkness of a room beyond. He felt his left elbow splinter, and sent a hundred slugs into that room, pumping round after round into the darkness, hoping, praying his hidden assailant was Zirp. He waited as a bloody form toppled forward into the light.

It was not Zirp. It was hardly more than a boy. Gus felt the horror of slaying the innocent, even though the dead boy still clutched a bulldog .38 in his hand. Gus looked at his putty-colored features, pencil-line mustache, oiled-down hair. He looked familiar. Gus had to be sure. He ripped a bloody wallet out of a breast pocket, read the name. Romulus Zirp.

The only son of Mickey Zirp was born to lose.

TEN

THE ORGANIZATION FUNCTIONED EFFICIENTLY, closing ranks and acting to protect its new boss. Gus was dimly aware that the main reason it was working was because young Babe Saltz, who had been put into the business early by his father, was making the right motions. He had a dozen men, including legal plainclothesmen guarding the penthouse on a twenty-four-hour-a-day basis, he had the right whiskey on the right trucks going to the right places on time. He had wired a coded progress report to Mr. Pendergast in Miami Beach. And he did it because he was trained to do it, because that's what organization meant. You could lose your top man to a bullet and your second top man to a severe wound, and still keep the business going as usual.

Mr. Pendergast made it back in time to be the chief mourner at Mr. Fitzgerald's funeral. His presence guaranteed it would be a lavish affair with truckloads of flowers arranged in beautiful symbols, a horseshoe of carnations, an Irish harp of cornflowers, a heart of bleeding red roses, decorated little hand-printed ribbons saying "Good Luck, Honeyfitz," "Goodbye, Old Comrade," "Heaven's the Winner."

"He's gone to the Top Bootlegger in the sky," Tiny said, coming to the bier, seeing that Honeyfitz appeared blooming with health and cheer. "That's why he's so happy."

Honeyfitz slept on, his rosy cheeks denying death, his pleasant smile indicating he'd just had a double Cordon Bleu.

Gus was unable to attend. His wound was too close to the lung, the doctor insisted, and he'd lost too much blood.

Bessie stayed by him, although she was overdue for a singing date in New York with Benny Goodman's band.

"Bessie," he said, trying to keep his tone firm and solid, "I'll be O.K. in a couple of days. I want you to get on that train east."

"If they can't wait a day or two, they can whistle," she replied.

She wouldn't budge until the doctor assured her the bleeding was stopped and the wound would heal cleanly.

"Gus," she asked, "you sure you want me to go?"

"Of course," he said seriously. "I want you to bust open Carnegie Hall like a Kansas City safecracker."

"It'll only be a month or so," she said.

"I only have one worry and that's you and your white candy. Back home I was raised up believing that stuff'd drive a person berserk, make 'em do all kinds of terrible things. And I can't quite shed the fear out of my mind."

"I'll be gentle," she said. "I never use it less'n I'm feelin' lower'n a worm's belly. And I ain't felt like that since you came back."

"O.K.," Gus said, "give 'em an extra chorus for old Gus."

"I promise." She laughed. "You listen on the radio, I'll sing a song for you."

And she kissed him long and lovingly.

Salty reported back that she'd made the City of Salina easily and was safely on her way east.

He didn't report, because he had no way of knowing, that Mickey Zirp's men had her spotted the minute she'd stepped into the limousine, and that Zirp, knowing her weakness, had set two of the slickest junk pushers in the business after her.

The pushers were a bright and amusing couple, young, dark and handsome, a boy and a girl who seemed to be living a grand, carefree life. And like a worm in an apple, they grew fat on what they passed.

They'd made Bessie's acquaintance by the time the luxury train reached St. Louis. And by Cincinnati, they were sharing pops, and they had Bessie stretched out in a heavy heroin sleep by the time they hit Pittsburgh, and they fixed her again before the train pulled into New York. The Big Apple.

"Hey, wait, kids," she tried to say, "I got things to do."

But they were noodling along, the bright guy and his girl, saying, "Lookie, happy Bessie, she got something to do," laughing as if it were a joke.

They went together to the Van Wingerden Hotel in groggy bliss, and then they had her. The tough stretch of health she'd cold-turkeyed while she was with Gus had been wiped out, and the need, the physical, chemical need for the new narcotic, was redoubled. They played it very well. They got her up for the afternoon rehearsals and she sang beautifully because she was high and she was trained well.

But none of this Salty knew, nor could Gus know. A postcard from New York told him all was fine—wish you were here—and that was all he expected.

Gus had more than enough to occupy his mind when Mr. Pendergast visited him secretly.

A big, heavy gentleman of the old school, Mr. Pendergast may not have been a gentleman at all beneath his rich clothes, but he certainly was the boss of the big city.

He didn't waste time. "First of all," he said to Gus, "I appreciate your taking the quick decision against the Chicago machine."

Gus stared at the ceiling. "Yessir."

"But these things get blown up by the newspapers."

"I guess you can handle the newspapers," Gus said. "My idea was to hit 'em hard and fast, before they split up."

"All right, Gus," the florid-faced, paunchy gentleman said, lighting a big cigar, "a decision was made, it was put into operation and completed very cleanly. On that account, you will remain in Mr. Fitzgerald's place. He wanted it that way, I know, and I think you can handle it."

"I'll be in the office tomorrow morning, eight o'clock," Gus said.

Mr. Pendergast rose like a great robin redbreast from his chair and walked to the door. He stopped to turn and say in a low, quiet voice, "Mr. Fitzgerald had a proper send-off."

"Thanks," Gus said.

"One more thing to think about," Mr. Pendergast said over his shoulder. "The next election will finish Prohibition. We have to be ready for it."

Gus took a moment before he answered, "Yessir."

That meant an end to bootlegging, and an end meant a beginning. The big booze money had to go to work somewhere else. He'd have to think. Prostitution was distasteful. Car theft and extortion was small-time. Usury was lucrative, but was essentially a strong-arm cheat. Construction graft and servicing ice were thin potatoes. Narcotics, though not large, paid well, but still he had a prejudice against profiting off the weak and sick, and that left gambling on horses, dogs and athletes.

He had to think about it. The turn was coming. He was glad he had the notice. Most people never even got fair warning that the bottom was going to fall out of their careers overnight.

There was still time, and Gus had a safety-deposit box packed solidly with a thousand hundred-dollar bills beside his regular five-figure bank account.

But there wasn't time for the constant, sudden and deadly attacks by Zirp's regrouped Mafia backed up by the Capone Syndicate.

There had been no notice in the papers that young Romulus Zirp was among the casualties in the City Garage.

But the gravevine said that Mickey Zirp was off his rocker, insisting that Gus had set the kid up, shot him down for the fun of it and laughed about it, and Zirp swore every morning over his horn of white lightning that Gus Gilpin would die like a gut-shot hog in the street.

For sure the attacks against his trucks and barges and bottling works were coming hard and fast. Hardly a week went by that Gus's men weren't in a bloody gunfight. Gus immediately equipped them with bulletproof vests and the latest weapons, raised their wages, and hired extra guards.

Gus had his old lieutenants lined up under young Babe Saltz: Lafe, Lefty, Catfish, Cracker Zack, Tiny, and Fid.

In three weeks of hit-and-run fighting, Zirp's losses were six killed, wounded unknown, while Gilpin men were three wounded, none killed. But the responsibility for his loyal friends was becoming too much for Gus. He couldn't sit behind a desk, ordering them to drive the night highways with so many chances of their not coming back.

"We're all right," young Babe Saltz said, "we're doing fine. They're eating our dust."

"I know," Gus agreed, pacing the big paneled office he'd arranged downstairs from the penthouse, "but it's only a question of time before somebody gets it. Could even be your dad."

Young Saltz put on his rimless glasses and studied an audit of the Wichita Alcohol Unit a moment, but disturbed, glanced up at Gus and said, "He should retire. He's pushed his luck farther than anybody in the organization."

"I've tried to pension him off. He almost drew on me."

Young Saltz smiled. "O.K., how are you going to do it?"

"Get Inspector Moriarty on the phone."

It took only a second before Gus heard Moriarty's crunching crocodile voice come over the wire.

"Gus Gilpin, Moriarty," Gus said. "I want you to do me a favor."

"I dunno, Mr. Gilpin, about doing favors . . ."

"Look bull, you're paid a fat fee every month to do us favors and you've done darned few the past year. I'm beginning to think you might be taking a fat fee out of the Syndicate slush fund too."

"Yes, Mr. Gilpin, go ahead." The voice was guarded, playing it like a venerable old protector of the citizenry, just in case the grand jury was listening.

"Get ahold of Zirp. He wants a personal duel with me, I'm ready. I'll meet him back of the gas house. Just him and me. You see it's fair."

"What's this all about, Mr. Gilpin?" Moriarty's voice was cautious.

"I'm tired of risking my men's lives just because Mickey has a personal hate on me. I want to fight him man to man, fair and square. Tell him to meet me at daybreak and soon as one sees the other, start busting caps."

"I'll see about it," Moriarty said. "Of course, I don't condone this conduct at all, but I'll investigate the matter."

"Dawn. Back of the gas house," Gus said and hung up.

"You think he'll do it?" Babe asked.

"A chance. That's all."

"I'll have enough men to watch your back."

"O.K., but no funny business. We're playing it out fair and square."

"Meanwhile we've got schedules to work out."

They dug into the piles of paperwork that Gus hated so much but that had to be done to keep the organization going.

It was his job, and if there were some parts of it he didn't like, well, he was paid for it and he did it.

It was harder with Bessie gone. He couldn't help worrying about her. In some ways she was so vulnerable. She was no sap for any sob story, but a sucker for the happy-time sell. You could kid her out of anything if you knew how to make her laugh.

And he hadn't heard from her for several days now. He counted it up. A little lazy note a week ago. Seven days. Too long. The note was sleepy, every sloping dozing word seemed to say cocaine, cocaine, and more cocaine.

"You trust Moriarty, Gus?" Young Saltz's voice broke into his worrying wool-gathering.

"No," Gus said. "He's sold us out for the past two months at least."

"Why not give him a long bath in the Missouri?"

"It's better, Babe, to let him hang himself. He can't hurt us so long as we know he's a lugger."

"I can't figure how you spotted it."

"Experience. I can read him a lot easier than this quarterly statement from the Dodge City unit." Gus smiled and closed the last page of the ledger.

"Must be late," he said. "I was hoping Bessie would call. I think I'll turn in for a couple hours."

"Go to sleep," Babe said. "I'll keep the phone lines open and wake you at five. Give us plenty of time to be at the gas house by six."

"Thanks." Gus nodded and walked up the stairway to the penthouse.

It seemed too lonely without Bessie; he was about ready to move into a boarding house. A light was burning and old Salty was nodding away in a deep overstuffed chair.

Gus smiled, glad for a human presence, buoyed up by the knowing he had the best friends any man could ask for. He stopped at a low table and lifted the gold-framed picture of Bessie to the light.

Dear God, how he loved that strange girl, her beauty, her pathetic weakness, her voice which expressed it all in simple tones and easy phrasing.

One more week and she'd knock them dead at Carnegie Hall. That's all she'd ever need or want. The one supreme accolade. She was smart enough to know that to repeat it would be playing the rat-race game for nothing. But to bust open the hall, that was worth it. Bust it, then quit. Come home to old sewed-up Gus and be his woman, mistress, wife, and mother of his children.

Lying on the big bed, he looked into the darkness thinking a man liked to leave a son. Death moved quickly and crazily. There was never any sense to it. And where was the son of Gus Gilpin?

Until he heard old Salty's voice saying, "Come on, boss, it's five o'clock. Time. Time to kill."

"Right there, Salty," Gus said, sitting on the edge of the bed coldly clutching at his knees and shivering in the November morning.

Bessie, Bessie, is it so chilled there in New York City?

He'd already made his will carefully, setting up a trust in case Bessie should have a child.

He took a shower and shaved. His long yellow mane of hair curled up like a sun-dappled foaming wave of surf.

No use in dying or killing dirty. He felt better, as though his luck was nearly even.

He dressed in fresh clothes, not worrying about time. He strapped on his old comfortable .45s. Their pearl handles were beginning to reflect the wear he'd put them to. They were honorable pieces.

And they'd saved his life more times than he wanted to remember. By God, Gus thought, I must be getting old. Anybody in this business who starts remembering the early days is finished. He laughed at his ruddy, straw-topped face in the mirror, knotted the tie carefully, and went to the closet where the banjo case was stored.

"I'm ready," he said to Salty.

"Us too. Each man has a position, you're covered."

"Maybe he won't show," Gus said.

"I sure hope he won't," Salty growled.

"But if I lose, young Babe will take my place. He's as ready as he'll ever be."

"You're not going to lose," Salty said. "Don't talk like that. You give me the willies."

Gus smiled and patted the old driver on the back. "Saddle up, Salty, time to ride."

Going downstairs, Gus thought he heard the telephone ringing, but there wasn't time to go back. Salty was waiting.

The phone rang to the empty room and death was waiting at the other end of the long wire. Death was hungry in the Big Time.

Bessie was holding the receiver with both hands, listening to the ringing in the empty room.

"I'm sorry, that number doesn't answer."

"Please, Operator, let it ring some more."

Bessie was looking at death in the mirror of her bedroom. She was looking at her strange face. Good God, she looked like an old hag! She had to get hold of herself. That new junk she was shooting was tough stuff. Flashed you up like a mule kickin' you in the butt, but what a come-down. Oh my, what a down! She looked at the eyes of death, dully staring back at her. Greasy hammocks hung under those dull eyes. The color of her skin was opaque and scruffy, as if she'd been in the moldy dark too long.

Better start eatin' one of these times, she said to death.

Funny how that happy dust takes away your appetite. Why eat? Don't bother nobody, just stay high and happy, sleep easy with pretty dreams, sing to yourself.

My, my, I'm crackin' Carnegie Hall. Me and Benny—

Shoot, how you goin' to crack Carnegie anything with the load you're carryin'?

The load kept squirming in her long lonely body, kept eating away at her center, and the only thing that made it purr was a snootful of snow.

"I'm sorry, there is no answer."

"What time is it out there, honey?" Bessie asked.

"Five-oh-seven."

"You'd think a man'd be home by five in the morning less'n he was stayin' someplace else . . ."

"There is no answer, madam. Shall I try later?"

"Would you take a message for me? Tell him to get back here and gimme a big kiss and loan me his big freckled shoulder to cry on for a while."

"Shall I connect you with Western Union, please?"

"No, Mom," Bessie said, "connect me with heaven. I want to talk to ol' marstah God."

The connection snicked off.

Bessie smiled at death in the mirror and arched her back and purred. "Gonna crack 'em wide open, baby," she said. "Goin' back rehearsin' with Benny just as soon as I can get ahold of a couple friends of mine. Gus, damn you, where you sleepin' tonight?"

She started to cry softly, murmuring the worry and the horror of her own disenchantment.

"Oh, Gussie baby, why'n't you here long as you're someplace? Why'n't you here just holdin' me, s'long as you got time to hold somebody?"

Dawn broke around the gas house in a gray furry haze, the muggy mist coming off the river and curdling around the squat brick building. A few dirty windows looked out like cannon ports. Machine shops and cooperages and paint factories nearby were still as swamp ghosts, and no one walked the streets at night.

At the South end of an empty acre lot behind the broad brick building two big sedans were parked. Men with shotguns and telescopic sighted rifles stood alertly near the cars, watching the opposite end of the vacant lot. There was nothing there. No cars, no people. The Gilpin men were disappointed. They'd punished Zirp's forces badly over the past month and they were anxious to have another helping.

But apparently the Zirp mob was sitting this one out.

Gus stepped out of the car, carrying the submachine gun. He glanced at the faces of his men. Broad, cleft-chinned Lefty, solid as pavement, quick-eyed Lafe, and that deadly hunter, Catfish. They shook their heads slightly, not speaking. Gus stared across the area. It was a good spot for a stomp. Plenty big so no bystander need get hurt, unconfined except for the back of the gas house, which was more like a brick wall, pierced by dim windows. But it took two to do the Kansas City Stomp.

"Give 'em a few more minutes," Gus said. "Maybe they had a flat tire."

His men smiled thinly, their eyes alert and moving.

Beyond the gas house, across a glass- and cinder-littered yard, was a blocky, brick school. If possible, he thought, it looked less hospitable than the gas house. If you were a kid going to school, you'd prefer the street. He was aware that this was an all-black neighborhood, but he had thought that the schools would have trees and pleasant buildings the same as the west end, but there stood the outrageous truth, obvious as a scar on a woman's face.

"You know, Salty, we got to do something about that school."

"What about it?" Salty asked, puzzled, thinking Gus knew of an enemy hidden there.

"I mean it's got to be burned down and a new one, a good one, built."

"I'm for that," Salty said.

"We discovered in the accounts that Mr. Fitzgerald had sent an architect from Chi to Africa. We couldn't figure it out. But now I think I see why."

"Schools cost a lot of money." Salty nodded.

"Couldn't spend it any better than teaching poor kids how to change their world. We'll start as soon as we're back to the office."

"There's some folks like to keep things the way they are," Salty said.

"I know," Gus said, "and then there's human beings." Gus smiled and Salty chuckled deep in his craggy canyon throat.

"Boss!" Catfish called.

"I see 'em," Gus said, noting the big car pull up at the opposite end of the field. "Time for me to ride the elephant."

"Seems too easy," Salty worried. "And where's Moriarty?"

"Busy counting blood money," Gus said, seeing the tall hunch-backed figure slide out of the car, leaving the door open. The driver stayed at the wheel, the motor running.

Little light came through the smoky fog. Gus wondered if the sun ever did shine down here. No matter, for the moment he could see all he needed to see. The slim, spidery figure carried a pump shotgun.

"Twelve-gauge," Catfish reported. "May have rifled slugs in it for the first couple rounds while you're still out of range, then double-ought buck for short stuff."

"I'll stay with the banjo," Gus said, snapping off the safety and jacking in a shell.

He glanced along the route he'd travel to meet Zirp. He would keep the gas-house wall close to his right to avoid any special little snare Zirp's mind might have conjured up. His men would be watching for long-range sharpshooters. Catfish had his own long-barreled Springfield at the ready.

"C'mon, you sonofabitch!" Zirp's rusty, crippled voice carried through the pearly morning across the long lot.

"There's some names I don't take," Gus growled, "and that's one of 'em."

Gus moved away from the group, staying within arm's length of the brick wall, hardly hearing the voices of his friends wishing him good luck.

He kept the banjo cradled across his crippled left forearm at the ready. It would be a straight face-to-face brutal battle to the finish. Gus would squeeze the trigger as soon as the distant figure made any kind of overt move.

He passed a dark, dusty window and moved a slow step at a time, trying to draw Zirp in farther from his car.

He approached another window, just like the other, only it was wide open. He caught a glint of a face, a face he knew well, but even before it all could click into place—that the face belonged to his old enemy Moriarty—two hand grenades dropped out of the window six feet in front of him.

There was no time to think. If he ran, either the grenades or Zirp would tear out his back. His men couldn't see the steel pineapples fizzing away on the ground like innocent little vipers coiled to strike. There was only one chance. His body was already half through its motion before his mind caught up with it.

The banjo was abandoned as he dived with both hands outstretched for the bombs, rolled on his back, came up with a grenade in each fist and threw them simultaneously back into the window where he saw for one instant the disbelieving, terrified face of the redheaded cop, fat from free wine and painted women, and he saw the burgundy color change to mud yellow in that face, saw the mouth try to make a No.

Gus hit the base of the wall as the grenades went off and the No was never said. Even as the brick wall shook and the window glass and Moriarity exploded outward, Gus heard the slam of a heavy lead slug drive against the wall just above his head.

Rolling again toward the chopper in the dust, Gus saw the hunchback diving back into the car, which took off before the door was even closed.

The shots of Lefty and Catfish's rifles ricocheted harmlessly off the armor-plated rear of the car as it raced to the corner, screamed on two wheels in turning, and was gone into the swirling fog.

There was the cold, wet silence. Blood dripped from the window casement. No one moved. They stood alert, ready. But it was over. Thickening blood dripped from the casement.

A watchman in the front of the building was yelling timidly, "Hey, what's goin' on back there?"

Gus looked inside the blasted window and said a simple prayer. He'd hated Moriarty almost as much as he'd hated Zirp, but he wanted no one to be torn to pieces by hot, jagged steel hooks. And when a man died, any man, he was approaching purification.

Turning sickly away from the slaughtered mess of a man, he trudged heavily back to his friends.

"What was it?" Salty asked. "We couldn't see it."

"Pair of pineapples. Moriarty dropped 'em. I picked 'em up for him, and gave 'em back."

"Mighty close, Gus," the old man said. "I never saw anything move so fast."

"Let's go," Gus said. "Sooner we leave, the sooner the bulls'll be here."

"That scum of a Moriarty," Catfish said.

"That Moriarity in a way made me what I am right now," Gus said tiredly, the crisis over, the adrenalin in his veins ebbing.

He was remembering a ragged farm boy, his side plowed open and bleeding, hopping off a boxcar and meeting, instead of a friend, a cop on the make.

And thinking of the afternoon Jim died and a cop on the take, Moriarty taking his pay at Bessie's apartment. Scum, scum, yes, scum.

The fat mouth had flashed its yellow teeth, had bucked open wide to scream a No.

But this time, Moriarty, Death was on the take.

ELEVEN

"MAN TO SEE YOU," Babe said.

Gus, at his desk wading through stacks of reports and jotting down the balances, hardly heard the young man. He was determined to work out his worry over Bessie, and this was the work.

"Gus," Babe said again, "man to see you."

Gus looked up this time, hearing. "Frank Wright again?"

Babe grinned. "No, said his name was Fats King."

"Fats. Not much difference from Frank," Gus said, remembering the roly-poly piano player. "They both make their own kinds of music."

In the waiting room he found his old friend looking a little rounder, a little more pop-eyed, and a little more worried.

"Fats," Gus said, grabbing the small, slender hand, making sure not to break it in his rush of remembrance.

Fats grinned his porky pencil mustache smile. "Hi, there, Gus. You're still as skinny as ever. Don't you never get any barbecue?"

"At least I'm getting three squares a day now." Gus smiled. "How are you? Where've you been?"

"Now wait a minute, Mr. Gus," Fats said. "I'm still fakin' a barrelhouse piano player. 'Course I play Bach in church every Sunday too. That keeps me right with the Man upstairs and I don't want to waste your time, Gus. I know you're a big man now and that means you're busy."

"Forget that stuff," Gus said. "You got it just backwards."

"But I heard what you're doin' for the kids down by the gas

house. Likely even a couple of those rascals is mine and, Gus, I think they ought to name that new school after you."

"Nope. It's called the Jim Crispus school. All settled. Getting the sign made already."

"Too much, Dad." Fats laughed. "Old Jim is rolling over in his banjo case right now."

"But how about you, Fats? I'm never going to forget what you did to get Bessie started. We owe you more than you'll ever know."

"That's why I'm here, Gus. It's about the Lady."

"Level with it." A cold fear gripped his heart.

"Well, everybody's got some kind of a grapevine. Bootleggers got one, musicians got another. Sometimes they don't cross. But I'm cuttin' across. It ain't much, only that Bessie ain't goin' to make that Carnegie Hall set because she's bonked on the conk ever since she went east. That's it."

"Heroin."

"Big."

"Damn," Gus said. "That concert's tomorrow night."

"They'll dump her. I just got the word about an hour ago from a gut-bucket in from Philly. He heard it from a hide-beater hop-head."

"If I could get back there in time . . ." Gus said, his thoughts working at top speed, trying to put together a plan, a schedule that would work.

"Maybe you could call her," Fats suggested.

"I've been trying to call her since yesterday," Gus said. "I knew something wasn't right, but I thought maybe she was rehearsing extra hard, or jittery on account of the big performance and wanted to be left alone. No, we've got to go."

"We? Go?" Fats' bulbous eyes bulged out like a frog ready to croak.

"There's airplanes," Gus said, and yelled to his assistant. "Babe, call up somebody and get me and Fats on the fastest airplane to New York."

"Right away," Babe answered, totally unruffled, knowing that no one flew those planes except if they were in the flying business themselves or were faced with a life-or-death emergency. The casualty rates were too high for people interested in staying alive.

In a moment he relayed the information. "A Ford Trimotor

Scout can head east in ten minutes from the airport. Be in New York tomorrow afternoon."

"C'mon, Fats, we're flying."

"Mr. Gus," Fats croaked, "I ain't never flew except on the wings of song."

"Me either, but we're going to give it a try."

Gus told Babe to wire Bessie they were coming, and hustled Fats downstairs to the big La Salle Salty had warmed up and waiting for them.

Driving at high speed down the brick streets, Salty grumbled over his shoulder. "I think I could beat your flyin' machine and be a lots safer too."

"Don't worry, Salty, my marker's not up yet."

"I know, but up there in the air, your engine stops, you fall down. Happens all the time."

"Tell that to Fats," Gus said. "He needs something to cheer him up."

The aluminum craft's three motors were already turning over. The waiting pilot had a black patch over one eye. He wore a sheepskin coat. Indicating a couple of parachute packs in the seats, he made sure that his passengers were strapped in.

"Might be a little rough up there." He didn't smile much. "Thunderstorms passing through."

To Gus he looked like a one-eyed grease monkey hanging around the truck garage, trying to learn a trade.

"You ever flown this thing before?" Gus asked.

"No, but I read a book." The pilot suddenly laughed back at him. "And you want to get to the big town, don't you?"

"By tomorrow."

The pilot nodded. "Do my best."

He caught a signal from the airport manager and said, "All set. Let's see if I can remember that first chapter."

On each wing and on the nose, the propellers were whirling, and the great radial engines were deafening.

Gus had a moment to wonder: There was nothing on earth he feared, but he didn't know about the sky. Fats was right. Up there you depended on the pilot and his instruments and the workers who'd built the plane rivet by rivet and the men who'd refined the gasoline, hopefully with total purity. Had the maintenance men loafed on the lube job? Was there a dry bearing right now burning out?

The huge engines thundered; the pilot released the brakes and drove the plane bouncing down the runway.

Gus waited for something to happen, but after an eternity and about a half mile of dirt road, the wheels lifted gently off the land, and they were airborne.

As the plane rose, Gus looked down and saw the ugly, writhing mass of the stockyards and train tracks, and his city on each side of the river, and on the east until there was no city, no smoky bricks, only the patch by patch of green farmlands.

Gus grinned at Fats, who was pale, slick black.

"Wonderful! How fast?" he yelled at the pilot.

"Hundred and forty," the pilot yelled back, handling the stick with the sensitivity of a conductor with a baton.

"Hear that?" Gus yelled at Fats. "One hundred forty miles per hour!"

"I'll settle for a waltz," Fats said.

"We stop in Indianapolis for gas," the pilot yelled.

Gus realized too that the sun was setting, and ahead of them great towering thunderheads boiled like gas-house steam.

The Trimotor came in low, below the clouds, in the gathering darkness. It took the pilot a minute to get his bearings and find the field, but once he'd located his position, he brought the plane in without delay. It was too simple. There was the airport, so you came in downwind of it and landed upwind, taxied to the hangar, and killed the engines.

"When do we leave here?" Gus asked.

"Depends on the weather ahead," the pilot said. "I'll check in the office."

"No wonder you're the Satchmo of bootlegging." Fats smiled faintly. "You move ten times faster'n anybody I ever knew."

"Time's important," Gus said.

"Not much we can do, even if we make it before the gig."

"Nobody knows till they try."

When the pilot returned he held a sheaf of flimsy papers in his hand, his face no longer that of a prankster.

"No luck," he said. "The whole east route is socked in solid."

"So?" Gus asked, feeling a sense of loss, a feeling of fate snipping at his heart strings.

"In the morning. Daybreak. Maybe."

"I'll add on five hundred dollars," Gus said, "if I make it to New York before dark tomorrow."

"There's transient's quarters inside no one's using," the pilot said. "We can save a few minutes staying here."

He showed them into a room with half a dozen cots made up. Gus and Fats tried to sleep. Gus hardly knew it happened until he felt the hand on his shoulder. His own hand instinctively went toward his shoulder holster when he heard the dry, casual voice.

"C'mon, let's fire up the bird."

Fats hadn't slept. He was lying there, round as a plum, his eyes open, his day-old stubble white.

"The weather report," the pilot said, "is fifty-fifty."

"Let's go," Gus said.

"We can take off," the pilot said. "After that, things start getting a little murky."

"When in doubt, fly," Gus said, swallowing the hot coffee the pilot held for him.

A thick mist hung a few hundred feet above the airdrome.

A mechanic was pumping gas into the plane's tanks. Another was socking the fittings with a grease gun.

In a moment the pilot with his passengers were in the cabin, strapping their seat belts and beating their cold hands together.

The huge radials roared; the pilot gunned the angular, boxy craft across the ramp and lifted it off into the lowering murk. In a matter of seconds they were wrapped in a heavy, smoky fog. Visibility zero. The pilot watched his instruments like a hawk, kept the plane climbing due east.

"Any mountains up this way?" Fats asked.

Gus tried to smile, saying, "Just a few big ones."

In a few minutes the murk gradually thinned into patches of gray and blue, and at last, with a small sigh of relief, the pilot cut completely through the fog and winged on upward into the clear blue. The fog was like a great roll of cotton batting beneath them, shimmering in the sun, and all the rest was pure clear cold sky.

He held his compass course, trying to estimate wind drift.

His radio worked if someone on the other end was there to make some noise. Once in a while he contacted a station on the ground to confirm his position. It seemed so easy Gus was considering buying a plane for his own use.

In no time at all the pilot announced they were passing over Columbus, Ohio. Gus looked down but could see nothing but the solid white batting below.

"We can make it to Pittsburgh," the pilot yelled. "Plenty of gas to there. And the weather may break open by then."

The steady beat of the Ford engines put Fats to sleep, and Gus was nodding off when he dimly heard the pilot saying, "Hello, Pittsburgh, this is Ford 126 Bravo, ten miles northwest for landing."

"Roger, 126 Bravo. This field's closed. Visibility zero. Repeat, field closed, visibility zero. Suggest you try Washington."

"Thanks, Pittsburgh." The one-eyed pilot started whistling a little tune between his teeth.

"Can you make Washington?" Gus asked, looking at the gas gauge.

The pilot glanced around at Gus and winked his good eye. "Hell with it, let's try Philly. Five hundred skins will just make me a down payment on my own airline."

"Got a route?"

"I'm all set," the pilot said. "L.A. to Kansas City. All I need is a little luck."

"I'm loaded with luck," Gus said and smiled.

"Use some on that thunderhead yonder," the pilot said grimly.

"You can drop me off here," Fats said.

The pilot held to his heading and tried not to think about the bruised tower of spume directly ahead.

Gus admired the steadiness of his eye and the sensitive touch on the controls. He could just as well be pushing a baby buggy through the park instead of ramming this cloud of freezing darkness.

Gus felt the craft swinging hard off to the left, then turn back like a leaf in a vagrant wind, tossed across to the right and up. His stomach was down around his knees.

Fats was clutching his tummy, his eyes closed, singing a little song to himself. "Baby, can't stand you, 'cause your feet's too big . . ."

Suddenly the plane was locked in the grip of the storm; they were not only flying upside down, they were being smashed sidewise. It seemed their three beating engines were meaningless. The storm vortex had them and was spinning them however it wished. The pilot kept his calm attitude, even when hanging upside down, still trying to control the craft he captained, still trying to deny that any larger force existed outside of those mighty three engines which were governed by the throttle in his hand.

They were blown a thousand feet upward across the enormous black sky, the struts of the wings quivered in an agony of metal, the howls of the plane's skin and bone were like screams of a pig under a gate, and Fats was singing his little tune, "But, Baby, I hate you, 'cause your feet's too big," and Gus was trying to see everything that was going on.

Lightning flashed white brilliance close by.

Gus could see the altimeter spinning crazily and the air speed rise to three hundred as the winds sent the plane soaring.

The pilot did his best, using all he had, expecting no more but not expecting any less either from his own chosen universe, and, as they spiraled through the infinite sky, a blast of sunlight seemed to smash into the cockpit. The pilot grinned.

In another twenty seconds the thunderhead was behind and the pilot had the craft on the right course at the right altitude and was calling in Philadelphia.

Gus looked at his watch. Just two o'clock. The gas gauge said Empty.

"Baby, you're awful, 'cause your feet's too big . . ." Fats sang, his eyes still shut tight.

"We're O.K., Fats," Gus said. "We're landing for gas. The weather is great from here on. Heck, you can practically see New York from here."

The pilot eased her down into the smog over the city and scooted her into the airport, where a gas truck was already waiting.

Gus and Fats and the pilot walked around the stoutly built aircraft, patting its silver skin occasionally, complimenting it on its beauty and strength under duress, and after a short lunch and a cup of coffee, they were airborne on the final leg of the trip.

And there it was, the greatest city in the world, its skyscrapers rising up from the island of rock. The Empire State Building needled the heavens and the Statue of Liberty stood there to welcome the downtrodden and idealists from abroad.

The airport was more modern than any they'd seen, but its location was away from the city. The pilot let them out of the door and Gus put a thousand-dollar bill in the brave man's hand.

"I'll be back," Gus said.

"Lots of luck." The pilot winked his one eye.

Gus shook his hand and hurried with Fats to the terminal cab stand.

"The Van Wingerden, fast as she'll go," Gus ordered as the two men settled into the back seat of the Terraplane.

"Right," the driver said and hit the gas.

In Manhattan the driver drove uptown, up Sixth Avenue, turned off on 44th Street, and pulled up before the expressionless concrete hotel noted for the excellence of its service to artists.

"Here you are, sir," the driver said, taking Gus's ten-dollar bill and reaching for change.

"Never mind," Gus said and hurried on inside to the desk.

"Miss Crispus? Yes. Three-oh-eight. I'll ring."

The clerk plugged in and waited, speaking even as the bell was ringing. "No answer, sir. Would you care to leave a message?"

"I want the key," Gus said.

"I'm afraid that isn't . . ." The clerk looked into the haggard face and burning eyes which brooked no nonsense, and quietly slid the key across the counter.

Fats trotted along as Gus hurried to the elevator. The uniformed octogenerian closed the door and punched the button.

"You seen Miss Bessie Crispus lately?" Gus asked.

"No, sir. I used to see her, but she ain't been around for two or three days."

"You think she's out or in?"

"I dunno, sir. She's got a couple friends come visit her sometimes."

Gus tried to fathom if something deeper lay behind those ancient, rheumy eyes.

He glanced at Fats. The tired pianist shrugged his shoulders.

Gus found 308 a few steps down the carpeted hall. Quiet. Almost cold.

The door unlocked, opened, and closed behind them. A sitting room, immaculate. Musty. A closed door.

Gus knocked. Nothing.

He opened the door and in the darkness of the shaded room he saw his beloved on the bed. She wore a white silk robe.

She seemed asleep. Her mouth was slightly open.

Ah now, Gus felt the relief flooding over him. He'd been afraid to admit to himself that if she were not here, he'd have an impossible job of finding her anywhere else in this enormous, brittle city.

He touched the shoulder of the sleeping woman. Her face had aged in a way he couldn't understand, not by time, not by sudden cruelty.

"Bessie," he said, "wake up. It's Gus and Fats. C'mon, Bessie." She didn't stir.

Gus tried to feel her pulse and couldn't. He put his ear to her breast and picked up a faint, very faint, beat.

He saw then the needle marks on the inside of her arm.

"Call an ambulance, Fats," he said softly. "Be fast."

"Right." Fats used the house phone and made the order explicit.

"An overdose," Gus said. "Somebody's really been throwing the junk into her."

"There's hope," Fats said, feeling a dreadful weight with hooks pulling inside his round tummy. The sorrow that such an artist should be so destroyed was unsupportable. The why demanded answer and there was none.

"Bessie . . ." Gus rubbed her wrists, trying to wake her, but she dreamed on.

The white-jacketed internist was interested. He liked class and he liked the twenty-dollar bill in his hand. He might have let her sleep on through to the cold, cold earth, but these little things made a difference. He made a quick examination. He listened to Gus's suggestion and drove a shot of adrenalin into her arm and only then was she carried out on a stretcher.

Gus was pale-faced, grim, and dazed. It was over so swiftly.

"Attempted murder or suicide. I can't figure it," he said at last.

Fats shook his head. "I know a lots of hoppies, I even used some myself, and I could maybe explain all of them and me, but this ain't the right beat. It don't swing."

They took a cab to Bellevue, numbed by the dull brain-pounding of the desperate flight and the bitter end of it.

The internist had passed the word on to the staff. She was already out of emergency and in a private room.

Gus made the financial arrangements at the desk before going on up. There was no hurry. She'd be sick for weeks. She'd be climbing walls and screaming. She'd be sneaking pills and shots of whatever.

She was a lost Nefertiti seeking the peace of the pyramid tomb with golden bracelets and sacred cats. In everyone's mind except Gus's, she was a goner.

On the next floor they met the doctor in charge, a man whose bulbous head was shaved clean.

"Close," he said. "Very close. An hour later, she'd have gone too far to come back."

"But how is she right now?"

"We've antidoted the drug and she's out of the coma," the doctor said carefully. "I'll have to notify the police, of course."

"You'll what?" Gus asked, puzzled. He thought of her as being sick, not a criminal.

"It's the law. We'll have to have a policewoman in her room before she goes to jail."

"What the hell are you talking about?" Gus stared at the doctor, who was looking off at a wall.

"Hopheads is illegal," Fats explained, " 'specially here."

"So what?" Gus asked. "Everything's illegal if you want to make a case. Maybe you better not make a report like that for a while, Doctor."

"I'm sorry," the doctor said, "we have our ethics and obligations."

"You just think saying sorry is sorry, but, Doctor, you'll feel a lot sorrier with a nice forty-five-caliber hole between your eyes," Gus blazed.

Gus was tired, he was shaken, he was bitterly disappointed, but he could stand all this. He just couldn't stand mealy-mouthed piety.

"Are you threatening me?" the doctor asked coldly.

Gus whipped out a .45 and laid the barrel against the shiny pate, utterly disgusted with the politeness of official murder. He knew what life was behind bars, knew what it would do to Bessie.

"I'm telling you just once," Gus said, "you make a peep, you're a dead doc. You do anything less than the best, you're wiped out, and that's my promise to you."

"I see," said the doctor carefully. "Well, you know papers get lost unaccountably every day."

"Of course." Gus slipped the pearl-handled Colt back in its holster. "We'd like to visit her now."

"Right this way," the doctor said, leading them down a linoleum corridor to an open doorway. "Try to cheer her up."

She was in a white cotton robe in the white bed in a white room staring at the ceiling.

"Hi, Lady," Gus said. "How are you?"

"I'm not sure, Gussie," she said, a tear gathering up and falling like dew from a cornflower. "I'm alive. Worthless, but alive."

"You'll make it back ten times over," Gus said.

"No," she said, "I just blew it on goofer dust. That's just what I did. What did they say when I didn't show?"

"They don't know yet," Gus said.

"How come?" she asked, her voice reedy, near to singing.

"The show doesn't start for a couple hours yet," Gus said.

"Can I still make it?" she asked.

"Not this time," Gus said. "But there'll be other dates."

"I tried to call you, Mr. Beautiful," she said softly. "I tried to tell you I was losin', but you wasn't home."

"I had a meet with Mickey Zirp," Gus said.

"Oh, you big doll," she murmured. "I figured you was out two-timin' your old lady."

"Crazy," Gus said. "There was that day in the room where Jim died I saw you and I knew right then we belonged to one another, and nothing can ever change that."

Another tear welled up and roamed down the sleek bronze of her cheek.

"I dunno why I did it," she said. "I used to kind of go for a little coke, but never heroin. Seemed like my friends would sniff a little coke, and then switch onto the H. They really go with that hard stuff, but I'm just not all that much."

"They have names?" Gus asked.

"Wally and May, but don't blame them. They just do what they feel like doin'. You want to punish someone, take it out on me."

"Nobody's going to punish you," Gus said. "You'll stay here awhile till you get your strength back, then back to good old K.C. with me."

"Sounds so beautiful," she said, singing it instead of saying it. "You sound so beautiful. But, Gus, how can I live if I don't keep that date?"

"You will." Gus shook his head. "Get some rest. I'll be by to-morrow morning and see how you're doing."

"Good night, Mr. B.," she said, closing her eyes.

"Hey," he said gruffly, "I get a kiss, don't I?"

"Darlin', darlin' Gus." She tried to hold back her quicksilver tears.

He kissed her warm lips gently, longingly, a seal of promise.

In the hall, Gus held his forehead in his hand. He had to lean a moment against the white wall. He heard Fats saying, "Can you think of how many people have leaned against this wall, thinking that their lives had gone busted?"

"Why can't a man be a man?" Gus nodded. "Why can't people just be people? Their business is to help each other to a better life, why don't they do it?"

"Let's go, Mr. Gus," Fats said. "You'll be stuck in the hospital yourself if you don't get some rest."

They rode in a cab back to the Van Wingerden and took a dou-ble room.

In the shower Gus washed the muck of soul sweat off his red skin and out of the pitted scars of his body, feeling the terrible loss of something. Not Bessie, surely, she was all right now, but a rare loss of hope.

He was reaching for a towel when Fats answered the phone. Gus couldn't hear what was being said, and Fats managed to keep his face away.

Hanging up the phone, he turned to Gus and said simply, "She's gone."

"Gone? What the hell you mean, gone?" Gus yelled.

"Disappeared. She had a hundred-dollar bill in her sock, grabbed a cab, and that's all they know."

Gus was dressing as fast as he could. Where would she go? Where could she go? Gus couldn't believe she'd go out hunting her suppliers, and yet wondrous were the ways of junkies. Sleepily terrifying were the ways of hopheads. You never knew: to each his own and God bless the child.

He knew right then where she'd gone.

Gus checked his watch. Ten of nine. "Call a cab, Fats, we're going."

"Yessir. Where we going?" Fats had the phone to his ear.

"Carnegie Hall."

Fats stared at him. "It'll kill her," he said, his voice cracking. "The doc said her heart was too ragged to do anything."

"It's her game," Gus said.

The cab was waiting and ready. Fats gave the cabbie the order and the driver hit the gas and burned rubber.

"You got tickets?" the hook-nosed driver asked once they were sailing at top speed up Park Avenue.

"No," Gus said, "we'll try the door."

"Heck of a big crowd. May not even be standing room."

The cabbie turned in alongside the curb near the great brownstone and granite-slabbed hall.

Gus, big and chesty, and Fats, a ball of butter, hurried into the milling mob before the great doors. Policemen were trying to lend an air of authority as the mob swirled and howled for admission.

Gus made it to the door, where a man in soup and fish stood repeating tiredly, "Nothing left. Nothing left, not even standing room."

Gus screened his movements by moving in close to the man. He slipped a fifty-dollar bill into his hand, glared at him, ready to strike him dead.

Two tickets materialized into Gus's hand.

The man said loudly, "Nothing left. Nothing left. Admission to ticket holders only," and, glancing nervously and wisely at the mob, said in a stage voice, "You have tickets, sir?"

"Tickets," Gus said, handing back the pasteboards.

"Very wise of you to think ahead." The man smiled and rolled his eyes at the angry and disappointed mob. "Prudence always pays."

The tickets were supposed to be for standing room, but inside the foyer was so packed, there actually wasn't even that.

"That gent's coining himself a fortune," Fats said.

Their words were overwhelmed by a burst of applause as the great golden curtain opened though they could barely see through the tiptoed mob.

"Have to get closer," Gus said.

"A long time back I played organ here," Fats said. "I can get us in some more, but we'll miss the first set."

"Go," Gus said.

Using his round body like a tugboat, and maintaining a steady stream of gentle apology, Fats assaulted the solidly packed mob straining to hear a note of music, or see a spangle of performer. The mob resisted them en masse, but Fats knew his work and intended to go where he aimed.

Gus heard a lovely note that only Bessie could sing, but it was lost in the coughs and grunts and rumbles and whispers and shushings of the mob.

They squeezed through the ranks of people until Fats had to stop for breath. He had to jump high to see over the bodies ahead of him.

"Murder," he groaned, "even the aisles is packed. Anybody yelled fire, there'd be ten thousand casualties."

But getting his bearings, he gallantly barged off again toward the side aisle so crowded Gus didn't think humanity could squeeze so close without breaking bones. Every tactile contact was made as they moved through. Those standing and watching enrapt were spoon to spoon, their legs and abdomens and entire bodies moving together to a rhythm set up by the band on the stage and bounced back by the solid man-and-woman audience locked together.

But it was too slow-going. Another set was finished. There was wild applause for something Gus hadn't seen or even heard, except for the one true note which assured him Bessie was there and would sing her heart out one way or another.

They made it through another section of chockablock folk to a small island where he could see and hear. The crowd was transfixed as she sang, as she phrased, as she lived. The big band was reveling, playing its own music, forgetting the stage, ignoring the prestigiousness of the occasion, showing a bare behind and a black back of the hand, not scoring, not paying off old marks, but wildly living it up among themselves and for those who could wildly listen, well, welcome all!

Oh, and she looked lovely away down there in a white polka-dotted blue silk gown with the white gardenias in her tall coiffed hair.

She was singing high, wide, and handsome, recklessly, playing back to Pres's sax, bouncing off Cozy's hides, noodling with Teddy's rippling keys and Basie's one finger on the eighty-eight, and getting it all in, all her own joy sounds and dying beats too, jousting with Eldridge's horn, cakewalking with Benny's licorice stick and Jack's slush-pump.

The hall echoed with applause when she finished "I Can't Get Started with You," and in the clamor the duo was able to move to another small area at the side.

Now she was singing "Them There Eyes," and catching them all up in her net of harmonies, her flashing eyes and the ultra-feminine stance she unconsciously gave away.

From Gus's viewpoint, over the round heads of thousands of attentive people, he could still see the thrust of unconquerable thigh and the demanding accent of her tall neck, insisting that this was a human moment, and if it weren't, she would make it so, and that those with eyes and ears would participate or she would die trying to give it to them without a sense of contempt. It was that vital. She encompassed them all truly, sharing it all out with them. Without any tricks, she opened the veins and filled the cups and asked for nothing except this moment of union with her.

She seemed more alive than ever in the long view but you could see only the stance and gesture, and only hear that voice carrying like the poignant cry of mankind aborning.

She ended the set with "I'll Never Be the Same," and you could laugh or cry, you could smile or die, it was so great.

When the curtain closed there was a rustle and rumble and a writhing of the multitude, but not one gave up his seat or moved from this place.

Valiantly Fats made a last effort, elbowing down a sloping aisle, trying to bear to the right, knowing where he was going in the peapod of humanity, but having no sure way of getting there.

Until at last, with Gus jammed close behind, he reached a small door in the corridor's wall.

"Only room for one," Fats told Gus. "Get going."

Gus slipped through the unobtrusive door, found himself in an ancient dark tunnel. It was so much like the hole in Leavenworth it gave him chills, but a small point of light beckoned at the other end. At the end of the tunnel, a series of steps led up toward the light.

He hurried. The night was late. The evening nearly done and the

unvoiced question hard in his mind: Could she finish? Could she
sustain the rainbow high she'd built, and send it off the top?

Now he could hear the band echoing down into the tunnel and
her own incredible voice swinging. Cautiously he climbed to the
light. His eyes came level with a floor, across the floor he saw a
pant leg, then he saw the doubled-up bands and Bessie right in
front of his eyes.

Great beads of sweat poured off their faces and they were moving in unity and playing in their own bubble of harmony. The
great Count, the great Pres and Ben, the great Art and Benny, the
great Jack, the great Satch on horn, the great Walter on bass. And
in front of them all, she stood in silken polka-dot sheath, fresh
gardenias as always in her hair, smiling like a happy kid and working like a horse, bringing her entire life and soul to bear on this
moment, a moment she couldn't be cheated of come hell or high
water.

As Gus's eyes adjusted to the light, he realized he was actually
onstage, in the prompter's box normally used in the opera season.

She was singing again, coming in like a bird, touching a twig
and taking off again, carrying the melody, passing it around for
the rest of the swingers to riff and jam on.

Once she stepped back so that he could see her face. Her eyes
looking out at the vast audience were hard set to do the work and
keep command, but oh, they were tired. He could see the force
of muscle in her face keeping those eyes open and alive, he could
see the strength it took of the body to put the gesture into the moving head and hands, the enormous effort it took to make the legs
move loose in the knee and ankle and send along some bounce
to the toes.

Oh yes, she smiled, oh yes, her eyes glittered brightly, but she
was a dying creature.

Gus wanted to leap out of the box, hold her and say, "No, no
no, no more, you've given enough," but it was her game, not his.
Her life, her death, hers alone.

She noticed the new shadow in the box, and, perhaps thinking it
was Marster Death himself, gave him a wink and a wave of an
arm, a magnificent gesture of energy, and the band swung into
the tune "I Can't Give You Anything but Love, Baby," and that

"baby" she sang shook the whole hall, just shook it like an earth-
quake.

And stepping back again, she saw it was Gus in the box, and
made the sign of thumb on forefinger, saying, it's all O.K., her
eyes terrifyingly tired, but squeezing up the last ounce of energy
she had, she sang the last time to him, to the crowd and to the
funny little world out there that for her had come and gone, and
come and gone.

O and she sang love to them all—love, love, love. That's all
I've got plenty of and all you've got, baby, and that's all I can give
you and it's all yours—until that lucky day, baby . . .

And the great golden curtain slowly closed across the tumult
of applause.

It would have ended on that had the audience not wanted more
love, more and more. Encore! Encore! She started to kneel or
crumple like an ancient papyrus husk of a creature, but Benny
lifted the band into the killing encore number, "Longtime Love."

The music fired her, lifted her again beyond physical endur-
ance. The heavy golden curtain swept aside and she stood in the
spotlight, a vibrant, energetic, laughing, swinging black dame giving it all she had.

> "I live a long long time, baby
> Because I love a lot
> I love a long long time, baby
> Because all I've got—
> Is my longtime love for you."

The band members couldn't see. It was their business to make
the swing, and the husks drifted off her being as she died swinging
like a gate with a great grin and a meaning and a shot of coke and
a lotta life, baby, and that's how she went out singing one helluva
high note.

The curtain closed as she started to fall. Gus leaped out of the
box to the stage, catching her before she hit the boards.

"What is it?" the Count asked, his burnished, sweat-running
face utterly confused, his concentration unable to accept death
into the music-charged night. But seeing how it was without answer, he signaled that the curtain should remain closed, and as

the greatest jazzmen in the world congregated about Gus holding
the wasted body of his love, the burned-out husk of her who had
been once magnificent, his tears soaking into her black hair, the
Count struck the note on the piano.

Gus was conscious that she had died the way she wanted to die.
But he couldn't quite believe the word, or the act, or the meaning
of death as related to his woman. She was still young, still powerful, and now he held her while she passed from change to change
and shade to shade of times he could only dream about when there
would be another day and another night and that love again.

Every man onstage loved her. And when the Count punched
the key note with his stubby first finger, Artie took another note
and Shirley another and Pres another, behind the curtain as the
applause on the other side rolled and beat as a surf storming, and
their upbeat tune rambled and stomped back through the opening
curtain and Gus stood fixed there in the spotlight, cradling his
only woman.

Jamming, all of them jamming for Bessie, right on to "The Saints
Go Marching In."

"Oh, when the Saints . . . when the Saints . . . go marchin'
in . . . " Jack's tailgate trombone blasting it out in a fury, Ben
razzing it with a spurious joy, Satch's horn and all the gates screaming a high mad wail, swinging, baby, baby, swinging for her.

"Oh, when them Saints! Oh, Oh, them Saints! Go marchin'
in . . . !"

In the audience no one stirred. They saw the heavy gold curtain
opening, they saw a big blond man facing them, holding their dark
angel like a sleeping child. They saw him turn and slowly carry
her away, the curtain closing for the Lady.

TWELVE

MOLDY, DRIPPING HOURS. Stiff face and empty mind. His grief never changed; it overpowered him.

One warm morning Fats went with Gus to the big river and sowed the heavy stream with her ashes.

As they walked from the bridge ramp, Gus's mind was so overwhelmed he hardly noticed the gray folks keeping warm in wrappings of old newspapers which promised prosperity around the corner. Now there were soup lines and bread lines, now there were human beings trying to grin in the teeth of the cold nights, bucking each other up, and a searing drought had come across the prairie.

So overwhelmed was his mind he hardly heard the headlines being shouted in the street: "Prohibition repealed! Booze legal!"

Men, not schoolboys, were selling papers. A nickel was a nickel, if there was no truck to drive or house to build, a man could sell a Kansas City *Star* and make a penny, or he could lay down and die.

"Boss, I'm 'sposed to cut a platter in Chicago next week," Fats said. "I'm goin' to have to leave you with old Salty and the boys."

"I'm all right," Gus said. "You go ahead. It's all over anyway. If you ever need something, look for me in Dodge City."

"Dodge City?" echoed Babe Saltz, staring at Gus from behind his desk. "You've still got enemies—and we ain't settled the score for Miss Crispus."

"You find that pair, Wally and May, let me know," Gus said.

"And tell the boys, I'll see 'em in the garage on my way out."

Gus packed the worn old machine gun in its banjo case and went out the door to the garage.

Salty had spread the word and they were morosely smoking and chewing tobacco, slouched against the wall, studying the greasy brick floor. Gilpin's Gang, as tough a bunch of men ever put together to fight or work. They didn't look up at him. They rubbed their hands together and gnawed at wooden matches and would not look at him. The sick silence of the garage rang like a bell in Gus's consciousness. He couldn't bear to leave them like that.

Gus straightened his back, his eyes flashed, his words roared out harshly. "Look, you guys, we been friends, but if you're going to go sullen on me, I'm going to have to knock the tar out of a couple of you, so you'll remember who's boss! You ain't a gang of sec-ond-raters, you're my gang and that means you're first class all the time—good times or hard times—so shape up!"

The men came to attention, their eyes flashed with manly re-sponse.

"You work for Babe like you've worked for me or I'll be back here on somebody's tail! Now—any time any of you ever get in a bind you can reach me in Dodge City. I mean it."

He shook Babe's hand first, and, going toward the door, he seemed casually to pause by each man standing at attention, pat a shoulder, shake a powder burned hand, saying, "So long, Guns. So long, Lafe. So long, Lefty. So long, Cracker. So long, Catfish. So long, Fid. So long, Steve. So long, Pinetop. So long, Johnny." And they, not speaking, simply telling him with their eyes. "So long, Fats. So long, Cirilio. So long. So long."

At the door old wizened Salty stood, taking care of the heavy money satchel, and before Gus could speak, he growled, "You ain't ridin' no cab so long as I can drive. I'll take you to the station."

"Thanks, Salty," Gus agreed, and put the banjo case next to the satchel on the seat, turned and faced each of those hard, blood-stained men, fixed them with his eyes, his tough glower saying plainer than any spoken word never to let down the principles they had fought for.

The open Packard roadster roared off. Salty never ceased trying be the hottest driver in town.

"We have a few minutes to spare," Gus said. "Go by way of the gas house. I'd like to see the school."

"Sure, boss," Salty said and swung off on Fourteenth Street toward the gas house.

The building shone through the slum jungle like a vision of the holy grail. Its long, floating arches of polished granite were inspired by an Axum temple of another age, a Masakin five-turreted dwelling, a Basuto theater. Frank Wright had put it all together the way Gus had said Mr. Fitzgerald wanted it. Not just a box of bricks full of desks and a couple of bathrooms. Wright had found his design and brought it back and built it as an uncorruptible temple of the black. Its presence unwittingly made the gas house one of the seven monstrosities of the world.

Arches, intersecting vaults and arches, reminiscent of minarets and Kilimanjaro, and long flat planes of open glass like infinite deserts and buttes all nearly obscured by cool hanging gardens and jungle growth. A fountain of pure water splashed into a long pool mirroring the black flag of Mohamat and Old Glory flying side by side.

Wright had insisted it should be an entity of itself, a work of art in three dimensions because of its importance in the lives of the people, and Gus had not only given him carte blanche but had gone directly to Mr. Pendergast, insisting that the project not be pirated by white bosses, nor sabotaged by the whites of other neighborhoods who preferred things to be as they were or worse. Mr. Pendergast paid his debt to Gus with his absolute backing of the integrity of the project, not only of the building but of the faculty and its wide-ranging program of black sociology, though it cost him a few dollars and a few friends.

As a memorial for Jim Crispus, it was more than a school; it was a monument to a million poor uneducated good people who had lived so that their children could have this chance.

Near the entrance walk, by the pool, was a simple granite slab upon which was carved "Jim Crispus School" and the motto: "*Tarika sufiyya*"—the Sufi way.

"People are coming from a thousand miles around just to look at this," Salty said.

"I hope they see it," Gus said.

The green-turfed junglous playgrounds were full of rousting,

yipping children. A little boy in a tree waved at them as they
drove slowly by, and as Gus waved back, he flashed the bright-
est smile on earth.

"God bless the child that's got his own," Gus said.

He didn't let Salty come into the station. He punched his old
friend on the shoulder and said, "Take care, Salty—don't get any
parking tickets."

And he was gone before Salty could even start to cry.

"Dodge City! Dodge City!" the conductor hailed. "Dodge City
next!"

He came along and spoke the word pleasantly to Gus. "Your
stop, sir."

Carrying the satchel and the banjo case, Gus stepped off the
steel tread to the brick ramp. Home. How does it feel? Everyone
feels it and knows it, too. The alien returns to familiarity.

An old man sold him a paper, and Gus saw the headline:
"G-Men Kill Dillinger, Betrayed by Lady in Red!"

"Betrayed by a bribe," he said aloud and threw the paper away
in disgust.

But the day of the hunter was coming. You could feel it. The
old mavericks were being swapped off for the syndicate's safety.
Mr. G-man could build up a sensational name as a crime stopper
by ambushing the maligned Robin Hoods, while hiding the organized Syndicate as they devoured the country from within.

Well, that's the way they work the shell game, Gus argued with
himself as he got into a cab, aware that only a few insiders like
himself were in on the secret take-over.

"I'll try the old hotel," Gus answered the cabbie's question.

"That'd be?"

"The Stockman's Rest."

" 'Fraid that's before my time. They must've tore it down in
'twenty-nine."

"Is the Dodge House still standing?"

"Yessir. It ain't too fancy, but it's reasonable and clean."

The old cab turned a corner and came onto Front Street where
the familiar hotel still stood. An ugly sign—"ROOMS FIFTY CENTS
AND UP"—hung above the original stained-glass fan window over
the door.

On the porch facing the street was a glider and other benches

for idle men to sit upon in the warm weather and watch the action
go by.

Inside, he found the hotel was comfortable as an old shoe, and
his room was large and clean with a high, wallpapered ceiling.

The first morning, after a breakfast of steak and eggs at Del-
monico's, he sat on the porch, hoping to see an old face or a cheerful event. But the great Depression was locked as hard upon
Dodge City as it was upon Kansas City or New York City. Skinny
old farmers walked the streets in patched overalls, their wives in
hoarded ancient dresses and their children inconspicuously bare-
foot.

There'd been no rain, the young wheat was already burned off,
and the topsoil was shifting under the constant winds.

Out of the corner of his eye he saw the desk clerk at the door
with an older, heavier man bearing the obvious stamp of the lawman.

Gus had expected it. His name was not a screaming headliner,
but he was known. Especially in this town, he was known.

The marshal came over to him, cleared his throat loudly, so
that Gus would turn and acknowledge him.

Gus wanted no trouble, no more bloody storms, no more hate,
no more pushing and elbowing to the trough. He kept his face calm
and friendly and spoke first.

"Hello, Marshal Darby. Marshal Grover Darby."

"And you're Gus Gilpin."

Gus didn't extend his hand. "Nice morning," he said.

"Let's not beat around the bushes," the paunchy lawman said.
"What are you doin' here?"

"This is my old home town." Gus said.

"Your kinfolks all gone to California. Ain't nothin' here for
you."

"Couple headstones out at St. Olaf's," Gus replied mildly.

"You sure you ain't carryin' any grudges?"

Gus smiled. "No. Life's too short."

The marshal's lawful eyes bored into Gus's, trying to find out
what was truth and what was not. "Lemme tell you somethin',
Gilpin. You may be a big man in Kansas City, but in my town
you're no better than anyone else. One funny move outa you, you'll
regret it."

"Goes both ways, Darby," Gus replied. "You're elected to protect the citizens and I expect the same protection as anyone else."

"The way I hear it you don't need any help."

"I'm retired. Hung up the Colts and took the firing pin out of the old banjo. I'm goin' to set here and rock in peace."

Gus leaned back in the chair and closed his eyes as the marshal left.

Down the street was the Valley Bank, where, so long ago it seemed more like a story he'd read in school, he had horse-whipped a ruddy, lecherous usurer. He wondered if Hundertmarx were still alive.

A bowed-over, thin-necked woman came out of the bank with a bucket of soapy water and dumped it in the street. She dabbed at the brass door handle tiredly, and went back inside with the empty bucket. Somehow the scrawny old scrubwoman had stirred a memory in him.

After the raucous whistle over the city hall howled high noon right on the exact second as it did every day except Sunday, Gus strolled up and down the low hills of the business district. He looked for the old saloon Donald Dodge had kept for so long, where Lu had found the only welcome and comfort, but it was as empty as the livery stable next door.

There were still plenty of horses and wagons though. For most farmers it was all they had for transport. And those who'd let their wagons rot in the fields while they splurged on flivvers found that you could hitch a team to a Model-T chassis and it would serve as a wagon rolling on worn-out rubber tires filled with wheat.

No matter how ludicrous, they could do it because they had a basic sense of humor. You had to be able to smile to drive an old retired team of draft horses ahead of a gutted-out car body with a steering wheel and stuffed seats.

He paused in front of the bank. There once had been an iron rail where old men had hunkered and chewed and ruminated, but no one sat on the railing any more, because the banker had bolted spikes upright into the rail.

Gus noticed a figure at the plate-glass window staring at him. The figure moved to the door and came down to the sidewalk. A big-bellied man with a pleated neck and scanty wisp of hair combed forward over the bald pate.

Again Gus refused the hand.

"You're Gus Gilpin. I heard you were in town," the banker said jovially. "I'm J.J. Hundertmarx, still running the old hometown bank."

"I'd suppose by now you'd be running a little more than that," Gus said dryly.

"I don't know what you mean." Hundertmarx' smile thinned to a sliver.

"Oh, I'd guess you'd own the grain elevators and the feed yard and the sales yard. I'd guess you own most of the buildings on this street and are taking up tax lands as fast as the people leave."

"You sound like a radical to me," Hundertmarx said. "And coming from a common hoodlum, it spells trouble."

"Yeah," Gus said. "And speaking of trouble, who's that lady scrubbin' your floors?"

The banker flushed and turned away. "That's none of your business." Stopping at the door, he added, "Gilpin, you better move on while you still can."

"Don't push me too hard. I'd hate to take the horse whip to you."

Again the banker flushed dull scarlet.

Gus grinned at the beefy back of the banker. He felt a little better, getting something off his chest. His blood was starting to circulate again. He took a deep breath and walked on down the street with a stronger stride and a new bounce to his step.

In the afternoon Gus sat on the porch and watched the people moving to and fro on the street. He could see the marks of privation, either in their clothes or on their thin, pale faces.

And Gus was very aware that no man was more law-abiding or more patriotic than the American farmer who now restlessly roamed the streets of Dodge City. Gus had seen too many violent scenes sparked and played out not to be aware of how this one was building.

What the prisoners had done to Leavenworth could be as justifiably done by the dispossessed farmers to the city of Hundertmarx.

Gus promised himself he'd stay out of it. Surely he could find a way of life where one could do the right thing and still stay out of trouble.

"What are you lookin' at?" Marshal Darby's voice interrupted Gus's thoughts.

"Why?" Gus asked, startled awake.

"Hundertmarx's worryin' about his bank. You been studyin' it mighty close."

Gus laughed. He laughed until Darby growled a curse at him. A moment of anger hit Gus inside.

"Beat it, Darby," he said. "Go pick up your split off the dice game behind Poffenburg's Cleaners."

Darby's face dropped a second. How could this sleepy gangster know about that game so soon?

"Sure, Hero," Gus said, "don't forget to pat some trusting little kid on the head as you go."

Never make friends that way, Gus told himself and then cheered as he thought of Hundertmarx over there in his bank worrying about the K.C. gangster. He'd better be worrying about these little knots of faded farmers trudging up and down the street.

Again his musings were interrupted, this time by a slight man wearing a tweed suit with a tiny scimitar in the lapel. The man wore a Masonic ring, and his black shoes were shined. His eyes were straight and unafraid, and his nose had once been broken and set improperly.

"Mr. Gilpin," the man said, "I'm Ross McClanahan. We went to school together a long time ago out east of town."

Gus shook Ross's hand. "Hi, Ross," he said mildly. "Lot of water over the dam since we learned our ABCs to the tune of old Stuffy's hickory stick."

Ross laughed, glad to be remembered. "I'm glad you're back," he said. "Town needs some new blood."

Gus looked at him sharply, then relaxed.

"My guess is Mr. Hundertmarx has his hooks into you like he has everybody else, and if you don't want to be foreclosed on, you better speak low to me," Gus said quietly.

Ross's eyes swept swiftly over to the bank's window. "Hell with him. I been up, now I'm down, so I'll get up again."

"What do you do?" Gus asked, glad someone in town wasn't totally whipped.

"Ford agency," McClanahan said.

"Could you tell me who's the scrubwoman at the bank?" Gus asked.

"That's old Sally McCoy. She was in school with us, as I recall."

"She was." Gus felt tired and weary.

"I was wondering, so long as you was stayin' in town, you might be interested in buying a car. Then you could travel around some. See the country."

"Ford?" Gus asked. "Well, I don't know . . . They any good?"

"The best. All the big bank robbers drive 'em. Heck, they can outrun anything. Ain't a sheriff anywhere can catch 'em."

"I guess I'd like a yellow one," Gus said.

"I think I might have a yellow one." Ross smiled.

"A sedan with the top that folds back?" Gus asked.

"I been stuck with that touring phaeton all year," Ross said. "But Henry said take it or get out, so I took it."

"I need a driver. Not any kind of a driver, but one that knows all the back roads, and one that can keep his mouth shut, and one that's honest and wants to stay honest."

"Happens my boy Jack is exactly that. He's just the one."

"Jack?" Gus asked, thinking it over. "Well, I've always had good luck with them. They name the best ones Jack."

"Just say when," Ross said.

"No hurry. Tomorrow morning's fine. I'll pay cash," Gus said mildly.

Ross's eyes bugged out. "Cash? This car'll come to near two thousand."

"I know the price of 'em, Ross," Gus said. "How old is your boy Jack?"

"He's sixteen. And he's free all summer. And probably all winter too, if you need him."

"Fine," Gus said. "I'm glad you ain't worried I might teach him how to rob old widows."

"Gus," Ross said, "we faced old Stuffy, I ain't worried about you any more'n you're worried about me."

In the morning, when Gus stepped out on the porch, he saw a group of gray men in their washed-out, pale overalls gathered around a bright mustard-yellow touring car. It looked like a tinny flivver compared to the big armored limousines Gus knew.

Ross was on the curb by the car with a leather briefcase, talking conversationally to the men who were admiring the audacity of the color and the machine's powerful engine.

Nearby was a youth in corduroy pants and sport shirt, a nondescript kid, unformed, unnoticeable except perhaps for his big jug ears. Gus caught the boy's steady eyes and decided he could see the road and then some.

Ross greeted Gus on the step, a big smile shining with gold crowns. "There you are, Gus, right on time."

"Just put all the papers in the glove compartment," Gus said.

"Yessir. I'll give you a receipt." Ross wanted the money, but he didn't want to push.

"Don't bother." Gus pulled two thousand-dollar bills out of his vest pocket and put them in Ross's hand.

"Holy smoke," Ross whispered, staring at the denomination.

"They're good," Gus said, "and they're clean too."

"I'm not a bit worried. I just wish I could keep 'em for souvenirs," Ross said. "You know, I've got the fork that Teddy Roosevelt ate with when he was out in Colorado."

"I travel light myself." Gus smiled. "This your boy?"

"Jack, this is Mr. Gilpin."

"Call me Gus, Jack."

Gus looked into each of the gathered men's faces and saw no malice or hatred, only the forlorn, stunned look of the man separated from his earth.

"You fellas like to go for a ride?"

They looked at each other.

"Don't see why not," they finally agreed. "Ain't nothin' else to do."

Gus put one of them in between himself and Jack and the other three in the back seat.

The man in front said, "I don't guess you remember me, but I'm Benny Peacock. I was a friend of Lu's."

"I remember now. You married Maudie Koberman," Gus said. "Drought kind of hard on you?"

"Wiped us out. Cows took pneumonia. Dust won't let the seed germinate. Had three hundred twenty acres of good ground, but Hundertmarx's got it now."

"What'll he do with it?"

"He'll match it up with the rest of our farms, get federal loans and then hire a man with a tractor to work it. Used to be able to keep a whole family on a quarter section, but if Hundertmarx gets his way, it'll be one sharecropper every square mile."

"And the families that used to live out here—the Brewers, the

Zitzmans, the Lunquists, the Poffenburgs and Veitgengrubers—what about them?"

"On relief. Or off to California. Ain't nothin' to do about it."

The scene that met his eyes as Jack tooled the yellow phaeton down the back roads was sickening. Empty dwellings, small monuments to enormous labors, leaned like forgotten sepulchers over the dark, dusty plains.

"I think she'll be a little prettier after it rains," Benny Peacock said.

"It'll all come back," one of the men said. "A little rain and these fields'll bloom like the garden."

"Next time we'll have sense enough to lay a little by."

Occasionally they would see a diehard family, still hanging on. Threadbare washing whipping on the line, a few scroungy chickens scouting for grasshoppers, thin cattle gnawing at the fence posts. A farm wife, wearing her husband's overalls to save her last dress, would wave, and the man out wandering the shifting silt with his sons wouldn't even look up.

Half a mile on down the road toward the Goshen Hills, Gus saw a little knot of people in a farmyard where cars and wagons were parked.

Ben sadly shook his head and explained, "That's the Armsbury's farm. Looks like they're bein' sold out."

"Better pull in, Jack," Gus rumbled. "Might be something there we need."

Jack turned into the once prosperous farm and parked beside Marshal Darby's official car.

Gus nodded to Darby, who was fiddling with a proclamation and a list of goods.

Hundertmarx stood to one side, counting the crowd, and counting the line of farms he was picking up alongside Goshen Road. You couldn't beat that little worker named Interest. He looked so small, but he never quit working for you.

Gus looked over the goods for sale. Set on the kitchen table in the yard was the family china, and stacked neatly by were the patchwork comforters and the beds that had slept a family of honest Americans. The old man and his helpmate stood by their little pile of goods, the last they had, expecting nothing except the ritual of squaring accounts, dispossession and abandonment.

"All right," the marshal said, "I hate this as much as anybody, but it's the law." He glanced at Gus. "You want me to read the proclamation?"

"Does it say you're goin' to sell these folks out?" Gus asked.

Darby looked at the banker.

"Minimum bid on this quarter section of land is two hundred fifty dollars, plus eighty-three dollars' interest. Altogether that makes three hundred thirty-three dollars cash money," Hundertmarx said.

" 'Sposin' nobody bids that much?" Gus asked.

"I'll bid that much," Hundertmarx said, "don't worry about that."

"I'm ready to start the bidding," the marshal said, looking around at Moses Peterson, the local junk dealer, and a few neighbors.

Gus studied the little crowd. The old farmer's wife looked too much like his own work-broken mother had looked. The farmer looked too much like a human being who is shaking to pieces because he'd done what he was taught to do, and Gus couldn't stand to see any honest man break. Heck with it, do or die.

"Mind if I say something, Marshal?"

Gus didn't wait for an affirmative; he simply stood as tall as he could and spoke as softly as he could.

"Seems to me you all are in the same fight. Somebody start to pass a hat around to help these poor neighbors out. You are all going to have to start stickin' together or go under separately, so dig deep and share out all you can."

Ben Peacock took his sweat-stained straw hat off and found a silver dollar in his pocket to start the collection. As the hat went from hand to hand, Gus continued to speak his thoughts.

"First thing I'd like to say is that I learned in the big drought of 1921 that out of the business end of a gun comes power. That ain't to say power by itself is any good—you can see how Hundertmarx is usin' his—but any man can have it, and it don't take much more'n a couple shotgun shells to even things up some."

The hat returned to Benny Peacock, who counted out thirty-four dollars in coins. The people were silent, wondering what was going to happen next.

"Put the money on the table, Benny," Gus said. "Now I'm not threatening anybody here because I know we all believe in de-

cency and helpin' our neighbors like always, so I'm makin' a bid
of thirty-four dollars for the whole shebang."

Gus moved close to Hundertmarx, who shifted his shined shoes
in the dust.

"Go ahead, Darby, see if you can get a higher bid."

Darby avoided the banker's eyes. He looked around at the
group. They were all standing straighter and their eyes were suddenly awake.

The dazed old farmer and his wife still couldn't believe a gangster would ever come to their aid and say the awful things he'd
just said. "Even it up." he'd said, and there right next to Momma's
comforters was the old twelve-bore goose gun and a half box of
shells. Why hadn't he thought of it? The old man nagged at himself. They break us like gelded horses. They break us like we was
mules or sheep.

Darby glanced at Gus and said loudly, "I'm not going to have
any trouble here. There'll be no threats of violence. I'll have law
and order or somebody will go to jail. Now, I've got a bid for
the land, anybody want to buy the household goods separate? The
stuff is worth fifty dollars easy."

"My bid was for the whole lot," Gus said. "Thirty-three for the
land and a dollar for the goods."

"You better take that fat banker out of here, Marshal, before
he opens his fat mouth." A young voice spoke.

One of the younger farmers, only a moment ago a faceless atom
of the shifting earth, now a determined man who saw how he
and his whole community were being looted by the person they
had most respected and admired and tried to imitate.

"Now look here, Marshal, I don't care about the money," Hundertmarx said, "but there's a principle of law here. This man is
conspiring armed rebellion, and that's the same as Bolshevism or
anarchy."

"Beat it, you blood sucker," the tall man said. "And when you
come around to foreclose on me, you better have the goddamned
Army with you, because I'm goin' to have every able-bodied friend
of mine in the county backin' me up."

"Boys, don't get too upset," Darby said. "The law is the law."

"Laws are made by men," Gus said, "for men. Likely neighbor
Hundertmarx can discover there's ways of extending your loans."

"Come on, Marshal, I've heard enough of this," Hundertmarx said. "I'm going to swear out a warrant for Gilpin, charging him with conspiracy to incite riot."

"You do that, Hundertmarx, and I'm goin' to have something to live for." Gus put his eyes flat onto the banker's shifting gaze. "I might just find out if you can bleed as hard as you can suck."

Hundertmarx's face fell apart under the words so easily modulated.

"You're all going to pay up or move out!" Hundertmarx yelled.

The crowd of ragged farmers started to move as a single mass toward the marshal and the banker. Their docile patience was not endless after all.

The marshal and the banker retreated. They roared their engines defiantly and drove down the road toward town.

The old lady pulled at Gus's sleeve and said, "I just can't believe it yet, young man. You done something I taught my boys was bad."

Little neighbor boys dressed in clean but hand-me-down overalls ran happily around the farmyard, sensing the worst was over.

Gus gestured toward them. "That's what it's all for. You teach 'em sometimes the law is right and sometimes it's wrong, but human, man-to-man decency is never wrong."

"We surely are much obliged," the old man said.

"What do you say we have a drink," Gus said, "and wish our neighbors well?"

He produced a quart of old honest bourbon and handed it to George Kaupke, the tall, lean man who'd spoken for them.

Kaupke lifted the bottle and said, "Well, by golly, here's to freedom!"

He tipped the bottle up and passed it on. "Now, boys," he said after he got his breath, "we got to watch the papers and see when the sales are comin' up and make damned sure we don't get sold out no more."

"But we still have to have some money," one little man said. "I ain't got thirty cents left."

"There's supposed to be federal aid to farmers on the way—"

"Chances are it's already available, but old Hundertmarx's been keepin' it quiet," Gus said. "I'll put up a stake to carry the work along till you can get the federal allotments and everyone gets on their feet."

"Well, I'll be go to blazes," Kaupke said. "You're square. I say we ought to run you for marshal."

"Well, I sure wouldn't sell you out," Gus said, grinning, "but I'm afraid my history's against me ever wearin' a badge."

"You sure have my vote," the old man said.

"Come on, Jack, let's roll," Gus said. "Anybody want to go along?"

"No, I guess not," Ben Peacock said. "We're goin' to have us a meetin'."

Jack had the engine warmed up and, as soon as Gus was settled, drove out the dirt road to the Goshen Hills Road.

"Mr. Gilpin . . ." Jack said tentatively.

"Gus," Gus said, "and don't say anything if it's about me."

"Yessir," the young driver said.

Next day Hundertmarx retaliated. The Dodge City *Sentinel* carried notices of several farms and chattel goods to be sold.

Tension in the town grew. The threadbare farmers were numerous, they talked more, grouped more, and planned their campaign.

Gus secretly put enough into the kitty to protect those most close to disaster.

Gus never attended another auction, but he heard the results. A thousand blue-dressed, organized farmers and their families would be waiting for the marshal and Hundertmarx. Nothing was sold and nothing foreclosed, and the kids would chant: "Banker, banker, you're a chancre, thank yer," or, "Marshal, Marshal, be my friend, go back home and try again."

Jack, the jug-eared boy, was the only one who knew how much Gus traveled through the country, checking up on the desperate situation with the countrymen and the poor people in their Hoovervilles by the hobo jungles. There was always a load of groceries to be delivered. Often they would stop at a poverty-stricken farm and beg a meal, and Gus would slowly draw out the host's problem. Often it was a widow woman who couldn't keep her family going because her man had worked himself to death trying to make wheat grow without rain, and under the plate Gus would leave a bill.

The banker was distraught and the doctor treated him for possible ulcers, but Marshal Darby was a cooler head. All he had to do was make a phone call.

"Give me Chicago," he told the operator. "A Mr. Michael Zirp at Daly's Soap Company."

He waited for the long call to connect across the country and find the man he knew could eliminate his problem.

"Zirp here."

"Marshal Darby calling from Dodge City."

"The merchandise there?"

"The offer still good?"

"Ten Gs. But it's got to be right."

"It's right, bring the money," Darby said, thinking that he could live a long time as a righteous old cowboy in Hollywood on ten thousand.

Hardly aware of Darby, and forgetting long ago his enemy, Zirp, Gus was in Abilene asking the district chief of the Federal Farm Loans Office, "When can they get their loans?"

"Just as soon as the local banking authorities cooperate."

"You're kidding," Gus said. "The banker's bleeding us dry."

"That's the law. The aid money passes through the banking channels so there's no mistakes."

"We can't wait for channels or red tape," Gus said. "It's life or death."

"Could you get a cooperative started?" The federal man knew the problem well enough.

"It's already started," Gus said, "but it's never had a name."

"Name it and bond it, then if you can get copies of the bank's records," the official said, "I'll personally see the loan money is deposited to your co-op."

"Let me use your phone," Gus said, and, without waiting for permission, called Benny Peacock at the Dodge House and told him what had to be done. Benny agreed to try.

Jack was parked at the curb.

"Back to Dodge," Gus said. "I just have to explain it to the co-op and they're on their way."

Jack didn't know what Gus was talking about. Once he asked, "Gus, why don't you drive yourself?"

"Bad arm," Gus said quietly, not wanting to talk about the bullet Romulus Zirp had put through the elbow. "You pick up my mail this morning?"

"Yessir. There's just this one letter," Jack said, handing over a plain dime-store envelope.

It was postmarked Kansas City.

"Dear Gus, How are you? We are fine. Regarding your query, we been looking and we finally caught up with Wally and May in Havana. Their last words was they was hired by Zirp to put down Miss C. Grapevine says Z has 10 Gs bounty on you. We're ready when you are. Your friend, Babe."

"Bad news?" Jack asked hesitantly, seeing the muscles go rigid in Gus's jaw.

"No," Gus said after a moment. "Just urgent business. Highball it for Dodge."

"Yessir," Jack said, and tramped on the hot V-8 until the speedometer was wobbling around eighty.

"That all she got?" Gus asked.

Jack eased it on up to ninety. "That's tops," he said.

"We oughta be back home in an hour then," Gus said, and closed his eyes, trying to get his thoughts sorted out.

They had deliberately overdosed Bessie just to get back at him. Only one mind had that capability, a mind Gus had never been able to understand because it thrived on pain and death.

"Jack, some day you may want to tell a story about how it was in the Middle West of the Twenties and Thirties, and maybe somebody'll bad-mouth me for killin' some folks. So remember I never killed anybody that didn't mean to kill me first, and I always gave them the first shot." Gus's voice was slow and weary.

"Yessir," Jack said, hardly listening, trying to keep cool as the overpowered phaeton threatened to take to the air.

Gus saw the rest of the pieces coming together. He'd fulfilled a purpose he hadn't known he was expected to fulfill, but it was nearly done.

The nucleus of co-operatives would spread out; the people would see the advantages of controlling their own lives and not leaving their destinies to unknown and distant traders, or be manipulated by the local bankers, hand in glove with the lawmen.

The price of freedom is eternal vigilance against the bankers, Gus thought as the little car hurtled up the road, its pale yellow lights hardly any help at all to the boy holding the throttle wide open.

"Do or die, Jack," Gus said so softly he didn't think the boy heard him.

But Jack replied, "Yessir, I believe it."

Soon the boy could see the glow of lights from Dodge in the distance, but he held the car to a full, flat-out ninety until Gus stirred.

"O.K., Jack, let's ease into town quietlike. I been thinking about some things that never added up right till just now. Cruise down the back street instead of Front."

"Yessir." Jack nodded. "Can I help out?"

"Look, Jack, you're a little young to get mixed up in gunplay."

"Mr. Gus," Jack said, "I know everything and everybody in Dodge and there's only two men who don't just plain-out worship you. And that's the marshal and Mr. Hundertmarx."

"There's one other somewhere," Gus said. "A monster. An honest-to-God, stinkin' animal, and he's got to come for me. The only reason he hasn't is because he never knew where I was," Gus said.

"How could he find out?"

"You just told me," Gus said suddenly. "That's it. Pull up."

Jack was totally confused but he pulled the car to the curb.

Gus put a bill in his hand. "Jack, you go to college next year on this. Now take the car and make sure it's greased and gassed and all ready to go tomorrow, because we may be going on a long, fast trip. I'm depending on you."

"You ain't firin' me?"

" 'Course not," Gus said, "but don't do anything dumb tomorrow, Jack. I mean, keep your head down."

"You need help, Mr. Gus?"

"No. That's what I'm trying to tell you," Gus said patiently, "don't mix in it. I'll handle it alone or die tryin'."

"Yessir, but you only got the one arm."

"Go on, Jack, get some sleep." Gus grinned. "You made a honey of a drive."

Gus sauntered off into the darkness, acting a lot more carefree than he felt. All the old senses that signaled danger were buzzing in his bloodstream.

He knew for sure he had to get those .45s under his arms again.

Easing quietly down the dark alley, he saw a cigarette glow behind the old hotel. He stopped and saw the shadowy figure of a man alone, watching the back of the hotel.

Gus had to know if it was a local countryman or an outsider. He needed some evidence, the last piece of the puzzle which at the moment existed only in his imagination.

The spotter was situated on a little platform where milk cans used to be delivered to the back of the creamery which faced the street behind the hotel. He couldn't be approached from behind or surprised from either side.

A bit of moonshine glittered on glass, and Gus picked up an ancient, heavy milk bottle. Carrying it by the neck, he lurched down the alley singing drunkenly, "Oh, Kaiser Bill went over the hill . . ."

The cigarette coal disappeared as Gus took to talking to himself. "Hey there, soldier, march straight. You been drinkin' on duty, sojer? Nosir, I ain't had a drop, hee hee. Hey, anybody like a little snort with a vet?" Hardly waiting for a reply, he answered himself, "Ain't nobody wants to drink with you, sojer, so you might as well drink by yourself."

Gus tipped the milk bottle like a quart of booze, coughed, and said, "Whooeee! That is good stuff! Prewar, sojer."

Staggering on, he came to the platform where someone with a gun waited and watched. Gus brought himself to a full halt and demanded of a telephone pole where he was and what was he doing out so late and who was his commanding officer and, getting no answer, Gus yelled, "By God, sojer, you want a drink of good rye whiskey? Or shall I just pour it out?"

"I'll have a drink," the shadowed presence said.

The voice shook him. It was Eastern. It was gutter. It was outside.

Pretending confusion, he said, "Hey, yessir, Cap'n, where are you?"

He saw the blue steel shine of gun in the darkness, saw it slip into a serge pocket, and watched the city man step forward on the platform.

"Gimme a little snort, buddy."

"Yessir, Cap'n!" Gus said, and, before the eyes could pick his face out of the darkness, swung the thick milk bottle as hard as he could. The bottle smacked; the city man fell without a sound.

Gus quickly dragged him into a coal bin and lighted a match over the face with glazed eyes.

No mistaking that map. It was Buzz Bonnanoes. No left ear. Starved-out face. Brow like an ape. A hit man. Straight from the Murder Incorporated catalogue. Gus tried to take his pulse, but there was none. A thin skull. Death was closed again. The gun in the pocket was a .38. Gus checked the bullets. Carved into dum-dums and rubbed with squashed beetles to make sickness along with maceration. Buzz Bonnanoes had lived many years by cold-blooded murder, and Gus felt no remorse about beating him to the punch.

He dragged the man back to the creamery platform and put the milk bottle in the stiffening claws. Give them something to worry about. At least it was out in the open.

Opening the rear door of the hotel and going up the stairs, Gus felt a great relief.

He knew his enemies. That was half the battle.

He could fight Zirp for pure joy.

He paused in front of his door and sniffed the air for cigarette smoke or a strange scent, but so far they just wanted to know where he was, and he'd fouled them up by being gone all day and most of the night.

He double-bolted the door inside and pulled the window shade down before turning on the lamp.

He broke down the pearl-handled .45s and cleaned them care-fully. He took the mellow old banjo out of its case and went through its pieces with just as much care. The firing pin was brand new.

Satisfied that he was armed, he massaged the stiffened elbow and went to bed. Tomorrow in the daylight Mickey Zirp was going to die or Gus Gilpin was going to die.

He slept like a log. He had nothing on his conscience. It was after four.

It was eleven when he awakened and he was half through shav-ing when he heard a knock at the door.

"Yes?" he said, gripping a .45 and standing by the door.

"It's Ben," the voice said. "Ben Peacock."

"You alone, Ben?" Gus couldn't fathom it. Ben surely wouldn't betray him. Yet he'd been certain the first knock on that door would be that of an enemy.

"I'm alone," Ben said. "I'd like to talk to you."

Gus opened the door and placed the .45 barrel on Ben's chin. "Alone?" Gus asked again.

Ben could only nod and barely that.

Gus let him in and bolted the door. Ben saw the other guns ready for action.

"How did you know?" he asked, his eyes wide. "I knew you were smart, but I didn't think you knew."

"Knew what?" Gus asked.

"About Reineke, our co-op man, going over to Hundertmarx's side last night."

"That's dynamite," Gus said. "Why would he do a thing like that?"

"Because Hundertmarx wouldn't release his files to us."

"That's not so bad as it sounds." Gus laughed. "I was expecting something else."

"Every farmer in our co-op will go wild. They'll figure Reineke took a bribe."

"Probably did," Gus said, trying to settle down his thinking.

He had to handle Zirp first, then he could settle the banker's hash. But suppose his luck ran out? Who else would bust those farmers out of their grooves?

"Where are they?" Gus asked.

"They been comin' into town since daybreak," Ben said, "and I'm afraid 'cause there's a lot of state cops been rolling in, too. Must be twenty extra cops loaded down with bombs and guns."

"Our boys got their fowling pieces?" Gus smiled.

"You're darned right," Ben said, "but they don't look like much against the troopers. What can we do?"

"What do you want to do?" Gus forced the question.

"We got to get ahold of those files," Ben said. "No way out of it. We don't mean to cheat anybody, but we got to have 'em or suck hind tit."

"So?" Gus pushed some more.

"You're asking family men with birdshot to try to fight a trained army."

"That army come right out of the prairie, just like you or me," Gus said.

"You mean you don't think they'd shoot us?"

"Maybe they would, maybe they wouldn't. If you talked to 'em first, though, if you tried explaining how it is and they still kill you, then I guess it's worth facing up to it, just to find out what is what and who is who."

"Family men?"

"Yes, by God, family men! What the hell are they living for if not to educate their children about the way the world works? I

don't know about them troopers, but for now I'd give 'em the bene-
fit of the doubt that they ain't completely turned into murdering
dogs."

"Will you lead us?"

"I can't," Gus said.

"I know," Ben said carefully, "if I know anything at all, you
ain't yellow."

"Thanks, Ben. Happens there's another string being pulled in
this town today. Kind of messes up everything, but when the time
comes, I'll side you. You got to all stand up, about ten abreast,
and march without a leader. You tell the troopers your story
and appropriate that bank and all your documents and all your
money. That's all there is to it."

"I don't believe our boys will do it. They believe in law and
order," Ben said.

"So do I," Gus said.

"I see," Ben said, his old eyes studying Gus's shining guns.

There was another knock at the door. Gus went through the same
careful procedure.

"Who is it?"

"Marshal Darby. Open up."

"You alone?"

"I'm alone."

The door opened, the .45 on the chin, and Darby slowly entered the room.

"You know better'n to pull a gun on an officer of the law,"
Darby said coldly.

"State your business, Darby."

Gus noticed Darby was wearing two .44s, the holsters tied down
to his thighs.

"Was a killin' in the alley last night. I'm takin' you in for ques-
tionin'."

"Why me?"

"Because the man killed had a connection with your past."

"How do I know," Gus asked, glancing at old Ben, "that you
can keep me alive?"

"I guarantee your safety," Darby said.

"Ben is my witness. I don't think you've got guts enough to kill
him. I'll go peaceable, after you make one phone call to a pal of

yours name of Mickey Zirp. You tell him we're coming out, and
I want to meet him face to face on Front Street."

"You're out of your head," Darby said, his mouth twisting.
"Crazy."

"Sure, Darby. Like a con. Ben will see it's honest. And I think
Zirp'll remember how he tried to hustle me at the gas house. Just
make it be somewhere near a fair fight. I give him first draw."

"Never heard of him." Darby's face was weak and sick. "You're
coming with me."

Gus put the .45 in the marshal's nostril and said, "You brought
it on. Now you're goin' to live with it. Lift his guns, Ben."

And as Ben warily complied, Gus said, "I think you ought to
make a phone call."

The marshal wilted. Cold sweat beaded his brow. His eyes were
crossed, trying to see Gus's trigger finger.

"O.K., O.K.," he whispered, "a call."

Gus nodded at Ben. "You see? Out of the business end of the
gun comes truth, too. I said that."

The marshal gave the operator a number. His devious eyes were
exploring the room like a cornered rat, assessing the advantages
and disadvantages.

"Mr. Zirp, this is the marshal. I'm under a gun. Have no choice.
He'll meet up with you on Front Street, give you first draw when
the fire whistle blows at noon." A pause. "Me?"

He glanced at Gus.

"You're going to be right alongside me."

"I'm just settin' it out. Ain't any choice of it," the marshal
said, and hung up.

"You're smart," Gus said, "you can accept a fact when you see
it. Now, Ben, you got the notion. Goin' to be a little fracas and
some dust fly down there. Their newspapers are bound to say
you're a gang of outlaws if you associate with me."

"We know different, Gus," old Ben said. "Every man jack on
our side of the street would back you."

"No. It's my fight. All the way, start to finish. Now watch the
marshal while I finish shaving." Gus grinned and went into the
bathroom.

Ben held the marshal's .44s on full cock.

"Darby," Ben said, "make a move and we won't need to bother

with the election. You found out we was going to run Gus for marshal of Dodge City, and that's why you tried to set him up."

"You dumb dirt hog," Darby said, "another week and I'll have you in chains breakin' rocks. You're barnyard dirt. Takes more'n a gun to make a man of a dirt-grubbin' sodbuster."

"Keep talkin', Darby. Sure, I farmed all my life, and I'm goin' to keep it up, too."

Gus came out of the bathroom, dressed in a clean, pressed suit, his great shock of yellow hair shining from the brush.

"Come on now, Ben," he said, "I been tryin' to tell you, never argue. The only thing to do is boot 'em out."

Gus looked out the window at the street below. Strangely, there was no automobile traffic. Nor any cars parked. Word traveled fast. He saw lanky red-necked farmers milling around the sidewalk across the street. Dear God, Gus wondered, why can't they move? It's right in front of their noses.

Then he saw the troopers carrying short shotguns, patrolling in front of the bank.

No wonder they can't make up their minds. None of them wants to get his head blowed off, especially if he don't figure he's going to win anyway.

Down the street the youngsters watched and waited, sizing it up. Making up their own minds as to what happened or didn't happen and, whether they meant to or not, they sat as judges of their fathers and their country. The clock on top of the firehouse said five minutes to twelve.

"Ben," Gus said, "you've got to talk to those troopers. You've got to tell 'em we're all the same people out of the same ground, looking for the same hopes and rewards for our work as anybody else, and we can't bear to see our own hopes busted, nor the hopes we have for an honest-to-God justice from our laws and our government. Ben, you have to hurry and you have to be honest and straight out with 'em, because if somebody gets killed at least they knew what for."

"I'll do my best, Gus," Ben said, handing over the .44s, hurrying through the door.

"Don't break a leg, old-timer," Gus called after him.

Gus watched through the window and saw the old farmer in his patched overalls talking to the nattily clad troopers who stood formidable and obtuse as concrete, so that it seemed never a word of good sense would get through, but old Ben was trying, talking to them with slow farmer gestures, as if talking to his own sons, as if explaining that the field must be plowed on contour or it'd wash away, that the field must lie fallow to rest, or that the field must have water to grow anything at all.

Gus watched the top officer in his stiff cavalry hat, frozen and wooden and petrified, as the old citizen spoke to him, telling him that all they wanted was to remain on their lands, to form a co-operative bank and mill, and to pay their debts as soon as the rains came.

The officer didn't listen. Petrified. Galvanized. Prehistoric. Muscled.

Ben, in his own good time and sense, knew he was talking to a fossil and, changing his direction, addressed his words to the young troopers, the men not yet cast into crystals by the machine.

"Would you shoot your neighbors for crossing a street and entering a building? Not a church, not a state capitol, simply a commercial building. Not disturbing anything or hurting anyone except to take over the paperwork? Would you use bombs and gas against your neighbors? Would you blow the heads off your own people?"

Gus couldn't tell. He saw the officer remain frozen and guessed he was afraid to command his troopers for fear they mightn't obey, and then what could he do?

It was a minute to twelve and Ben saw that he'd done what he could. He'd not begged, he'd not commanded, he had reasoned on the simple basis of man to man, for human decency. If he couldn't win with that, there was no point in trying anything else. Better to walk across the street and die.

Gus saw him cross back to the multitude of awkward farmers, those with the silt ground into their pores, and the sun burned into their faces, and a simple earthy humor burned into their mouths.

"O.K., Marshal," Gus said, "time you and me take a little mosey up Front Street."

Gus shucked the bullets out of the marshal's guns and handed them back empty.

"Maybe you feel better with a little extra weight on your hip," Gus said.

Proceeding down the stairs, Gus carried the loaded banjo and the marshal kept close to his side.

"Hope you make it through, Marshal," Gus said, meaning it.

"I hope you don't," the marshal snarled back.

They came to the front porch of the hotel. Gus sniffed the air. It smelled fine, like dewy white gardenias. It smelled as though blue rain could come to this dry street some day.

"You just stay to my left and keep wide, Marshal," Gus said pleasantly, and, walking down the steps, he passed the congregation of silent farmers and stepped off into the middle of the dusty street.

Jack was watching from his father's garage. The yellow Ford was greased, watered, oiled, and full of gas. Its engine was tuned to run like a Swiss watch, just in case.

Gus felt a sort of sorrow, a sort of prairie-wind melancholy, as the old clock started its heavy chime which would in twelve seconds blast off the noon whistle.

The marshal lagged a step behind and drifted off to the left.

"You get behind me, Marshal, I'll have to kill you," Gus said.

The marshal jumped forward.

Gus's lips were tight, his eyes set on one thing. He flexed the stiffened elbow, keeping his eyes moving all the time. Zirp would never fight fair, but if he'd only show himself, the rest of it made no difference.

The old clock springs wheezed and the chime rang—six, seven, eight, nine . . . And Gus walked up the middle of the street, coming up by the bank toward the police station, going slowly, wanting Zirp in the wide-open street.

He saw Hundertmarx at the open bank window, his hands folded across his chest, smiling, counting it out. Another three steps and the whole county, the whole West, would be smack in his money pocket.

On the other side of the street, the mass of hungry farm faces, fixed in their awe of entrenched law and order, stood like a river choked with ice awaiting the hot breath of spring to crack loose and flood to their destiny.

Gus took another step and another . . .

Another step. The noon fire whistle howled, and the street exploded. A heavy rifle bullet came out of nowhere and caught Gus in the back, driving him to his knees. They'd worked a perfect double-cross. Zirp'd used Hundertmarx to do his dirty work. There was the banker hidden back in the window aiming for another shot as Gus knelt blasted in the dust, the banjo out of his hand, a sick, gut-shot feeling paralyzing him.

And the crowd on either side of the street stood disbelieving.

Gus groped for the banjo as the banker raised the .30-30 for the *coup de grâce*. He had the buckhorn sight lined on Gus's stubborn face when suddenly a hard, leathery arm shoved the rifle up and the shot went wild.

The banker snarled at the scrubwoman, old Sal, the old whore, the old sot, the old bum.

"By God," the banker yelled, "you've had this coming a long time!" and clubbed her frenzied face with the rifle butt, knocking her to the floor.

But she'd given Gus the moment he needed. The right fist that had grown so powerful by milking twenty cows every morning lifted the weapon, and the heavy finger touched the trigger, strumming a staccato tune through the plate-glass window with its gold-relief letters, spinning the paunchy usurer behind the window into a solo buck and wing, and then he was bowing off dead.

Darby dropped, reloaded, and tried to roll and fire. He got off one shot before Gus stitched him up as neatly as a tailor. Darby's bullet finished the lousy elbow. No matter. Stitch him up. Finish the magazine.

A strange warm silence fell over the street. Gus got to his knees again, a gout of blood bursting out of his side, his left arm dragging like a broken wing. He found a pearl-handled .45 in his good milking right hand and staggered, lunged, falling and heaving until he could stand erect. Keeping only one thing in his mind, he aimed for the marshal's office.

"Come on," he croaked, "come out, Mickey, and give it a try!"

And suddenly down the street Mickey Zirp leaped into the open. His slanted hunchback was twisted to the side, his sliced smile was locked tightly for the death of Gus Gilpin.

His slender fingers maneuvered a sawed-off automatic shotgun, and he was already spraying buckshot up the street.

Gus fell again.

He had nothing much left, he decided. Just ain't much left. Just ain't much.

The double-ought buck slugs were splitting the air, driving through the dust and burning into his body.

Do or die, Gus said to himself, lining up the .45 with both bloody hands, sighting down the blade to catch the scrawny, scarred spider, catch him solid, catch him and mash him.

Gus squeezed the trigger and saw the bullet hit its mark, right smack in the teeth. A pink ice-cream mess smeared the jailhouse wall behind the exploding face.

Like a blinded giant, Gus crawled toward the curb through the dust. He'd done his business, would his friends do theirs?

The yellow Ford phaeton came around to the corner where the bleeding, ashen-faced man clutched at a telephone pole and saw Jack what's his name, that dumb jug-eared kid who couldn't add two and two, stop the car, open the side door and reach for him.

Looking backward, Gus watched as the threadbare farmers, ready to live or die in their work clothes, walked quietly across the street. They left him alone. They left the troopers alone. They left the dead alone. They simply walked en masse, as a group of men, not as raw material of an industry, not as brain-dulled troops told what to do, they simply walked as free men walk in concert on the surface of the single blue world, walked past the blood of Front Street into the bank, took the documents in wheat sacks, helped the old scrubwoman to her feet, and observed the troopers take off their helmets and join the people.

Gus watched it all happen as the yellow car picked up speed and, chasing the westering sun, smoothly topped the first long hill.